THE REARRANGED LIFE of OONA LOCKHART

THE REARRANGED LIFE of OONA LOCKHART

Margarita Montimore

GOLLANCZ
LONDON

First published in Great Britain in 2020 by Gollancz
an imprint of The Orion Publishing Group Ltd
Carmelite House, 50 Victoria Embankment
London EC4Y 0DZ

An Hachette UK Company

1 3 5 7 9 10 8 6 4 2

A CIP catalogue record for this book is
available from the British Library.

ISBN (Hardback) 978 1 473 22760 6
ISBN (Export Trade Paperback) 978 1 473 22761 3
ISBN (eBook) 978 1 473 22763 7

Printed in Great Britain by Clays Ltd, Elcograph S.p.A

www.gollancz.co.uk

For my mother, Olla Vaisman
Who encouraged me to dream hard
And let me read books instead of doing chores

For my husband, Terry Montimore
Who encouraged me to write hard
And gave me the time and space to do so
(Sorry about the book hoarding and messy house)

Time heals all. But what if time itself is the disease?

—Wim Wenders and Peter Handke, *Wings of Desire*

Prologue

Oona stopped trusting the mirror years ago. After all, it told only a sliver of the story.

This isn't me. I am not this woman.

The mirror exposed time's passage, yes, but eclipsed her heart's true mileage. The lined face, the extra pounds, the hair chemically treated to hide its gray. Each year the body was hers, but her mind was out of sync with her reflection. Always playing catch-up, trying to rearrange the scrambled pieces of her life.

It was nobody's fault she had met her future too soon. It should've been decades before she wore this funeral dress.

Oona threaded the chain of her necklace through her fingers, sunlight glinting off the gold gears of the pendant's clockwork parts.

At first the lost years were agony, the instant loss unbearable. And when the stolen time was returned to her, it was rearranged. Always something else taken from her. Someone else. But life had a system of checks and balances, and the bad breaks were tempered with good fortune. Even on this bleak day, hidden delights waited to offset the sorrow. She just had to be patient, open.

For Oona, the pendulum could swing either way; next year, the face in the glass could be older or younger. It was the closest thing she could imagine to immortality, a game of existential roulette, even though the wheel would eventually stop spinning.

I'll see them all again. Eventually. And lose them all. Again.

She tried to accept the mirror's current verdict, to look at herself here and now. To *be* here now. But today, when her loss was tremendous and threatened to engulf her, she allowed herself to step out of this moment and rewind to a brighter one. Her muted dress replaced with sequins. Her bedroom swapped for a mirrored basement. A room brimming with music and color and light. A love like a supernova. A party like no other.

I can still get it right.

Someday she would pick up the thread and return to the party. Not a do-over, only a disrupted continuation. No telling when.

Someday.

"Are you ready?"

PART I

The Party's Over

1982: 18/18

1

The party flowed with cinematic choreography: plastic cups and beer bottles tilted back in a syncopated rhythm; clusters of guests bobbed heads and danced to a new wave soundtrack as if the floor were a giant trampoline, a ribbon of tipsy laughter running through the room. It might have been only a basement in Brooklyn, with mirrored walls and tan carpeting, but tonight it was their Studio 54, their Palladium, their Danceteria. A group of fifty with the noise and energy of hundreds—most on their college winter break—they'd come to celebrate New Year's Eve and Oona Lockhart's nineteenth birthday. And they showed up in style: in leather and frills, spangles and mesh, eschewing subdued fabrics for ones that glistened, glimmered, popped with color. The looks flirted with glam, goth, new wave, and punk, even as those who wore them refused to be labeled as one thing.

In the corner, Oona knelt beside the stereo, sifting through a crate of records. She paused to check her watch, an anniversary gift from her boyfriend, Dale. It had no second hand, which gave the illusion of time moving slowly, sometimes even stopping. A single black diagonal line bisected the silver face dotted with tiny black stars: 9:15 P.M. In less than three hours, it would be 1983 and she'd be a year older.

She stood, a record in either hand, as Dale—tall and sleepy-eyed, favoring his Brazilian mother's golden complexion, curly pompadour gelled back at the sides—ambled over. The sight of him quickened her breath.

"Hey, gorgeous. Whatcha got there?" He pointed at the records.

"I can't decide which one to play next. Yaz or Talk Talk?" Shoulders tight, she raised and lowered the records as if weighing them.

"I've never seen anyone look so serious about picking a record. It's adorable." He gave her a quick peck on the cheek. "How about I take over as DJ and you go dance? I'll play them both."

While she allowed him to take the records, her shoulders remained stiff. "Okay. I just need to bring down more napkins and ice—"

"I'll take care of that, too. Your only job is to enjoy the party." A wink belied his stern tone.

Suddenly, one floor up, there was a crashing thud and shatter. Everyone stopped dancing and gazed up at the ceiling. Was it a noisy intruder? Something thrown through a window? Oona and Dale rushed to the foot of the stairs.

"Stay here, I'll see what it is," Dale said to her.

"I'll come with you." Forced assertiveness as a cold dropping sensation overtook her. *Not again, please.*

He paused on the stairs, turned around. "I'm sure it's nothing. But if it'll make you feel better, I'll go find Corey to check it out with me."

"Found him." She pointed over his shoulder.

At the top of the stairs Corey's lanky frame was hunched over in dread, his black liberty spikes casting geometric shadows on his face. "Dude, I'm so sorry. I was showing off some dance moves for these girls and the rug got in my way. I fell on top of your coffee table and it, um, broke. Nobody's hurt, but I'm a dumbass. I'll clean up the mess, replace the table. Promise." Cowering behind Corey were two petite girls wearing too much mascara and lamé dresses like liquid metal.

Dale thundered up the rest of the steps. As his chest puffed out with a slow indrawn breath, Oona crept up behind him and touched his back. Finally he sighed and said, "Hey, it's not a real party until something breaks, right?" He stepped aside, waved through Corey and the girls. "I'll clean it up. Just try not to break anything else."

The contrite trio headed downstairs as Oona followed Dale to the kitchen.

He grabbed a broom and dustpan and grumbled, "The guest of honor shouldn't be doing cleanup. I can handle the mess."

"Let me help. I've barely seen you since the party started." She pulled a trash bag from under the sink.

"I know." Softened by her kindness, Dale dropped his voice to a sexy husk. "Good thing we saw plenty of each other earlier."

They shared a suggestive chuckle. "I think at one point the mailman saw plenty of us, too." She leaned in and nuzzled against his neck, breathed in his tangy scent of Drakkar Noir and Dep hair gel. "Serves us right for leaving the curtains open."

"And still less embarrassing than your mother walking in on us last week," said Dale.

"Oh, it got even more embarrassing after you left." She flinched, remembering. "Once she made sure I was still taking the pill, she offered to let me borrow her copy of *The Joy of Sex*."

"I love it." Dale's booming laugh forced his head back. As much as she would've liked to join in, she could muster only a weak smile.

Having a liberal mother had its advantages, but Oona would've preferred more boundaries. Her father, a banker, had provided those until she was eleven (weekly chores, study plans, limited TV time), but once he died, she'd had to set certain rules for herself. Which left her mother, a flight-attendant-turned-travel-agent, in a role more friendly than parental. She often teased Oona about taking things too seriously, whether it was her college courses or band practice, or even her relationship with Dale, urging her daughter to be young and frivolous once in a while. As if you couldn't be serious about something and still enjoy it. As if being young meant being foolish.

"I have an idea," said Dale, dropping the broom and dustpan with a clatter. Running over the scales of her sequined dress, he teased the zipper down a few inches and murmured, "How about we go upstairs?"

He kissed her exposed shoulder and walked his fingers beneath the hem of her dress, up her thigh. "We could lie under the stars . . ."

The "stars" he spoke of were indoors, his bedroom ceiling strung with a nest of cables and telephone wires he'd scavenged from his father's electronics store and splattered with phosphorescent paint, creating a three-dimensional cosmic effect. The first time Oona had seen that ceiling, it made her gasp in wonder; two years on, she still found it awe-inspiring. To say nothing of the man running kisses down her neck.

"Tempting, but it would be rude to the others." Reluctantly she stopped his hand from moving any farther up her leg. "With school and the band, it's been ages since I've seen anyone besides you, Corey, and Wayne."

"We saw a bunch of people at CBGB's just a couple of weeks ago."

"Yeah, but we were so busy playing the holiday showcase and meeting with Factory Twelve's manager, we barely got to talk to our friends."

"Considering what came of it, I don't think they minded. You know what a tour like this could do for our band? After opening for the Pretenders, Factory Twelve got signed to Chrysalis, and their first single just hit the Top Forty."

"They're still not the Pretenders, though. I mean, it's not like we're going to be playing stadiums."

"Right . . ." The word drawn out as he took a step back, his eyebrow inching up. "But we've never played for more than a couple hundred people—we've never even left the tri-state area. And Factory Twelve could still become huge. Opening for their spring tour is the kind of break most bands never see. I thought you were excited about it."

"I am. I just— I'm not . . ." She fought to keep a stammer out of her voice. "It's exciting, but it's intimidating. Visiting new cities, playing bigger venues . . ."

"It's more than that," he said with a knowing nod. "You don't have to keep it from me, you know."

Her stomach plummeted. *Did he know?* "Keep what from you?"

"You're still shaken up from the mugging after Wayne's party. I saw how you jumped at the crash earlier. You thought it was a burglar.

And you're worried about touring, scared something bad might happen again."

"Oh." Relief ran through her like a faucet turned up full blast. "Well, it *was* pretty terrifying." It happened last month, on the subway back to Bensonhurst. At first she'd laughed at the man who approached them because he wore swim goggles. But she'd stopped laughing when he pulled a switchblade.

"Listen to me." Dale's voice dove down a few notes as he pulled her in close. "Nothing would've happened to you. I was ready to do whatever it took to keep you protected. Face a knife, a bullet, anything."

"Thank god all it took was handing over our money." She shuddered, recalling how paralyzed she'd been, how Dale had to reach into her own coat pocket to remove her wallet and pass it to their goggled assailant. "And good thing I wasn't wearing my watch that night."

"Nothing bad will happen to you on this tour. As long as you're with me, you're safe." The promise was echoed in his steady gaze and the determined set of his jaw.

"I know." Her voice caught in her throat at his vehemence. "You don't have to take a bullet for me to prove it." She traced a finger over the bump in his nose.

"I'll also take a hammer if you wanna straighten that out for me." Despite his overall swagger, his nose was the one part of his body he felt embarrassed by.

"Shush. I have the hots for your nose. And not just because of what they say about big noses." Oona's hand hovered at his belt buckle, wanting to travel farther south, but remained still; it would be too easy to lose track of time. "Let's go take care of this mess. But first, a little help?" Draping her long chestnut hair over one shoulder, she offered her exposed back so he could zip her up into the dress. "Do you think we should've rehearsed more earlier? I know we're just playing for friends tonight, but I still want to impress." After a gig, she'd once overheard someone say she was "decent, but hardly the next Joan Jett." Oona wasn't sure how much she agreed—given the chance, she could be a better guitarist than keyboardist, and she was as solid on vocals as Dale—but that comment stuck with her.

When she turned around and finished adjusting her dress, he gave a low whistle. "God, you're a knockout. You have no idea." Even beneath the harsh fluorescent kitchen light, his skin glowed as he shook his head in awe.

Pinned in place by the intensity of his dark eyes, words escaped her and narcotic elation flooded her veins. All she could do was squeeze his hand in response.

Dale moved in and spoke low into her ear. "For the record, you're *always* impressive. I've been impressed by you since I first saw you. And every minute I get to spend with you is the highlight of my motherfucking life."

In the living room, the coffee table lay in a pile of twisted chrome and glass shards.

"Fucking Corey," Dale muttered. "And you wonder why I talk about finding a new drummer."

As they carefully collected the mangled metal and pieces of glass, Dale continued the now-familiar refrain. "He's getting out of control. I don't know if he's been doing more coke, but the drinking alone is a problem. We don't even have a record deal and he's already acting like Keith Moon. Maybe we should replace him now before he blows the tour for us."

"You can't kick him out. He messes up, but he's a great drummer and he loves the band." Oona smoothed his furrowed forehead. "Have more faith in him."

Back in the basement, Dale headed over to the turntable and Oona got herself a drink. She sipped cheap champagne from a plastic cup and observed the colorful crowd before her.

Someone tapped her shoulder.

"What's with the moping?" It was Wayne, wearing red leather head to toe, his Jheri-curled Afro shimmering in the light.

"I'm not moping." But in her voice, a hint of defensiveness.

"Oh, come on. You're usually dancing your ass off, smiling like a lunatic. What happened? You and Dale get into a fight?"

"Of course not. I was just thinking about how much I'll miss everyone." She hurried to add, "When we all go on tour."

"I'm not really buying it, but I'll let it go."

Oona pointed at her empty cup. "I need a refill. Back in a sec." She stepped away from Wayne, her mouth dry, faint queasiness undulating within her. What she really needed was a place to quiet her thoughts and set them aside, so she could get lost in the festivities.

Across from the basement stairs was the bathroom. A knock on the door yielded no response, so Oona turned the handle and stepped inside, where Corey was hunched over the sink.

"What the hell?" He bolted upright, eyes bulging.

"Oops, sor—" That was when she saw the hand mirror dusted with white powder. She closed and locked the door behind her. "Are you kidding me right now?"

"It's not a regular thing, I swear." A blur of his white, panicked hands waving against the orange backdrop of his jumpsuit.

"That's what you said after you wrecked our Hoboken gig. Do you want out of the band?"

"Of course not. You think I want to wait tables at Beefsteak Charlie's my whole life?"

"I don't know. I *do* know Dale dropped out of college to focus on the band and convinced Wayne to do the same. I know they expect me to take a semester off from Stern to go on this tour. If you want to be part of this, you need to start taking it more seriously." *Maybe I should take my own good advice.* She winced at her hypocrisy. "What do you think would happen if Dale or Wayne saw this?"

Anguish contorted his face as he slumped down on the lidded toilet. "You can't tell them. The band is everything to me."

"I know." Oona stood over him, hands on hips. "But band policy is no hard drugs. We all agreed to it. If you can't respect that, maybe you should get out now so they—we have time to find a new drummer before the tour." A prickle of guilt propelled her to rip off a square of toilet paper and wipe stray powder from beneath his nose. "I'll keep my mouth shut, but you need to get your shit together."

"This was the last time. For real." He went to the sink, rinsed the remaining cocaine off the hand mirror, and held it up. "See?"

Her own hazel eyes, raccooned with black liner and heavy with worry, reflected back at her. "Don't let me down." The words aimed as much at her reflection as her friend.

He rattled off more promises, gave her a grateful smile, and left.

Once she was alone, the confining space felt hot, oppressive. Maybe a brief solo respite upstairs would set her right.

She was so intent on leaving the basement unnoticed, she failed to spot a figure at the bottom of the stairs until they nearly collided. Oona stopped short, inches from knocking her oldest friend to the ground. Instead, she used the momentum to pull the shocked girl into a hug.

"Pam! I can't believe you're here. I hoped you'd show up to one of these eventually."

"Wow." She gaped at Oona and did a sweep of the room. "I didn't expect everyone to look so . . . glamorous." Where the other guests tried to look older and more progressive, Pam was a few years behind in both trend and maturity. Hair in the same wedge she'd worn since Dorothy Hamill won gold in '76, narrow shoulders overwhelmed by the white Peter Pan collar of her brown velveteen dress, freckled face bare except for a smear of Vaseline across her mouth. "Maybe I shouldn't have come."

"What are you talking about? You look so pretty." Taking her friend's hand, she gave a gentle pull. "Let me introduce you to everyone."

But Pam wouldn't budge. "I called your house earlier and ended up talking to your mom. I said she must be so proud and would probably miss you so much, and she got totally confused. You didn't tell her about London?"

London.

The word was like a syringe of adrenaline shot into Oona's heart. Reversing course, she yanked Pam away from the party, up the stairs into the empty kitchen.

"Jeez, Oona, you practically dislocated my shoulder."

"Nobody knows about London. Not Mom, not even Dale."

"Why not?" She tugged on her earlobe, a nervous habit since childhood.

"It's hard to explain." Oona's throat was so parched, she could barely speak. "Hold on." She got a Coke out of the fridge. A metallic snap as she popped the can open and foam gushed over the side. Hurried sips to tame the spill. "I haven't told anyone because I want to make this decision without anyone's input. Especially Mom's or Dale's."

"What is there to decide? We've been dreaming about going to London since we saw *Mary Poppins* in third grade. And now we get to live there."

"I might still get to see London this summer. Dale and I talked about backpacking through Europe. We even started a list of where we'll go. Paris, Berlin, Brussels, London, all the major cities." They'd also made a list of lesser-known European destinations and sights. The ancient seaside villages of Italy's Cinque Terre, Kastellorizo's castle ruins in Greece, Kutná Hora's chapel decorated with human bones in Czechoslovakia. "Of course, this was right before we got the Factory Twelve offer, and there's no telling what'll happen on tour. Dale's convinced some A&R rep will go nuts over us and we'll be recording an album for a major label over the summer. Who knows?"

"Are you serious?" Bafflement contorted Pam's features. "I know this music stuff is exciting, but it's not *real life*. You could spend months on a sweaty tour bus and come home broke, or you could spend a year in London and have every door open for you." A heavy sigh as she glanced down at her Mary Janes. "I'd hate to see you throw away a golden ticket. And you're running out of time. The paperwork is due in two weeks."

"I know." Oona pressed the soda can to her hot forehead. "But . . . I haven't figured it out yet. And I'd like one night off from worrying about it. One night to enjoy this party before things get more complicated. Can we go back downstairs and just have some fun tonight?"

Hesitation in the long breath she took before answering. "Fine. But I need the powder room first."

"There's one up here. Down the hall, to your left."

"Don't wait, I'll come find you."

"You better not run off on me."

Downstairs, Oona glanced at her watch: 11:40 P.M.

She went over to the beverage table, where Dale was opening a bottle of Cold Duck.

"You're drinking soda when we have the finest cheap champagne money can buy?" He popped the cork and filled two plastic cups, offering her one. "Come on, let's celebrate. You're gonna be the hottest keyboardist in rock 'n' roll history."

"Nobody cares about the keyboardist." Her eyes flickered to her discarded Coke before she took a swallow of champagne. "It's all about the lead singer or maybe the guitarist, so either way, it'll be all about you." *It can't be about me. I might not be there.*

"No, it'll be about *us*." Dale hooked an arm around her waist. A firm promise that whatever came next, he'd be there for it. Oona leaned into him and smiled, believing the promise, reciprocating it.

The floor rumbled beneath her feet. Did the subway run below the house? Maybe it was the energy of the partygoers, dancing so hard they were shaking the foundation. Maybe it was the champagne she had earlier and the hyper-focused adoration of her boyfriend. Oona's and Dale's eyes glittered when they locked on each other, as if privy to a secret, connected with a bond as intense as murder accomplices. Their faces drew together and liquid sloshed from their plastic cups as they joined for violent, oblivious kisses that cast the rest of the room in shadow. They kissed like lovers reunited after a battle, even though they spent all but two days of winter break together, even though they both lived in Brooklyn and saw each other all the time. Maybe they weren't reuniting after a battle as much as preparing for it.

Dale brought his mouth to her ear. "I have a birthday surprise for you. Come on."

He led her to a screened-off corner of the basement used for storage. On top of a stack of plastic lawn chairs was a rectangular box wrapped in silver paper.

"It's not my birthday for another half hour," she protested, even as she smiled.

"I can't wait any longer. Open it." He held the box steady as she peeled back the wrapping.

Inside, a layer of tissue paper revealed a black motorcycle jacket with gleaming silver buckles.

Her breath hitched. "It's too much. You should be saving up for the tour," she said while fitting her arms through the sleeves over her sequined dress, enveloped by the heaviness and smell of leather.

"Eh, Dad's been giving me extra shifts at the store, and everyone bought Commodore 64s for Christmas, so I've been making good commissions. Does it fit okay?"

"It's perfect." Head tilted in mock suspicion, she asked, "Is this because you're sick of me borrowing your leather jacket all the time?" She'd tell him it was her New York City armor, that she felt safe wearing it.

"No way. I just thought you could use some of your own armor," he said.

Her heart a hummingbird flying frantic circles in her chest. She wrapped her arms around Dale and murmured, "I'm so damn lucky."

"Because I spoil you rotten?"

His warm breath made her knees soften and her blood hum. "No, because I get to spend the rest of my life with the coolest guy on the planet."

"Goddamn right." He kissed her with a fierceness that made the room go dark and quiet. "I have another surprise for you, but you'll have to wait until after the countdown for that one."

"Don't tell me, don't tell me!" Holding up a hand, she turned away.

While she normally loved surprises, between the Factory Twelve tour, Dale's and Wayne's leaving school, and London looming, Oona was reaching her saturation point.

"Come on, let's rejoin the others," Dale said.

The basement was illuminated by clear Christmas lights kept up year-round. White dots of light bouncing between mirrored walls put Oona in the center of a giant disco ball, or a star on the verge of explosion. The room blurred as she blinked back confused tears. This was the culmination of a perfect year. But it wouldn't last. It couldn't. Not long after this party, the scales would tip. If Oona said no to London and took a semester off, she'd lose her academic momentum. But would she lose even more if she said no to the band? If Early Dawning went on tour without her, she'd have to contend with Dale's absence that spring—which would be painful enough—and his disappointment. And that would just be the opening act for her England departure. Could they survive such disruption?

Oona was at the mercy of a clock whose ticking grew louder and faster with each passing hour. A clock that was about to betray her.

She checked the time: 11:55.

In the corner of the room, a small color TV broadcasted the ball drop from Times Square. Corey pointed at the screen. "Is that lit-up thing a cherry?"

"This is why people think drummers are dumb. It's an apple, you doofus," Dale said. "You know, like the Big Apple? New York isn't known as the Big Cherry."

It wasn't all that funny, but Oona craved a break, so she threw her head back and laughed. Dale took advantage of her exposed white throat and dove in teeth first, playing the amorous vampire. The room tilted as he dipped her—the tips of her hair brushing the floor—then shifted further off its axis. Her laughs morphed into squeals of protest, then quieted into murmurs of pleasure. They engulfed and consumed each other, but wasn't that love? She couldn't imagine it being anything less. And now that she had it, she couldn't imagine choosing to leave it behind.

There was that tremor beneath her feet again, the shift and blur at the edges of the room. Had she overdone it with the champagne? Hopefully, she wouldn't be sloppy behind the keyboard and mic when Early Dawning performed a few songs after ushering in 1983.

Remember this party. Every second of it. Every person here.

They were a motley bunch. As she gazed around the room, Oona took mental snapshots of her friends, each strange and talented in their own way. She was sure they would all go on to do great things. But would she?

I wish I didn't have to choose.

A recurring wish she'd had these last few weeks and one she made again now, unaware that every granted wish comes with a hidden cost, every blessing shadowed with a curse.

The countdown to 1983 began.

"Ten!"

She tightened her hold around Dale's waist, felt this was the pinnacle of her happiness. A panicked voice whispered at the edge of her mind: *There's nowhere higher to go.*

"Nine!"

The jacket made her too warm, but she wouldn't take it off for the rest of the night. She also wouldn't tell Dale it wasn't his jacket's heft that made her feel safe as much as wearing something that belonged to him. Any talisman could've guarded her—a class ring, an old T-shirt, a ratty shoelace—as long as it was his.

"Eight!"

Unfortunately, there were some things her leather armor wouldn't protect her from.

"Seven!"

The tremor intensified, up Oona's legs to the base of her spine, an unseen force that threatened to turn her body into a metronome, setting a new rhythm for her life.

"Six!"

She tried to ignore it.

"Five!"

Perspiration trickled down her temples as she counted down the last seconds of 1982 and her own eighteenth year.

"Four!"

She followed the red glow of the ball descending on TV, crying out with the others, though hers was a cry of pain.

"Three!"

A sharp sensation exploded from the top of Oona's head and spread down the center of her body, an invisible broadsword cutting her in two.

"Two!"

Escalating heat stirred within her as particles scrambled to escape and rearrange, but not now and not here.

"ONE!"

PART II

Under Ice

2015: 51/19

2

Oona came to with a long gasp, as if breaching the surface after being trapped underwater, left to drown.

A second earlier, she'd been surrounded by people and light and noise and warmth. Now she lay on a plush carpet in a dark room lit by a fireplace, silent but for the crackle of flames heating the drafty space.

How much champagne did I drink?

"Hey, are you okay?" asked an unfamiliar male voice.

The light, though meager, hurt her eyes; the room wavered before her. She blinked as if recovering from a camera flash. *Focus.*

A man kneeled over her, lean torso clad in a Pink Floyd *Dark Side of the Moon* T-shirt, the album cover's prism and rainbow bedazzled with small rhinestones.

Oona propped herself up on one elbow, groggy. "Where's Dale?"

That's when it hit her: she wasn't in Dale's basement, or even his house.

Instead, she was in a room that could've been the library out of the board game Clue: high ceilings, dark wood paneling, leather wingback chairs, an antique globe, a bar cart laden with crystal bottles faceted like large jewels. Shelves of books dominated one wall, a rolling ladder offering access to the ones beyond arm's reach. The sort of room where stylish academics could mingle, enjoying fine scotch and murmured conversation. A walnut desk faced a bay window, framed by velvet emerald curtains eclipsing the view beyond.

A thread of unease wove through Oona's murky mind. "What is this place?" She gazed at a painting above the fireplace: an elegant woman doing her best Holly Golightly impression, pulled along by three large wolves on a leash. A small trail of blood dripped from the corner of the woman's mouth. "Creepy, but pretty."

"That's exactly what you said when you bought it."

Her brain fog thinned out. "Who are you?" She touched her throat. Her voice sounded different. Not overtly, but definitely pitched deeper by a few notes.

The man was in his early thirties, with dark, friendly eyes, high cheekbones, and dyed apricot hair styled like a miniature tidal wave. "I'm Kenzie. Your personal assistant—and friend. This place is your home. And your voice is different because—well, there's a *lot* to explain. It's gonna be weird and shocking. But I'm here to help."

Oona shuddered and closed her eyes. This was too vivid to be a dream, but what a strange mirage. Surely she was still at the party with Dale and her friends in the mirrored basement. This new reality must be a false one, so better not to give in to the hallucination.

Except . . .

A roiling in her body made her double over, as if her inner organs were reassembling themselves. She swallowed hard to keep from being sick, breathed in, and—

The scream was jarring to Oona, even though it came out of her mouth. The last time she'd shrieked at this decibel, two men were dragging her father back onto a boat, his clothes hanging off him in tatters, blowing air into his waterlogged dysfunctional lungs. Eleven years old, staring into the purple face of Charles Lockhart, who stared back at nothing. That scream was one of alarm at seeing the familiar become foreign. This scream, shaded with decades of maturity, retained notes of that girl's high-pitched plaintive wail.

"Whoa. Calm down. Please. You're not in danger."

But Oona got to her feet and scurried away from him. This action came with terrible new surprises, which distracted her from the stranger. Why was her body heavier, full of twinges, like she was wearing a rusty suit of armor? With no mirrors in the room, she couldn't take in the full effect, so the horror was revealed by degrees. There were her hands, which couldn't be hers. These hands had prominent veins, blue road maps extending from the knuckles, and a spatter of brown sunspots. She ran these hands over her body, now clad in a dark skirt and sweater, over the looser skin on her face and neck, over a midsection significantly thicker. None of it belonged to her: not the hands, the clothes, definitely not the body.

"Oona, don't lose your shit. I need you to listen to me." Kenzie stood.

Only there was no time to listen and Oona had her own needs. *I have to get out of here.* Except the stranger blocked her path to the door, so she dashed to the window. If they were on a ground floor she could—

A hand on her shoulder. She whirled around.

"Take it easy," he said. "You know me."

Shrinking back against the curtain, she crossed her arms. "No. No way. A minute ago, I was . . ." Her eyes drifted over to a framed photo on the desk and she nodded at it. "There."

In the picture, Oona was back in her gold dress and leather jacket, shiny-eyed and grinning, surrounded by Dale, Corey, Wayne, and Pam. The camera's flash reflected off the mirrored walls behind them.

Kenzie handed her the photo. "This is one of the things I'm supposed to show you."

"I don't . . ." She glanced from the photo to the man before her, back and forth. "I don't remember posing for this."

"I'm trying to explain."

"Did you hurt them? Are you going to hurt me?" Oona pressed the frame to her chest, a useless makeshift shield.

His eyebrows shot up and he stepped back. "Of course not. I'm here because you trust me. I'll prove it. You told me about that New Year's party a hundred times. Stuff it should be impossible for me to know." Kenzie reached for the picture. "Relax, I'll give it right back. Okay, so that's your band's badass bassist Wayne. And that's your drummer Corey, right? You caught him doing coke in the bathroom, he got all emo, swore he'd never do it again, so you promised not to tell the rest of the band. That's front man Dale, your boyfriend, who gave you a leather jacket just like his—adorbs—which you called your New York City armor." Oona's mouth formed a stunned *O* as he tapped on Pam. "That's your childhood friend with the questionable haircut—I can't remember her name, but that wedge will forever haunt me—who gave you shit about keeping the London thing hush-hush and tried to convince you to go the nerd route with her. Let's see, what else? Oh, right before the countdown, Corey thought the big apple was a cherry, and I can't even with that one."

Though puzzled by some of his jargon, his placid tone mesmerized her. As he replayed events Oona had lived through moments before, she shivered and her knees softened. She staggered over to the desk, clutched it for support. "I need to sit."

"Shit. Was that too much all at once?" Hastily setting down the picture, he held out an arm.

Oona didn't take it, but allowed him to lead her to the wingback chairs.

"So . . ." His pants, made of a shimmery fabric more typical of a prom dress, rustled as he took a seat. "Now that we're caught up on your recent past, how about I bring you up to speed on the right now?"

The ache in her knees made her grimace as she perched on the chair beside him. "Have I been kidnapped? Why do I look like this?" Her expression was fierce, but her voice wobbled.

"It's all going to be okay. I'm here as your co-captain. We're gonna navigate this mess together."

"So I'm not a prisoner?"

"Of course not. I work for you. And we're besties."

"Besties?"

"Friends."

"I don't have any friends as old as you."

Kenzie let out a startled laugh. "Hey, I'm only thirty, take it easy."

"What the hell is happening?" Oona closed her eyes. This new world had already exhausted her. If she wasn't dead, she must be in a nightmare. In which case, she could play along, wait it out until she woke up. A grim sigh and she opened her eyes, faced the stranger. "What's your name again?"

"Kenzie."

"Why are you here? Why am *I* here?" Even if this was a bleak fantasy, some framework had to govern it.

His pose was serene except for one foot tapping out an erratic rhythm. "You're . . . home. And you asked me to be here."

A silent laugh shook her chest. This room, this person, all of it was like learning a new language. "This isn't my home. And I don't know you."

"It's gonna be a while before any of this makes sense—if it ever really does. But I'll help you through it." Kenzie put a hand on her arm, gave it a reassuring squeeze.

It wasn't painful, but it was too much; she winced and jerked away. "Please don't touch me." Hurt flashed across his face as Oona got to her feet, backed away toward the door. "I have to go. I have people waiting for me. They'll wonder where I am." Inch by inch, she moved closer to the exit, hoping he wouldn't lunge for her.

"Hang on a sec." Kenzie rushed to the desk and returned with an envelope, handing it to her from a safe distance. "If you won't let me explain, maybe it'll be better coming from you. Still, there are things in here that'll be hella bizarre."

"*Hella?*"

"Right, sorry. It means 'very.' My bad."

"*My bad?*"

"Shit, I did it again. *My bad* means my mistake. I use silly outdated slang when I get nervous."

Curiosity interrupted her escape plan. "How outdated? I've never heard any of it before."

"I don't know, early 2000s?" Kenzie looked away from her widened eyes and fortified himself with a deep breath. "Here's the thing . . . You're no longer in 1982."

"I know that. It's 1983 now."

"Not so much. It *is* New Year's Day, but the year is 2015. So while you just turned nineteen on the inside—Happy Birthday, by the way—your body is the age it's supposed to be in 2015. So chronologically you're . . ." He paused to calculate the number, but Oona beat him to it.

"Fifty-one?" *No. No no no. HELLA no.*

"Right. You're fifty-one on the outside, but on the inside, you still have the mind and memories of yourself at nineteen. So it's like you've swapped bodies. Only with yourself. At a different age." He gave her an apologetic look. "You told me to memorize a speech explaining all this, but I was sure I'd be able to wing it. Sorry."

Oona stared into the fire. Her face could've been made of marble, it was so pale and still. Ten seconds. Twenty. Her lips moved as if reciting a silent prayer, except they formed no real words.

A glance at Kenzie, whose dark eyes reflected an inner tug-of-war between panic and serenity.

The edges of her mouth twitched down. "So you're saying I've been through . . . a time machine or something?"

"Or something."

"Did you do this to me?"

"God no. You've never been able to figure out how it happens or why."

"You know what I think?" Her voice was a shaky whisper. "I think one of us is insane, and I'm not going to stick around to see if it's you." She turned and fled the room.

As she ran down the hallway, her fingers brushed against silver-and-blue-striped wallpaper, reminiscent of gift wrap.

I need to get back to the party and unwrap my presents.

Hurrying down a curved staircase, Oona caught flashes of modern paintings in primary colors and a chandelier made of bicycle parts. She ended up in a marble-tiled foyer facing an eight-foot mirror. Its reflection made her gasp.

What is this?

An overweight middle-aged woman gaped at her. When Oona put her hand up to her face, so did the woman. And when Oona turned her body this way and that, the woman mimicked her gestures. It was like she'd been transported to a sadistic fun house.

This can't be me.

The face was older but unmistakably Oona's. The skin along her jaw sagged, parentheses-shaped grooves lined either side of her mouth, and her once-pouty lower lip was deflated. Her nose looked larger and her hazel eyes had crow's feet. There was no gray in her hair, but it was less lustrous and dyed blond.

"Oh my god, I'm *old.*"

"You're not *that* old. You're just not . . . young," Kenzie said behind her, then shuffled back at her terror-glazed stare.

"I can't be here anymore. I have to go somewhere . . . else. I have to find Dale."

"Look, I know this is all cray, but—"

"*Cray?*"

"Crazy—god, I'm giving you the worst of modern culture tonight." He uttered a frustrated growl. "I'm fucking this whole thing up. You warned me it was gonna be tough, but I was all, 'I got this.' I shouldn't have been so dismissive. But now that we're here, please stay. Take a minute to process. I'll tell you what I can about—"

"No. I'm leaving." Even a nightmare would allow you to exert some control, wouldn't it? If she couldn't wake up yet, at least she could go somewhere else. She went to open the door, but the handle wouldn't budge. Of course.

"Am I locked in?" A glare like a laser beam directed at Kenzie.

He ran a hand through his hair, scattering the perfect wave of it. "2014 You thought it would be better to spend some time in this house. You know, acclimate a little before you went out and saw what else has changed."

She let out a disgusted chuckle. "I don't know what that means. Just let me out." Eyes darting, they settled on a large glass vase; she'd use it if she needed a weapon.

"I wish you'd reconsider. But I won't keep you a prisoner in your own house."

"My house?" Her head snapped up, and she took a fresh look

around. "Nope. I've never been here before." She tugged on the door handle again. "And I don't want to be here now. Please unlock the door." Her words were meant to be assertive, but they sounded more like pleading.

"Can I come with? I don't want you to get lost."

"No way."

Kenzie darted into a side room and came out with a long black coat and red leather handbag. "At least take these with you? Your wallet is inside with your address, so you'll be able to find your way back. Your phone is in there, too—it's silver, about the size of your hand—hell knows if you'll be able to figure out how to use it," he muttered and handed her a slip of paper. "That's my number and the security code for the front door, but I'll be here."

The second digits on the paper caught her eye: 0628. Dale's birthday. Where *was* Dale, anyway?

She slipped on the coat and took the bag. It was time to find him.

As she stepped across the threshold, a frigid gust of wind hit her like a slap in the face.

"Please don't wander too far," Kenzie said. "If you get lost, call me."

"Yeah, right," Oona called over her shoulder, intent on never seeing him again.

3

Outside, Oona bolted down a short flight of steps, mystified at her sore knees. A quick backward glance at her supposed house. *This* was where she lived? This miniature-castle-looking brownstone? Uh-uh. She and Dale were supposed to settle down in a SoHo loft, a raw expanse they'd turn into a giant living/creative space. No way would she end up in such a stately abode. Of course, it might not be true. Not this house or anything else Kenzie told her. She still didn't know the real story. She barely knew the first sentence.

A curtain on the first floor fluttered, revealing an anxious Kenzie peeking through the window. Oona waved him away and began to walk as a merciless wind whipped around. Her fingers grazed the edge of the envelope in her pocket. A letter sure to contain bad news.

Forget the letter. I need to find Dale.

The block contained nothing but other brownstones, some with gaslights out front, creating an effect more antiquated than futuristic.

2015? I don't think so.

But the cars were more modern and streamlined than the ones she was familiar with. Less angular. Some more compact, others significantly larger, the vans and station wagons she'd known having received a so-phisticated makeover.

So the cars are different. That doesn't mean anything.

Except other, smaller differences nagged at her, like street signs with bolder fonts and pedestrian crossing lights that flashed a white silhouette of a person or an orange hand instead of WALK or DON'T WALK.

The tip of her nose and ears went numb as she walked, and her wool coat protected her body against the bracing temperature only so much. Hopefully, she'd find someplace warm soon.

A short while later, she reached an avenue filled with shops, bars, and restaurants. Outside a corner café with an iron crow hanging above its door, a man and woman stood smoking, coats open to the wind. They had the unsteady stances and glassy eyes of the inebriated, and their breath created small patches of fog indistinguishable from their exhaled cigarette puffs. Nothing about their appearance screamed futuristic, ei-ther. If anything, the man's vaudevillian handlebar moustache and sus-penders and the woman's top bun and prim schoolmarmish dress made them seem more suited to an older era.

Oona approached the couple. "Excuse me, where's the closest sub-way?"

The man pointed down the street. "Five blocks that way."

"Happy New Year," slurred the woman.

"Is it really 2015?" Oona couldn't resist asking.

"I know—last year totally flew by, right?" An eye roll, a short sigh, and she flicked her cigarette into the gutter.

It still didn't mean anything. The drunk woman could've misheard her.

Ever since Oona and Dale had been mugged, she'd been scared to ride the subway alone, especially late at night. She focused on this fear as she headed down Seventh Avenue, which diverted the bigger fear at the threshold. Had she really ended up thirty-two years in the future, robbed of her potential and her rightful place in time?

In the station, she did a double take at the subway map; it no longer looked like it was designed on an Etch A Sketch, though the modern curved lines did little to improve its clarity. "F train to Fourth Avenue, switch to the N," she murmured, memorizing the route to Bensonhurst.

There was an agent inside the station booth. Oona gave the middle-aged man behind the safety glass a relieved smile and handed over a five-dollar bill. "One token, please."

"We haven't sold tokens in years. This'll get you a MetroCard good for two rides."

She fought a panicked frown. "Okay . . . I guess I'll take one of those."

Moments later, "Here you go, ma'am." The attendant handed her a plastic card.

Ma'am?

Such a small but jarring reminder: she was no longer nineteen to this world.

A rumble below signaled an approaching train.

It took a few card swipes, but Oona made it through the turnstile in time to catch the F. Her brain was overloaded with information that refused to be sorted into tidy shelves. Maybe she should read the letter? Not yet. Whatever it might explain, the arithmetic was impossible; she couldn't tackle it right now. It was easier to dwell on smaller things without adding them up. Like this updated subway car—so bright and clean, graffiti-free, with no broken windows or flickering neon lights. Or the surprising number of people taking public transportation this late, the N train even more crowded once she transferred. If this really was the future, at least it was safer, less gritty. And not wholly unfamiliar. Even the clothes weren't dramatically different—no puffy sleeves, shoulder pads, or ruffly skirts in sight, but nothing like the *Jetsons* attire she would've envisioned for 2015. The silhouettes were sleeker, with many formfitting outfits which looked constricting, uncomfortable. Other ensembles were collages combining several decades of past trends.

Enough. Stop procrastinating. Read the letter.

She took out the envelope. *OONA LOCKHART: 2015* was spelled across it in block letters. Inside were two pages of unlined paper covered in tidy script with an upward slant, her penmanship recognizable by the quirks of the letters—*g*'s like figure eights, oversize loops on the *l*'s and *h*'s.

A high school English teacher had once told Oona her uphill handwriting was a sign she was an optimist. As she unfolded the letter, she wondered if this still applied to the version of herself who'd written it.

Dear Oona,

Welcome to your future. It won't be so bad once you get to know it.

Don't panic. You're not crazy or dead or dreaming. This is your true reality. It really is 2015 and you really are 51 years old (on the outside). The sooner you accept it, the sooner you'll adjust. But there's more to it.

What is "it," exactly? If Kenzie was able to keep you from running off, he's filled you in, but you're probably reading this on the subway, so I'll tell you.

First off, know that none of this is your fault. Or anyone else's. There was no science experiment gone wrong, no other explanation for it. And there's no way to prevent or fix it. Here's what's going on:

Every year, on your birthday, right at midnight, you travel through time to inhabit your body at a different point of your life. For exactly one year. Then you "leap" to another random age you haven't lived before (could be older, could be younger). You're physically and mentally healthy, but you're experiencing your adult life out of order.

Oona lowered the letter and stared up at an ad for a storage company. The train's motion shook her down to her bones, as if she were made of glass and would shatter to pieces at any moment.

Now. Please. Let me wake up now.

But the train continued rattling on its tracks, and she continued being jostled by people sitting on either side of her during turns and stops. When the train went aboveground, the passengers took out small, flat devices the likes of which she'd never seen and began tapping on and speaking into them.

This isn't the eighties.

The cold hadn't woken her, the noisy subway hadn't woken her, and her surroundings were painfully tangible, despite her wishes to the contrary.

No more denial.

This isn't a dream.

Deep breath in, deep breath out. Oona tried to check the time, but found she wasn't wearing a watch. A flash of color on the inside of her wrist made her pull up her sleeve. She gasped and revealed a tattoo: an hourglass with swirls of galaxies in place of sand, a ribbon across its base spelling out *M.D.C.R.*

She brought her wrist in for a closer look.

When did I get this? What do the letters stand for?

M for her mother, Madeleine; *D* for Dale; *C* for her father, Charles . . . what about the *R*?

Perhaps the letter would offer more clues. She resumed reading.

I'm sure you're bursting with questions, and I'll explain a few things, but you'll have to discover the rest yourself. I won't be able to protect you from all the bad surprises, but I don't want to ruin the good ones for you, either. There's this popular modern expression: no spoilers. *It's a warning not to give away key plot points (or endings) in movies, TV shows, or books. That's how I feel about our mixed-up life; I don't want to give away too many spoilers. It might take the fun out of living it. That's why I don't keep diaries. Instead, I try to write a letter at the end of each year, to prepare you for the next as best as I can.*

You have a lot of incredible things to look forward (backward?) to, but this first leap will be rough. To make things easier, I've laid out some . . . guidelines (I won't call them rules, because as much as you think you love rules, you also kind of hate them). Some of these might seem odd or annoying, but you need to trust me. After all, I'm Future You.

Here's some good news: you're rich. I'm talking ridiculously, buy-anything-do-anything-you-want rich. This is thanks to savvy investing and some educated sports bets (Croeso winning 1983's Florida Derby, at 85–1 odds, was a great start). So you can still get a SoHo loft if you want, but in the meantime, that Park Slope mansion you woke up in is yours. As is a nine-figure bank balance and a stock portfolio you must manage carefully. You'll need to memorize a lot of information in order to make/sustain your fortune, since whatever you learn in future years, you retain when you travel to the past. It can get complicated, though, which is why you have the binder (Kenzie will show you when you're ready; more on him later).

Let's get into these guidelines.

1. *You can't tell anyone about the time travel. Mom and Kenzie know, that's it. Right now, convincing anyone else would be tricky to impossible, and a doctor might sooner put you in a padded room than believe it. It'll take a while for you to believe it yourself, so for now, better to process quietly. This rule applies only to 2015. We'll have a little more wiggle room in other years.*

2. *Don't get too rich. If you make too much money, you might get unwanted attention, either from the IRS, the SEC, or people looking to take advantage, especially if you're mentioned in* Forbes' *list of wealthiest people. These days, that means keeping your fortune to under a billion (yes, billionaires are now a thing) and less than that in earlier decades. It means giving to charity and making some bad investments on purpose from time to time.*

3. *Avoid publicity. This applies to every leap. You're a philanthropist, but the last thing you need is people sniffing around, so don't draw too much attention to yourself (or your money). Kenzie helps you find good causes and can show you how to make donations while keeping a low profile.*

4. *Try to avoid having your picture taken, so you won't know what you look like year to year (again, no spoilers). Easier said than done these*

days, but do your best. If you can't avoid it, don't keep any photos taken
after 1982. The one in your study from Dale's party is an exception.

Oona's stop was announced before she could read the rest. She stuffed the letter back in her pocket and hurried out of the station. As she walked, she refused to button her coat against the brutal wind, refused to acknowledge that this was really her coat. That this was really her life. With each step, threads of confusion wove into a thick coil of determination.

As soon as I find Dale, we'll make sense of this together.

This Bensonhurst wasn't too different from the version she remembered. Some new storefronts—a bagel shop, a Laundromat, a nail salon—but as she turned off Bay Parkway, the sand- and earth-colored brick apartment buildings and two-family houses looked the same. She was infused with desperate optimism as she hurried up Dale's street.

It was the same house. Mostly.

Same house, different trimmings. The tiny front yard, once bearing rosebushes, had been replaced with a single blocky hedge. The black wrought-iron stair railings now looked as if they were made of silver pipe. And the front door, formerly crimson, had been painted brown.

No lights on inside, but Oona still rang the bell, lightly at first, then with more insistence.

The door swung open.

A short Asian man with rumpled gray hair squinted at her. "Who are you? Why are you here?"

Oona's legs grew wobbly and she put a hand on the front of the house for support. "I'm looking for Dale D'Amico."

"Nobody here by that name. You have the wrong house."

She pressed her palm into the brick's sharp grain, took in staccato breaths. "Do you know when the D'Amicos moved out? Where I could find them?"

"I've never heard of them. I've been living here ten years. Please go away now." He closed the door in her face.

An ambulance wailed in the distance as Oona collapsed on the top step, wheezing. Shallow breaths wouldn't satisfy her hungry lungs. The wind picked up, rattled through skeletal branches of nearby trees, yet she still couldn't take in enough air.

Finish reading the letter.

5. *Trust Kenzie. He may be a stranger to you now, but I've known him for years. He's more than your personal assistant, he's a loyal confidante. Younger than you, but wiser in many ways, and just plain fun to be around. He'll help more than you can imagine.*

6. *Don't trust technology. Think of it as your fair-weather friend. Learn to use computers, smartphones, and tablets (Kenzie will teach you). You can find a vast amount of information on the Internet about anything, anyone. It's awesome, but don't get carried away. Also, try to avoid social media. Don't get too attached to these modern conveniences, because next year you might have to live without them.*

Those are the main things you need to know for now except . . . Dale.

This is the hardest part. Even after all these years, it hurts to think about. Dale had a stroke, young. He's . . . I'm so sorry, but he's gone. Please don't look up his obituary. In fact, it's better if you don't look up information on anyone you know.

But you still have Mom. You'll see her tomorrow. She's fine, healthy. Has lots of boyfriends, takes lots of vacations. Hard to keep up with sometimes. She's living her best life. That's all she wants for you, too.

I'll stop here. Take some time to grieve and process but don't drown in the depression. You'll get through this. Trust me, it's me. Just take it one year at a time.

Love,

Me

P.S. You're probably wondering about the tattoo. All in good time . . .

Oona's fingers cramped from holding the letter so tightly. She wanted to tear it up and throw the pieces into the wind. Maybe that would make it less real. Instead, she refolded the letter and returned it to the envelope.

None of this is happening.

A youngish couple laughed as they climbed the steps to the house next door. "Happy New Year," they called out to her before going inside.

Fuck the New Year.

Fuck everything.

A black sedan pulled up and its driver gave two short taps on the horn. Kenzie.

Oona took leaden steps down to the car. Her bones felt like struck tuning forks. How was it possible to feel so heavy, yet so hollow?

"Thank *god*," he said once she was in the passenger seat. "You must be frozen solid. No hat, no gloves, coat all unbuttoned." He turned up the heat.

"I'm not cold at all," Oona said.

"What's that? I can't hear you over your chattering teeth."

As Kenzie drove, he kept looking over at her but said nothing. Not until he parked the car. "Are you all right? Dumb question. Of course you're not all right. What can I do?"

"Teach me about the Internet. And social media." *Fuck 2014 Oona, too.*

"Now?" Kenzie's hands fluttered like small panicked birds. "It's late and—"

"*Right now.* Please."

4

"You sure you don't want to start this in the morning?" Kenzie punched in the code to disable the security alarm.

"Yeah. I'm sorry to make you work so late, and on a holiday." Warm lily-scented air greeted Oona as she crossed the threshold.

"No sorries necessary. This isn't a nine-to-five gig. I'm around whenever you need me. It's not about that, more that this is *a lot*—"

"I live in this huge house all by myself?" Her boots clicked against black-and-white-checked marble as she circled the foyer in a daze.

"Um . . . right now, yeah. I mean, I'm here a lot—you have a sweet home office setup—and you fixed up one of the guest bedrooms for me to stay over whenever—you're a cool boss like that—but I have my own place in Cobble Hill." He followed her as she wandered down the hall toward the kitchen. "It's only a couple miles away, so if you wanted to take the rest of the night to, you know, absorb everything, I could come back first thing, bring you a soy latte . . ."

"No thanks. Whatever that is, it sounds gross. Maybe some coffee, though? If people still drink coffee in . . . wow." She entered the kitchen, which managed to be both lavish and cozy. Mint-green cabinets were complemented by chrome appliances and monochromatic granite counters. A breakfast bar and butcher-block island sectioned off the kitchen from the dining area.

"I know, right? Martha Stewart would cut a bitch for a kitchen like this . . . which is a compliment. Let me make the coffee."

"We had coffee makers back in the eighties, you know. It's this one, right?"

"Right, but—"

"Kenzie, I didn't grow up in the Middle Ages. If you could just show me where the coffee and filters are . . ." The annoyance in her voice faded as she scrutinized the sleek appliance's unfamiliar buttons. "And where they go . . ."

"It doesn't take filters, it takes K-Cups. They're like individual coffee pods." At her bewildered stare, he offered a calm smile. "It's easy, but how about you let me do it tonight so we can focus on Internet stuff? Coffee 101 can wait."

"Sure." Shrugging, she dropped her bag on a counter and sat at the kitchen island, concentrating on the granite's speckled pattern to avoid the blurred jumble of her thoughts.

After he made them coffee, Kenzie laid out three slim rectangular devices before her. "Phone. Tablet. Laptop."

Pointing at the phone, she said, "Well, at least I know what that is. Though it's a lot different from the ones I used."

"It's also a computer. They're all computers. You ever use one of those?"

She shook her head.

"Let's focus on the laptop for now." He flipped open the MacBook and began to type.

"How can it work if it isn't plugged in?"

"Wireless technology. It's a beautiful thing." With a flourish, he turned the computer toward Oona. On the screen was a video of a tabby cat in a blue satin shirt playing the keyboard. "Behold, the Internet . . ."

After a quick and dirty primer on the World Wide Web, he let her browse, but she kept accidentally closing out of windows and clicking on random hyperlinks. Frustration mounted on both sides.

"For now, I think it's gonna be easier if you just tell me what you're looking for and let me search for you," Kenzie said.

"Let's start with Dale. I want to know when he died. And how." Staccato clicks as Oona drummed her nails against granite.

"Didn't your letter mention that?"

"The how, yeah, but I don't believe it. Young people don't die of strokes."

"I don't think 2014 You would've lied about that." His fingers edged closer to hers, but she pulled back her hand.

"I want to know for sure. And I want the exact date of his death." The tone was meant to be stern, but her voice cracked with the threat of tears.

"Okay. I'll look him up. But even if I find the obituary, it may not mention the cause of death."

It didn't, but it did have his date of death: February 27, 1984.

"He was only twenty," Oona whispered, an ache in her throat. "He would've been someone great, but he never got to be . . . anything." She wiped at her wet face.

Kenzie exhaled audibly and slid over a box of Kleenex. "I'm so sorry. This is why you weren't supposed to—"

"I don't care what I'm supposed to do. 2014 Oona doesn't rule my life, *I* do. And I want to know what happened to everyone. All my friends."

"Then let me make us more coffee."

Once they were armed with refills, Kenzie took his place at the computer with a resigned hunch. "Who's next?"

"Pamela Lipscombe."

Her childhood best friend went on to Harvard Law School, worked as an assistant district attorney in New York, and ended up a federal judge.

"I always knew Pam would make it big. Look at this—she was even short-listed for the Supreme Court in 2010. And her daughter's an over-achiever, too, ranked one of the top twenty chess players in the world." Somewhat bolstered by her friend's success, Oona nodded at the screen. "Let's look up Wayne Sumpter."

The former Early Dawning bassist now lived in Baltimore, owned a private security company, was married to a petite redhead, and had two grown sons.

"How is all this personal stuff so easy to find?" she asked.

"Believe it or not, people post a lot of it themselves. Social media is . . . complicated. It's like people live their private lives in public now."

Oona tilted her head at the Facebook photo of Wayne on the beach with his family. "So ordinary people act like they're famous?"

"And many of them actually become famous for nothing. Don't get me started on celebrity culture. Who's next?"

"Corey Balcerak."

Early Dawning's former drummer was twice divorced (no kids), ended up in real estate, and was in the middle of serving an eight-year sentence in a federal prison for embezzlement.

"Oh my god." Horrified, she leaned in to get a closer look at the screen. "That can't be him." But the orange jumpsuit he wore in the news photo was eerily similar to the one she'd just seen him in at the party. And even with smoothed-back hair and the addition of wire-rimmed glasses and a grooved forehead, the resemblance to his younger self was undeniable. "But he was a good guy. A sweet dork, even if he was kinda dumb. I can't imagine him being a criminal."

"Considering he got caught, he's obviously not a very smart one."

"I can't even picture him working in an office. He was all about having crazy hair and playing the drums." She saw a flash of his quirky grin, his sweat-drenched face after rehearsal. "Does that mean nothing came of the band? Look up Early Dawning opening up for Factory Twelve."

While the latter went on to massive success, there was nothing about the 1983 tour mentioning the former, nothing in any other search results.

Does that mean I chose London? Did the band break up because of me?

Oona rubbed her bleary eyes.

"Maybe that's enough for tonight," Kenzie said.

"No way. I might as well know about everyone else."

Eventually it all became a blur of careers, marriages, divorces, children, grandchildren, diseases, and, in a few more cases, early death. These people were supposed to be extraordinary, yet most ended up with mundane, marginally successful, or flat-out tragic lives. Aside from Pam, none of the others had accomplished anything truly great.

"What about me?"

Pages of results filled the screen; websites, blogs, and social media profiles from around the world. Melbourne's Oona Lockhart was a tattooed vegan with three kids. Cleveland's Oona Lockhart was in college and collected antique board games. Oslo's Oona was biracial and photographed reindeer.

"None of those are me," she said. "I didn't think my name was so common."

"It isn't. I pay for special services to create fake Oona pages to flood the Internet. Makes it tougher to find the real you and easier to bury any info we can't erase. We're careful about you keeping a low profile. Sometimes you use aliases."

"And I've lost touch with all of them? All my friends?" She stared down at the laptop's keyboard, the letters swimming before her. "I must be so lonely."

There was a loaded pause before Kenzie replied. "You form other friendships over the years. And you've gotten a lot closer with your mom. For what it's worth, I'm here, too."

Right then it wasn't worth much, but it was better than nothing. "Thank you for . . ." Her hand wove through the air, unable to pluck out the right words. "Just thank you. I think that's enough for tonight. You can stay over if you want." There was a tremor in her voice.

"Of course. I'll show you your room. We should try to get some rest."

"Yeah." Though how could she sleep? The new information coursed through her head like cars on a busy freeway.

But when Kenzie led her to a bedroom dominated by a chrome four-poster bed piled high with pillows, she slid beneath the covers, curled up into a ball, and dropped right off. It would've been a small solace to dream of Dale, her friends, that mirrored basement, to return to 1982 for even a little while—before she knew how the story ended for all of them—but her sleep was a deep inky void.

Oona woke up after a few hours, oddly rested. Early morning's pale yellow light illuminated the room. She blinked at the celling.

I need to tell NYU if I'm going to London.

I need to tell the band if I'm going on tour.

I need to decide—

Except it was the wrong room. Instead of the popcorn ceiling of her teenage bedroom or the tangled wires suspended over Dale's bed, above her was an ornate tin ceiling.

Shit.

There was nothing to decide. She was in 2015.

Oona got out of bed, still in last night's skirt and sweater, eager for a fresh set of clothes.

Is this really my room?

She took cautious steps around the bedroom, like a guest snooping in someone else's house. Too nervous to touch anything—the nightstands resembling aluminum cubes; the glass shelves lined with silver vases, each containing a single violet calla lily; the iridescent lavender walls. A small display case in one corner of the room bore the only personal traces. It was filled with colorful knickknacks: a pyramid inside a snow globe, a porcelain Venetian mask, a model car made of crimson crystal, a Fabergé egg, a glass igloo, dozens of other items. *Gifts? Souvenirs?* Above the display case was the anniversary wristwatch from Dale, mounted and framed.

Why is it behind glass? I should be wearing it.

A desire to break the glass rose within her, only to be extinguished as the answer came:

It's too precious.

She turned away and refocused on finding a change of clothing, only there were no dressers or wardrobes in the minimalist room. There were three doors, though. One opened to a hallway and the rest of the house. The second revealed a bathroom done in creamy marble and mother-of-pearl. The third led to a humongous walk-in closet. It housed a wardrobe of classic styles in neutral colors for a range of body types, which made it easy to find something to fit her current size. At the far end was a rack containing more colorful pieces like vinyl catsuits, crinoline skirts, bustiers in metallic fabrics, and dresses made of improbable materials (Christmas lights, duct tape, plastic shingles . . .).

Are these leftover Halloween costumes?

As she changed into black jeans and a gray turtleneck, there was a knock on the bedroom door.

"Be right there," she called out.

When she opened the door, her mouth fell open. Her mother stood before her, smiling a crooked, expectant smile. Oona had anticipated wrinkles, frailty, gray hair, a stooped posture, but instead found a woman in leather pants and a low-cut sweater, brimming with bawdy vitality.

"How's my little time traveler?" Madeleine hugged her, enveloping her in a cloud of dark curly hair, periwinkle mohair, and Chanel No. 5, the same perfume she'd worn her entire life.

A stunned silence gripped Oona as she gawked at a woman who'd surely been trapped in amber. True, the decades had left some finger-prints on Madeleine: they added a plumpness to her petite form, framed the mouth and eyes with lines, made her neck tendons more prominent. But her face was pulled tight, copper-green eyes still bright, even if tilted at a new feline angle, eyebrows higher by a few degrees, lips fuller. And where Oona covered up her older body, Madeleine showed off ample cleavage, the loose skin of her bustline only faintly discernible.

"How is this possible? How do you look younger than me?" Oona put a hand to her face, as if she could read the mark of years like Braille.

"You're afraid of needles, my dear. To say nothing of knives." A kind chuckle at her daughter's perplexed expression. "Plastic surgery. You frown upon it. I adore it. In fact, you've accused me of being a little obsessed with it. But look at me. You'd never think sixty-eight, would you?" Madeleine twirled around.

"I don't know what to think, period. Why weren't you here last night?"

"I'm sorry, sweetheart, but you—2014 You—thought it would be best that way. I may be well preserved, but she—you thought it might be frightening to see me older so soon, before you had a chance to read the letter and let it all sink in a bit. Goodness, I can't imagine how try-ing this first leap must be for you. Come, let's eat, and then we'll have a little adventure."

Madeleine stepped aside to reveal Kenzie in the hallway, bundled in a royal blue scarf. "Good morning." He held out a lidded plastic cup. "Before you say or do anything else, try this."

Was it always going to feel this way, like being thrust onto a treadmill, running to catch up as everyone around her calmly walked? Oona took a sip from the offered cup—coffee, but with a creamy, nutty flavor. "It's good."

"Soy latte. See? Not gross at all," he added with a wry smile.

"Plus you don't have to worry about me breaking my robot coffee machine." Oona smiled back. The coffee and friendly faces added a normal patina to the morning, crammed the darker feelings away like closing an overflowing junk closet. It would all come tumbling out eventually, but the door would hold for now. "Mom just told me we're going to have a 'little adventure.'" She graced Madeleine with a quick eye roll. "Because when I woke up today, thirty-two years into my future, you know what I decided I needed most? *Adventure*."

Madeleine swatted her shoulder. "You don't even know what it is." A shake of her head, a look as if she were trying to find her daughter in a crowded room. "It's going to be like having a moody teenager again."

"I *am* a teenager. Who just lost decades of my life, so excuse me if I'm a little moody." Oona rubbed the back of her neck. Her body ached like she'd slept on boulders, not on a high-end mattress.

"You haven't lost decades, sweetie, your life has just been . . . rearranged."

"You make me sound like living room furniture."

Forming his hands into a T, Kenzie stepped between them. "I have an idea. How about less arguing and more birthday brunching? I made a reservation for you two at Applewood. Understated, but just fancy enough."

"You're not coming?" Trying to hide her disappointment, she covered with "Not that I'd expect you to. You should take today off."

"Oh." Warm surprise colored his cheeks. "I just thought you and your mother would want some time to . . ."

"Catch up on the last three decades?" The idea of which made Oona want to go back to bed. "I, um—I don't think I'm up for a fancy brunch right now. Maybe some toast in my fancy kitchen instead?"

"Fancy kitchen toast, coming right up," he said.

"It's bad enough I kept you up late last night. I can make it. Or have Mom show me how to use whatever high-tech contraption toasts bread nowadays."

The three went downstairs and, after checking to make sure Oona didn't need anything else, Kenzie left, and the two women headed to the kitchen.

Madeleine took out a loaf of bread and some plates. "If it makes you feel any better, toasters haven't really changed."

"That makes me feel *so much* better. Makes up for everything." It wasn't intentional, this tendency toward sarcasm; Oona never understood how her mother triggered it so easily.

"So how are you . . . handling everything so far? Did you read the letter?"

"Yeah, and it doesn't mean anything. I could be insane or have Alzheimer's or . . ." She placed her hands on the kitchen island's cold granite, overcome. *Wake up, wake up, wake up.*

But the stone was unyielding and her mother's stroking the back of her head offered little comfort.

"Listen, sweetheart. I know this is going to be a tough year for you—you told me so yourself last week. But you can't remain in denial."

"*This* is denial? How do I know you and Kenzie aren't trying to make me deny my true reality?"

"Why would we do that?"

"Maybe because . . ." The lump in her throat made it tough to dislodge the words. "Maybe soon I'll forget all of this anyway. Maybe it doesn't matter what you tell me, so you're taking the safe route, trying to keep me from totally cracking up."

Madeleine's head jolted back. "Does that sound like something I would do? Take the safe route with you? If you recall, I've done everything to encourage you to take more risks. I'm the one who told you to give Dale a chance when you were uneasy about dating an aspiring musician. Who made you play hooky once in a while so we could go shopping. Who bought you clothes you said were too loud or too slutty."

The toaster clicked; the bread popped up.

"True." Oona thought on this for a moment. "That was pretty messed up. Why would you do that?"

"You were always a cautious kid, but after Charles died, you walked around like the world was made of eggshells. So scared of making a misstep—"

"I'm scared to go on boats. I think that's understandable, seeing what happened to Dad."

"It's more than that. I wanted you to be open to taking risks now and again."

"Oh, like the kind of risk that made you get a fake birth certificate to land your dream job at Pan Am only to lose it because you got knocked up at seventeen?" Her hand flew up to her mouth. "That was mean. I'm sorry."

An eyebrow twitch and a smirk. "Apology accepted. Yes, my teenage daughter is back, all right."

"I didn't mean it. I'm just—I wish I could make sense of all this." Oona closed her eyes and forced her brain to pluck a memory from the void of missing years. But no matter how much she strained to cast a light into the dark corners of her mind, the most recent time she could illuminate was the party at Dale's. And, god, it was so vivid. The Christmas lights, the rough scales of her sequined dress, the astringent gel Dale used on his rockabilly pompadour, the whispery scratch of the Talk Talk record before the cascade of drum machines and synthesizers ushered in a string of *hey-hey-hey*s. But when she opened her eyes, the scene before her was less vivid. The pale green kitchen, the cold counter, the smell of buttered toast, her mother calling her name.

"Oona, listen to me. Hard as it is to believe, you *do* still have your whole life ahead of you."

The toast was brittle and scratched the roof of her mouth as she chewed. "How would you even know?"

"Because you've hinted at things. Fabulous things." Madeleine's inflated lips curved into an enigmatic smile.

"What things?"

"Why ruin the surprise? You have some hardships ahead of you, but you also have some marvelous experiences on the horizon, ones that would be robbed of their wonder if I told you."

The plate screeched against the granite as Oona pushed it away. "Then just tell me the bad stuff, so I can avoid making the same mistakes again. Did I end up going to London? Was that a mistake? Tell me, so I can choose the band next time, if this insanity is even real and I ever go back to the eighties."

Madeleine shook her head. "It doesn't . . . you can't. You've learned not to play with your fate. Apart from the stock market, but maybe it's your fate to be wealthy. I'm sorry, Oona, but I have to respect your own wishes not to reveal your past or future."

"Can you at least tell me about my tattoo?"

"I can't."

An invisible hand tightened around Oona's throat. "Why do my earlier self's wishes matter more than the me in front of you right now?"

"Because that you is wiser. She's had more time to consider how to craft a meaningful life. And because you once told me something about my future that hurt me deeply. I vowed I'd never do that to you." Her mother looked away. The dish trembled in her hand.

"I'm sure I didn't mean it." How strange, to feel contrite for something impossible to recall.

Madeleine rinsed off the plates. "It's fine now." She turned back around. "Now let's take a break from finding order and do something a little wild."

"We're two old ladies, Mom. Both probably lacking in mental faculties." Folding her arms across her chest, she shifted her weight to one leg, the pouty teenager pose at odds with her middle-aged body.

"Wrong on both counts. Now stop sulking and open your birthday present." Her mother handed her a flat package, its wrapping paper covered with antique clocks.

"Nice touch on the wrapping. If I'd been attacked by a shark, would it have had a *Jaws* theme?" She tore into the thin cardboard box. Inside was a black fifties-style halter-top bathing suit. Beneath that was a folded paper, a printout confirming a two-week stay at the St. Regis Princeville Resort in Kauai.

"We leave on Saturday. Might as well start the year in paradise, right?" Madeleine winked.

"What day is it today?"

"Thursday. Go try on the suit. You're going to need it for today's adventure."

Oona's muddled mind struggled to process the exchange with her mother, though it had revealed little. "That's still happening, huh?"

A serene yet mischievous grin played across Madeleine's face. "Yes. Yes, it is."

"And what kind of adventure are we talking about? Like the one in Coney Island when you forced me to ride the Cyclone until I threw up? Or when you took me to see Pink Floyd and I had to babysit you while you tripped on acid? Or how about that *adventure* we had on my sixteenth birthday when you nearly gave me and my friends alcohol poisoning after spiking our punch? Do you mean one of those types of adventures?"

Madeleine's face glossed with the boredom of hearing the same grievances repeatedly. "Go put the suit on. Wear your other clothes over it."

Grumbling under her breath, Oona did as she was told.

Thirty-two years of instant aging above the neck was one thing, and the weight gain was evident from the larger clothing sizes and her sense of the extra bulk, but this was the first real look she had at her body. Once she caught sight of her naked form, she couldn't keep from staring. In her youth, she hadn't been exactly thin, but her curves had been proportional, and she'd been comfortable with her fuller figure. It helped that her mother always told her that all bodies were beautiful, no matter their shape or size, no matter what the movies or magazines dictated. It helped that she was raised to expand her aesthetic boundaries and to value smarts over looks. And it helped now, when she felt like she was wearing someone else's heavy skin. Where she had once been shaped like a cello, she now pushed double bass proportions.

Fifty-one years old overnight and she'd have to make peace with it somehow, find beauty in the way she looked today.

"Come on, Oona," her mother called out. "Adventure awaits!"

5

Madeleine parked a few blocks from the boardwalk, removed a tote bag from the trunk, and led the way to Stillwell Avenue.

"Normally, I'd think nobody would be crazy enough to go to the beach in this weather, but I have you for a mother, so I shouldn't be surprised."

There was no rebuttal, but Madeleine's smirk was full of secrets.

"If you want to walk on the beach, that's fine," Oona continued. "It'll actually be nice to be somewhere quiet, by the water, away from people. But if you think I'm going to strip down and go swimming in January, well, I don't want to disappoint you, but—"

"It's not going to be quiet," Madeleine interrupted.

"Huh?"

As if in response, a cacophony of hooting greeted them when they rounded the corner. The beach swarmed with people.

The last time Oona had been to the beach was with Dale—months ago, now decades in the past. After watching reruns of Carl Sagan's show *Cosmos*, Dale had become obsessed with astronomy and his greater place in the universe.

"Take all the beaches in all the world"—he'd grabbed a handful of sand and let it seep through his fingers—"and count all the grains of sand."

"I know, I know. The stars in the universe would still outnumber the grains of sand," Oona finished for him.

"By a factor of five to ten." He'd held out a fingertip coated in sand, which Oona blew on to disperse the granules.

"Okay, Sagan, you've made me feel tiny and insignificant. What's the point of being in a band, then, or going to college or doing anything at all?"

"That's all the more reason to make our mark on the world, leave a legacy."

A tug on Oona's arm and she was back in 2015.

"Come on, let's find a spot to leave our things," Madeleine said.

Surrounding them were thousands of people, cheering, dancing, laughing, jumping up and down. Most were in sensible winter wear, while others dressed in costumes ranging from superheroes to sea creatures. Then there were the people in swimsuits.

"Mom, this is not going to happen. Why would you bring me here?"

Madeleine, a few steps ahead, turned around. "I'm part of the Coney Island Polar Bear Club. We do this every Sunday from November to April. I wanted you to join me today. The New Year's Day Polar Bear Plunge is an annual tradition and open to nonmembers. I think you'll find it refreshing. I think you need something to . . . wake you up."

There was no point in resisting Madeleine once she set her mind to something.

A detached, floating sensation came over Oona. She watched as if from the sidelines as she stripped off her clothes and shoes, put on the neoprene booties Madeleine gave her, and allowed her mother to slather her with sunscreen ("You can still get a sunburn, even in these temperatures").

Participants were split up into groups by color and given corresponding wristbands. Oona and Madeleine were in the blue group, slated to swim first.

I could let the tide carry me away. I'd be reunited with Dad. And Dale.

Needles of cold pricked Oona's arms and legs. The towel she

wrapped herself in helped little by way of warmth or modesty. It didn't matter; she wasn't getting many looks from the crowd, not the way the bikini-clad younger women were.

I was one of them only yesterday. Now I'm practically invisible. Maybe that's it. Maybe I'm not here at all.

"You're probably thinking the water will be freezing, but it might actually feel a bit warm because the air is colder . . ." Her mother continued a cheerful patter about how "awake" and "alive" these swims made her feel as Oona stared at the horizon, a sheet of white broken up by the undulating gray line of the Atlantic Ocean.

"It's almost time. Try to relax your mind and body as you go in," her mother said. "Pretend it's a hot August day and you're taking a dip to cool off. The more you can put yourself at ease, the more you'll enjoy it."

Yes, how lovely to pretend, to revert to those summers with Dale. Yet the fantasy was like a vinyl record; it would play out only so long before it ended and needed to be flipped. She'd never been susceptible to nostalgia before—she tried to believe the future held better things than the past. *Is this what it means to get older, replaying happy memories because the best times are behind you?*

Before long, the blue group was called forward. They charged the water, whooping and splashing. Oona let herself be carried forward by the people, then by the tide. Her mother was right, the water was warmer than she expected, but it still stabbed at her.

"Splash some on your wrists and neck," Madeleine urged. "The sooner your pulse points acclimate, the sooner the rest of your body will."

If only acclimating were that easy.

Oona waded farther out and dove into the water. Maybe if she swam far enough she'd drown or get washed onto a shore where time hadn't taken such a big bite out of her life. But the waves resisted, pushed her back where her feet could touch the ground.

The real cold didn't hit until she was out of the water, when icy winds chilled Oona bone-deep.

"The car has seat warmers, so we'll be nice and toasty before you know it," Madeleine shouted over the noisy crowd. She led the way off the beach, taking several solo steps before she circled back to her daughter, who was rooted in place with her head bent down. "What's the matter?"

Oona gazed at the sand at her feet, not thinking of planets or stars or of being young or old or average or extraordinary. She tried to hold on to the numbing effects of the winter swim, even as each shiver commanded her to feel *something*.

"What is it, Oona?"

If only she could rush back into the ocean and fight against her natural buoyancy. But the tide had navigated her here, so she had to say it out loud. Oona took in a jagged breath and forced the words from her mouth:

"Dale is dead."

Oona came home bundled in reticent sorrow, and went upstairs to her bedroom, inconsolable.

"I'm so sorry. I thought the swim would invigorate you. I shouldn't have pushed," Madeleine said through the closet door as Oona changed into dry clothes.

Do I still have it?

Running a hand across the garments suspended from the long rack, Oona paced the length of the walk-in until her fingers brushed against the jacket Dale had given her. She pulled it off its hanger. The leather was more pliant all these years later, soft and weathered, the black material now shaded with gray. Its rich scent was also faded, though still prevalent, with notes of cedar and cinnamon. Years of wear and exposure had made it only more beautiful. But she was unable to get her arm all the way through the sleeve. Her armor no longer fit her.

When Oona emerged from the closet, clutching the jacket to her chest, she stepped around her mother and made straight for the bed. Slipped beneath the covers without a word.

"Let me go make you some tea."

Oona buried her head in a pillow, hugged the leather tight, and closed her eyes.

It was easy to ignore the cups of tea and bowls of soup brought to her in the ensuing days. It was easy to turn Kenzie's and Madeleine's concerned murmurs into ocean roars and drift away into a dreamless darkness. And when she woke, it was easy to dismiss the iridescent wall before her. All she had to do was shut her eyes.

Maybe I'll sleep the year away.

In the blackness, a sweet-voiced soundtrack played, urged on the slumber. A candy lullaby sending a little boat off to stormy seas. No matter that her boat had already capsized, that the water had frozen with her beneath it. She preferred submersion.

"Wake up!"

No.

"You must wake up!"

Must I?

Reluctant, her eyelids fluttered open. The room was empty. What was this music? Disjointed, melancholy, a soaring voice filled with longing and regret. Where was it coming from?

Oona's head felt so heavy, a steel globe, the pillow a magnet. Sleep the tide, quick to seduce and pull her under. Her cherished leather jacket more anchor than life vest.

Yet the music dragged her to shore, pleaded for her to rise. Inertia fought a tug-of-war with melody and the latter prevailed. It coaxed her to a sitting position, released her grip on the jacket, drew aside the blanket, tugged her to her feet. It commanded her to stop drowning.

A lap of the room revealed the source of the music on a glass shelf: a white device slimmer than a pack of cards, a vein of a wire, the sound projected from tiny speakers camouflaged in the corners. Beside the device, a note:

Take a shower, get dressed, come downstairs.—K.

One last glance at the shipwreck of her bed. It was time to find her land legs.

She showered. She got dressed. She went downstairs.

The scent permeating the kitchen wasn't coffee or tea—it was something more complex: spicy winter treats hidden in the woods.

"Chai. And that's portable." Kenzie handed her an aluminum mug with a screw-on lid.

"Are we having an adventure? Because if I'm getting pushed out of a plane today, I'm going back to bed."

A soft snicker. "We're just going for a walk. I think Madeleine over-estimated your tolerance for adventure. I promise we'll keep it low-key."

She took a sip of the warm liquid: surprised delight allayed her suspicion. "Yum."

"I know, right?" A conspiratorial grin as he held up a plastic bag. "I also got us éclairs. It's impossible to hate life after a good éclair, and these are the best. Let's get our coats."

The sweetness on her tongue turned sour. "Hawaii. Mom planned a whole trip for us."

"Postponed. Don't worry about it. And if you're not ready then, I'll take your place." He winked.

"Is she mad?"

"Of course not. She's gonna meet us for lunch, after Zumba." At her puzzlement, he added, "It's a dance aerobics thing. I figured you'd prefer a quiet park to a room full of middle-aged women sweating to loud Latin music. Of course I could be wrong." There was an impish glimmer in his eyes.

Maybe it was the lingering effects of the music or the serene way he regarded her that said, *You can do this*. Or maybe it was his sweater that resembled teal cotton candy and begged to be touched. Regardless, Oona set down her mug and gave him a long hug. What a relief—the sweater was as soft as it was bright. An even bigger relief that he hugged her back.

They walked through Prospect Park, following the track down to the lake. A fallen log provided a makeshift picnic bench, where they ate their éclairs, watching ducks and geese float and waddle along.

"So do you hate life a little less now?"

"I think it's going to take more than French pastry for that, but thanks for trying," Oona said. "What was that music playing in my room?"

"Ah, 'The Ninth Wave.' The second side of Kate Bush's *Hounds of Love* album. A concept piece about a girl stranded at sea."

"I've never heard anything like it."

"Actually you have, but . . . you know." The corner of his mouth twitched up. "It's a friggin' masterpiece. Came out in 1985. There's a lot of great music for you to catch up on."

A stirring within her, a hunger after all the days in bed, but not for food. For something intangible, something momentarily satiated by the music. "Maybe that's what I'll do, then. Instead of spending the year sleeping, I'll spend it listening to music."

"It doesn't have to be one thing, you know."

"I should see a doctor," she murmured into her travel mug. "I might be sick."

"You're not sick. If you want to get a checkup, get some tests done, we can do that, but doctors won't find anything."

"I still don't believe it."

"The world doesn't care what you believe." He raised a finger to placate her. "Sorry if that sounds harsh. I care, of course, and your mom cares, but the world is gonna carry on whether you spend the year moping in bed or exploring it."

"Don't I have good reason to mope? What am I besides old and useless?"

"You're not old or useless. You're rich and generous. And you have more of your mother's rebellious streak than you think, regardless of age."

Oona slapped her thighs and stood, returned to the track with brisk steps. "You know how messed up it is to be told what you're like by someone who's a stranger to you?" She picked up the pace, ignoring the twinges in her joints. "Not as messed up as wondering if what's happening to you is actually happening. Every time I go to sleep, I pray I'll wake up from this nightmare, a teenager again, with Dale beside me."

"If that's what you want, I hope that happens."

"Oh, come on, don't be condescending. However much I've changed in the last thirty years, I'm sure I still have a low tolerance for bullshit."

His bewildered laugh curled around them like a ribbon.

"What's so funny?" she asked.

"It's nice to see moments of my old friend. It's not entirely you and yet it's still you."

Her pinched heart sent a sharp volt through her, demanded more room to expand. How gracious for him to persist and sidestep her barbs. "How did we meet, anyway?"

"It's a long story. We bonded over music. I promised not to tell you more than that."

"No spoilers"—air quotes and a smirk—"right?"

"That's right."

"What about the girl lost at sea?"

"What girl?"

"In that Kate Bush album." She cast her stinging eyes up to the sky, which was white as paper. "Does she ever get rescued?"

"She does," came the reply. Earnest, firm. "She definitely does."

6

It would be a difficult year for Oona, though she'd do what she could to make it better. The money helped, as money often does. The financial cushion was welcome, but it also felt like a lawsuit settlement or insurance payout for whatever accident or act of God resulted in those years lost. At least any struggles awaiting her wouldn't be monetary. But being able to buy anything put a spotlight on the things that couldn't be bought (lost friendship, lost love, lost time), human nature being prone to focus on what was lacking.

Hoping to find a medical cause for the missing years, Oona got a full medical work-up. Apart from the extra weight, she was in fine health, and a brain scan revealed no abnormalities. She considered a psychiatrist but heeded the letter's warning not to reveal her true condition to others. Better to be insane in the comfort of her home than a mental hospital.

And what a home it was—vast but designed for comfort. There was a rec room with classic arcade video games and pinball machines. There was a home theater with red velvet couches and a projection screen across an entire wall. But her favorite was the music room, with its shag carpeting, beanbag chairs, and massive stereo. Custom shelving housed a staggering collection of vinyl, and the opposite wall held guitars that had belonged to Lou Reed, David Gilmour, Prince, David Bowie, and other music legends. At first, reverence kept her from touching them, but after a few days, she grew emboldened and took a turn at each guitar. She strummed chords and picked out melodies the way Dale had shown her on his own guitar, imagined stadiums full of cheering fans and intimate recording sessions. It lifted her up and up and up—until a stab of guilt sent her plummeting down. She returned the guitar to its spot on the wall.

The guitar is Dale's instrument. Keyboards were mine.

Yet there were no pianos or keyboards in the house, and her fingers thirsted to strum and pluck and pick at guitar strings, anyway.

But what if—

No. It would be disloyal to Dale.

She vowed to keep the instruments as nothing more than a display, a dream out of reach.

In the days that followed, Oona wandered through her house like a marble rolling around an empty box, often retreating to the music room. Despite her extensive record collection, she fixated on that one side of that one Kate Bush album, played over and over. She'd lie on the floor and pretend the carpet was an ocean, close her eyes, and wait for stormy seas to carry her away.

Until one day the music stopped mid-song. When she sat up, Kenzie was standing beside the silenced record player, a laptop under one arm.

"Mind if I sit?" Without waiting for an answer, he dropped onto the carpet beside her and opened up the computer. "I want to show you something."

"If it's another cat playing the piano, I'll pass."

"No, it's your music collection."

"I can see it from here." She gestured to her record shelves.

"That's only part of it. There's more in here." After a few taps on the keyboard, he turned the screen toward her. "This is your iTunes library. That's the total number of songs you own."

"Forty-two *thousand*? And is this how long it would take me to listen to all of them? A hundred and twenty-four *days*?" A film of sweat broke out on her forehead.

"Yeah. And look, you can play any song just by clicking on it." With the push of a button, jangly guitars filled the room, followed by a man's sultry croon.

Oona's eyes darted to the corner speakers. "It's like some kind of magic trick. Hey, is this Roxy Music?"

"Bryan Ferry. He's released some great solo albums since your time. And not just him." He spent the next few minutes showing her the basics of digital music.

"I still don't know where to begin." A trill of alarm in her voice. "With any of it."

"All right, step away from the panic attack. Breathe with me." Once he staved off her hyperventilation, he continued. "Nobody expects you to know all the things. It's not like there's gonna be a big test. Start with the bands you already know, or with some of these playlists I made for you. As for the rest of it . . ." Cautious optimism wrinkled his brow. "Wikipedia's a good place to start." He pulled up the website and explained how it worked. "Maybe do a quick overview of each decade first?"

As she clicked around, she bobbed her head slowly. "Seems a little less overwhelming."

"You got this. Just learn a little something new every day. And let me show you modern conveniences once in a while. Though they can be inconvenient, sometimes—I spent two hours picking out a new pillow the other day."

"Two *hours*? How many pillows are there?"

"Too many. The curse of plenty. But we'll save online shopping for another time. And we'll need to talk about your money at some point, but I don't want your head to explode. For now, give iTunes a chance?" He held out the MacBook until she nodded and took it from him. "Holla if you need anything. You've got a few hours before your mother comes by for dinner. After we eat, we'll watch *Purple Rain*."

"*What?*"

"It's a movie. You're gonna love it."

*   *   *

She did love *Purple Rain*, as well as *Back to the Future*, and all the eighties
John Hughes movies Kenzie chose ("Next week, we'll start on the nineties. Two words: *Pulp Fiction*"). While she got accustomed to cable, DVR,
and Netflix, she preferred he take the reins of what they watched so she
could focus her exploratory energy on music. After the initial intimida-
tion of her iTunes collection, she rejoiced at catching up on decades of
discographies from her favorite musicians, though she still often opted
for the lush crackle of a vinyl record. But she also gave the playlists a
chance, which enlightened her on some new genres that emerged in
recent decades. She warmed to the rhythm and cadence of hip-hop, the
raw growl of grunge, the mechanical seduction of electronica.

Heeding Kenzie's advice, she used Wikipedia to get up to speed
on key events of the past decades, following many rabbit holes when
a particular person or event sparked her curiosity. She became profi-
cient at online research, though she resisted the urge to look up her
old friends again. Instead, she distracted herself with decades of scien-
tific and technological advancement, historical conflict, and popular
culture. The loss of time was less painful when it was less personal,
though the deaths of musicians she admired saddened her: Freddie
Mercury, Joe Strummer, all four original Ramones . . . Lou Reed's
passing especially stung.

While she took walks with Kenzie in the park every other day,
she stayed in the rest of the time, glued to her laptop or tablet, picking
a different room of the house each day to settle in. Kenzie joined her
when he didn't have calls or errands, and she picked his brain about
the modern world. She brimmed with endless questions like a hyper-
curious child, only instead of asking why the sky was blue or where
babies came from, she asked why 9/11 happened and where society's
progressive attitude came from, still in awe that a black man was pres-
ident and gay marriage was legal.

"There's been a shit-ton of progress, but don't go thinking we're
in some kind of liberal wonderland," he said. "There are still parts of
America where I'd be scared to flaunt my . . . fabulosity."

They were in her study that day, Kenzie at the desk and Oona nestled into the bay window, three floors up, high enough to spy the tops of the park's snow-covered trees across the way.

"Is it rude or weird if I ask . . . ?" Awkward hand motions.

"How long I've known I'm gay? When I came out?" He nodded like he'd been expecting this.

"Yeah."

"Known as long as I could remember. Didn't really come out as much as coaxed out by my lesbian mothers when I was ten. There was this popular show on at the time, *Blossom,* and I practically wallpapered my room with posters of Joey Lawrence, one of the stars. So it was pretty obvious."

Oona smiled along with him, as if tapping into his memory.

"Did you get picked on at school?"

"Not that much, surprisingly. Sometimes when you're sure of who you are, it kind of . . . I don't know, protects you in some way. And I hung with a more alternative crowd, so that helped. Plus, nobody messed with me because of my moms. They were fierce women."

"*Were?*"

"Yeah." He plucked at his sweater, collected invisible lint. "They both died a while back. Drunk driver. No real extended family, so I've been on my own since then."

"Oh, Kenzie."

No wonder he'd formed such an attachment to her and her mother. No wonder he was so attuned to her loneliness. His mellow presence was a balm, even when they sat staring into their respective laptops for hours, taking turns picking what music to play.

"My turn for a question." Kenzie cocked his head. "Why haven't you asked me about your money? Aren't you curious about how you made all these millions and how you spend them? Don't you wanna know what I do day to day when I'm not going out for bagels and explaining stuff like apps and podcasts? Just yesterday you asked a bunch of questions about the Mars rover and reality TV and *The Da Vinci Code*—nice to see you're making your way through the 2000s, by the way—and we talk about more serious things, too, like AIDS and climate change. But you've never asked about the market crash of '87 or the subprime mortgage crisis or anything related to economics or your investments. How come?"

"I don't know." Her shrug was noncommittal.

"Come on, you went to school for this. Even when you were a kid, didn't your dad teach you and your Dorothy Hamill hair—"

"Pam," she snapped. "Her name is Pam and that haircut looked cute on her."

"Sorry. Pam." His tone softened. "Didn't he teach you and Pam about interest rates playing some board game?"

"Pay Day. He got it the summer I was eleven. Pam and I would play for hours, and when we got tired of it, we'd make up our own games pretending to be bankers." A bitter smile curled her lips. "That was a couple of months before Dad died. I still remember what the box looked liked. The cover said, 'Where does all the money go?'" She looked at Kenzie with weary eyes. "I used to care where the money went. What does it matter now? Game over."

"You need to care or you won't have all this." He swept an arm around the room. "Didn't your letter mention the binder?"

"Yeah, but with everything else going on . . . I couldn't handle the thought of doing *homework*."

"Don't all of a sudden hide your geek roots and act like you hate doing homework." His voice dropped to a dramatic hush. "I think you're ready. Come with me." Kenzie led her to one of the bookshelves and removed an armful of hardbacks, revealing a small safe built into the wall. "The combination is six left, twenty-eight right, sixty-three left. I keep telling you using Dale's birthday for all your security needs isn't the best idea, but whatever." There was a metallic click and the safe opened. Kenzie pulled out a black three-ring binder.

"What else is in there?" Oona asked.

"Nothing. And to be honest, this thing would be useless to any thieves without a time machine, but you're allowed your foibles."

Back at the desk, Kenzie opened the binder, which was filled with sheet protectors. Each plastic sleeve contained a single piece of paper and had a tab with a year on it. "You know how you don't keep diaries? Well, this is kind of a money diary. Each year shows the stocks you bought and sold, winners of big sporting events, and any relevant socio-political events affecting the economy. This is your homework. There's no telling which year you'll leap into next, so you need to be prepared for any of them."

"Assuming this leaping business is real."

"It's real. Trust me. Trust *you.*"

Trust me, it's me.

"If nothing else, memorize everything about Apple, Microsoft, and M&T Bank."

She glanced at the first page, following Apple through the years:

1983–Oct: Apple (AAPL) buy limit order at $21, wait for stock to split in 1987.

1987–July: Apple (AAPL) stop-loss order at $60 (will take effect in 1991).

1991–April: Apple (AAPL) buy limit order at $17, wait for stock to split in 2000.

2000–July: Apple (AAPL) stop-loss order at $60 (will take effect in August).

2000–August: buy limit order at $15 (will take effect in December), wait for stock to split in 2005.

"Jesus, how many times did this stock split?" she asked.

"Four. And just last year, it split seven to one."

"Holy shit." Her eyebrows shot up.

"Holy shit is right. If you invested a thousand dollars in Apple in 1995, you'd have something like ninety-five thousand today. You invested way before that, and more than a thousand."

"There's something I don't get," she said. "If I use limit orders and stop-losses, the stocks are bought and sold automatically, so where do you come in?"

"I do some of the less glamorous work, like market trend research, bookkeeping, taxes. I also make some of my own trades—your portfolio might look fishy if there aren't losses reported, so I keep it real. And I balance your capital gains with your charitable contributions—sounds sexy, huh? That's where a lot of my time goes. There are countless good causes and your millions can't help them all."

"But I do help some?"

"A *lot*." At her hopeful smile, he offered a list. "Military veterans, the homeless, animal rescues, special-needs children, refugees from war-torn countries. Then there's all the medical research you help fund: cancer, AIDS, Parkinson's, you name it."

"Wow." She stood a little taller.

"That's not all. There's this thing called crowdfunding, where people set up websites to get donations over the Internet. Some have a serious financial crisis, like medical bills or impending foreclosures, and some are looking to fund a creative project—comic book, movie, et cetera. You've even put money toward a museum celebrating Nikola Tesla—I did, too, because Tesla was the bomb. Anyway, I try to make sure these people are legit, but you don't care—you're like the freakin' Oprah of Kickstarter and GoFundMe."

"Oprah Winfrey, I know that one." Recognition flashed in her eyes, and she pointed a finger around the room, shouting, *"You get a car, you get a car, you get a car!"*

He laughed. "Exactly. It's insane how much money you give away."

"It sounds like fun. I'd like to see these websites."

"You will." Kenzie closed the binder.

"Aren't you gonna make me do my homework first?"

"No, I'm putting this away. And you're putting that"—a nod at her laptop—"away."

She offered an agreeable shrug. "Park?"

"No park. It's almost February and we haven't left a five-block radius in weeks. We don't have to go far, but we could at least explore the city." It was something her mother would say, though Kenzie's adventurous spirit was less daunting.

"You don't . . ." She began to formulate an argument, but could only conjure feeble excuses. "You're right. I'll go put on some shoes."

"Great. But before that, could you do your Oprah for me again?"

They got the obvious things out of the way first. The Brooklyn Bridge. The Met, MoMA, the American Museum of Natural History. Central Park. Rockefeller Center. Times Square ("It looks like a sci-fi movie!" Oona exclaimed). The Statue of Liberty (from a distance, because she refused to ride the ferry; for posterity, she bought a small souvenir statue for her display case).

At the top of the Empire State Building, Oona gazed south, and her heart went somber at the sight of a single skyscraper standing in place of the Twin Towers.

"Did you know one of the towers had a bar called the Greatest Bar on Earth?" she told Kenzie. "Dale always talked about bringing me there once I turned nineteen—that was the drinking age back then." She closed her eyes and tilted up her chin to meet a gust of wind that blew back her hair like a flag.

"I knew someone who worked there. As a waiter at Windows on the World."

"Was he . . . a friend?"

"More than that. I was in New York the summer before my senior year of high school, a few months before the planes hit," Kenzie said. "We met in Washington Square Park and hit it off. He was nineteen. Wanted to be an actor. We spent a week together and did sort of a long-distance thing when I went back to Boston. Emailed, IM'ed, and called a lot." He ran a hand up and down his arm, as if massaging a sore muscle. "He worked the breakfast shift so he could go on auditions."

Oona whipped her head toward him. "Was he there that morning?"

Something sharp flickered across Kenzie's eyes. "Yeah, I think so. I never heard from him after that. For a while, I told myself he found out I lied about my age—got freaked out I was seventeen, not eighteen—and that's why he stopped talking to me. He was never online, so I told myself he blocked me. I thought about looking up the list of names . . ." Kenzie chewed his lower lip. "But I haven't, because . . ."

"Because that leaves a chance he might still be alive."

"Yeah. He meant a lot to me. I'd rather not think of him as a victim of something so awful."

"God, Kenzie." She pulled him into a long hug. "Why didn't you tell me this before when I asked you about 9/11?"

He stepped back and jerked a shoulder up. "I don't know, you were so caught up in your own grief, I didn't think you'd want to hear about it."

Shameful tears sprang to her eyes. "I'm still caught up in my own grief. But I won't let that make me a crappy friend."

In the months that followed, her friendship with Kenzie deepened. Between their outings, playing catch-up with the decades, and studying the binder, she usually had enough to keep from being swept away by wistfulness for her earlier life. But sometimes nostalgia would deal her a mean sucker punch, like the one afternoon in April when she and Kenzie were walking around Little Italy. There were more souvenir shops and fewer restaurants than she remembered, but as they reached the intersection of Mulberry and Hester, she gasped and pointed across the street.

"Oh my god, Caffe Napoli is still here? Dale took me there on our second date."

"Do you want to . . . go inside? Run far away?" Concern folded Kenzie's forehead.

"No. It looks fancier now." Staring up at the gold and black signage, she blinked until the tears receded. "Did I tell you how Dale and I met?"

"Tell me again."

"A month before my junior year of high school, I was in a bookstore reading the latest *Rolling Stone*. This guy came up to me—sleepy eyes, rockabilly hair, leather jacket, super-cute—and just started talking to me about music. Asked me what bands I was into, teased me for liking Pink Floyd, but then we bonded over Velvet Underground. He introduced himself and when we shook hands . . ." Her face softened into a dreamy smile. "I *knew*. This was it. *He* was it. He asked if he could give me his address, if I'd write to him, even though he lived in Brooklyn. I agreed, and Dale handed me a piece of paper that already had his name and address on it, with 'guy from bookstore' written on top. We exchanged a few letters, and when school started again, I saw him in the hallway. He was a year ahead of me—I don't know how I hadn't noticed him before. He finally asked me out, and our first date was dinner and a movie—fried calamari at Rocco's followed by *Private Benjamin*." Though of course they hadn't watched much of the movie. As soon as the lights were dimmed, their lips sought each other's out, months of anticipation overshadowing any inhibitions. Their kisses tasted of marinara sauce. Bright light burst behind Oona's closed eyelids and the hairs on her arms stood on end as everything around them faded to black.

"And for our second date, he took me for dinner in Chinatown, followed by dessert. Right here." Oona gave Kenzie a fortified look that promised she wouldn't cry. "That's when he told me he was starting a band and wanted me to be in it. By that point, I was so in love, he could've told me he was starting a circus and I would've joined it."

"And I'm sure you would've made a damn fine trapeze artist or lion tamer."

That was something about Kenzie she cherished. He could always brighten a situation without disrespecting its emotional weight.

A final look at the restaurant's window and she nodded up the block. "Want to check out Chinatown? I could go for some wonton soup."

When he wasn't working for Oona, Kenzie wrote freelance articles for music blogs and often got free concert tickets. It took a bit of coaxing, but in the late spring, he convinced Oona to see a folk-rock band play a small club in Williamsburg. The music was decent, and she enjoyed the show while fighting invasive what-if thoughts, wondering about her own short-lived music career, staving off resentment at being relegated to spectator.

In the cab home, Oona channeled her irritation into something less existential and more tangible. "What's the deal with all the phones?" she asked Kenzie. "It was so annoying, having all these little screens reflect the performance onstage. You were done taking photos for your article after a minute. Some people were recording the whole thing! Does *everybody* have a music blog?"

He chuckled. "Probably not. But they do have Facebook, Instagram, Twitter . . ."

"Right, and people have to share everything they do in order to feel important."

"Or to feel a sense of community. Like I said, social media is complicated."

"And cluttered. There's so much white noise and distraction. The girl next to me didn't even watch the show—she spent the whole time texting. I get why people are so obsessed with their phones . . ." Turning hers over in her hands, she still couldn't wrap her head around all its capabilities. It seemed inconceivable something so small offered endless information and convenience. "I just wonder if it's making us a little lazy and rude. How much real life do people miss out on because they're focused on a screen? How much have I missed out on?" She put her phone away.

"It's an epidemic. But you're a special case. And you're mastering the art of living in the moment. Hashtag truth."

Maybe not mastering, but Oona did her best in the following months. She spent more time attending concerts and other local events with Kenzie, and less time behind her screens.

One day in September, they went to an art installation in Williamsburg called *Hiraeth*. A series of rooms showcased family portraits spanning multiple eras, the heads swapped out for mirrors so the viewer became part of the picture. As Oona's reflection joined these families across time, her somber face matched the painted ones around her. In the last room, a digital screen took up an entire wall. Above it, pink neon script spelled out, "Hiraeth: homesickness for something that never was and never could be." The screen reflected whoever stood before it and warped them, swapping their heads with the people beside them, changing their hair or skin color. Oona stood transfixed and marveled at the different permutations of her image. But when it morphed into a version freakishly identical to herself at eighteen, she snapped her eyes shut and covered them with her hands.

I can't take any more.

Kenzie put an arm around her and led her outside. She spent the next week in bed, silent, immobile.

Every night before bed, she told herself, "Tomorrow I'll be home." Every morning, her hope waned. What if she'd never return to her true time, her true self? What if she remained trapped in her own future?

On her good days, she thought of herself as a truncated female Rip Van Winkle and treated the decades of catch-up as an embraceable challenge. On her bad days, she was an interloper in a foreign country, a prisoner in a foreign body.

As temperatures dropped and daylight hours shortened, she fought the fog of depression, pushed through, kept it at bay with anticipation that the following year would bring her to a better place, a better time.

Madeleine decided to spend the latter half of December at a yoga retreat in Java and urged her daughter to join her, but Oona declined. She remained averse to traveling beyond the city limits and was apprehensive about ringing in the new year far from home, not knowing what to expect at the stroke of midnight.

On New Year's Eve, she made mulled wine with Kenzie—piercing oranges with cloves and setting them afloat in a sea of red wine, brandy, cinnamon, and nutmeg ("the chai of boozy beverages," they agreed). They took turns stirring the pot, adding amber dollops of honey until the mixture was just right, then sat in Oona's library beside the fireplace, drinking mugs of the stuff.

"Are you excited about your next leap?" Kenzie asked.

"If it means waking up from all this, yes. I'm excited to resume my old life, with my friends and my boyfriend and my band. Take that semester off, go on tour. Of all the things I missed, school wasn't one of them."

A long sip while he measured his words. "Let's say you don't wake up. Let's say this time travel stuff is real and the next leap isn't to the eighties. Can you handle that possibility?"

"Not if it's another leap forward. I'm not ready to be a twenty-year-old in a senior citizen's body." Oona inhaled the fragrant scent of her wine, savored how heavy it felt on her tongue. "But if I go back to an earlier part of my life and get to live out a year when I'm younger, that might not be so bad. If nothing else, it might convince me I'm not crazy."

"You're not. You'll see."

Oona regarded Kenzie. Would it be years before she saw him again, or moments? Something tugged inside her at the thought of leaving him behind. Had she been a good friend to him, all things considered? She tried, but she could've done better.

They spent the final moments of 2015 in her study, nursing mulled wine, which left a fuzzy coating on Oona's tongue and made her warm and woozy. In her lap was the framed photo from the 1982 New Year's party. If only she could will herself back there.

What's next? Will I continue as a tourist in my own life? Will any of it ever make sense?

She watched the clock and prayed she'd been told the truth about her strange circumstances, prayed her blind optimism wouldn't prove fruitless. She vowed not to be ruled by nostalgia and grief after this year. Wherever and whenever she ended up next, she'd make the most of it.

At 11:59 P.M., she sat back in her chair and gripped the armrests as if preparing for a turbulent flight. She closed her eyes, tensed her body, took a deep breath, and held it.

PART III

Let's Go Crazy

1991: 27/20

7

An immersion of sound, white noise that could've been breaking waves pounding rocks instead of the roar of cheering. People surrounded Oona, pressed against her in a darkness punctuated with purple and white strobe lights. A haze of smoke. A blizzard of confetti. The crowd bled into a blur of wild eyes, dark lips, bright teeth. It enveloped her from all sides, a human vise tightening.

She pushed her way through the masses like a dull needle piercing stiff fabric. A new noise filled the space: electronic beeps and a clanging of metal on metal joined by a bass and drums. As she wove an escape path, the frenzy surrounding her grew. Dancing limbs were new obstacles to maneuver. "Excuse you!" someone shouted when she accidentally elbowed them.

Once she got clear of the crowd, it became evident it had been propping her up. Her limbs were rubbery, and she grabbed a wall to keep from falling over. She adjusted her eyes to the darkness, but it was still like peering at a smudged aquarium tank. Not much she could make out through the blurs and trails, the images swimming before her.

Am I drunk?

She hadn't been a heavy drinker in her teens—a vodka cranberry

with Dale here and there, a beer at a party, champagne on New Year's—
and in 2015, she'd rarely exceeded two glasses of wine, even on nights she
felt especially lost and lonely. But this was more than a light buzz. She
felt loose the way alcohol made her feel loose, but less in control of her
movements, unable to steady her vision. She felt . . . altered.

I'm fucked up.

No way to tell what was coursing through her body.

"Excuse me." Her hand was incredibly heavy, but she latched onto
the arm of a passerby, a girl in a transparent raincoat and white pageboy wig. "What year is it?" She could barely speak, her words low and
garbled, and she had to repeat the question several times before she was
understood.

The girl grinned. "You must be more messed up than I am. It's
1991. Happy New Year."

Goodbye, 2015; hello, 1991.

A heady surge like a bright yellow light flooded through Oona. Her
mouth opened wide, caught between wonder, laughter, and confused joy.

I know the when. On to the where.

Down a red-lit hallway, she gripped the side of the wall, made
steady progress until she tripped over a pair of feet. She clutched at the
first thing she found to keep from falling: a shoulder.

"Oops, sorry." Her vision and hearing became more focused, but
balance was still a bitch. *What kind of stupid shoes am I wearing?*

The shoulder keeping her from tipping over belonged to a man in
his twenties, a hair taller than her and well built, with a square jaw and
brown curls falling into his eyes. He took hold of her arm to steady her.
"Don't worry about it. I don't need all ten toes."

Oona looked down, adjusted her stilettoed foot so the heel was no
longer planted in the man's shoe. "Oh, wow. Sorry again." Her tongue
still too big in her mouth, too slow to form words. "Where's the exit?"

"I can't tell you."

"Why not?"

"Because if you leave, I can't buy you a drink. Give me five minutes, if only to make up for my lost toe." His crooked smile triggered a
dimple.

Oona was still disoriented, but the light within her glowed brighter when she stared at him. The smart thing would be to get her bearings and go home—or at least somewhere safe and quiet. Sober up. Figure out what to do next.

But the way this man looked at her—enticing and a little dangerous—made her forget about being smart. Nobody had looked at her that way in a year. Not since before . . . and a year was such a long time to be alone. Invisible.

"Okay, you can buy me a drink. But I need to find a bathroom first."

He pointed down the hall. "Second door on the left. I'll be here. Promise not to run out on me?"

His curls undulated before her and she blinked slow and long. "I promise."

As she wobbled toward the restroom, a guy in a camouflage vest brushed by her. "Sorry, beautiful," he said.

Beautiful? This she had to see.

In the bathroom, a poster advertised an upcoming party, "Bloody Valentines," at a Chelsea club called Pandora's Box, "where the freaks fly high." Beside it, a beaky-nosed woman in a minidress made of aqua feathers teased her hair into a big black cloud.

"Are we in Pandora's Box?" Oona asked.

"Yep. You know it's a good party when you forget where you are." The woman waved a comb at Oona's mouth. "Girl, that lipstick is outta this world. You get it at Patty Field's?"

"Probably?" She angled toward the mirror for a look and gasped. "Holy shit, I'm pretty."

The woman gave a throaty cackle. "I wish *I* reacted like that when I looked in a mirror." Giving her hair a final fluff, she turned on her heel, leaving two feathers in her wake.

No wonder men were ogling her. Hell, she couldn't stop ogling herself. Her face was wrinkle-free, youthful, and painted to draw attention: electric blue eyeliner, thick fake eyelashes, cherry-red lips that glittered and matched her hair, which was worn in two long ponytails. Her (slim! sexy!) figure was squeezed into a purple velvet tuxedo jacket over black fishnets.

It was over-the-top, garish, and she only vaguely recognized the face in the mirror, but she'd never felt so damn alluring in her life. A quick check of her wrist confirmed the *M.D.C.R.* hourglass tattoo was still there. But never mind the tattoo, back to the mirror. Back to the reflection, mesmerizing, incredible. Better not blink in case her fifty-one-year-old self reappeared behind the glass.

"I'm young." She touched her cheek.

"Not that young, honey," said a drag queen in a pink sequined turban from behind her. "You're lookin' late, maybe mid-twenties at the youngest, which is a *hundred* in club years. I'm twenty. *That's* young."

"Me too!" Oona's eyes lit up. "It's my twentieth birthday." *At least on the inside.*

The queen squinted at her. "Yeah, keep tellin' yourself that." She reapplied her lipstick and left before Oona could retort.

It didn't matter. The catty queen didn't bother her. Nothing bothered her. Her blood flowed in glorious surging waves, secret hot coals glowed in her bones, and she would not be a slave to numbers and calendars. Not tonight. She was young again. Closer to who she used to be, closer to her true age. Right then, nothing else mattered.

Well, one other thing mattered: the sexy stranger waiting for her down the hall.

She rushed out of the bathroom, tottering as quickly as her heels would allow.

"You're still here," she said with too much enthusiasm.

"And you came back. I wasn't sure if the bathroom was a ruse to run away."

"I just needed to splash some water on my face," she lied. "The crowd, the heat, the noise, it was all getting to me. I had to catch my breath." Quick double check to ensure he was as cute as she'd first thought through her narcotic blur. She could make her eyes behave now, and yes, even cuter. A moment to admire the sharp line of his nose and his pale blue eyes. *Like the Velvet Underground song.*

"Do you feel better now?" he asked.

"Like a new person."

His mouth curled in a lazy way that made the coals in her bones glow brighter. "Let's get you that drink then." An outstretched hand, eyebrow raised in a challenge.

She took it without hesitation, a grip that meant business.

"We'll never get past the crowd at the main bar, so I'll take us to a VIP room."

"Ooh, I didn't realize I was with a VIP. I would've curtsied or something." Her smile equal parts sarcasm and lust.

"Aren't you a little firecracker." A hungry wolf flash of his eyes. "Let's go, this way. Careful going up."

After ascending a narrow metal staircase, they emerged on a catwalk suspended over a dance floor.

"Can we stop and watch for a while?" she shouted over a techno song's crescendo.

"If you want."

What is this place and why am I here?

From her vantage point, she gauged the space as a converted warehouse. Below, a shimmering kaleidoscope of bodies trailed dazzling colors on the dance floor. At the opposite end was a stage where performers with duct tape covering their private parts juggled and swallowed lit torches. Occasionally one would spit fire. Before Oona's altered gaze, the flames made filigree patterns of orange, red, and yellow, fireworks in slow motion, hot tongues teasing one another.

"Ladies and gentlemen, freaks and freakettes, you're one hot crowd, but you're getting a little *too* hot," a disembodied voice boomed through a megaphone. "It's time to cool down. Which means it's time for Flying Fiona."

A pale, petite bald woman came out to hoots and hollers. Naked except for a white thong, she turned and showed off a scarred back as two assistants came out carrying cables attached to hooks.

"What are they gonna do to her?" Oona's knees buckled. A firm hand caught the small of her back.

"Exactly what you think. Don't watch if you're squeamish. You shouldn't miss the final effect, though. I'll tell you when it's safe to look again." Curls tickled her face when he leaned in to ask, "So you wanna tell me your name, or should I just call you Red?"

She tilted her face toward his, stubble prickling her cheek, but she relished the sensation. Craving more textures, she put a hand on his arm, tried to absorb the silk through her fingers. Cool, slick. She stroked the fabric, almost forgot there was an arm under it, and moved her mouth to his ear.

"Red is fine." Red was better. No need to be Oona tonight.

Another wave of heat as he moved closer and pulled her in. Her tongue darted out, eager to taste the tender skin of his earlobe, suck on it. When this elicited a positive murmur, she continued down to his neck. Her hands were aimless wanderers traversing the sea of his shirt, up to his shoulders, across his back. She needed more sensation, more textures, more tastes. *More.*

His hand skimmed the back of her neck, and a rush of animal need spiraled through her.

"If you don't let me kiss you right now," he said, "I'm gonna throw myself off this catwalk."

The words barely made it out before Oona pressed her open mouth against his, tasting gin and cigarettes on his tongue. His hand crept beneath the hem of her velvet jacket, stroked her upper thigh. She kept her eyes open. She wanted to see everything.

It's like I'm in a crazy movie or music video.

Onstage, the assistants hooked cables into the woman's scarred back and raised her off her feet. A push, and she sailed over the crowd holding a bucket. Each time she went flying, she threw its contents onto the people below. She doused them with silk flowers, glitter, confetti, water. When the assistants took her down, her back was streaked with blood.

On the catwalk, Oona and the stranger continued to devour each other, lost in sloppy kisses and roaming hands. A full year since she'd kissed a man. Famished for affection, she'd kiss this man raw, until—

A tap on her shoulder.

"Excuse me, kids, I gotta get by." A man in a bodysuit covered with paper butterflies made impatient circles with his hand.

Oona and her companion separated to let him through. The stage was now empty.

"Is there more to the show?"

"Show's just getting started, Red. Come on." He pulled her off the catwalk and down a corridor to an unmarked door, up more stairs, to a roped-off area where a dozen people mingled, most paired off and in various stages of foreplay. The space overlooked the dance floor, a ledge jutting out high above it like an afterthought, dotted with low tables and leather couches.

A bored bouncer nodded and unlatched the rope.

Oona's companion led her around the clusters of amorous duos to the bar, where two flutes of champagne awaited them.

Adding alcohol to the intoxicants already in her system? Probably not smart. Water would be more sensible, but why interrupt the flow of the moment? The elation of returning to her younger body, the confirmation of her sanity—this needed to be celebrated. She was the girl in the movie who has reckless fun with a handsome stranger, and that girl doesn't choose water over champagne.

They clinked glasses and downed the bubbly as if doing tequila shots.

Taking her hand, the man led Oona around a bend, where the VIP area curved into an L-shape. A shorter ledge with a single empty couch faced a DJ booth suspended in a giant transparent bubble twenty feet away.

"Nobody's gonna bother us here." The man sat in the center of the couch, stretched his legs out.

Oona remained standing, taking in his admiring gaze, his hands running up and down the sides of her legs. The music changed—a sound like robots playing with children's instruments. A fast, heavy drumbeat echoed the rhythm of Oona's heart, thrummed under her skin. The pale blue eyes invited her to come closer. She obliged, straddled him.

Her thirsty fingers continued their exploration, across silk, leather, stubble, skin. He was keener to explore with his mouth, beginning with her lips and continuing down to the tender spot where her jaw met her throat, farther down to the groove of her collarbone. She arched her back, delicious synapses firing inside her. Strobe lights flashed, created a slow-motion illusion of their movements.

Oona undid the top button of her jacket, revealed a black lace bra. The man buried his face in her cleavage, ran a tongue down its center.

Over the sound system, a remix of Frankie Goes to Hollywood's "Relax" started up, prompting the writhing duo to laugh.

"Do you think the DJ can see us?" Oona asked.

"Oh yeah, and this song is definitely for us."

"We better put on a good show." Oona unbuttoned her jacket the rest of the way and tossed it aside. The man had big hands, his touch slightly rough, igniting her skin like a match across a striker strip. In her haste, she fumbled with the buttons of his shirt and popped one. He tugged his arms out of the sleeves without removing his tongue from her mouth. Red and yellow laser lights painted stripes across their bodies like Technicolor zebras.

"Do a bump with me, that'll make it even hotter." He removed a small brown vial from his pocket, unscrewed the top, and poured out a mound of white powder onto the webbing between his thumb and forefinger. A quick sniff and he poured more, gestured to Oona.

Cocaine? It would've been wise to verify (wiser still to politely decline). But the girl who doesn't say no to champagne doesn't ask what the powder is; she inhales. So that's what Oona did. Sharp and clean. A jolt like a shot of espresso. She clenched her jaw and swallowed hard. Everything looked and tasted and felt *so good*.

The man took one of her ponytails in each hand and pulled her back down to him, mouth open, tongue waiting to meet hers again. He grew hard grinding against her, and Oona unzipped his pants to release him, unconcerned who besides the DJ might see them. She was lost in her hunger for *more*, had to pour gasoline on the fire simmering within her.

The stranger put his hand between her legs, tore a hole through her fishnets, and moved aside her underwear. A finger inside her and . . . *yes*. Exactly what she wanted, to be filled up after an abstinent year. Except a finger wasn't enough.

Her brain's pleasure center was so overloaded, it missed the pragmatic memo as to whether unprotected sex with a nameless stranger pushed the boundaries of recklessness too far. The flicker of caution was quickly extinguished, any lingering concern wiped out the second he was inside her, swept further away with each upward thrust of his hips.

"I'm going to come," she groaned after only a minute. Behind closed eyes, colors flashed as her mind's light show took over.

"Good girl. Come hard for me. Do it." He lifted his hips to meet hers, tugged down her bra, took a nipple between his teeth.

Her moans were lost over the frenetic cacophony of music, a gospel choir singing over factory noises. She felt like she was in a warm bath shot through with a mild electric current. Her body twisted into a tight knot of anticipation, then burst free, releasing the pressure in a flood.

More than pleasure—relief, like sleeping for a full day after a bout of insomnia. The orgasm brought a clarity to her high, honed its blurry edges.

What the hell am I doing?

Her capricious urge abated, she waited for him to finish before climbing off him and readjusting her clothing.

"That was fun." He zipped up his pants.

"Would you excuse me for a minute?"

She didn't promise she'd come back and he didn't ask her to.

I didn't cheat on Dale. Dale is dead. Has been for years.

She swallowed down nausea.

As she left the VIP area, someone knocked into her, spilled a drink across her chest. Oona kept walking. At the top of the stairs, she checked her pocket for a tissue and found a Post-it with her handwriting:

Tonight you'll meet a curly-haired guy w/pale blue eyes. DO NOT HAVE SEX WITH HIM.

8

Oona turned over the Post-it:

You're here w/boyfriend Crosby—tall, blue hair, red tux jacket. Great guy. FIND HIM. Full letter at home.

Up until now, as with the last leap, none of it had felt real. All of this was happening to somebody else, a puppet whose strings Oona was at the end of, whose marionette skin she inhabited. No wonder it was so easy to make questionable decisions. Like leaving a mess in a hotel room; someone else would come clean it up. Except she was both the careless rock star trashing the room and the maid. The puppet and the one pulling the strings. Accountability was unavoidable.

A glance at the inside of her wrist.

M.D.C.R. Madeleine, Dale . . . Crosby?

The first step in sorting through this mess: finding the bathroom. Oona launched down a flight of stairs, snagged her heel, and nearly did a nose dive. She twisted an ankle but caught the banister before gravity caused further harm.

In the restroom, she inspected the damage. It was like she had to cover up someone else's crime. A dead body foisted upon her, and she had no choice but to bury it.

The lower half of her face smeared red like she'd been sucking face with a clown, traces of white powder beneath her nose, jacket buttoned crookedly with one breast threatening full exposure. She tucked it back in and adjusted her clothing.

In her other jacket pocket was a compact and tube of lipstick. She made use of both, then fixed her smudged eyeliner. Her eyes were bloodshot, frenzied, her jaw tight. Her brain a runaway horse, with her barely able to hold on to the reins. All she could do now was find Crosby.

How long had they been separated? No clocks anywhere.

Locating him wouldn't be easy. Hundreds of people swarmed the three-story club, which was permeated with dark corridors, staircases, and alcoves. It could be a while before she caught sight of her boyfriend.

Maybe she should follow the same advice given to hikers lost in the woods: stay in one place. Surely Crosby was looking for her, too. Yes, that was best. She limped through the crowds in search of blue hair or a place to sit.

If only she had her cell phone. It was so much easier to lose track of someone in 1991. *Could he have left?* She admonished her earlier self for not setting up this leap better. Drugged out in a packed club, separated from her boyfriend, the lame Post-it she didn't see until it was too late— *What were you thinking, Earlier Oona?*

Should she go home? She couldn't. If Crosby was as great as the note claimed—if he was the *C* in her tattoo—he'd keep searching and worry if she didn't turn up. Besides, what if she hadn't bought the Park Slope brownstone yet? And who knew where her mother might be living these days?

As the drugs lessened their hold, euphoria was replaced with unease. She was waiting to be rescued by a stranger. All she had to go on was a name, a hair color, and the top half of an outfit. Oh, and that he was a "great guy," one she'd just cheated on.

At a lounge area overlooking the dance floor, Oona searched the crowd for blue hair. Violent flashes of white light and sweeping green lasers made it impossible to make out anyone. She found an ottoman to perch on and scrutinized everyone who walked by, fidgeting like a little kid after too much chocolate. Under other circumstances, she would've enjoyed the people-watching: shirtless men in leather harnesses led around on leashes, sparkling, statuesque drag queens, couples in corsets and waistcoats right out of a Victorian portrait. But rather than savor the eye candy, she scanned the passersby with impatience and disappointment. No one matched the description in her note.

Before long, a tall man in a red tuxedo jacket rushed over and knelt beside her. "Jesus, Oona. Where did you go?" His voice couldn't decide between anger and concern.

"I fell down the stairs and hurt my ankle." Tears poured down her powdered cheeks like expert skiers down a fresh snowbank.

Crosby examined her ankle, as if he could do anything but note it was swollen. "I was going nuts looking for you. I thought you had a bad reaction to the E and passed out somewhere—or worse." He raked a hand through his blue hair. The face was new to her but not displeasing, with intense brown eyes and angular, androgynous features. *At least Earlier Oona has good taste.*

"I'm fine, I just want to go home," she said.

"I'll get our coats."

"No way. I don't want to be separated again." Though she didn't know him, she instantly imprinted on Crosby like a baby duck.

He helped her to her feet.

"We'll need to go slow," she said.

"You and your crazy shoes." He shook his head and supported her as she leaned on him.

They got their coats and made their way outside, onto a side street lined with more warehouses. "Stay where you are, I'll get us a taxi," Crosby said.

"Why not an Uber? The surge pricing will be ridiculous, but it'll be faster."

"I don't understand *anything* you just said."

She clamped a hand over her mouth. Right—1991. "I don't, either. I had a drink at the club, and maybe someone put something in it. I feel kind of sick."

Crosby gave her a quick hug and kissed the top of her head. "I'm sorry. This is all my fault. You said coming here was a bad idea, but I insisted. Hang tight, I'll get us home."

His kindness brought forth a new wave of tears, but she held them back, clenched her jaw. Ground her teeth so hard, it made her temples throb, a matching beat to the pain in her ankle. She glowered at her stilettos, wondering how much tonight's footwear would contribute to her creaky joints decades from now.

Eventually Crosby hailed a taxi. He helped Oona into the back seat and gave the driver an address she didn't recognize.

"Are we going to my place? I'd really like to go home," Oona said.

"I thought we were going back to mine tonight." Hand up to wave away his disappointment. "What am I saying? You're injured. Of course you want to go home." He gave the driver a different address, but she couldn't hear it over a passing police car.

Now that they were in a quieter space, Oona chewed her lower lip and fended off dread. She was a body snatcher, an impostor that had to pass as her host. This meant watching every word out of her mouth, avoiding any more slipups—nothing about post-1991 technology or any other knowledge she'd accumulated last year.

Problem was, the drugs made her want to talk talk talk. Impossible to curtail the verbal deluge that slipped past the dam of her lips.

"I thought I was insane the last time this happened," she blurted, scooting up against the door to look at Crosby. "Or at least—I don't know, senile or something. I had to wait a year to find out for sure, and tonight I did, and you know what? I'm not insane. I did the math and today is my twenty-seventh birthday. I get to spend the next year being *twenty-seven*." She made wild gestures with her hands. "Do you have any idea how happy this makes me? I'm *young*." Her elation made

Crosby watch her with bemused, uncertain eyes. "And I'm here with you, and you are gorgeous. I mean, *wow*, you are a really, *really* good-looking guy, with an aura of cool about you. You've got kind of a young Jack White thing going on."

A nervous laugh. "Uh, thanks? Who's Jack White?"

"From the White Stripes." *Shit*. "A local band I was into in high school. You're much cuter than Jack, though."

"Well, that's good. I'd hate for you to be pining over some teenage crush." He slid over, closed the space between them.

An image of Dale flickered into Oona's mind: winking at her during band practice as Corey and Wayne argued about a song's tempo, crooking a finger to bring her over, only to whisper something silly into her ear. The flash in his eyes before he kissed her.

The same flash now in Crosby's eyes. Crosby was her boyfriend now, and he was going to kiss her.

Oona put an arm out to stop him.

It made no sense. An hour ago, she'd been so quick to have frivolous, drug-fueled sex with a stranger. Now here was a stranger that actually *wasn't* one, here was an attractive man who cared about her, and she wouldn't let him near her.

"I'm sorry," she said. "I think hurting my ankle put me off my high. And then losing track of you, and the lights, and the people . . . it was too much. Amazing and surreal at first—but then it got weird and scary when I couldn't find you, and I wasn't sure I'd even be able to recognize you." She pressed her lips shut before anything else escaped.

Taking the hint, he slid back. "Why wouldn't you recognize me?"

"Well, you know . . . it was dark, and I was kind of seeing things. People looked like they had all these weird Instagram filters on them."

"Insta-what? What are you even talking about?"

I have to get out of here.

They were in Brooklyn now, but how close to home? How much more time to say baffling, incriminating things?

"That drink I had, I think it *was* laced with something," she said.

"I'm sorry I'm being so weird. I . . . don't feel like myself." At least that part wasn't a lie.

Crosby reached out and rubbed the base of her neck. She stiffened, but forced herself to accept the gesture, though she wanted to squirm away. *You don't deserve his comfort.* She could still feel that other man's hands on her, inside her, bringing her so much pleasure then, making her queasy now.

The taxi pulled up to a familiar corner. "Oh, thank god. It's the same house," she said.

"Why wouldn't it— Never mind. Hang on, I'll come around to help you out."

"I'll be fine. Really. I just need to sleep it off." She opened the car door, letting in a gust of cold air.

"You don't want me to come in? We were gonna spend the night and go out for a big birthday breakfast tomorrow. I mean, I should at least be around in case . . . with all the drugs you took—in case you have a bad trip."

"You're really one of the good ones, aren't you?" She put a hand to his cheek, which was shaved smooth. "I'm sorry, but I have to be alone right now. Could we postpone that breakfast?"

"Yeah, okay." His voice was tight. "I'll call you tomorrow."

A stab of remorse, for hurting his feelings, for the other ways she'd hurt him he wasn't even aware of.

"Tomorrow." She lunged forward and gave him a peck on the lips, hoping to conjure instant familiarity, a modern fairy-tale curse broken to unlock the love she'd felt for him before midnight. But his lips were as foreign as the stranger's at the club. Only this mouth was a little fuller and firmer with disappointment.

Once inside, Oona took off her shoes and threw them across the foyer.

Stupid shoes.

Stupid girl.

It took a beat to register the quiet of her house. The *sameness* of it. Same checked marble tiles, same chandelier made of spokes and gears and crystal and light, same blue glass vase on the entrance table filled with white lilies. Such a sweet scent from those funereal flowers. Such relief to have some consistency.

"Hello?" she called out. "Mom? Kenzie?"

Silence.

The kitchen should've been her first stop, for an ice pack, but instead she limped upstairs.

The library was also the same, though the armchairs, red leather in 2015, were currently brown suede. A series of shivers cascaded through her body. She built a small fire and moved one of the chairs over to it.

On the mantel, a sealed envelope with her name and the current year, followed by DO NOT READ IF UNDER THE INFLUENCE.

Seriously?

She rolled her eyes and was distracted by the carved wooden ceiling, its ornate grooves rippling like water disrupted by a thrown pebble. A quick jerk of her head, attention forced back to the envelope, block letters wavering before her eyes. Okay, maybe 1990 Oona had a point. Better to wait, read the contents sober.

But.

Something about the warning grated on her. Made her want to read the letter then and there.

"Future me is one bossy bitch." She tore open the envelope, tossed it aside, and unfolded the letter. Yawning, she lay with her legs across the arms of the chair and began to read.

Dear Oona,

Congratulations on getting through that first leap, I know it was tough. This year will be a lot more fun, though not without some drama.

I hope you got my earlier note. Maybe this time was different and you didn't cheat on Crosby. If you did, well, things will play out the way they have to.

Except . . . I don't want them to play out that way. I want a redo. If you fucked that random guy in the club, DO NOT TELL CROSBY.

Sustaining a relationship from year to year is hard enough with-out our bullshit time sickness on top of it, and I know it feels like you just met him, but Crosby is incredible . . .

Oona's eyes drooped, her chin dipped to her chest, and the letter slipped from her fingers as she fell asleep.

9

Oona woke up with a happy murmur, as if somebody was whispering her name. Except she was alone, which made her sit bolt upright. A moment to remember the where and when as she rubbed the back of her stiff neck. Acrid remnants of smoke and burnt wood tickled her nostrils. *Shit. The letter.*

It was on the floor beside the fireplace, intact. Oona slowed her panicked breathing and skimmed to where she'd left off the previous night.

. . . Crosby is incredible. Thoughtful and romantic, but with an edge. Not the most ambitious, but more importantly, he has a big heart. And we have great chemistry—you've already seen how hot he is.

Having an instant boyfriend may be unsettling, but I wouldn't push you to hold on to him if I didn't think he was a keeper. At least try.

To make this year easier, I've included a cheat sheet, which is the smaller folded-up paper in the envelope. It includes key info on Crosby and your current friends. I tried to balance need-to-know items without giving away too much of 1990, so you can still enjoy the year whenever you leap into it.

What's this about "current friends"? you may wonder. Just wait until you see Cyn, Desi, and the rest—they put the "fab" in fabulous. They can't know about the time travel (neither can Crosby), but you'll have some epic outings with them. NYC nightlife is taking a wacky turn, so get ready.

That said, I do need to warn you about drugs.

Oona huffed and muttered, "A little late for that."

I won't play Mom and tell you to stay away from them. Let's be honest: if I were Mom, I'd encourage careful and moderate experimentation and offer you a pot brownie to kick things off. But something recreational and fun can easily become a dark habit. Being young again after a year trapped in a much older body, you'll be tempted to go wild. Just . . . remember you often prefer to hide rather than tackle problems head on. Be careful about using drugs to avoid things. Enjoy the year, but not too much.

I also need to warn you about sex. You got an IUD years ago, so you don't need to worry about pregnancy, but AIDS and other STDs are prevalent. You and Crosby have been tested and are both clean, but if you have sex with anyone else, condoms are a must.

Another drawback to this year: lo-fi tech. Hope you didn't get too hooked on your gadgets . . .

As you've noticed, there's no Kenzie. He's busy being a kid in elementary school. You'll miss him, but his absence could be your chance to get closer to Mom. Since he won't be around to handle the financial nitty-gritty, the Rubin brothers at Chestnut Investment Services will do so in the interim (their card is on your desk). You're still responsible for the binder, though, so be sure to update it accordingly. Fill in everything you remember for each year including this one (hint: ditch any remaining Japanese holdings before that bubble bursts).

Every leap will have its advantages and disadvantages, things you'll gain and lose—relationships, youth, modern conveniences, etc. No year will be perfect. But I do think this year will be better if you have a little more love in your life. And boy, does Crosby love you (and vice versa). I hope you can make things work with him. Please try.

Love,
Me

P.S. Crosby is taking you out for your birthday dinner tonight, so brush up on those notes before you see him.

As she lowered the letter, there was a faint pounding behind her forehead, a drumline in the distance, headed her way. She stood and checked the mantel for the envelope to read the cheat sheet. It wasn't there. Scrambling to her knees, she searched under the chair. No envelope.

Oh no. Please, no.

The drummers neared, their persistent rhythm echoing through her skull.

A glance at the fireplace. A triangle of white amidst the ashes.

Fuck.

Oona pulled out the corner of the envelope, but the rest was in cinders. She wanted to bang her head against the brick fireplace, to punish herself for being so careless. Again.

Instead, laughter bubbled out of her—dark, bitter.

"I'm such an idiot." Arms around her stomach, kneeling on the carpet, she giggled helplessly.

Once she caught her breath, she stood, cringing as she put weight on her bad ankle.

Now what?

The room held no further answers.

A possible solution came to her: *Mom.* Madeleine might not be able to fill her in on the intimate details, but she could provide basic information on Crosby. Hopefully, enough to get Oona through this birthday dinner.

In the living room was a cordless phone/answering machine

combo. A red light blinked, indicated a new message. She pressed play.

A chorus of "Happy Birthday" was followed by, "Oona, darling, it's your mother. I hope you had an easy leap. I went up to Vermont for a few days with Leonard—he's a sweetheart, I'll tell you all about him— and we were supposed to be back today but got snowed in. It's been quite an adventure! The power went out last night and phones are still down—we had to drive five miles to find a pay phone that works. Roads are a mess, but we should be able to return tomorrow. I'm sorry to miss your birthday, but I'm sure Crosby has something fabulous planned. I'll call again when we get home. Oh—I snuck a birthday gift for you behind the cushions of the gray sofa. Love you!"

So much for that.

Oona ransacked the house for any hint of Crosby or her new friends. There were no photos, no notes, no phone numbers, nothing. Had it all been in the cheat sheet?

All she found during her search were reminders that she'd traveled back in time. Her clunkier electronics involved more wires. The music room was still dominated by a record collection, but also contained shelves of CDs and cassettes. In place of her screening room was a den with a boxy television and racks of VHS tapes. She didn't even own a computer.

"Maybe lo-fi will be better," she mused, examining a *Jaws* Laser-Disc.

Getting her homework out of the way, Oona spent hours poring over the binder. She flipped to various years and filled in gaps in the notes. That done, she reviewed 1991's financial instructions and followed Qualcomm's predicted upward trajectory from its December IPO (*Buy at $16, hold until after third split in December 1999, sell in March 2000 at $70, buy again at $13 in August 2002, wait until fourth split in 2004, sell at $78 in 2014*).

Later, as it got dark outside, Oona fastened the clasp of her mother's birthday gift: a gold necklace with a pendant made of interlocking gears and other clock parts. It dipped below her collarbone and complemented her emerald-green velvet dress and red hair, which she wore slicked back, a crimson curtain shimmering down her back. The watch from Dale was in a jewelry box, but after seeing it in a display case for a year, she felt it was safer not to wear it. She also found the jacket from Dale, its sleeves stiffer and the leather less worn than it had been when she last saw it. While she was pleased it fit her again, she opted for a more formal wool coat that night.

"I can't tell you where we're going, except it's somewhere special," Crosby had said when he called that afternoon.

Another surprise? Why not.

Last year's loneliness was still fresh in her mind, so Oona promised herself she'd try with Crosby. Especially if he was the *C* in her tattoo. This was her chance to have everything: youth, money, and a man who loved her. A man Earlier Oona already loved back; this Oona just had to catch up. True, her negligence with the cheat sheet made tonight a step shy of a blind date. But how hard could it be to pretend to know a man intimately familiar with her? To pretend to be in love with him? Maybe she wouldn't have to pretend for long. Maybe she'd be smitten by the end of the night.

But what if I'm not?

If only she could talk to Kenzie (if only Kenzie wasn't currently in grade school). Or Wayne or Pam or another friend from her past. *How long before I'm reunited with any of them? And what if I can't find any of my current friends?* The doorbell rang as she swiped on a final coat of mascara.

When she stepped outside, Crosby swept her into a tight embrace, smelling of cold air, mint gum, and sharp citrusy cologne.

"I was worried about you today," he murmured into her hair. "I thought you might cancel on dinner."

"I'm so sorry about last night." So much weight and sincerity in the words, her eyes glossy with tears.

"Hey, it's okay. You weren't feeling good and wanted to be alone. Gotta respect the birthday girl's wishes. Now let's get on with the main event. Surprise number one." He stepped aside and swept an arm out.

A black limousine was parked in front of her house, sleek and shiny as a panther.

"Wow, you don't exaggerate when you say *special*." Oona gaped as the uniformed driver opened the door for them. They settled into the leather seats, and the car pulled away.

"Here, hold these." Crosby handed her two champagne flutes and reached for an ice bucket with a bottle of Moët & Chandon.

"This is so thoughtful. But it isn't even a major birthday. I'm twenty-seven, not thirty or forty." Except on the inside she was twenty, so she was pleased. "Why the special treatment?"

"Because every birthday should be special. And I wanted you to know your boyfriend is so fucking cool, he planned an unforgettable night for you." The cork popped.

I get to spend the rest of my life with the coolest guy on the planet. She recalled the weight of the leather armor Dale had given her, the armor of his embrace.

Oona shook off the memory. "To an unforgettable night," she toasted.

"I also got you this. It's something small that made me think of you." He handed her a white box that fit in her palm.

Inside was a miniature red sports car made of etched crystal.

"It's a little red Corvette, like the Prince song," he explained. "I thought you'd get a kick out of it."

"It's adorable. Thank you. I have the perfect place to put it, too."

She gave him a quick peck on the cheek and drained her glass. Her mouth was dry, and the champagne did little to abate her thirst. It should've been easy to accept the romance of these gestures, but the limo felt more like a giant moving coffin. All this unspoken pressure for the night to be perfect, for *her* to be perfect. How was that possible? How many leaps had she made before meeting Crosby, and what had she done/seen/learned by then? Was that version of her funnier, kinder, wiser? And what kind of person was Crosby? How would she get to know him without giving herself away?

Conversation was minimal during the drive to Manhattan; instead, they watched the city skyline. The cold made the buildings gleam like they were made of gemstones, and the resurrected Twin Towers filled Oona with sad wonder.

Up to the West Side, to the edge of Central Park. The car pulled up to a red awning surrounded by trees wrapped in a multitude of white Christmas lights, a blanket of electric snow.

"Tavern on the Green? No way," she whispered.

Oona took slow, reverential steps inside the restaurant, through a wood-paneled foyer, into a mirrored hallway. Her darting eyes took in her multiple selves. What if each reflection was actually a separate version of her, trapped in time? All twenty-seven years old externally, all with cherry hair and a green dress, but while Oona on this side of the glass was twenty internally, maybe that other Oona was forty-two, and that one thirty-seven, and that one seventy-three. Maybe each Oona had a different chronology. Maybe one was living her life in order. If only this Oona could find that one and swap places with her.

The hallway led to a dining room with enormous chandeliers suspended like earrings on a pretty bohemian girl. Heads turned as they were seated. From the neck down, Oona and Crosby blended with the conservatively dressed diners, but their primary-colored hair made the duo unmistakably Other. Patrons stared without staring, peripheral glances that pretended not to linger, except for a little girl in a lavender princess dress who gaped with openmouthed wonder. The girl raised a bandaged finger to point at them and an adult hand slapped it away in admonishment.

Ah, so this was how being the center of attention felt. The previous year, she'd treated Kenzie and Madeleine to meals at some of the city's finest restaurants, but if they got any lingering looks, Kenzie had always been their target, with his youth, striking bone structure, and vibrant wardrobe. At the time, Oona had felt mild envy at being relegated to the background. She'd forgotten the spotlight's flip side: stares came with judgment. For every gaze that admired, another assessed, criticized, made assumptions.

She shifted in her seat. If only they were in a cozier, more casual setting. A dive bar or diner. Not this historic epicurean behemoth, and not a restaurant that had connotations with Dale.

"You know, when I was a teenager"—she pretended to look at her menu—"I used to dream about coming here."

A puzzled smile from Crosby. "Why do you think I chose this place? I know it's not to celebrate a record deal, but—"

"I told you about that?" She fired out the question before she could hold it back, an errant arrow that flew wide of its target.

"Of course."

"What else did I tell you about the band?" *What else did I tell you about Dale?* Had she played down her depth of feeling for her first love? Dismiss him as a passing teenage crush? Maybe so many years had elapsed before leaping into 1990, she hadn't needed to downplay it. Maybe by the time she met Crosby, she seldom thought of Dale.

"What did you tell me about the band?" Crosby repeated. "Did you get sudden amnesia or something?" His smile wavered.

A waiter came over before she could answer. They ordered shrimp cocktail, steak, and a bottle of Cabernet.

"So what's up with you tonight?" Crosby took her hand across the table, ran a thumb across the inside of her wrist, over the hourglass tattoo. "I'm sure the hangover is part of it, but something else is off. It's almost as if . . ." His eyes dropped down to the tablecloth. "As if you don't like me as much anymore."

Fixing her mouth into a tight smile, she tried not to betray the ugly, twisting emotions inside her as she searched his face for something to ignite a connection. At least he was nice to look at, with translucent paper-white skin and a cool indigo pompadour that recalled sixties-era Elvis. The square jaw, wide dark eyes, Roman nose—all added up to a geometrically attractive face. Even his scars—one dash above his left eyebrow and another across his chin—contributed to his allure. It was easy to appreciate him on a superficial level, but conjuring genuine emotions? For now she'd have to fake it.

"Of course I like you." She placed her fingers over his and squeezed them. "I . . . more than like you." Nope, she couldn't force out those other words. "Last night messed with my head—*a lot*—and I'm still getting over it. But it's also the new year. I feel all this pressure to . . . make it great, better than the last one. And I always have a tough time on my birthday. It's not about getting older or anything like that . . . I can't really explain it." She could, but why ruin dinner?

"You warned me about all that, how you get moody and distant at the beginning of each year. I thought something like this might get you out of your funk." A gesture to their grand surroundings.

Was last year's Oona worthy of Crosby? Because surely this year's Oona wasn't.

When their wine was served, Oona gulped hers without tasting it.

Uncomfortable silence fell over them like snow. They regarded their ornate surroundings, searching for something to comment on. The room had a soft glow from the chandeliers; their silverware and plates gleamed as if underwater.

Say something.

Yet neither one did.

A pull at the back of her throat. Her fake smiles weren't passing for the real thing, but Crosby didn't prod. Instead, he reassured her with careful glances that said he'd listen, that he'd understand.

Oona didn't trust those glances; no way he'd understand if she gave voice to the unspoken between them.

The waiter brought over their appetizers, and they bit into giant shrimp. Maybe good food would take the edge off their disappointment.

I have to turn this around. I'll die if this dinner gets any more uncomfortable.

"So you know how the new year is a new beginning and all that?" she asked.

The corners of Crosby's mouth twitched, uncertain. "Sure."

"Well, with my birthday, new beginnings are magnified for me. Can we try something?"

His fork paused halfway to his mouth. A crimson dollop of cocktail sauce dropped onto the white tablecloth. "Depends on what that something is."

"Can we pretend this is our first date?"

"What?" He set the fork down.

Eyes on the centerpiece, she coaxed her voice into a breezy lilt. "I know it's silly, but I thought it might be fun to, you know, pretend like we just met and it's our first date. Kind of get to know each other all over again." She pressed her fork tines into the pads of her fingers.

"Oh." A shrug and his body relaxed. "I mean, I guess. I thought you were going to say you wanted us to see other people or something."

"No! God no. I have no interest in seeing other people." The bigger concern was sorting out her interest in him. "I just thought—just for tonight—we could have a blank slate. Is that too weird?"

Head tilted, he squinted in exaggerated concentration. "Too weird . . . hmm . . . on the grand scale of weirdness, this ranks fairly low. What the hell, let's try it."

"Awesome." The word came out in a breathy sigh.

"So how do you want to do this?"

"I think we just dive in. Like . . . how did you get those scars on your face?"

He rubbed the one above his eyebrow, smirked. "I walked into a glass door."

"Were you drunk?"

He was taken aback for a beat, but resumed his role. "No, I was six. Playing with a neighbor's kid, running back and forth between their living room and backyard. Someone closed the sliding doors when I wasn't looking. I went crashing through them."

"Yikes."

"Yeah, it was pretty scary at the time, but I ended up with a nice insurance settlement that my parents invested for me. Which is how I can afford a decent Manhattan apartment on a retail salary. What about you? What's the story behind your tattoo?"

"What?" A glance at her wrist, as if the ink would reveal a clue. *Maybe this wasn't the best idea.* "I would love to tell you . . ." She coiled her lips seductively. "But that's something I never reveal on a first date."

Their steaks were brought out and Crosby ordered a second bottle of wine.

"Let's see . . ." Oona continued. So many things she wanted to know, deeper questions to ask, but she had to maintain their first-date role-play. "Who are your five favorite bands or singers?"

Restrained impatience tightened his face, his eyes asking, *How long do we have to keep this up?* "Bowie, New York Dolls, Sisters of Mercy, Depeche Mode, Bob Dylan."

"Bob Dylan? But he can't sing."

"Says the girl who loves Lou Reed." The glint in his eyes was playful yet barbed.

"So you work in retail . . . Do you want to own your own store one day?" she asked.

He hesitated, as if he had to talk himself into continuing the charade. "I don't think so. Working at Vamps is fun—and St. Mark's Place is awesome—but it's not like retail is any great passion of mine."

As Oona listened, she tried to calculate a formula for the quickest way to fall in love. How could you apply mathematical logic to something that defied numbers? Good-looking man plus fancy restaurant plus wine plus friendly banter might not equal a pounding heart and undying devotion. Love at first sight was too ambitious (even if it had gone that way with Dale).

She and Crosby exchanged polite, bewildered smiles, her secret a barrier between them. What had her first kiss with Crosby been like? No way had it sent her into a similar free fall as Dale's.

But a new set of firsts with Crosby awaited. A new first date (in progress). A new first kiss. A new first fight. Other firsts, both good and bad, but weren't the earliest days of a relationship some of the best? Sure, technically this was a continuation, but she'd also experience the novelty of their relationship, even if it was one-sided.

Maybe I've been looking at this all wrong.

"I guess it's my turn to ask questions," Crosby said. "Do you like your job at . . . what is it you do again?" His delivery wooden.

"Um . . ." *Crap.* She stalled by cutting and chewing a large bite of steak. "I, uh . . . I have a trust fund, so I'm lucky . . . I don't have to have a regular job . . ." Maybe that answer would fly.

It didn't.

"A trust fund? I thought you're a personal financial advisor." He narrowed an eye.

Damn that incinerated cheat sheet. "Yeah, I do that, too." Not a complete lie, since she advised herself. "On the side. I've always liked numbers and seem to have a knack for it . . ."

"Did you keep the trust fund a secret because you thought I'd take advantage of you?"

"Of course not."

"Because I'd never do that. If you remember, you had to talk me into accepting that Vespa you got me for my birthday."

"I remember," she said through dry lips.

"I don't care about having lots of money. I have enough to be comfortable. And I don't have expensive tastes—tonight's an exception and more for you. I think wanting more than I have would just make me unhappy."

A stirring within her, a whisper of tenderness. "That's a very . . . Buddhist way of looking at things." She tried to numb the pinpricks of shame with more wine. "So if making a lot of money isn't your thing and retail isn't your thing, what's your big passion?"

The hurt and suspicion in his eyes softened. His face flushed and he shifted an eyebrow, implying he didn't need to vocalize his great passion because he was looking at it.

No question about it. There was no way she deserved a man like Crosby. And she had no idea how she'd hold on to him.

"That was a lovely dinner. Thank you," she said as they exited the restaurant.

"My pleasure." He slipped an arm around her waist. "I'm crazy about you, you know that?"

"I'm starting to get an inkling." The end of her sentence was muffled as Crosby pressed his mouth against hers. It wasn't as intense as kissing the blue-eyed stranger, but then again, drug-fueled kisses with sexy strangers will intrinsically be more intense. Even so, Crosby's kiss contained something more important: a profound feeling, a promise of devotion.

"Let's get a cab to your place," Oona murmured.

"We have the limo until midnight."

Back in the car, he called to the driver, "Could you take us around the park for a little while and put up the privacy window?"

"Yes, sir." The tinted divider rolled up.

"Are you sure he can't see us?"

"Are you sure it matters?" Crosby pulled her in. He kissed her beneath her jaw, then scraped his teeth along her neck. An instant heat coursed through her. How perplexing, he knew her body so well when she was exploring his for the first time.

As the car rolled through Central Park, Crosby's touch grew less tentative. He stretched her out beneath him on the dark leather, his ribs and hipbones pressing against her. This made her open her mouth wider, inviting his tongue. He matched her fervor and reached beneath the hem of her dress, the tips of his fingers cold against her thighs, tickling her skin, growing warmer as they explored higher. They paused at her underwear.

Even though caution had eluded her the previous night, the dangers of AIDS and other STDs popped into her head. What if she picked up something nasty from last night's indiscretion? It wouldn't be fair to put Crosby at risk. "Do you have a condom?" she asked.

He sat up with a start. "Have you been taken over by a pod person or something? We never use condoms."

Shit. Oona propped herself up on her elbows. "I just thought . . . there's no harm in being extra careful."

He rubbed his forehead, trying to make sense of the soured moment. "We just got tested last month . . ."

Shit shit shit.

"Oh." His nod was slow as the grim truth emerged. "You fucked someone else."

It would've been more insulting for her to deny it. She tilted her head downward, affirmation enough.

"Are you bored with me?" he asked.

"No, of course not—"

"Or am I too much of a nice guy?" Slumped in his seat, his long legs angled like an insect's. "When you told me about the creeps you've been with, who lied and took advantage of you, I thought you'd be happy with someone more decent." As the car moved through the park, streetlights reflected off his pale face, alternating with patches of darkness. Each time Oona saw him in the light, his eyes grew shinier and filled with more resignation.

"You're *not* too much of a nice guy, and I *am* happy with you." Her voice was strangled, desperate. It was like holding on to a ledge with the tips of her fingers.

"Then can you explain why you cheated on me?" Tears trickled down his face.

Crosby pushed a button to lower the privacy partition. "We can leave the park now," he told the driver. "There'll be two more stops. The nearest subway station, then back to Brooklyn."

"No problem." The driver nodded.

"Crosby, please." A sick plummeting like the ledge had given way. "You have to let me explain."

"It doesn't matter." He made no move to wipe his damp face, stared straight ahead.

"It mattered up until five minutes ago. You can't all of a sudden stop caring."

"Up until five minutes ago, I didn't know you cheated on me."

She opened and closed her mouth. Only one option left. "Listen, this is going to sound like the most insane thing ever, but . . ." The words spilled out in a jumble as she told him about her time traveling while they exited the park and drove down Fifth Avenue. ". . . it would mean starting over in a way, and forgiving me for last night, which I realize is asking a lot." A hesitant peek at his profile as the car pulled up to the Fifty-seventh Street station. *Look at me, please.*

Cold air swept over them as Crosby opened the door. He turned his head toward her but kept his eyes down. "The car's paid for, except for the tip. You can give him this." A twenty-dollar bill placed in her lap.

"Wait," she pleaded. He had one leg out of the car. "There has to be something I can do."

One final look at her, but there was nothing behind his eyes. "Please don't come to the store anymore." A crack in his voice and he turned away. "And don't call me." His shoulders shook as he exited the limo.

10

Although, as it turned out, her one-night stand left her free of STDs, she did wake up the following morning with the flu.

"At least let me bring you some soup," Madeleine urged when she called later that day. "It's only your second leap, and I don't like the idea of you being alone."

"I might as well get used to it, right? Sorry, I'm just not up for company."

But the doorbell rang an hour later as her mother arrived bearing flowers, Tylenol, juice, and soup. She wore an electric blue coat over a lime-green dress—both padded at the shoulders, giving her top half a boxy silhouette—and her curly hair was sprayed and teased, bigger than ever.

"I don't care if you're contagious, I'm coming in for a hug."

Oona didn't resist and rested her head on Madeleine's heavily re-inforced shoulder. "Thanks for not listening and coming over anyway." For once, she wasn't being sarcastic. She stepped back to get a better look at her mother. "You're a lot younger than the last time I saw you." Yet she also looked oddly older in her mid-forties than she would in her sixties. Her face wasn't pulled taut, so her pre-Botox forehead could furrow with worry, and the groove between her eyebrows deepened, still a brow lift away from eradication.

"But I bet I was still a foxy mama, right?" Madeleine gave a little hip wiggle.

"Always."

"Find something trashy for us to watch on TV while I make you some tea." With a wink, she headed off to the kitchen.

They settled in the living room watching *The Sally Jesse Raphael Show*. Oona on the pale gray sofa cocooned in a blanket, an untouched mug of tea on the glass coffee table, marginally soothed as her mother brushed her hair.

"It's gotten so long. Do you think about cutting it?"

Oona shrugged. "The last thing I'm thinking about is my hair."

During a commercial break Madeleine asked, "How's Crosby?"

"We broke up."

"Oh. Did you end it?"

Her shoulders slumped. "Mom, I love you, but please don't push. Talking about it isn't going to help." Because talking would mean lying or confessing the actual despicable reason Crosby left her and reliving the confusion and humiliation. Problem was, not talking also made her feel shitty, an unbearable heaviness pressing and pressing. "It doesn't matter who ended it. It wasn't going to work and it was stupid of me to try. The me he knew isn't the me I am now."

A final smoothing of Oona's hair and Madeleine put down the brush. "So what are you going to do?"

"Mope some more and then get on with things, I guess. It's weird— like I'm grieving for someone I never knew *because* I won't get to know him. At least with Dale, I know what I lost. With Crosby . . . it doesn't make sense for me to be sad about him."

"The day love makes sense, check the pork chops for feathers." A weak grin at her own corny joke.

Oona twisted the satin hem of her blanket. "Last year I was in denial about the time travel stuff, but now . . . now that I believe it, it's different. I have to figure out how to manage this. The more I think about it, the more I realize I won't be able to have anything lasting in my life. Any boyfriend, band, friend—it all comes with an expiration date. What's even the point of getting attached to anyone, anything? Or even getting up in the morning."

"That's always been the biggest struggle for you."

Oona shed the blanket and sat up straighter. "Of course. Why didn't I ask you right away? You've been with chronologically younger versions of me, but also older ones. Did I ever figure it out?"

"Not what causes the leaps. But how to manage them? I suppose. As much as any of us figure out life."

"Do I ever find any kind of stability? Or do I live life year after year like some kind of existential hobo?"

Teeth bared in a grimace, Madeleine said, "You know I can't tell you. Some years will be more volatile than others. But you have me for all the stability you want." The way she squeezed Oona's hands begged for no more questions.

On TV, a woman with badly permed hair and a missing front tooth sobbed. Sally Jesse crouched beside her, the red of her lipstick—a perfect match to her glasses—making a sympathetic *O*.

Oona took the remote and muted the sound. "Mom, you know I love you . . . but I need something more."

A tug-of-war took place behind Madeleine's eyes, and her chest inflated with a deep breath. "Okay, I can tell you this. You like to assign a theme to some years."

"A theme? Like a prom theme? Like 1991 Under the Stars?"

"Not quite. Well, for example, the theme of one year was travel. You found such a sense of peace exploring foreign countries."

"I can't even imagine. Everything feels like a foreign country right now."

"I know. But you'll figure it out eventually."

"Will I?"

Once she recovered from the flu, Oona still couldn't shake off her muddled emotions. She'd known Crosby for less than twenty-four hours before she wrecked their relationship. Not enough time to reestablish true intimacy, but she'd had a taste of it. A good man had gone from adoring her to despising her in the span of one night. Something precious was now destroyed and unknowable. Guilt and disappointment haunted her for letting Crosby and her 1990 self down.

Then again, why had 1990 Oona left her letter so close to the fireplace if she knew the cheat sheet would get incinerated? Was a flimsy warning on the envelope supposed to be enough to prevent that? And why go to the club with Crosby on New Year's Eve if she knew she'd end up having sex with another man? Had she really believed a Post-it note could change her fate? If this Oona had let last year's self down, it was because Earlier Oona had set her up to fail.

Either way, despite the promises of a year full of fabulous people and wild outings, Oona found herself alone, unsure of how or when she'd see any of her friends again, hesitant to venture into New York's nightlife scene in search of them.

Instead, she kept to a familiar limited radius, though after a year spent being fifty-one, Oona felt revitalized physically. Her bones and muscles were stronger, and her skin had a flawless sheen. Last year's fatigue was replaced with an urge to move move move, as if small motors powered her limbs. She expelled extra energy by taking walks in Prospect Park, which were typically soothing, but now made her restless, uneasy. People gawked at her, candy-colored hair being uncommon in the early nineties and rarely seen in Brooklyn. 1990 Oona must've wanted that kind of attention, but 1991 Oona couldn't handle it. So she went to a salon in the East Village.

"I'd like something that'll make me look like a different person," she told the stylist. Pointing to a wall covered in black-and-white photos of Old Hollywood starlets, she added, "Like that black bob with bangs."

"One Louise Brooks, coming up."

Once Oona's hair was chopped off, colored, shampooed, and blow-dried into a sleek new style, she didn't look like a new person, only like herself wearing a flapper wig.

"It suits you," the stylist told Oona.

Did it? She didn't know what truly suited her anymore.

As she was about to leave the salon, the stylist called out, "Hang on," and handed Oona a glossy electric green postcard. On it was an image of a bald man with flower petals for eyelashes and an *X* of black masking tape over his mouth. Glittery blue letters spelled out *SOMA 3000* above his head. "My brother's a club promoter. This new weekly party at Antenna should be pretty hot. I bet you could use a fun night out."

Outside, Oona gave the flyer a closer look. *I could use a fun night out.* The dress code demanded "fab, funky, or freakish" attire. Unsure if anything in her current wardrobe would qualify, she went shopping. Obeying Crosby's wishes, she bypassed St. Mark's Place to avoid the store where he worked, swallowing bad feelings and a lump in her throat. Instead she went west on Eighth Street, past countless shoe stores and shops selling bongs, Zippos, and other tobacco/cannabis paraphernalia, until she reached a window display whose mannequins were adorned with vibrant, skimpy clothing: Patricia Field.

She entered the basement level of the colorful store. Ten feet away, sifting through a rack of rhinestone belts, a tall black woman with spindly arms and a pastel-pink Afro wig greeted her with a grin. "Look at Miss Thing and her new haircut."

"How'd you know?" Oona put a hand up to her freshly shorn hair.

"Because no wig looks that good except the ones we sell upstairs, and I know you don't buy those. Now are you gonna give me some sugar or do I have to come over there?"

She cautiously approached the woman, who pulled her into a suffocating hug.

"What happened to you? You haven't been out in ages. I was starting to think you and Crosby ran off and took that trip to Japan you're always talking about."

Did I just find one of my friends?

"Crosby and I actually broke up. Then I got sick. I've been . . . taking some time."

"Oh, baby girl. What a shame." She scooped Oona into another hug, enveloped her in a cloud of perfume that smelled of lilacs and baby powder. "I thought the two of you were the real deal. He didn't play around on you, did he? Because Jackie Hammer has a mobbed-up uncle—we can get his kneecaps busted if he needs to be taught a lesson."

"No, no, Crosby was great. It just didn't work out. After the breakup, I needed to be a hermit for a while. And now I need to stop moping." She fished out the SOMA 3000 flyer. "I was thinking of going to this tomorrow."

"The new night at Antenna? There's nothing to think about." She zigzagged an admonishing finger. "You're going, period. We're all getting ready at Jenny's. Now let's find you something to wear."

A man behind the register called out, "Hey, Cyn, do we have the snakeskin pants in an eight?"

"We're out of eights, but should get more next week."

"Cyn?" One of the names in the letter?

"What is it, sugar?" Her eyes ran up and down Oona's body. "You got skinnier. Breakups are the best diet, right?"

Grinning, she answered, "Right. So is the flu." What a delightful surprise, to stumble across one of her friends.

"I bet this would look great on you." She held up a minidress made of fuchsia mirrored tiles.

Oona followed Cyn around the store, collecting bright, skimpy outfits before modeling them for her friend. In the end, she settled on the fuchsia dress but still bought the other clothes, in case Cyn worked on commission.

Is that why she's friends with me? Because I buy lots of clothes? Is that why I buy the clothes? So she'll be friends with me?

It didn't matter; it was worth it to find someone allegedly familiar. Someone who didn't accuse Oona of behaving like a different version of herself. Maybe she could actually carry over a friendship from the previous year.

"So we're meeting up at Jenny's between nine and ten, then heading over to Antenna around eleven. We'll be going all night, so take your disco nap. Oh, Jenny just moved. I'll give you her new address." Cyn scrawled it on the back of Oona's receipt.

"I don't know . . . I'm still . . . Maybe I'll just meet you all there." While she was pleased about this reunion, the thought of trying to pass as her 1990 self to an entire group of people was nerve-racking.

"Uh-uh. You've been away too long. Now you know I won't come to Brooklyn to drag your ass out, but I expect to see you at Jenny's. She has a special treat planned, so you better be there."

When Oona got home, there was a message on the answering machine from her mother. "Just wanted to see how you were feeling. Call me, kiddo. I miss you."

But Oona didn't call her back. Instead, she went upstairs to try on all her new clothes again.

11

Jenny's ground-floor studio was in a run-down sliver of a sooty gray building on Avenue B, next door to a redbrick tenement with broken windows. This was years before gentrification would take full effect in the East Village. This Alphabet City still had drug dealers on corners outside of bodegas, hunched-over junkies weaving up and down the street, and cracked sidewalks decorated with debris: empty cigarette packs, Styrofoam cups, used condoms, broken bottles.

Some would've been scared off, but Oona had a bystander's appreciation for the urban grit. Knowing how New York would be transformed in the ensuing decades—the cleanup, the influx of money, the reduction in crime—made this version surreal and cinematic. Though the man with a bandana tied around his face like a cartoon bandit, casually strolling down the block with a baseball bat, was very real indeed. A reminder Oona wasn't watching actors on a screen but real people from behind a transparent and very breakable taxi window.

As if to punctuate the thought, there was a shatter of breaking glass in the distance—almost musical, like out-of-tune wind chimes—followed by a volley of shouts in Spanish.

She paid the driver and got out of the car.

Maybe going to Jenny's wasn't the best idea—not because of the neighborhood, but more Oona's inability to shake off her sense of being an impostor. Granted, she wasn't a phony as much as circumstantial amnesiac. Even so, the idea of passing as someone who knew these people—who were strangers to her current self—caused a tightening at her temples. She'd failed with Crosby; what made her think she'd do any better with her friends?

Pessimism notwithstanding, she went to the door and rang the bell.

A drag queen with a blond bouffant and a cigarette dangling from the corner of her mouth answered the door. The thump of house music blared behind her.

"Well, well, well, it's about time you showed your face again. Love the whole silent-film-star-meets-space-disco look. I have those in red." She nodded at Oona's white go-go boots. "Come on in, Desi's mixing up margaritas. I'll take your coat."

Here goes . . . something.

"Look who I found loitering." The queen announced Oona.

"Dressed like that, I'm amazed you didn't get picked up for solicitation. Just kidding, dollface." A slender man with olive skin and dark, slicked-back hair handed her a hurricane glass filled with frothy blue liquid. He stood on tiptoes to kiss her cheek.

"You're just jealous because you could never afford me." Oona instinctively understood a certain amount of attitude was required. She regarded the cocktail. Would alcohol make her behave more like the Oona they knew or less? *I guess we'll find out.* She took a long sip of the drink, which tasted like oranges and lighter fluid.

"Coat's not off and the claws are already out. Welcome back, girl." Cyn swooped in and gave her air kisses on both cheeks. She'd swapped her pink Afro wig for a glossy purple pageboy.

A buxom brunette with her hair in large curlers stepped out of the bathroom. "Sorry things with Crosby didn't work out." She had a thick Long Island accent.

"Have some couth, lady!" scolded the blond bouffant.

Oona glanced between the two of them. Which one was Jenny? "Hey, Jenny," she called out.

"I'm standing right here, I don't know why you're shouting."

Okay, Jenny is the blond bouffant. Who's the brunette?

"I, uh . . . I love what you've done with the place." Oona glanced at the apartment's bare-bones decor, gray boxy furniture framed by walls like cracked eggshells. Not an interior design any normal person would compliment, so she drowned the idiocy of her statement in several long swallows of her drink.

Desi, Cyn, and the brunette cackled with laughter.

"You can shove your sarcasm right up your ass, missy," said Jenny as ash from her cigarette dropped onto her chest and she flicked it away.

"Hey, our girl is nursing a broken heart, give her a break. She can be as bitchy as she wants." Cyn kneeled over a coffee table, cutting up pale yellow powder on a Deee-Lite CD case.

"Oh yeah? What's your excuse, Cynthia?" Hand on hip, Desi went around the room with a blender pitcher and refilled everyone's glasses. He purposefully bumped Cyn, causing her to scatter some of the powder.

"Careful with that, Cyn. I'm not getting more till next week." Jenny turned to Oona. "Wait till you try this shit. It's gonna blow your mind."

The brunette squeezed Oona's shoulder and rolled her eyes. "Oh my *god*." She drew out the word: *gawwwwwwd*. "All week long, it's all we've heard about, like Special K is the best thing since E."

Patting a spot on the sofa beside him, Desi said, "Oona, come sit next to daddy and tell us what's new."

She perched on the edge of the cushion. "What's new with me?" Tongue numb, brain going fuzzy, she kept sipping her blue drink. "Let's see . . . Crosby found out I fucked another guy and dumped me. That's new." So nonchalant, like mentioning a dentist's appointment.

"Shut your mouth," said Cyn, hers hanging open. "I assumed you broke it off."

The brunette, sitting at a card table covered with cosmetics and balled-up tissues, paused while applying glue to a false eyelash the size of a tarantula. "I thought you were serious about Crosby."

"I was. It was a one-time thing. I didn't even get his name. God, I'm such a slut." Oona touched her hot cheeks, fingers cold from the frosted cocktail glass. Her buzz softened the edges of the room, softened everything.

"You're not a slut, sugar, you were just ready to move on." Cyn rubbed her arm. "You always said you weren't sure if you could settle down with Crosby."

"All right, kids, gather 'round." Jenny cut a three-inch segment off a drinking straw and gestured at the CD case with pale yellow lines of powder. "You're up first, Oona."

Am I really going to do this?

Oona took the straw and paused. There was a time such a scene would've horrified her. She'd made her disgust plain any time she caught a whiff of marijuana on Madeleine's clothes. And what about the way she came down on Corey when she caught him with cocaine? What would either of them say if they saw her now? Not to mention Dale.

What did it matter? Nobody was around to judge or admonish her.

So she leaned over and snorted a line. The ketamine smelled soapy and had a bitter aftertaste. After she inhaled, there was a roar in her ears like a plane taking off. She returned the straw to Jenny, settled back on the couch, and closed her eyes. Her body floated up to the ceiling, past the ceiling, through each floor of the battered building, up to the smoggy city stars. She hovered in a tactile darkness, a velvet she could put her hands through, dotted with pinpricks of light. All sound became muffled and garbled, like deep voices underwater.

Beep. Beep. Beep.

"Can someone pass me my pager?" Jenny asked. "We gotta go. My customers are waiting."

How much time had passed? Oona opened her eyes, but her lids were heavy, like waking up from sedation. A white-hot light pierced her retinas, a bare bulb dangling from a rusted chain.

"Don't move, I'm almost finished," said Desi.

There was a feathery dabbing at Oona's mouth, then a finger pressing along the outer ridge of one eye socket, then the other.

"The breakup has been great for your body, but your makeup skills have gone to shit. Have you forgotten everything I taught you about contouring? Okay, open."

She squinted as Desi brushed loose powder along the bridge of her nose.

"And she's back." He held up a hand mirror.

"Jesus, how long was I out?" Oona did a slow wink to take in the peacock effect he'd created, replete with blue and gold stick-on rhinestones and tiny green feathers glued along her lash line. Her cheekbones appeared higher, her nose thinner. She was a dazed, half-starved, glamorous cartoon rendering of herself.

"Just tell me you love it and get your coat on."

"It's amazing." Who was this wide-eyed, spaced-out girl staring back at her?

Another series of beeps as Jenny's pager went off. "Come on, Oona. Unless you want to party with my cats, you better mosey."

Oona grabbed her coat and followed the others out.

They arrived in the Meatpacking District, their destination a graffiti-covered, squat beige building with columns two stories high flanking the entrance and arched, bricked-over windows. Where some of the other nearby clubs were converted slaughterhouses and fostered a BDSM scene, Antenna was a converted bank and dedicated itself to more diverse debauchery.

The club was reaching capacity as they entered. Some of the original interior had been preserved, including marble plinths dotting the cavernous main room, a teller window repurposed as a coat check, and a massive silver vault door. A pulsing throng of colorful bodies moved in choreographed chaos to a techno remix of a Madonna song, its bass so heavy it pulsed through Oona's fingertips. Streams of tiny bubbles blew over the horde like iridescent snowfall.

A giant panda in a sparkling red vest waved at Oona.

"Are you real?" she asked.

"I'm Johnny Panda. Of course I'm real," he answered. "I bring joy and delight. Want a hug?"

Arms stretched wide, she let herself be embraced by the panda and was flooded with affection and relief.

"Everything is gonna be okay, right?" she asked.

"Of course, sweetie." An oversize paw patted her head. "Nothing bad ever happens here."

And nothing I do this year will matter, because I know how it all turns out.

"Thank you." Oona stepped back and hurried to catch up to her friends.

She wove through a motley crowd, some in goth and bondage gear, others in striped Adidas jackets and soccer shoes; some in drag pageant regalia, others in little more than body paint.

Jenny was chatting with two teenagers dressed as Catholic school-girls wearing small backpacks. A nod and she handed each one a heart-shaped lollipop from her *I Dream of Jeannie* lunch box in exchange for a folded-up bill, which she slipped into her bra.

"Refreshments first, dancing later," Jenny called out to the group.

The vault door led to a basement labyrinth of VIP rooms, mini dance floors, and shadowy nooks. Jenny navigated them to a room cordoned off with a velvet rope, guarded by a goateed man with arms the size of Oona's thighs. When he saw Jenny, he unlatched the rope and bent down to let her plant a kiss on his cheek. She slipped a plastic packet into his palm as she ushered them inside.

The room was black-lit and painted in floor-to-ceiling Keith Haring murals, neon outlines of sexless people framed in squiggles on a glowing white background. The sweaty, skunky odor of marijuana permeated the space.

They headed for an empty banquette. When all were seated, Jenny began to cut more powder on a low glass table. Across the way a woman in a red leather harness snorted lines off a hand mirror, and in the corner, a group of skinny men in gold hot pants passed around a glass pipe.

Be cool. Stop gawking. A tremor of uncertainty coursed through her.

A magnum of champagne was brought over and Desi uncorked it, filling and passing around glasses.

"You must be pretty important," Oona said to Jenny.

"Oh yes, darling," she replied. "They named the VIP room after me, don't you know? Very Important Pussy."

Everyone but Oona howled with laughter. Their teeth glowed white, faces lit with glee, eyes glittering, bodies decorated like birthday parties on acid. Oona brought a glass of champagne to her face and let the bubbles tickle her nose.

I don't have to be lonely this year. I have friends. People who like me. A silly giggle to herself and she joined the group's laughter, magnified by alcohol, drugs, and the need to have an uproarious, fabulous time. And if the real thing evaded them, they had ingredients for artificial fun.

Jenny waved an open palm with a flourish, presenting a row of five neat lines. She handed a rolled-up twenty-dollar bill to Oona. "The prodigal doll goes first once more. Don't leave us for that long again, missy. The party's not as fun without you."

Was this powder more K or something else? It didn't matter. She belonged here, belonged with them, an impostor as much as the others.

Oona snorted the line. Her lips, fingers, and toes went numb. This time she floated backward, the room receding into a long dark tunnel.

As the images before her warped, so did the music. It slowed, the vocals faded to nothing, and the bass line pounded louder and louder until it merged with her heartbeat. Muffled, whooshing as if underwater. She traveled with the flow of her blood, propelled herself forward. Her Frisbee-sized red blood cells swam past her, grazed her bare arms like firm Jell-O. Everything around her red, so very red. She swam through another dark tunnel and emerged among her nerve cells, violet nuclei housed in neon-blue cytoplasm, which gave way to a network of dendrites like twisting tree limbs. Tiny explosions went off around her, and she became tangled in nerve branches.

"I don't want to be here anymore," she muttered.

A great white flash, and she was in a nest of wires painted with Day-Glo stars; another flash and she was among real stars, in deep space, gliding past a nebula. Its pastel cloud of dust and gas morphed into shapes: an eye, an hourglass, a pinwheel. It was the most beautiful thing Oona had ever seen.

Dale, can you see this? You should be here with me.

As she continued to float, the stars formed outlines of people, a celestial connect the dots. Though they were gender-neutral silhouettes, Oona could make out one of Dale and another of her father.

In her head, a disembodied voice whispered, "We all start here, and we all come back here. You are only stardust."

From a distance, other voices grew clearer.

"Is she breathing?"

"Yeah, but we may need to carry her out."

"Hold up, she's moving."

Oona's eyes fluttered open. "I died and it was so beautiful," she murmured. Four faces hovered over her. "Is it still 1991?"

All four nodded.

"Are you still my friends?"

"We sure are, baby doll, but it's past last call and we need to leave." Cyn bent down and eased Oona to her feet. "You good to walk?"

"Not good. *Great.*" Her limbs were helium light as she exited the club.

Outside, Desi, Jenny, and Whitney walked ahead in search of taxis.

"Oona, you're gonna want to step it up," Cyn said. "The Meatpacking District isn't the best place for a four A.M. stroll."

Old metal awnings further darkened the dimly lit streets, and the few cars that drove by did so with slow and seemingly sinister purpose. Layers of grime and graffiti coated the industrial buildings, some of which still bore hand-painted signs advertising wholesale meat distributors.

"In ten years this place is gonna be filled with designer boutiques." Oona marveled at the neighborhood's squalor, as if parading through a sepia-toned photo.

"Yeah, well, I don't think that's Calvin Klein drinking a forty on the corner." Up ahead, a heavyset man in a bomber jacket sat on a stoop taking swigs from a paper bag. Casting him a furtive look, Cyn added, "Button up your coat."

"But I don't feel cold. I feel . . . *magnificent.*" Twirling around, Oona spread her coat open wider and laughed.

"And I feel like you're gonna get us into trouble."

As if on cue, the man looked up as they passed, sneered, and yelled out, "Tranny faggots."

Cyn grabbed Oona's arm and tried to quicken their pace, but Oona shook off her friend's grip and confronted the man.

"I don't know what's worse," she said. "How rude you are, or how ignorant."

At that, the man lurched to his feet, showing his full refrigerator-like proportions. He grabbed Oona by the throat and threw her against a storefront's steel rolling shutter with a tinny rattle. "You think I'm gonna let a little bitch like you talk to me like that?"

"She's sorry. Oona, say you're sorry." Cyn tried to pull the man off her friend, but he swatted her away effortlessly, keeping a firm grip around Oona's neck.

"I'm not sorry," she wheezed. Unable to breathe, Oona's earlier euphoria morphed into a dark confusion. She didn't have enough air to say anything else. Her eyes darted to a sign across the street advertising frozen oxtails and back to her attacker, a looming, menacing shadow. As his hand clamped tighter, the edges of her vision blackened, and two contradictory thoughts raced toward each other.

No! Don't hurt me!

Yes! Do it!

There was shouting, so much shouting, and the scramble of people running, but the only thing she saw was a giant fist coming at her face.

12

"You sure you don't want to go to a hospital?" Cyn asked.

She and Oona were in the back of a taxi permeated with body odor and pine air freshener.

Bringing a hand up to her nose, Oona hissed as a bolt of pain shot through it, joining the throbbing chorus of her left eye and jaw. She tasted blood, but running her tongue over her teeth proved them intact. "I don't think anything is broken." Her voice was hoarse and it hurt to swallow. Wincing, she turned to Cyn, whose arms were folded tight.

"I'll get you cleaned up at my place, then. You can crash on my sofa."

"Thanks."

Neither said another word as the car made its way to the Lower East Side.

"I really don't want to put you out," Oona said as they climbed the stairs to a second-floor apartment in a building above a luggage store.

"It's fine." But her tone and movements were clipped as she unlocked the door.

It wasn't until Oona was sitting on the edge of the tub having her face dabbed with hydrogen-peroxide-soaked cotton balls that Cyn let loose:

"You want to explain what the hell happened back there? And don't give me no excuses about drugs, because I've seen you more fucked up, and you've never done anything stupid like that before. Did you want to get killed? Because my skinny ass couldn't stop him from beating on you, and if I didn't get the others back in time, he might've snapped your neck, then come for me. What. The. Fuck." Cyn tore open a packet of gauze.

The antiseptic seared her raw wounds and Oona gritted her teeth. "I don't know where that came from. He was so—it was such an ugly thing he said. And so stupid—I mean, we're both women."

"Girl, I know I'm a stunning lady, but you can't tell me you forgot I was born a man."

These were the slipups Oona dreaded the most, the social land mines she tried to avoid. "It's just . . ." Was there any explanation that didn't sound lame? "I only think of you as a woman." So many questions, but better they remain in 1990 Oona's purview.

Cyn allowed a grudging smile. "You're sweet, but it was dumb and dangerous for you to talk back to him. You think I don't hear shit like that all the time?" Her face tightened again. "I worry enough about getting jumped without your smart mouth."

"I'm sorry," Oona croaked, her split lip trembling.

"No need to boohoo about it, just be happy he didn't break your head open and keep quiet next time." She secured a bandage across the bridge of Oona's nose. "You feeling dizzy or nauseous?"

"No. Just cold."

"Hopefully you don't have a concussion. Now let's get some ice for that eye."

"Thank you." The words a strangled whisper.

Oona followed her to the living room, which was dominated by an overstuffed sofa covered in a quilt patterned with orange and green triangles.

"You lie down right there," Cyn instructed, firm but not unkind.

The quilt wasn't enough to subdue Oona's shivering, so Cyn brought her a pair of wool socks and a second blanket, followed by a bag of frozen peas and a mug of hot chocolate.

Cyn took an armchair beside the sofa and held out a plastic baggie. "Jenny said to give you this. Vicodin. You in any pain?"

"Tons." Oona popped one of the pills. The hot chocolate soothed her ragged throat.

"I'll let you get some rest . . ."

Resting quietly would've been safer, posed less risk for slipups. But Oona craved a real connection with another person. "Can you stay and talk to me for a bit?"

Cyn crossed her legs and entwined her fingers over her knee. "What, you want me to bore you to sleep in case the Vicodin doesn't work?"

"Something like that." She offered a weak smile. "It's just nice to be with a friend." This elicited an appraising glance from Cyn. "What?"

"You're real different from how I thought you were when we met." *Uh-oh.* "Different how?"

Leaning forward, she lowered her voice. "I'll be honest—I wasn't sure how much I liked you the first time Desi introduced us. And even in the weeks after . . . I couldn't help thinking there was something phony about you."

The Vicodin was painting everything over with a soft-focus brush, but this made Oona sit up straighter. "Really? Like what?"

"Well, there was the way you dressed. It seemed too polished, you know? Not your own style as much as someone dressing you. But now I get it, you're trying things out, and that's okay. It wasn't fair for me to judge."

"Was that it? The way I dressed?"

"Well . . ." Cyn scratched the back of her head. "Okay, there was also the way you talked. Some things you said sounded made up. Like, you have all this money and claim to be a financial advisor, but you don't look like anybody I seen on Wall Street and change the subject any time I ask you about it. But I thought, *Hey, she doesn't want to talk about where her money comes from, that's her business, leave her be.* But that made me question other things you'd say. Like, did your mom really work for Pan Am as a teenager in the early sixties?"

"She did."

"Oh." In a more subdued tone, she asked, "And did your dad really drown in a boating accident?"

"Yeah." In an instant, Oona was back on the boat, which reeked of fish and the cigars the men smoked while they waited for a tug on their lines. The combined odor was foul, but she'd take extra-long breaths of it, perched on a bench with a Nancy Drew book. A few feet away from her father, who'd been leaning over the railing when the boat jolted. He toppled over like a cartoon character, and she'd laughed at first, because his bewildered face was so goofy. But the hollers that followed eclipsed her giggles.

"The stuff about my dad is true. And I *am* a financial advisor of sorts, but I also kind of inherited the money, and I don't like to talk about it. Not to be rude, it's just something I'm private about."

"You don't have to explain it to me, girl. We're friends now, right? When I was growing up, Mama used to say what you dislike in other people is really what you dislike in yourself. That had me wondering if I'm phony—I mean, parts of me are, obviously"—she pointed to her chest—"and we all adopt club personas. But we're all just trying to figure it out. And once I talked to you more, I knew you were a sweetie. We've been having a blast partying together ever since. Not counting tonight's beatdown."

There was a pressure on Oona's head, an invisible heavy hat. "I bet we have so much fun."

"You were there, honey . . . or do you get more fucked up than you let on?" A playful wink.

Another slipup; she *had* to be more mindful. "I mean, I hope we'll have more fun when this"—she waved a hand over her face—"is back to normal. It was great to get out of my head tonight. I could use more parties." Eyes at half-mast, so tough to keep them open.

"We got a whole heap of parties coming up." Cyn's grin was fleeting. "But you know you can only stay out of your head for so long, right?"

The words came at Oona from a distance. Her chin dropped to her chest as she fought to stay awake. "I know."

Cyn shook off her faraway gaze. "Girl, I need to let you rest."

Permission to relax granted: Oona's spine softened. "No, it's okay. I like talking to you." Sentences took more effort to form. Random thoughts swam through her head and popped up like feisty fish. "I should really call my mom."

"I've got a cordless you can use. Though maybe you shouldn't wake her up?"

"It's okay, she's"—Oona inhaled a giant yawn like a vacuum—"at some craft festival in New Paltz. I'll get the machine. I just want to hear her voice."

"Of course you do, sugar. Hang on, I think it's . . . here you go. There's some water and a bottle of juice on the end table. Give a holler if you need anything else."

"Thank you."

Cyn nodded and left the room.

The phone felt heavy when she picked it up to dial Madeleine's number.

"Hi, Mom. Looks like we keep missing each other." Such an effort to keep her voice steady, the tightrope between slurred and choked up. "I'll call again when I can. Love you." It would be a few days before her mother returned, but Oona wouldn't tell her about the incident, wouldn't tell her much at all, and wouldn't see her until long after her face healed. Was shame making her punish herself, denying her mother's consolation? Was the avoidance an emerging defiance? Maybe both.

A slump, a sigh, and she pulled the covers tighter around herself. When she closed her eyes, she saw the dirty warehouse advertising frozen oxtails, felt the air being squeezed out of her by an angry fist. What had driven her to such a confrontation? Could be she'd been testing the limits of her known future by putting herself in harm's way. The attack should've served as a warning—her life was like tissue paper, easily crumpled up and tossed aside. It should've sent her scurrying to her sensible roots. But surviving it had the opposite effect. It made her feel ironclad, invincible.

In the dark, she brought a hand up to her tender face.

I'm still here.

I have time.

* * *

Cyn wasn't wrong about that heap of parties. The months that followed were full of excess, fun, and superficiality.

After the attack, all Oona wanted was to recapture the high-wire exhilaration of her outings to Pandora's Box and Antenna. This would require an elixir of alcohol, drugs, and a smattering of danger, but time travel would be her safety net.

So she became a staple of the club scene. Cyn, Jenny, Desi, and Whitney made friends faster than a virus finds a new host, and Oona expanded her circle of acquaintances as a result, people to whom she was connected via venues and costumes and drugs, flimsy and fragile as a spiderweb. Though at the core were the five of them.

They established a social routine: Limelight on Tuesdays, Antenna on Thursdays, and occasional weekend outings to the Roxy and Tunnel. Their favorite spot was the World, a former wedding banquet hall with peeling gold leaf and an aura of faded opulence. Going there was a special treat because it opened sporadically and operated without a liquor license. It played house music, hip-hop, rock, and punk, attracting a crowd that erased the boundaries between genders, races, subcultures, and sexual orientations.

"I spilled a drink on Prince once," Desi boasted one late night at the World, from a balcony overlooking the cavernous dance floor. "Right where we're standing. Someone shoved into me and I dumped my vodka cran all over his white ruffled shirt."

While the others gave impatient smiles, having heard the story one too many times, Oona's eyebrows shot up and she asked, "Did he get mad?"

"Oh, honey, no. He just took off his shirt and threw it over the railing. Walked around bare-chested the rest of the night."

Oona herself had some smaller brushes with the present and future (in)famous, though she didn't always recognize them for who they were or would become. When they went dancing at the Pyramid—a shoebox of a club on Avenue A—and she spotted Lady Bunny and RuPaul's big blond wigs, Oona was tempted to sidle up and tell them they'd be world-renowned drag queens (though they probably already knew that). At the Limelight, a Gothic church turned disco, when a man with clownish makeup and a diaper/corset ensemble offered her champagne, Whitney told her to turn it down. The champagne turned out to be piss and the man was Michael Alig, club promoter and ringleader of the Club Kids, whose antics would become the stuff of legend and nightmares in a few years when he'd be indicted for murder.

"And who *is* that?" she asked Desi one night at the Roxy, pointing to a boyish man waiting for the bathroom. "I keep seeing him around and he looks so familiar."

"Oh, that's Moby. I think he's a DJ? He'd be cuter if he shaved his head."

Sometimes there were after-parties at Save the Robots and sunrise breakfasts at 7A or Sidewalks—Bloody Marys more often than eggs since Ecstasy, coke, and K killed the appetite. Then there were underground parties at unconventional venues: Burger King, Home Depot, a subway car. They swarmed like rainbow-colored bees, with Johnny Panda leading the charge. Someone would bring a boom box and tinny techno would punctuate their outlandish cheer. The parties were fun in concept and amusing for the first half hour, the Club Kids dazzling in a mundane setting. Then there was the rush when the police arrived and they scattered before being rounded up for disorderly conduct, disturbing the peace, or indecent exposure.

While technology had been her umbilical cord to the world in 2015, this year's Oona was happy to disconnect from screens (not that she had a choice). The novelty of convenience was replaced by the familiarity of the analog: going to stores instead of shopping online, hailing taxis instead of ordering Ubers, using landlines and pay phones instead of her cell. It was nice to see people out and about living their lives rather than curating them for the Internet or hiding behind their devices. It also made it easier for Oona to drift apart from her mother, to return fewer of her calls.

Yes, Oona was happy to disconnect.

Her days and nights took on a flipbook's repetition, each image the same with minor changes. One night she came home covered in glitter; another in fake blood. One night she came home with a broken heel;

another a broken handle on her Wonder Woman lunch box. She developed a taste for house music, techno, freestyle, and breakbeat, finding appeal in the rhythm. She conjured clocks ticking off the seconds and tracking her pulse, each song an erratic metronome that stated she was both moving and standing still.

Her nights were full of so much sound, silence balanced out her days. She recovered from these outings in her music room, splayed out on the fuzzy carpet, often ignoring her records. Sometimes she'd sneak a wistful look at the guitars, but she never touched them.

"Music should be our biggest high," Dale often said—so fervent, quixotic, naive.

Sorry, baby, but I need something stronger.

The calendar might've put her at twenty-seven, but inside, she was barely out of her teens, with so little accountability and so much disposable income. And so it was the year of color, artificial highs, and staged recklessness.

Building off her silent-film-star haircut, Oona adopted a club version of a flapper look, wearing low-waisted dresses fringed with unconventional materials: chains, dollar bills, bones, bacon strips, syringes. She had long necklaces made of pill capsules and candy, cocktail rings with jeweled skulls and insects trapped in amber. The classic style of a bygone era made modern, warped. Her look wasn't as extreme as some others, but it still caught the attention of a producer for *Geraldo*, who stopped her one night at the Limelight and asked if she'd like to appear on an episode about Club Kids. Oona politely declined. She also avoided being mentioned in Michael Musto's nightlife column in *The Village Voice*.

Once in a while she wondered if she should be doing something more substantial with her time, but forced her focus on the inconsequential: the next outfit, the next party, the next drug and alcohol combo that would bury her in a blizzard of chemicals.

It was a temporary fix, but she felt at home among these oddballs. That would have to suffice, at least for 1991. Who knew what year would come next? She could be twenty-one and middle-aged again, or even a senior citizen. No telling when she'd revisit her youth, so she turned the year into one long party.

The party got interrupted three times.

The first time was a Friday morning in March. Just after eight, Oona was exiting a taxi dropping her off at home, still in last night's garish outfit.

Coming up the street, a grocery bag in each hand, was Madeleine. "I thought we could finally have breakfast together. Unless you want to keep avoiding me?"

"I already ate breakfast." Two Bloody Marys, but surely the tomato juice counted as nourishment.

"You look like you haven't eaten in months. Cocktail mixers don't count."

Is she a mind reader now? Her mother's sarcasm was like a Brillo pad on Oona's bare skin. "If we're gonna fight, can we do it inside?" Trudge trudge trudge up the steps, into the house.

"I come bearing bagels. You don't bring bagels to a fight. Why don't you go change while I lay out the food and make coffee. Nice outfit, by the way. Never saw a dress made of duct tape before."

Oona entered the kitchen a few minutes later, face scrubbed, wearing clothes made of actual fabric. Her mother slid over a plate piled so high with smoked salmon, the bagel beneath it was barely visible.

"I like the new hair. What else is new?" Madeleine asked. Getting only a shrug in response, she said, "I was in Home Depot the other week when it turned into a spontaneous party. I saw you there." A sharp click as two bagel halves popped out of the toaster. No eye contact as she focused on spreading them with cream cheese.

"Why didn't you come say hello?"

"Because you looked high as a kite and were busy dancing with a giant panda. I figured you didn't want to see me." She waved the cream-cheese-covered knife as if conducting an invisible orchestra. Bafflement made her mouth wide and mirthless.

"I just needed to—I don't know, enjoy myself. Be someone else. Get out of my head."

"Mission accomplished, from the looks of you."

"See, this is what I didn't want." Oona pushed her plate aside. "The veiled judgment. Motherly wisdom. Last year was . . . not easy. I just want to have a good time while I can."

"Are you sure that's all it is?" The paper-thin slice of salmon glinted as Madeleine popped it into her mouth. "God, this lox is so good, it melts in your mouth. Maybe you'll enjoy it when you sober up. You know, your father's mother was an alcoholic. And Charles was a heavy drinker. That type of thing is hereditary."

"I'm not an alcoholic." She rubbed her eyes with the heels of her hands, which came away dusted with glitter.

"I'm not saying you are. And how you decide to have a good time is up to you, but you should know addiction runs in your bloodline." A sigh when that provoked no reaction from her daughter. "You know I'm not a prude about drinking, drugs, sex—none of it. But I always saw you often enough that I knew I didn't need to worry. When you avoid me, I wonder what you're hiding."

To deny any obfuscation would be an insult to her mother. The least she could do was offer some transparency. "Maybe I need to hide for a little while, Mom. Maybe that's what this year is about for me."

"Maybe." A whimper of agreement.

How terrible it must be when the source of your pain is your own child.

"Whatever you're worried about, don't be," Oona said. "I've seen how things turn out and we're both okay."

"That doesn't mean you're bulletproof. It doesn't mean what you do today won't have consequences years from now."

"You don't need to tell me about consequences." She thought back to the birthday dinner with Crosby, the painful limo ride after. Would this year be happier if she was still with him? "I can't win with you, Mom. You give me shit about being too serious. Try to get me to loosen up and have more adventures. But now that I'm having them, you're giving me shit about that, too."

"Nobody's giving you shit." The corners of her mouth turned down. "I just miss how you used to open up to me. We were so close. It's . . . an adjustment for me, these different versions of you."

"Yeah, I know all about making adjustments." Oona poked at her bagel, with no intentions of eating it. "Sorry it's so hard on *you*." The harshness of her tone startled both of them. "I really am sorry," she said, chastened. "I'm just tired."

"Go get some sleep, then. We can have breakfast together some other time. I'll put the food away and see myself out."

The second time the party got interrupted was at the end of June, when the owner of their favorite club, the World, was found shot to death in one of its gilded balconies. The club closed for good.

The third time was in September at the Limelight.

While heading to the bar, Oona spotted a familiar blue pompadour. Crosby.

Seeing him shouldn't have triggered more than a twinge of regret, but instead his pale handsome profile flooded her with something stronger and more complicated: the loss of what might've been. *I was loved by him and now I'm not.* What would it have been like, feeling a natural high with him rather than chasing an artificial high with her friends?

Was it too late? Maybe enough time had passed that he could forgive her.

In her drunkenness, she decided it was a good idea to find out. As she approached Crosby, a redhead with Bettie Page bangs in a black latex dress slipped a possessive arm around him.

Recognition flickered across his features before a solemn mask slid down his face like a steel door slamming shut. Oona wanted to backtrack, but the redhead nailed her in place with a smug leer. "Can I help you?"

"I thought . . . never mind." Oona turned around and rushed to Jenny, who handed her a small glass vial and made it all better.

The drugs made everything more fabulous until they didn't, until the hangovers became increasingly brutal.

After seeing Crosby, Oona found herself in a vicious cycle of needing alcohol and drugs more often and earlier, to feel normal, to feel nothing. A hamster running on a treacherous wheel.

Next year. Next year I'll take it more seriously. Next year I'll try to make something of myself, do something meaningful.

She still gave to charity anonymously, donating exorbitant sums to children's hospitals, animal shelters, AIDS research, and other organizations.

"Do you know how much money you're throwing down the toilet in taxes?" Harold Rubin, one of her advisors at Chestnut Investment Services, complained. "You need to offset your significant capital gains. We're talking millions in potential deductions if you set up some kind of foundation."

"I'll set up a foundation later on." *When Kenzie does it for me. After he learns long division and gets a diploma or two.* "Not right now," she said over the phone, certain they'd had this conversation before. "Besides, I'm going to make more money than I could ever spend in a lifetime."

"Don't be too sure about that, Oona. I've seen how quickly people can make and lose money, how careless they get. You've been on a hot streak, but you can't predict how the markets are going to behave. For one thing, I think you're getting out of biotech too soon."

"I am, but that's okay. I have a good feeling about this Qualcomm IPO." She chuckled, knowing the stock would increase by nearly 12,000 percent in the years to come.

While she tried to maintain a low profile about her wealth on the club scene, rumors circulated that she was an heiress with millions.

"I heard her mother's related to the Astors."

"I heard it's mob money."

"I heard she was some kind of pop star in Europe in the eighties."

"I heard her grandfather invented the lawn mower."

Whenever someone asked Oona flat out, she'd give a mysterious smile and shrug. Except one time, after she'd chased two tabs of Ecstasy with copious lines of cocaine. She was with her usual crew, at Sidewalks at five A.M., on her second Bloody Mary.

"So come on, where does your money really come from?" Desi prodded.

Oona was slouched in the booth as if her bones had been rubberized. "I actually travel through time and memorize stuff that'll make me money. Mostly stocks, some sporting events, that sort of thing."

"Like *Back to the Future Part II*?" Jenny asked.

"Kinda."

Silence around the table.

Could it really be this easy?

A seed of relief—they believed her.

Oona waited for an onslaught of follow-up questions.

There weren't any.

Instead, an outburst of laughter. First from Whitney, then the rest of the table. Even Cyn laughed, though she was the first to stop as curiosity clouded her features.

A waiter came by, and Oona asked for another round of drinks and the check. She usually picked up the tab, which didn't bother her. If she spent more time sober, it might. She glanced around the table: these people would be strangers to her in a matter of months. Maybe she'd chosen them as friends because they were strangers to begin with. And there she was, little girl lost, with buckets of money.

On New Year's Eve, they went to Antenna, arriving early for "refreshments" in a VIP room before the countdown. Dressed in a black-sequined top hat, sleeveless shirttails unbuttoned to her bra, and glittery fishnets, Oona played a shinier, skimpier version of a modern-day Marlene Dietrich. She wouldn't be out long—only wanted to enjoy a few final moments of whimsy—and palmed the Ecstasy tab Jenny gave her, nursing her champagne for the next hour.

A little after eleven, she slipped out while the group was distracted by one of Jenny's stories.

Down the hall, a few feet from the stairs, a voice over her shoulder.

"Where are you sneaking off to?" Cyn asked.

"Just going to the bathroom."

"Upstairs? To the one five times as crowded?"

A breezy shrug. "I wanted to walk around a bit."

"It's not as fun when you're sober, is it?" Oona opened her mouth to protest, but Cyn clucked her tongue. "Don't even, girl. I saw you palm that E. And you've been sipping champagne looking like Michael Alig's pissed in it. What's the real story?"

"I'm just tired." But she owed Cyn more than that. "And it's becoming less fun even when I'm not sober."

"The law of diminishing returns."

"Yeah. Exactly. I keep thinking about a conversation I had with my mom a while back. Turns out, my dad drank a lot. I never thought about it as a kid, because he never got angry or violent, and he and Mom rarely fought. He liked his beer and would get a little loud after finishing a six-pack. Then he'd get sleepy and go to bed. It wasn't a problem, until the day he drank a six-pack and fell off a fishing boat."

A grim understanding darkened Cyn's voice. "And we've all been drinking our six-packs and getting a little loud. But you gotta go before you fall off that boat. I get it. I don't know how much more of this scene I've got in me, either." Her tone was unconvincing and they both knew it. "Not like I got anything better to do. I did just inherit five grand from . . . an older gentleman friend I knew. So that should keep me in wigs and lashes for a while yet."

But there was another way Oona could show her gratitude. "Cisco Systems. Forget wigs and lashes—invest some of the money. You missed Cisco's first split, but I have a feeling it'll split again." It was more than a feeling: the stock would split eight more times in as many years. She clutched her friend's wrists with urgency. "If you invest two grand now, in eight years, you'll have close to . . . half a million. Please trust me on this."

The purse of Cyn's mouth projected suspicion, but there was a glint in her eyes. "I'm not gonna ask how you know, but I'll believe you on this one." She whipped out a lipstick and scrawled *CISCO* across her bare arm in red. "Any other names you wanna add?"

"Dell, but ditch it in March of 2000. Oracle. GE. Apple—hold on to that one for a while." When her friend was done writing, she said, "Cyn, I need to thank you—"

"Uh-uh. You thanked me plenty. And I think you just gave me a future as a rich lady. Anything else you say is gonna ruin my makeup." Fervent waving at her damp eyes. "I'll take a hug, though."

The women embraced. "Happy New Year, sugar." Cyn winked and shooed her away. "Now get the hell off this boat."

And with that, Oona's year of frivolity was over.

It took fifteen minutes to hail a taxi, and once she climbed inside, she let out a long breath. She'd miss 1991. Would she ever have this much fun again? She probably wouldn't. She probably shouldn't.

"Traffic is bad. You might not make it to Brooklyn in time," the driver warned.

"It doesn't matter," she said. "I won't be here for the new year, anyway."

In the rearview mirror, the driver arched an eyebrow but said nothing.

He was right about traffic. She wouldn't get home in time to write her 1992 self a letter, but that was okay. That Oona would be far more wizened than this one.

They were on the Brooklyn-Queens Expressway when the countdown began over the radio. This time she didn't close her eyes. She watched the Manhattan skyline crawl past and wondered if it would look the same the next time she laid eyes on it.

"Three! Two! One!"

PART IV

Some Kind of Stranger

2004: 40/21

13

A rhythmic rattle and the ground beneath Oona lurched, sent her tumbling. On hands and knees, more rumbling as nausea roiled through
her. Blink blink blink. Focus. Yellow and orange molded seats with
wood panel trim. Strips of fluorescent light along the ceiling. Stainless-
steel poles running down a center aisle. A picture window bearing an
orange circle with the letter *F*.

Why am I on the subway?

Oona got to her knees.

There were a handful of passengers in the car, but their appearance
gave Oona no hints as to the possible year.

Am I still young . . . ish?

A twenty-something woman in a houndstooth coat rushed over.
"Are you okay, ma'am?" she asked.

Maybe not.

"I think so." Oona used a nearby pole to help herself stand. "I just
spaced for a second."

A deep male voice called over the loudspeaker, "Next station,
Fifteenth Street–Prospect Park."

"I found a pen," the woman said, holding out a ballpoint. When

Oona didn't take it, she added, "You were just asking for one. You seemed pretty upset."

The station came into view as the train slowed down.

"Why was I upset?" Oona asked. *And what did I need to write down?*

"Fifteenth Street–Prospect Park," the conductor announced as the doors opened. "Next stop, Fort Hamilton Parkway."

"I don't know," the woman replied. "I didn't hear all of it."

"Shit, this is my stop." Oona was half in and half out of the car. "What *did* you hear?"

"Please stand clear of the closing doors," said the conductor.

Oona stepped back to be fully on the platform as the woman's blank stare brightened. "Edward! You mentioned someone named Edward. And Peter."

Before Oona could ask anything else, the doors slid closed and the train pulled away.

As she exited the station, she checked her pockets. One was empty. The other contained a MetroCard, house keys, a few twenties, and the silver watch from Dale, which had stopped at three o'clock (*When did I start wearing it again?*). Nothing else. No letter, no Post-it, no clues as to why she'd been on the subway, who Edward or Peter might be, or what year it was. She was in a black lace dress and high heels. Maybe she'd come from a party?

Thanks for nothing, Earlier Oona!

As she approached her house, a man in a dark suit and gray coat was sitting on her front steps, his leather loafers glinting in the streetlight.

He sprung up as soon as he saw her, his face in shadow. "Oona, I'm so sorry. Are you okay?" Trepidation in his tone. A British accent. Less royal family, more Michael Caine.

"Who are you?" She backed away from him until she bumped a lamppost.

"Oona, it's Edward. Do you know who I am? Has it happened again?"

At least it was one of the names the woman on the subway had mentioned. She took one step forward. "Has . . . *what* happened again?"

"Your memory lapse. You told me about your condition. Have you forgotten who I am?" The trill of fear in his voice matched hers.

"I . . . yeah."

"It's okay, Oona. Why don't we go inside, and I'll fill you in."

Despite the dollop of reassurance, Oona narrowed her eyes. "Hang on. I need a minute here. I can't just invite you into my home. I can't even see you back there. If you could—that's fine, that's close enough."

Once he inched into the light, the face revealed was handsome: hooded blue eyes, stubbled square jaw, shallow groove bisecting the chin, brown hair sculpted into a faux-hawk. He gave a self-conscious wave and smiled, revealing a large space between his front teeth. "Hello there."

Is this my boyfriend? Her breath quickened. While Edward was conventionally attractive, she bet it was his gap-toothed smile that won her over. If he was indeed her boyfriend.

If. Until you know for sure, get a grip.

Oona put her arms behind her back and made it as far as the base of her steps. "Hi."

"Are you okay?"

"I have no fucking clue. About anything, really. What year is it?"

"It's 2004. Happy New Year."

"You too . . ." So let's see . . . twenty-one internally, but externally she'd gone from twenty-seven to forty. *Ugh.*

"There's a bottle of champagne chilling in the fridge. We can go in and celebrate properly, if you like, Oona." What was beneath the glossy surface of his voice? Nerves? Annoyance?

"You don't need to keep repeating my name. I feel like you're trying to hypnotize me or something."

"Sorry, I wasn't sure how much you'd remember. Particularly about last year."

Was she expected to enact some sort of charade? Too bad if she was, because she intended to play it straight. "Last year is a complete blank and I've never seen you before." At his stunned gape, she added, "Sorry if that's upsetting, but I'm tired of pretending. Are you and me"—she pointed back and forth between them—"friends?" Better not to make any big assumptions.

A gust of wind rustled the bare branches above them, nature's drumroll.

"More than that, I'm afraid," he said. "We're married."

She let out a peal of laughter. "Oh yeah?" Holding up her bare left hand, she asked, "Then where's my ring?"

"Ring*s*." He emphasized the *s*, digging into his pocket. "I've got them. May I?"

Her dubious smirk wavered. "You may."

When he reached her, he extended an open palm, which held two rings, both gold, one with a solitaire emerald-cut diamond.

Wow.

"You thought it would be better if I gave these back to you once you had some time to adjust to the news."

"Of our happy nuptials? Well, thanks for giving me all of ten seconds to adjust." Dazed, Oona plucked the rings from his hand and tried them on. Both a perfect fit. "Are they happy? The nuptials, I mean."

"I like to think so."

"And I'm really married?"

"You are. To me."

The news seeped in like a sponge absorbing water. *I have a husband. A husband named Edward.*

"Oona? Do you think we could go inside now?" His voice was professorial but beguiling, a resonant voice that demanded you listened. Now that the voice belonged to her husband, she decided she liked it. A lot.

But it was still too soon to invite him in. Except . . .

"Do you live here, too?" She nodded at the brownstone.

"I do indeed. That's typically what married people do, live together."

"And that's what we are. Married. To each other." She twisted the rings on her finger. It all made sense, yet it didn't, like a puzzle piece that fit, but needed to be banged into place, its edges out of sync with the rest of the picture.

Tilting his head, he gave her a searching look. "Not to bemoan the point, but you really, *truly* don't—"

"I don't remember you. At all. And to be honest, even though you've got the cute charming Brit thing going on, the thought of you coming into my house right now is freaking me out. Could we talk out here for a little while?"

"Of course. I can even sit one stoop over if that would put you at ease." His mouth's wry quirk belied his grave tone.

"You don't have to be a smartass about it." She swatted his arm.

"I can't help it, it's what us cute charming Brits do."

They sat on the steps, a courteous space between them.

"So. Edward. Where to begin? What's your last name?"

"Clary."

M.D.C.R. Madeleine, Dale . . . Clary?

"Any middle name?" she asked.

"No middle name."

That sparked an idea. "Do you know mine?"

"Stephanie Lynn." No hesitation. "Which is also Stevie Nicks's real name. Your mum was so obsessed with her, when you were a little girl, she dressed you up as Stevie for Halloween three years in a row. You were always so embarrassed, you told everyone you were a fortune-teller."

A wave of goose bumps erupted along her arms. The only way Edward could've known this was if he'd spoken to someone close to her. Or if she'd told him.

She wanted to trust him, but there were still so many question marks, so many dark corners.

"Tell me something else you know about me," she said.

"Your favorite movies are *The Wall*, *Pulp Fiction*, and *Purple Rain*. You have a collection of knickknacks in your bedroom, but you don't know where they all came from. You hate the color yellow. Do you need more?"

Do I? How much would it take for her to believe it, for it to feel true? As with Crosby last year, she felt the physical attraction but longed for a leftover twinge of shared intimacy. But, as with Crosby, it wasn't forthcoming. "I just wish I had something else to go on."

"Ah." He cleared his throat. "You said I should give you a letter you wrote—"

"You have my letter?" Oona shot to her feet. "Why didn't you give it to me right away?"

"To be honest, I thought you might remember something. I wanted to chat to you a bit first. I'm sorry. That was foolish." Reaching inside his coat pocket, he produced a sealed white envelope.

Oona snatched it up like a rope that would pull her back to safety. "I'll need a moment."

"Of course."

The sealed envelope bore her name in block letters, followed by the year. She tore into it.

Dear Oona,

I'm still figuring out the best way to navigate these leaps, how much to tell you, and the best advice to give. Finding happiness in this chronological maze shouldn't be so complicated. Maybe it doesn't have to be.

Last year, I met and married a lovely man. He makes me happy. He can make you happy.

You might be thinking, after the fiasco with Crosby, there's no way you can sustain an actual marriage. This will be different. Edward knows you experience time/memory lapses and that he'll be a stranger to you. He's willing to work with that.

I did put a different spin on the time travel specifically (you know how it goes when you try to tell the full truth). I told him I fell off a balcony at eighteen, which caused a condition where my brain resets itself every year, leaving big memory gaps. And the so-called accident happened on New Year's Eve, so that's when the amnesia kicks in. Crazy story, but not time travel crazy. Edward bought it and vowed to accept me the way I am, broken brain and all. How could you not adore a guy like that?

So what should you know about Edward? This time, I'm skipping the cheat sheet. The fun will be getting to know (and love) him on your own. Edward will tell you everything apart from some of last year's specifics, like how you met and got engaged, when you got married, etc. (say it with me now: no spoilers). He promised to be patient as you adjust to your time lapse—that's how much he loves you.

Peeking over the top of the letter, she caught Edward watching her from the lower steps, his shoulders curved forward and eyebrows pinched together.

"Good letter?" he asked.

"Still reading. Riveting stuff so far."

"Well, if there's anything . . ."

"Actually . . ." A kernel of suspicion popped in her head. "You're a British citizen, right?"

"I am. Though my grandmother was American, so I have dual citizenship. In case you thought we wed for my green card."

"Oh." She hid her flushed cheeks behind the letter.

"No need to be embarrassed. I'd wonder the same thing in your position." There was an arch lilt in his voice.

She turned back to the page.

You might think the marriage is doomed to fail, because of these extreme circumstances and because you were unmarried in 2015. Here's the thing. I still don't understand whether our fate is fixed or fluid. There's no telling whether our future will play out a certain way because of our actions or in spite of them. So I can't help but wonder if there's a way you could still be married to Edward in 2015 and beyond. Sure, you had a blast in 1991 with all the clubbing and drugs—and you deserved some wild fun—but don't you want more substance now? This is your chance to build on something meaningful, even if this version of you is starting from scratch.

And how do you do that? I'm hardly a marriage expert, but I can tell you there's effort involved. You have to make the relationship a priority, know when to set your needs aside to do what's best for the marriage. Be flexible and look for ways to enjoy your time together, especially when you have less of it. Be open with him. Talk to him. Let yourself fall in love with him.

A word of warning: I'm not sure Edward ever really won over Mom. She was supportive about the wedding in a whatever-makes-my-daughter-happy way, but something always seemed off. The year may start off shaky with her, but have some compassion. You're not a teenager anymore, internally or externally.

As for Kenzie, he still is a teenager, so you'll still work with Chestnut on the finances. As you'll see in the binder, apart from Google's IPO, you'll hold steady with the portfolio, since the post–9/11 markets have been volatile to flat. But don't let that stop you from continuing the donations and investing in passion projects, even if they don't pay off. Financial security is one of the few things you can count on, so allow others to benefit from your generosity. Don't shy away from risky ventures. Gamble on the unknown (hint hint: Edward).

Love,
Me

P.S. Ask him to make you toad-in-the-hole—it's your favorite!

Oona folded the letter and glanced at Edward. An expectant silence hung between them, interrupted by a melodic jangle as she took out her house keys.

"Hey, why was I on the subway?" she asked. "When I—at midnight."

"Is that where you were?" Edward rubbed the bridge of his nose. "How peculiar. We were at a party and around eleven-thirty I noticed you were gone. I asked if anyone had seen you leave, but"—a helpless shrug—"nobody had. I didn't know what to think. I'm just glad you came home and that you're all right."

"Relatively speaking." *I don't know what to think, either.*

"Would you perhaps be more comfortable if I spent the night somewhere else?"

I'd be more comfortable if I wasn't married to a man I never met.

Could a husband magically add substance to her life? Surely her existence would always feel transient and random as long as chronology eluded her.

Then again, maybe 2003 Oona was onto something. Maybe marriage would suit her.

"That wouldn't be fair," she said. "You live here. You can stay here. But . . . um . . ."

"I'm happy to sleep in one of the guest rooms." Edward sprung to his feet.

"Okay." There was some small relief in the way he anticipated her needs.

As she unlocked the door, something still nagged at her. That woman on the subway. Something about a pen and two names.

"Hey, do you know anyone named Peter?" Oona asked.

Edward thought for a second and shook his head. "I don't. Why do you ask?"

"It's not important."

But was it?

14

Oona went over to the foyer mirror before taking off her coat, inspecting her forty-year-old self.

"I guess it could be worse," she mumbled. Not as heavy as she'd be at fifty-one, but her thighs, upper arms, and midsection were thicker than last year. Her face held better news: smile lines and a faint crinkling around her eyes, but not immensely older-looking than her 1991 self. The hair, lightened to a caramel shade streaked with gold, gave her a more youthful appearance.

Cute.

"What are you on about? You're a stunner." Edward appeared in the reflection behind her.

This time she couldn't hide her blush as they made eye contact in the mirror. She turned around.

"Are you hungry?" he asked.

"Yes." Her stomach made a quick dip. "I'm told I should ask for . . . frog-in-a-hole?"

"Toad-in-the-hole." A wide smile and he held up his palms as if for a stickup. "You give yourself good advice. I could make it right now."

At least he seems easy to like. "I don't know. It doesn't involve any actual toads, does it?"

Head thrown back, he laughed deep and hearty. "No, I promise no amphibians will be harmed in the making of this dish. Let me hang up our coats first."

"Wait." She fished out the silver watch from her pocket. "I must've taken it off when the battery died. I'll need to get it replaced." Better yet, she'd frame the timepiece.

"Shall we to the kitchen?" He offered his arm.

It wasn't too late to run to her bedroom, lock the door, and lie in bed until her head stopped swimming. But she *was* hungry, so she threaded tentative fingers through the crook of his arm and followed him to the kitchen.

Taking a seat at the island, she watched him prepare the meal. There was a swift efficiency to his movements, and Oona couldn't resist checking out his trim but muscular body as he navigated her kitchen. When he reached for a casserole dish from a high shelf and his sweater revealed the red band of his boxer shorts, she thought: *I wonder what the sex is like.*

But that was 1991 Oona's mindset, the girl used to a quick buzz, a quick lay, quick distractions to help her forget poor decisions and bad circumstances. 2004 Oona had to behave more maturely.

How is a forty-year-old woman supposed to behave?

Edward whisked flour and seasoning in a mixing bowl, a shushing metallic scrape echoing through the room. "Can I ask you something?" Eyes down, forced casualness in his tone.

"Sure."

"Do you remember *anything* from last year?" He pressed his lips together, wanting to say more, resisting.

Silence as Edward cracked an egg into the bowl, added milk, and continued to stir.

"You know, I wish I did," she finally answered. "But no. Nothing."

"What's the last thing you do remember?"

"Um . . . the nineties. Yeah, a lot of years lost this time around." She cringed at her lie. "I'm sorry. I know it makes things difficult."

"Don't apologize." He got a package of sausage from the fridge. "It's clearly not something you can control."

"I feel bad when it affects other people." *Like people I married.*

"You mustn't blame yourself. I chose to be with you, and I take our marriage vows seriously, particularly the 'for better or for worse' bit." The sausages sizzled as he browned them in a copper pan. "Let's not even call this 'for worse' but 'for different.' You probably feel like you came to—woke up, however it happens—married to a stranger, but I'm not such a bad bloke. You'll see."

"In a way, you're married to a stranger now, too." Oona tried not to stare at his mouth. What would it feel like against hers? Would last year's chemistry carry over? "I'm different—at least mentally—from the person you knew just an hour ago. It's like we've found ourselves in an arranged marriage."

"Hey, don't knock arranged marriages," he said over his shoulder. "Their divorce rate is under ten percent. We actually have better odds of making it now."

A smile tugged at the corners of her mouth. "That's an optimistic way of looking at it."

Edward poured batter over the browned sausages and slid the casserole dish into the oven. "There, that's done. In a half hour, you'll have a taste of Britain's finest comfort food."

Her smile faltered. Having his full attention cast on her was like wandering into a spotlight on an empty stage.

"Now, I did mention the champers chilling in the fridge, yes?" he asked. Before she could reply, he took out the bottle. "Let's toast our new 'arranged' marriage."

Coming off an intoxicated year, she still desired the glorious numbness that came with being under the influence. She hadn't been addicted to the substances as much as their oblivion.

"I'd love to," she said.

While he retrieved crystal flutes and opened the bottle, she struggled with a thorny irritation that he was so well oriented in her kitchen. Reminded herself he wasn't an invader in her home, but a resident.

I hope I made him sign a prenup. Her neck heated at the unkind thought, though it was practical, since Edward would be out of her life by 2015. *Unless I can change my future.* Regardless, she made a mental note to search her office for pertinent legal documents.

The cork's pop brought her back to the moment, a sound that always struck her as more violent than celebratory. A glass filled with fizzy amber liquid appeared before her.

"To arranged marriages," Edward said.

They clinked glasses and Oona chugged hers, keen to alleviate her muddled thoughts.

"Need a top-up already, eh?" He grinned and refilled her glass with a flourish.

A doughy, meaty, hearty odor permeated the room. "That smells incredible," Oona said. "How'd you get into cooking?"

"My late mum was terrible in the kitchen, bless her heart, so I began making our suppers as soon as I was allowed to use the stove." He leaned his elbows on the kitchen island. "I can't blame her. She spent days on her feet as a hairdresser and came home knackered, so there were a lot of bland soups and stews set to die a long death in the slow cooker."

"And your father? What did he do?"

"He worked on cars. Retired now."

"Did he cook?"

"No, his palate is nonexistent. Probably wouldn't have noticed if his veg had motor oil on it instead of gravy. Which reminds me." Edward went to the fridge and removed a Tupperware container of gravy, which he heated up.

The second glass of champagne also went down quickly, but she turned down a third. She already had a light buzz and a headache.

"Happy Birthday, by the way," he said while sifting through the silverware drawer. "I should've said it sooner, but with everything else going on, it slipped right out of my mind. Last week, you said you wanted to keep things low-key, so I didn't make posh reservations anywhere. I hope that's all right."

"No, low-key sounds good." Oona had more than enough excitement.

When the meal was ready, Edward took out a single glass plate, which he set before her.

"Aren't you having any?"

"I like to prepare food more than eat it." He scooped a golden-brown brick onto her plate and poured gravy over it. "I promise it tastes better than it looks."

Oona took in a messy forkful. "Wow. I can see why this is my favorite dish." The sweetness of the eggy batter paired with the tangy pork sausage and rich gravy made for a bite she wanted to both savor and devour. "It's a shame British food gets such a bad rap."

"That's something I hope to change." He passed her a napkin.

"Do you cook for a living? Have your own restaurant?"

"Yes and . . . soon."

"Soon?"

"I'm currently a chef at a Carroll Gardens bistro, but I'll be opening my own place in Gowanus next month."

"That's exciting." She helped herself to more gravy.

"For both of us."

The fork paused a few inches short of her mouth. "How's that?"

"We're partners in the restaurant." He scratched at his collarbone. "Though granted, most of the financial contribution was yours."

She put her fork down. "Are you telling me I bought a restaurant?"

"I suppose that's the simplest way to put it, yes."

Oona's eyebrows shot up. She assessed her plate with a new eye.

"What do I know about running a restaurant?" Oona asked.

She and Edward were on their way to Clary's Pub, due to open at the end of February. As the taxi crossed the short bridge over the dingy green waters of the Gowanus Canal, they left behind the tidy tree-lined streets of Park Slope for a neighborhood filled with mismatched buildings, dilapidated warehouses, and auto repair shops.

"You're more of a backer, but I know this industry, and we've hired people to handle the design, construction, accounting, PR, you name it. I—*we* have a small army of skilled people."

Gamble on the unknown, her letter had said. Would their marriage survive even if their restaurant didn't?

They approached a converted redbrick carriage house. A shingle hung over the wide black doors, *Clary's Pub* carved onto it in Old English script. Beside the door was a sign that read: COMING SOON.

"Isn't this a great property?" he asked as they got out of the car. "We got a good deal on it, too."

"I can see why," she said. The desolate street contained warehouses, a sign-making store, and farther down the block, yet another auto repair shop. A dirty plastic bag blew in the breeze like a tumbleweed. "There doesn't seem to be much of anything around here."

"Maybe not yet, but the area is undergoing scads of development. Gowanus will become a trendy neighborhood before you know it." He unlocked the front door.

"And if it doesn't?" Because it wouldn't, not to that extent—at least by 2015.

Edward turned around, mouth pursed. "Are you getting déjà vu having this conversation? Because I am." Ignoring her blank expression, he continued. "If it doesn't—though I believe it *will*—this can be a destination restaurant. Look at Peter Luger. People have been coming to East Williamsburg for ages just for that steak house."

"Actually, Williamsburg would've been a better choice." That neighborhood's gentrification was already in progress—the struggling artists and musicians who enjoyed its inexpensive housing wouldn't be able to afford living there in a decade's time.

"Well, we didn't get a space in Williamsburg, now did we?" His voice was light, but his jaw twitched. "None of the places we saw there were quite right. Besides, Gowanus is right between Park Slope and Carroll Gardens, two neighborhoods with gobs of money. We're hardly asking customers to trek out to Staten Island. Now, can I get on with the tour of the restaurant, or would you like to stand out in the cold and bicker some more?"

It was like a teacher admonishing a grade schooler. As the one funding the restaurant, Oona had a right to voice her opinion, but she didn't want to kick off her marriage with a fight. So she put a hand on her husband's arm and adopted a conciliatory tone. "I don't mean to argue. There's so much I need to learn all over again—sometimes I get hung up on details."

"Well, don't." A quick squeeze of her fingers. "That's my job."

He opened the door and waved her in.

The raw space had a bar running along one side and an exposed brick wall on the other. Bare lightbulbs hung from electric cords, and exposed beams revealed a high ceiling threaded with ductwork like geometric aluminum snakes. The floor was covered in power tools and drop cloths.

"No furniture?" Oona sidestepped errant extension cords.

"It's coming in a few weeks. There's still some electrical work that needs doing, and the ceiling has to be finished, so that all needs to get squared away first. Come see the kitchen."

She followed him to a room with lots of brushed steel, pots and pans suspended from ceiling racks, a wall lined with fryers, flat grills, ranges, and other equipment gleaming under the harsh white light. Edward pointed things out with the enthusiasm of a little boy showing off his Christmas presents. ". . . and this tilting skillet is top-of-the-line . . ."

While he talked, her mind drifted. What were her friends from 1991 doing now? Recovering from some terribly fabulous party? Had any of them settled down? Had Cyn followed her advice and become wealthy? And what about Kenzie? He'd be in college now. How long before she saw him again? She meandered around the kitchen, running a hand over metal counters, smooth and cool to the touch. Everything new. Yet another blank slate.

Edward came over and draped a casual arm around her shoulder. The weight of it should've been disconcerting, but it felt natural. Nice. "You're making a childhood dream of mine come true." He gave her a quick kiss on the cheek. "I've said it countless times, and I'll continue to say it: thank you."

"You're very welcome." Her face burned with the lingering warmth of Edward's kiss. How could she not be moved by his excitement and gratitude? "Tell me about the menu."

"Oh yes." His eyes flashed, and his fingers splayed out, trying to create an image for her. "The concept is British meets classic French. Chateaubriand with béarnaise sauce and Yorkshire pudding. Shepherd's pie with dauphinoise potatoes instead of mash. Bouillabaisse with a side of bubble and squeak. That sort of thing."

Oona wasn't familiar with half the dishes he listed—and didn't know whether customers would be, either—but let herself be swept up in his enthusiasm as he led her back to the dining area and continued to share his plans for Clary's Pub.

"We're thinking of having a curtain separating the bar from the dining area. We can accommodate about a hundred, depending on how we do the layout." He took her around the room in a circle as he talked. "Let me show you something else." Down a short corridor at the back of the dining room, a door opened out onto a waterfront patio. "When it gets warmer, we'll serve food out here, let the guests take in the view."

And the smell. Her eyes watered at the potent stench: sewage, rotten eggs, garbage left out too long. How much worse would it get in warmer months? The view wasn't much better. The polluted canal was dark and grimy, speckled with patches of oil and litter. Beyond the water was an elevated subway, a building topped by a large gloomy water tower, and mountains of construction debris flanked by yellow cranes. The total effect would be dining al fresco in the postapocalypse.

"It may not look like much now, but remember, we're getting in on the ground floor," Edward said. "There's talk the canal will undergo a massive cleanup, and rumors of nearby condo developments. By the time the neighborhood picks up, Clary's Pub will already be a local establishment."

If it survives that long.

But Oona banished the thought and tried to see the horizon through Edward's quixotic lens. He had a vision, and she had the means to help him bring it to life. As his partner, her job was to have faith in him.

"I think the New York restaurant world is in for something special," she said.

Behind them, the patio door creaked open. "Oh! I didn't realize anyone else was here." A petite woman with a fox-like face, olive skin, and thick, wavy dark hair stepped out onto the patio. She had sophistication and poise like she was sure the world was going to deliver exactly what she demanded. Her features made her lineage tough to guess—could've been South American, Mediterranean, Middle Eastern, Spanish, even Southeast Asian.

"Francesca, what are you doing here?" Edward's frown deepened.

"Oh well, you know I never stop working." Leaning against the doorframe, she peeled off her leather gloves with the suspense of a burlesque dancer. Her faint accent was also tough to trace—Italian? Israeli? "Since we're meeting with the interior designer on Monday, I thought I'd come in and do another sweep of the place, without the noise of all the contractors. What brings you around?"

"Same." He turned to Oona, putting a protective arm around her. "You'd think my consultant would take a day off, but she's as much of a workaholic as I am."

How well am I supposed to know this woman?

Francesca gave Oona a sardonic smile. "You'd think your husband would remember how much is involved in organizing a restaurant launch. The opening-night party alone is a huge undertaking."

"Oh, I'm sure," Oona replied, sounding the furthest thing from it. "If there's anything I can do to help . . ."

Waving a dismissive hand, Francesca replied, "It's under control. Unless you've been hiding any celebrity friends who could attend the grand opening."

"I thought you already had big celebrities lined up," Edward said.

"Some, yes." There was a note of defensiveness in her voice. "Not *Friends* or *Sex and the City* big, but I have connections to David Blaine, Heidi Klum, and Kelly Osbourne. I may also be able to pull some strings to get Paris and Nicky, though so far I've only been able to get a direct line to one of their hanger-ons, Kim Kar-something-or-other. One way or another, we will have a killer launch."

"First I need to make sure we can actually open on time," Edward grumbled. "I'm still worried about the next MEP inspection. The mechanical should be fine, but electric and plumbing might have issues."

"We'll get there, don't worry so much. Listen, why don't I give you two some space? I can come back another time." Francesca turned to go.

After she left, as Edward locked up, Oona asked, "Does she know about . . . my condition?"

"No, why should she? That's a personal matter and she's just a business associate."

A very pretty one. Should I be worried?

Edward rubbed his bare hands together and blew into them. "Bad day to forget gloves. There's a diner on Smith Street if you want to get breakfast, have a chat, get used to each other some more."

Oona's head was full of so much new information, adding in a getting-to-know-you meal with her new husband was too much. "Actually, do you mind if we go home? I'm not really hungry and I could use some time to—settle in. And I'd like to call my mother."

"Madeleine is on vacation."

A sharp look of disbelief. "What?"

"She took a cruise with Nathan, her boyfriend. She's coming back in two weeks."

"Oh." Disappointment coursed through Oona like mercury, weighing her down. *She just left me to fend for myself with a strange man? Again? Is that what she does now?*

Noticing Oona's soured mood, Edward asked, "What can I do to cheer you up? Take you to a movie? Buy you flowers? Do a funny dance?" He did an impromptu jig on the sidewalk until she cracked a smile. "Or would you rather have a bit of time to yourself?"

Once again, his innate understanding released a pressure valve within her. "Yes. That. And maybe a movie later?"

The brownstone was usually her sanctuary, but going home felt odd now that her house held a new resident. She'd have to get used to the physical reality of a husband. The shared space, decreased privacy, another person beside her in bed every night (she couldn't let Edward sleep in the guest bedroom indefinitely).

Less than a day into the marriage and an unspoken expectation hung over her, for her to get back to normal or find a new normal.

Back home, Edward busied himself in the kitchen and Oona went to her study, locking the door behind her. She checked the safe for the binder. It was intact, its pages filled with her numbers and notations. At the top of the 2004 section, she'd written: *Edward doesn't know about this binder. No need to tell him.*

That made sense . . . though maybe she'd encourage him to buy Google stock when it went public in August. It would make for a nice buffer against any potential money lost in the restaurant.

What about money you might lose in the divorce?

Oona put the binder away and headed to her desk file cabinet. An apprehensive knot formed in her lower back until she found the pre-nuptial agreement. She waded through the legalese until its terms were clear: in the event of a divorce, neither party was responsible for spousal maintenance, and each would retain their separate income and assets. The house, bank account, and investment portfolio were still solely in Oona's name. A holding company in her and Edward's name jointly owned Clary's Pub and the Gowanus property housing it. So her main assets were secure, and she wouldn't have to pay Edward alimony when (*if?*) they split.

Next she reviewed the Clary's Pub paperwork. There were construc-tion contracts, insurance documents, copies of licenses, permits, and invoices. Most of the bills contained four- or five-figure numbers, but a few were into low six figures—customized build-outs, tableware, kitchen and bar equipment. A rough calculation tallied the costs to date at over a million dollars.

That is one expensive dream.

Judging from some of the bank records she reviewed, she funded more than that. There were big purchases at stores like Brooks Broth-ers, Ralph Lauren, and Salvatore Ferragamo—presumably attire for Edward. Additionally, she'd been writing him a five-thousand-dollar check every few weeks (*I give him an allowance?*) and paying his credit card bills, which also amounted to thousands per month.

Whatever she spent on Edward or the restaurant wouldn't affect her overall financial health. But if she supported him to such an extent, was the nature of their relationship transactional? Put more simply:

Am I buying his love?

It was a rational notion considering her circumstances, but in this case, the numbers couldn't tell the full story. If the marriage to Edward was going to work, she'd need to have more faith in her earlier self.

Oona put away the paperwork and headed downstairs to the music room. Once she put on a Velvet Underground record, she regarded her wall of guitars.

Growing up, she'd opted for rock music over pop. Where other girls were singing Olivia Newton-John songs into hairbrushes, Oona would grab a broom, crank up Brian Eno's *Here Come the Warm Jets*, and strum her makeshift guitar. She'd never envisioned herself as a rock goddess, but got a rush at the thought of performing music.

When she began seeing Dale and he enlisted her to be in his band, they'd gone to a store on Kings Highway to select an instrument for her. The curved gleaming bodies of the guitars immediately lured her, like mythological sirens.

As if reading her mind, Dale picked up a red-and-white Stratocaster and said, "I've had my eye on this one. Been saving up for months to buy it."

After working summers as a cashier at Genovese, Oona also had enough money saved for a guitar, but Dale discouraged that idea. "I don't see Early Dawning as a two guitars kind of band." He tapped a finger against his chin, musing. "We could use a different instrument to flesh out our sound."

Granted, they didn't have a "sound" yet because they were still forming the band, but Oona didn't point that out. Instead, she glanced around the store, tamping down her desire to hold one of the acoustic guitars, run a hand along its polished wood, strum its strings, and whisper her secrets into it.

Dale put a hand on the small of her back to steer her away, his resolute palm saying, *This is my dream, not your dream.* And she shuffled along, too indifferent to think of any new dreams, trying to block out the herky-jerky opening notes of "Hotel California" being plucked out behind her.

Until Dale came to an abrupt stop. "Hey, how about this?" He swept his hand across a silver Yamaha keyboard like a game show model. Before she could reply, he took her by the shoulders and coaxed her behind the instrument. "This is exactly what our band needs. You could be on keys and backup vocals."

"I . . . I never thought of myself as a keyboardist." One last longing look at the guitars as Dale continued to plead with her.

"Early Dawning needs you, Oona. Please be our keyboardist."

It was easy to look into his intense brown eyes and agree to anything. So she bought the Yamaha, took lessons, and got pretty good. She grew to love being in the band (which Dale described as "edgy rock with a post-punk soul"), but playing the keyboard was a marriage of convenience, and she never grew to love her instrument.

I do love these beauties, though.

She reached out to one of the guitars when there was a knock on the door.

"Oona, are you there?" Edward called out.

"I'm here." She opened the door.

"Is everything all right? I thought you might've gotten hungry, so I made you some lunch." He held up a tray with a domed lid covering a large plate.

"Everything's fine." Her expression of pleasant gratitude was a mask, tight at the edges. "I just got lost in thought. Come in."

"I made panko fried chicken and truffle mac and cheese with soppressata." He set the tray down on an end table and lifted the lid to let the rich food smells fill the room.

With all Oona was processing, there should've been no room for hunger, but her mouth watered as her appetite betrayed her. "This looks great."

"It really doesn't." A smirk at the beige, yellow, and brown meal. "I have a tendency to make food that tastes good but looks like a dog's dinner."

"I'm sure it's delicious. Thank you."

Edward nodded at the record player as the tinkling notes of "Sunday Morning" began. "This is my favorite song."

"It's sweeter-sounding and catchier than their usual stuff, but I love it, too."

"What's funny is that it's essentially a song about paranoia, warning you to watch out because the world is behind you, but I've always found it strangely comforting."

Her smile, now genuine, broadened. "Me too."

It was a diaphanous bridge, yet firm enough for Edward to step forward, push past her invisible boundaries, and embrace her. The hug was not perfunctory or patronizing, but tight with sympathy. A hug that superseded platitudes like "I'm here for you" and "everything will be okay" while still conveying those things. As if her body remembered what the rest of her had forgotten, her arms lifted up and tightened around him. She fit her head into the crook of his neck, which smelled of freshly baked bread and campfires.

That's when her body betrayed her for the second time: her muscles coiled with a desire for sustenance, a larger appetite surfacing, as she pressed closer to her husband.

Sensing the shift, Edward moved his mouth to the curve of her ear, breathed warm air against it. He ran a slow hand up her back, looking for red lights in her body language. Her small sighs told him *Go, go, go.*

She lifted her head until the sides of their faces were pressed together, her smooth cheek against his soft stubble. All the numbers trickled out of her brain like a window open to clear out a smoky room. There was only the geometry of her mouth and his, inches apart, then centimeters, then—

Their kiss was soft, tentative, filled with question marks. *Is this okay?* asked both sides. *Yes* was the answer. *Yes* on both sides.

Oona clutched Edward's sweater, responded to his kiss by opening her mouth. The tips of their tongues touched, asking more questions, but the resounding answer was always affirmative, the lights all green—*Go, go, go.*

Not since the stranger at the club had she felt such a dizzying attraction. Was it natural chemistry or a deeper need to satisfy her loneliness? Whatever the reason, she wanted him. She was coming off a year of parties and drugs and trysts, some of which had been fun, but all of which had been meaningless. Sex had been lost in a haze of chemicals that heightened or anesthetized or disassociated. She hadn't had sober sex—or sex signifying a deeper connection—since Dale.

Edward helped her out of her sweater and all worries of the year ahead faded. She needed his skin against hers.

He drew her into another deep kiss, pulled her down until they were kneeling on the shag carpet.

Her knees creaked, a backward echo of future aching.

Up above, mouth to mouth, their tongues did the exploring; down below, their hands took over. They shed layers of clothing with the same unspoken courtesy of their initial kiss. Their hands like gentlemen with top hats, asking, "Pardon, but do you mind if I remove this brassiere for you?" "May I cast aside these boxer-briefs?" And always the answer was yes, always the answer was go.

Kneeling above her, Edward offered a questioning smile. Even though her body was responsive—her skin experiencing déjà vu, eager for him—before he entered her, he asked, "Is this okay?"

She nodded, and he began slowly. But she craved a bit of pain, always did, found it gave a counterbalance to her body's pleasure receptors, the way spicy food hurts but can be so delicious. So she thrust her hips to be filled completely in one abrupt motion.

"I didn't know if you'd still want it a little rough." A low, throaty chuckle.

"I do."

She was less pliant than she'd been in 1991, but equally receptive. It helped that Edward knew when to slow down and when to tantalize her tender spots: a light scratching along her rib cage, biting beneath her collarbone, licking right behind her earlobe. He worked as if from a blueprint, privy to her hidden corners.

As she got close, he kept withdrawing, to build it up, tease. When she finally did come, it was unbearably intense, a prelude to multiple orgasms. His own climax followed.

Edward rolled off her. They lay on their backs several inches apart, breathing hard.

The carpet felt like fur against Oona's naked skin. "Wow. So that's what married sex is like."

"That's what it's like for us." His index finger sought hers out; their digits linked together.

But were they monogamous? Once again, the name Peter invaded her thoughts. "Do we have any special arrangements in our marriage I should know about?" She remained still. Could he read her murky thoughts, decipher the pounding of her blood like Morse code?

"Special arrangements? As in, do we have an open marriage? God no. Why would you wonder that?"

"I mean . . ." She scrambled for a reason. "We have this age difference."

"Five years, that's nothing. And I've always fancied women a bit older than me." He turned on his side and propped himself up on an elbow. "I appreciate being with a woman who's truly lived, truly experienced. I find all that a turn-on."

It confirmed what 2003 Oona said in her letter. But it also tugged at her like a fishing hook she'd swallowed and couldn't retrieve. Because she was a facade. Her face and body might hold history and character, but being twenty-one internally made her far from seasoned. Surely it wouldn't be long before Edward sussed that out and realized he was married to an impostor.

15

In the days that followed, Oona didn't see much of Edward, who rose early and came home late, drained of energy, filling her in on the latest catastrophes at the restaurant before passing out in the guest bedroom. A bathroom pipe burst. An electric socket that had to be raised two feet threw off the MEP inspection. There were delays getting a liquor license. A crate of pint glasses was delivered in shards. Something was always going wrong.

One day Oona set an alarm to get up before him.

"I thought we could have breakfast together," she said as he entered the kitchen, a newspaper under his arm. "I made a pot of coffee. How do you take yours?"

"Oh." A grimace flashed across his face. "I actually drink tea. Sorry."

"It's fine, that's good for me to know. One cup of tea, coming right up."

But before she could reach for the kettle, Edward said, "No, no. I'm a picky bugger about the way I like it—steeped exactly five minutes, one level teaspoon of sugar, tiny splash of milk. It'll be easier if I make it myself."

"Okay." She stepped over to the fridge. "I was going to scramble some eggs, unless you're a picky bugger about the way you like your eggs, too?" *Keep it light. This isn't easy for him, either.*

"If I'm to be honest, I am." There was a sound of rushing water as he filled the kettle, a click as he lit the stove. "But I usually start the day with kippers on toast. I can make you eggs."

"You don't have to make anything special for me. I can have kippers on toast, too. Whatever kippers are." Her hand hovered over the refrigerator handle.

Edward gave a hearty laugh. "They're smoked herring, and you hate them."

"Ah." Much as she wanted to be in on the joke, Oona could muster only a feeble smile.

"You usually skip breakfast, anyway." Scratching the stubble on his jaw, he searched her face. "Oona, what's this about? Are you hell-bent on making me breakfast because you think that's what a good wife is supposed to do for her husband?"

Embarrassed tears stung her eyes, and she turned away, occupied herself with taking the milk out of the fridge. "I don't know. Maybe?"

"I'd hate to think what Madeleine would say about you embracing such traditional gender roles," he teased.

"She'd probably curse the patriarchy, then make me burn my bras."

Edward took the milk from her, set it down, and put his hands on her shoulders. "Even if I wasn't a chef, I wouldn't expect you to cook for me. That's not how it works between us."

"How does it work, then?" Such a big question, it quashed her voice to a whisper.

"By understanding each other. Knowing when to step in or step back. Being patient—which you've been fantastic at."

"I've been patient? That doesn't sound like me."

"It's the you I know. I work long hours and don't always get to see you as much as I'd like." Guilt twisted his eyebrows. "But we try to find quality time together."

Oona thought back to her letter's advice. "What if I was more involved in the restaurant? What do you have going on today?"

"Today?" A frantic expression crossed his face as he reviewed the outstanding tasks. "I need to meet with a beverage vendor and a local butcher, review the latest interior designs, test a new recipe, and finish writing the employee handbook." He took a deep breath. "Last year you did help with a bit of the accounting and inventory, but you found it dull, and I don't want to subject you to that. Really, it's fine. This business isn't for everyone. You're much happier focusing on music and your philanthropic work, anyway. And with your memory condition and the opening six weeks away, I'd hate for you to get mixed up in all this madness and clog your head with rubbish."

It was like swimming upstream with no clear destination. The letter told Oona to make an effort, but her efforts seemed to hinder more than help. So she stepped aside and let Edward take care of his own breakfast and his own restaurant.

He did try to include Oona more in subsequent days—asking her opinion on paint swatches, wall decor, menu items—though it felt perfunctory, a polite gesture. If only she shared Edward's passion for food as an enterprise. Alas, she didn't want to know how the sausage was made or what kind of plates it would be served on, so mostly she kept out of restaurant matters while continuing to fund it.

To keep busy, Oona tinkered on her teal egg-shaped iMac, pleased to have the Internet again, though she still refrained from looking up any friends. The first time she'd done so, learning their fate left her more disconnected, lonelier. Lesson learned.

Besides, she wouldn't use technology as a crutch or excuse to remain cooped up. After the scrunchies and pagers of the 1990s and the leggings and smartphones of the 2010s, she was curious what details— large and small—would stand out to her from the 2000s. So she ventured into the city, where Manhattan's skyline was like a beautiful smile with a missing tooth, the Twin Towers gone, the Freedom Tower yet to be built. She walked everywhere, taking mental snapshots of today's society. Apart from the baffling proliferation of fedoras and trucker hats, fashion struck her as either too comfortable, with velour tracksuits as acceptable daywear, or too uncomfortable, with pointy heels squeezing the life out of female toes everywhere, except when it was both, in the case of low-rider jeans. Refusing to get swept up in clothing trends, Oona aimed her shopping dollars at record stores, many of which wouldn't be around in a matter of years. Cell phones were ubiquitous but more primitive, with social media and other apps still years away, so people were less absorbed by their digital devices (which would make seeing the Killers, Kanye West, Thievery Corporation, and others in concert later that year far more enjoyable).

When home, she spent a lot of time in her music room. In 1991, she'd ignored her records. Her personal soundtrack had been peripheral, party girl dance beats for nightclubs and wild gatherings, which left her ears ringing. But now she had a clear head to enjoy music again. Friends and relationships might slip away year to year, but she did have some continuity, a strong lineup of people whose songs would always be in her life: Lou Reed, David Bowie, Bryan Ferry, Kate Bush, Mick Jagger, Prince, Deborah Harry, Iggy Pop.

And others would reappear in surprising ways. A week into the new year, she received a postcard from Thailand. One side, a photo of limestone cliffs dotted with shrubbery like a patchy beard forming a circular lagoon around water the color of Midori and Blue Curaçao swirled together—like a cocktail awaiting a straw and paper umbrella. The back of the card read:

> *If you're ever in hell, go somewhere that looks like heaven. Sad today,*
> *but a little less sad than I was yesterday. Lonely, but this is what I need*
> *right now.*   *—Kenzie*

An initial gasp of delight was swept away with a frown as Oona reread the message.

The cryptic note contained no address besides hers and no clues beyond the Thai postmark. What did it mean? Why was Kenzie sad and lonely, and why did he need to be thousands of miles away? Hopefully, they'd cross paths again soon.

In the meantime, she still had Madeleine, who called when she returned from her cruise in mid-January.

"I want to repaint some of the rooms in my apartment. Will you come help me?"

No warm greeting, no niceties. Oona had expected a more conciliatory tone. Unable to keep the sulk out of her voice, she said, "That's
the first thing you ask? Not—oh, I don't know—how is married-to-a-
stranger life treating you?"

"I imagined we'd cover that while we paint."

Goody. We can also cover why you're never around when I need you most.
"Why don't you just hire a professional?"

"Because doing the work yourself can be more satisfying. When I
look around at my newly painted walls, the result of my labor—or our
labor, depending—I'll enjoy my home that much more. If I hire painters,
I might take these walls for granted."

"Will your boyfriend be there?"

"Nathan and I broke up."

"In the middle of your vacation?"

"I'd rather not discuss that. Now if you can't help me—"

"No, I will. Just tell me when and where. Are you still in Bensonhurst?"

"Bay Ridge. I'll text you the address. Wear clothes you don't care
about."

"You got it. Hey, I got a postcard from Kenzie. Do you remember
him?"

A pause. "I don't know who that is."

"Really? You never met him? I never mentioned him?"

"Oona, I have no idea who you're talking about, and I'm sorry, but
I really need to get started here."

Was the recent breakup causing her mother to sound so tightly
wound? Or was there something more? She'd have to find out in person.

An hour later, Oona arrived at her mother's penthouse apartment.
It had a sunken living room, a wide balcony with a view of the Verrazano
Bridge, and seemingly endless white walls.

There was something stiff in the way Madeleine hugged her. Reluctant. Her face held no clues: Botox treatments had left it smooth and
inscrutable.

"I thought we could start in the bedroom." Her mother led the
way, the word *Juicy* bedazzled across the rear end of her pink tracksuit.

"When we were in St. Kitts, I discovered this charming antique store decorated in the most divine colors. It brought the whole space to life and inspired me to add more vibrant color to this place."

In the bedroom, the furniture had been pushed to the center of the room and draped in drop cloths. Madeleine held up two paint swatches. "First, we'll do a base coat in teal. Once that's dry, we'll add a sponge effect with the magenta."

Taking a lap of the huge room, Oona said, "Mom, your ceilings are, like, twelve feet high. This could take days."

"Maybe you have something more important you need to do?" A sharpness to her breezy lilt.

"I wouldn't be here if there was." *Why isn't she being nicer?* They were two people crossing an iced-over lake; every treacherous step brought forth another crack, another fissure, until inevitably someone would fall through to the frigid waters below.

Madeleine opened a paint can, stirred its contents with a wooden spoon, and tilted a sea of teal into a roller pan.

"You weren't kidding when you said vibrant," Oona said. "That's . . . a lot brighter than it looks on the color sample. You sure it's not too much?"

It was a ludicrous question. Madeleine favored the bold, bright, exotic. Her apartment was decorated with a menagerie of trinkets and artifacts from India, Tibet, Africa, Japan. Her wardrobe was equally colorful: full of blinding saris, woven belts, kimonos (for a time, she'd even tried to pull off turbans). When she was a child, Oona didn't mind Madeleine picking her up from school wearing outlandish ensembles, until the kids snickered and nicknamed her mother United Nations. No amount of tearful pleading would get her to swap the global getups for simpler dresses.

"Too much?" Madeleine echoed, handing her daughter a roller.

The ice was getting thinner. The mature thing would've been for Oona to be direct, to tell her mother she felt neglected, but it was easier to add spikes to the tender emotions and find an alternate release for them. "I know you like bright colors, but . . . this combo is hideous. You'll be looking at these walls every day and it's gonna be—"

"Let me guess: *too much*." The words dripped with sarcasm. "I happen to know my taste quite well and chose these colors thoughtfully. I think they're beautiful. But since you find them so *hideous*, don't feel obliged to help me."

A grunt of incredulity. Her knuckles went white gripping the roller. "Mom, what the fuck? You keep making it sound like I don't want to be here, but *you're* the one acting like you don't want me here. Is this about your breakup? Because you've never let men get to you before."

"That's right, I'm the composed one. *You're* the one who falls apart whenever things don't work out with a man in your life."

Crack. The ice gave way and they both fell through.

Oona dropped her roller. "How would you even know? You're always trying to weasel into my personal life and be my best friend, but when I actually need you, you're on fucking vacation. And now, instead of being remotely sympathetic about my situation—having a brand-new husband I don't know and barely see—you're giving me shitty attitude."

Fists on hips, Madeleine huffed, "I didn't realize I needed to be at my grown-up daughter's beck and call. I thought she'd be able to act like a capable adult without my input. But it turns out I'm a neglectful mother with a *shitty attitude* who's not allowed to have her own life. Thank you *so much* for reminding me."

"Why are you being such a bitch?" The words hurt to say. She'd never called her mother names before.

As if expecting the insult, Madeleine's eyes lit up. "*I'm* the bitch? You have no idea. The things you said to me. *You're* the bitch."

Oona recoiled at the nasty boomerang. "What did I even say to you? Just now? I was only . . ." The lines in her forehead smoothed with realization. "Or do you mean before?"

No answer, but the sharp set of her jaw was affirmation enough.

"Mom, what's going on?"

Madeleine loaded her roller with paint and moved toward the nearest wall, but stopped shy of it. Her shoulders sagged. "We had a fight. It was awful. We've never fought like that before, not about anything. I booked the extended cruise to make sure we'd be away through

Christmas and New Year's, figuring you might not remember it when I got back. Did you leave yourself a letter?"

"I did, but it only said the year would start off shaky for us. No mention of any argument. I just got back from 1991." How casually put, as if announcing she'd returned from the grocery store. "I'm twenty-one. I haven't lived in this decade at all. What did we fight about?"

Madeleine's surgically paralyzed brow could betray no distress, but her eyes still conveyed bewilderment. "After all these years, I still can't get used to it. Sometimes you come to me as a child in an older body—"

"I'd hardly call twenty-one a child."

"—and other times you're this wizened soul, young on the outside but even older on the inside than I am."

"Mom, you're dripping paint on the floor."

"I can't imagine how trying it is for you, but it wears on me, too. I don't know how to be a mother to you sometimes. You were rarely a willful teenager, so to see you behaving like one in the body of a grown woman . . ." She shook her head. "I don't know what to make of it. I know . . ." Her voice caught in her throat. "I know there are certain things I'm supposed to forgive because of your circumstances, but sometimes . . ."

"You don't want to?" Oona took the paint roller from her mother's hand and placed it in the pan.

"I *want* to. But sometimes I feel like I can't." Madeleine sat on the edge of the bed, the plastic tarp rustling beneath her. She covered her eyes, inhaled through her nose. Unlike her daughter, she didn't cry easily.

Unsure, Oona remained standing, a stranger in her mother's home. "Tell me what we fought about."

"I can't."

"Why not? Maybe if you tell me, I'll be able to prevent it from happening in 2003."

"Your future is my past. I can barely get my head around it." A mirthless, machine-gun chuckle. "No, my dear. Your life shouldn't be about trying to prevent mistakes. Make mistakes, but learn from them and live with them."

A black, hissing voice in her head: *How many mistakes can you live with?* A mist of regret crept into her. She took in small gulps of air, released tears and more tears.

"Come sit beside me." More rustling as Oona joined her. "What is it? Why are you crying?"

"I. Wonder." Staccato words through jagged bursts of air. "I. Wonder. If." A hard swallow to quell the sobbing. "I wonder if I ever get things right."

"Do any of us? We all do our best. And even with your time travel, you still live through each year only once. You don't get any redos."

"But what if I could do better? What if avoiding last year's fight makes this year better?"

Madeleine took a moment before answering. "There's no telling whether it would change much. Maybe that fight needed to happen." A downcast turn of her mouth, but Oona nodded. "Another thing to consider—even if you could prevent it and ended up changing your future, you wouldn't know how because you already lived through that year. And if you start going on about alternate timelines again, it'll give me a headache, so please let's not go down that road. Make your life more about letting in the good things than preventing the bad things. You're not going to stop any wars or stave off any big tragedies. You're not Sarah Connor, and the Terminator is now governor of California. You . . . you do good by being a good person, making others happy. Embrace that."

"Do I make Edward happy?"

"You do."

How? "And does he make me happy?"

"Yes, I think so." Madeleine took the tone of a witness on the stand, measuring out her answers.

Recalling 2003 Oona's warning, she pressed on. "Are you sure?" Trepidation trailed like ivy up her spine.

Madeleine looked at her daughter, unblinking. "I think you make each other happy. The rest of it is none of my business."

They were back on solid footing, but still skirting the ice. Better not to risk another fracture. Oona walked over to the pan of paint, picked

up the roller, and began zigzagging swaths of teal across the nearest
wall.

"How is everything with Edward?" her mother asked.

Now that Oona had an opening to voice her marriage concerns,
she was more reluctant to do so. "I mean, it's weird having someone
around the house. It's not like it was with . . ." Kenzie. Perhaps because
they'd had more time to develop a friendship. Oona was lucky if she saw
Edward an hour or two a day with his hectic schedule. "I mean, it's not
like it was when I lived on my own and didn't have this other person
I'm legally tied to. But I'm getting the hang of it." Was she? "At first I was
worried it was gonna be a repeat of the Crosby situation, where I felt
like I had to pretend to be someone else. But I don't have to pretend
with Edward." A lie, but sometimes pretending was better than being
alone. "It's such a relief." It wasn't. But at least the sex was good.

"Careful, Oona, the paint is dripping. You're laying it on a little thick."

Oona gave her mother a look: *Really?*

"The paint. I swear I'm only talking about the paint. Use less on
the roller so it coats evenly." She got up and demonstrated on a second
roller. "You mentioned you don't get to see much of Edward?"

"Oh, that's only because he's so busy getting Clary's Pub ready for
the grand opening. I'm sure things will calm down once it's up and
running." Of course, Oona was sure of no such thing, but she wanted
to believe it and to see Edward's dream come to fruition. But it had been
easier when she and Dale had their band and shared a common dream.
Everything had been easier with Dale.

They worked in silence for the next few minutes, the only sound
the sticky slap of paint rolled onto the walls, as if the color was resisting
its new home.

Oona spoke first. "Is it terrible that I still wonder if anyone will
ever measure up to Dale?"

"It's not terrible. But it's . . . not realistic. Or healthy. Dale was your
first love, which is beautiful, but I think you sometimes put him on a
pedestal. He was a real person. He had flaws."

"I know he had flaws." Did she, though? "What do *you* think his
flaws were?"

"His table manners, for one thing. He'd talk with his mouth full, his elbows were *always* on the table. It drove me crazy."

Oona rolled her eyes. "How could you let me be with a monster like that?" But she'd never noticed these breaches of etiquette. And judging from her mother's hesitant look, there was more. How much did she want to know? "What else?" she finally prodded.

Keeping focused on the wall, she said, "He was a talented musician and certainly had drive and good looks, but he could be a little full of himself. And bossy. I worried about that sometimes. He had a power over you, like you couldn't make your own decisions without him."

"What?" Oona nearly dropped the roller. "What are you talking about?"

"You preferred to wear your hair short but grew it out because Dale liked it long."

"I was trying something new. Isn't that what being a teenager is about?"

Noncommittal murmurs from her mother.

"Are you saying he was controlling?" Oona asked.

"Not controlling. But a strong influence."

"Give me another example."

"You never wanted to be a keyboardist."

That was undeniable. "Yeah." The word came out between a whisper and sigh. "I thought I'd be happy playing anything as long as I was making music—and I *was.* I loved our band."

"You wouldn't have been happier playing guitar?"

"I didn't let it bother me. I figured Dale called dibs, it was his instrument, so be it." She attacked the wall with her paint roller, a new vigor filling her. "Ever since Dale died—these last two leaps, at least—I thought it would be betraying his memory to take it up. Like I was saying, *Oh good, now that you're dead, I can do this thing I've always wanted to do.*"

"But if he held you back from something you were so passionate about, maybe he was the one betraying you."

Madeleine's words were featherlight but detonated within Oona, sending her reeling forward. Palm to wall she caught herself as the epiphany ricocheted through her. While she'd held their love story as epic in her heart, part of her had been pretending with Dale, too.

She might be decades late, but at least there was one charade she could resolve.

When she finished helping her mother, on her way home, she picked up a copy of *The Village Voice*. Oona flipped through the back pages, checking the ads, until one caught her eye:

GUITAR LESSONS
ALL SKILL LEVELS
Reasonable Rates
Ask For Peter

16

How do I know this is the right Peter?

The question orbited Oona's thoughts as she made her way down Seventh Avenue and crossed Flatbush into Prospect Heights.

Since the start of her leap, she'd wondered about this second name the woman on the subway had mentioned. Maybe 2003 Oona hadn't wanted to spoil the surprise of taking up the guitar, but changed her mind at the last minute in order to reunite her with her music teacher. Except this Peter hadn't recognized her name over the phone when she set up the appointment. Would he recognize her in person?

Either way, the ad in *The Village Voice* had to be a sign.

Her hands were slick with sweat, and the guitar case nearly slipped out of her hand as she approached a beige row house. A few steps down to the garden level and she faced his apartment door.

"Are you Oona?" a male voice called out behind her.

She turned as an Asian man in black jeans and a leather jacket approached. He appeared to be in his mid-twenties, and his hair, which was overdue for a cut, flopped across his forehead.

"Sorry I'm late, subways were a mess. Hope you haven't been waiting long. I'm Peter."

Though he showed no recognition as they shook hands, she was immediately drawn to him. Yes, he was attractive, his frame long and lean, his mouth full and faintly smiling, his eyes kind. And yes, there was the leather jacket. (*Just like Dale's. Just like mine.*) But it was more than that.

When she stepped into his living room, the first image that greeted her was a giant poster of a yellow banana on a white background: Andy Warhol's Velvet Underground album cover. And when Peter took off his jacket and rolled up the sleeves of his sweater, along his forearm was a tattoo, a vertical row of glyphs Oona couldn't decipher.

"It's Korean," he said, noting her curious stare. "It means 'everything has its time.'"

The hair on her arms stood on end, and she *knew*. An unresolved puzzle in her life had been decrypted.

This had to be the right Peter.

That first lesson, when he put his elegant, tapered fingers over hers to demonstrate correct positioning, something within her began to glow. And when she played a series of chords that added up to an actual song—Tom Petty's "Free Fallin'"—her veins surged with a brand-new high. Inspiration and creative satisfaction were tinder, igniting dormant desire.

From then on, her days took on a new brightness and ease.

"Your strumming patterns are getting better."

"I bet you say that to all the girls."

Oona didn't mean to flirt with Peter, but it came naturally to her, just as learning the guitar did. Not that it was easy. At first she struggled to pluck out a single note correctly, then a scale, then open chords. In the first few weeks, more than fifteen minutes of playing left her hands aching. Sometimes she played through the pain; other times she had to set the guitar aside. But the better she got, the more she wanted to play, and the more she looked forward to her twice-weekly lessons. By early February, her passion for the instrument verged on obsessive.

"You must be practicing a lot," he said halfway through their lesson.

"Hours every day. I keep picks around everywhere and leave the guitar out, like you suggested."

"I wish my other students had your level of dedication."

"But then I wouldn't be your favorite student."

"That's true. How are the hands feeling?"

"Okay, but my wrist is a little sore."

"You're bending it too much." He massaged it with his thumbs, pressing into the upper bulb of her hourglass tattoo.

It wouldn't be fair to Edward. A persistent, pragmatic mantra. After the debacle with Crosby, a determination to keep libidinous impulses in check. She told herself it was displaced affection, like a patient falling for her lifesaving doctor. The guitar was her compass and light. The routine of practicing, the sense of purpose, the normalcy of it—all were tonics. As was the promised continuity. Regardless of her age or the year, she could play for the rest of her life. Given such a gift, naturally she'd feel a kinship with the man who gave it to her.

No, this is a gift I gave myself.

Peter knew she was married, though Oona wore her wedding ring only to the first lesson, found playing without it more comfortable.

"Let's take a five-minute break."

"Sounds good." She set the guitar down and turned to face him on his lime-colored retro-space-age sofa. His entire living room was decorated in a sixties vision of the future—boxy furniture with curved edges in soft blues and greens.

Oona always looked forward to these breaks. "What song completely out of my skill range are you gonna play today?"

"Let's see if you recognize this one." Picking up his own guitar, he launched into a jangly melody, upbeat on its surface, with a melancholy thread running beneath it.

"The Smiths, 'Girl Afraid,'" she said when he finished. "God, I wish I could play something that advanced."

"Keep going at the rate you're going, and one day you will."

A teasing grin. "Funny, I wouldn't have pegged you for a Smiths fan."

He chuckled. "Why's that?"

"Because you laugh and smile too much to be a Smiths fan."

"The Smiths got many teenagers on this planet—myself included—

through some tough times. And Johnny Marr is my personal music hero. My Lou Reed, you could say," he added with a wink.

"Why are you wasting your time teaching beginners like me, anyway? How are you not out there playing with your own band instead?" Was she leaning in too much?

"I tried, but could never get over my stage fright. Can't play in front of more than a dozen people without getting paralyzed." A kaleidoscope of emotions played across his eyes: frustration, disappointment, resignation. "But I've been lucky to get steady session gigs and to make a living doing this." He motioned to the space between them. "Which, for the record, is not a waste of time. It's a privilege. What about you? What made you take up the guitar?"

The way Peter asked questions was terribly endearing. He listened with his whole body, absorbing every word through small nods and head tilts, reacting without interrupting. He listened that way when Oona played guitar, too.

"It's been my dream to play for years, but my life has been . . . chaotic," she admitted. "Even so, music is one thread that's always run through it."

"Life can get in the way of our dreams. The important thing is that you found your way to your instrument. And what's better than the guitar?" He regarded her Carl Thompson 6-string as if admiring a beautiful woman. If only he knew it used to belong to Lou Reed.

Over the past month, Edward worked increasingly long hours to prepare for the restaurant's grand opening, so he was supportive of Oona's new hobby ("I was wondering if you'd pick it up again, seeing that you already played quite well when we met," he said). The more she played and the better she got, the less she minded his absence.

Seeing her husband sporadically made it easier to get used to marriage in general, as did Edward's eagerness to keep her satisfied when he was around, whether by bringing her leftovers as he developed the restaurant menu or fulfilling her needs in the bedroom. He even took her out on at least one proper date a week: a movie at the Pavilion or drinks at Brooklyn Social or brunch at the 12th Street Bar & Grill. Bit by bit, she got to know her husband. He loved Terry Gilliam but hated

Monty Python. All his friends worked in restaurants and every other Monday, a group of them played poker. He'd eat *anything*—organ meats, rotten fish, you name it—except for raisins ("bloody awful things"). His favorite music had grit to it: Pixies, Nirvana, Sonic Youth, and— thankfully—Velvet Underground. He could recite every line of every Tarantino film.

While Edward updated her on general restaurant business when they went out, he was tactful enough not to mention expenses. Instead, he left new invoices clipped to the fridge, which Oona replaced with checks.

One night in mid-February, high on having just learned Pink Floyd's "Wish You Were Here" and unable to wait for Edward to get home, she decided to surprise him at Clary's.

It was just after ten o'clock and Francesca answered the door. "What are you doing here?" they asked each other in unison and shared a tense chuckle.

Any signs of disarray in Francesca's clothes or hair? None that Oona noticed.

"I'm finalizing the grand opening details. Guest list, seating arrangements, that sort of thing." She didn't move to let Oona inside.

"You need to be here to do that?"

"Being in the space helps me get ideas on how to best utilize it. So yes."

"Can you let me in to see my husband, please?"

"He's in the middle of something. It's really not the best time." Her smile was pitying. "We only have a week until the opening and Edward needs to stay focused."

Oona ground her jaw so tightly, it was a wonder her teeth didn't crack. "I don't think it's your place to tell me what Edward needs. Now let me in."

A put-upon sigh and Francesca stepped aside.

Her boots thundered on wood, tile, and wood again as Oona stormed into the kitchen, which was empty, then upstairs to Edward's office. She opened the door without knocking and found him slumped over messy piles of papers.

He looked up, alarmed. "What's wrong?"

Maybe this was a bad idea. "Nothing. I just wanted to see you." It came out more needy than lusty.

Incomprehension in his eyes. "So . . . there's no emergency?"

"No. You haven't been around much this week, so I thought I'd stop by."

"Oh." A long sigh. "I have so much crap I need to sort out. I really have to focus if we're going to open on time. Sorry, love. I'll bring home some beef Wellington."

"Don't worry about it." Though she said it more to herself.

"Bear with me these next few weeks. Once we're up and running, I'll be around more."

"Of course." She kissed him goodbye and left the room.

At the top of the stairs, she ran into Francesca, who followed her back down.

"He won't, you know," Francesca said.

Keep walking. Ignore her.

But Oona couldn't resist. "Won't what?"

"Won't be around more. Prepare to be a restaurant widow for at least the next six months. Maybe nine. You have no idea how demanding it is running this type of business, how much he is responsible for."

"Well, if it gets too demanding, he can always hire more people to help."

A you-poor-girl grimace. "That is not the point. He thrives on the pressure, and he is meticulous about every detail. The restaurant is his baby, and he will not entrust it to other people to take care of."

There was no denying this. She left with a burning in her chest. Not only had Francesca gotten the last word in, but she'd painted such a lonely picture. Oona did the math: six months from now would put them at August, but nine would be November. That would leave little time before her next leap. How many years would it be before she returned to Edward, to their marriage? And what about these next months of being a restaurant widow? What might she miss out on in the meantime?

* * *

"Did you ever flirt with other men while you were married to Dad?"

Oona and Madeleine were browsing the Grand Army Plaza farmers market one Saturday morning, a few days before the restaurant opening.

"I flirted with other men all the time when I worked at the travel agency. Sometimes it helped me finagle discounts on hotel rooms or tour packages, or it got customers to upgrade their vacations, spend a little more. But it was harmless." Her mother ran a hand over a mound of beets. "Is it too cold for borscht?"

"You swim in the ocean in February, but you're worried about eating cold soup? I'll never understand you." Oona examined jars of organic honey at a neighboring stand.

"Is Edward giving you a hard time about flirting with other men? Is he jealous?"

"Not at all." *I wish.* Not really, though it would've held her accountable for any salacious thoughts about her guitar teacher. "But, you know, Peter and I have a vibe. Obviously it's nothing. He probably flirts with his students the way you did at work. Still, sometimes I feel guilty about it."

"Peter your guitar teacher? *Interesting.*" She drew the word out to extra syllables. "Is he cute?"

"He's—I mean—yes, he's cute, but it's not—I'm not . . ." A cold wind eased the heat rising to her face. "Most of it is just the two of us bonding over music. Which I haven't had since my first leap, with a friend you don't know yet." Another postcard had arrived from Thailand yesterday and Kenzie *still* hadn't said when he'd return to New York. *Shouldn't he have seen all the temples and palm trees by now?*

The brisk air was suffused with the pungent, peppery smell of fresh basil as they passed the potted herbs. Madeleine ran a finger across a sprig of rosemary. "Maybe it's more than bonding over music. You're also getting to know Peter in a different way than Edward."

"How so?"

"It's more balanced. With Edward, he knows more about you than you know about him, so you're playing catch-up. With Peter, you're getting to know each other more organically. Without being burdened by the gravity and expectations of marriage."

"It's not a burden." Oona rushed to defend her situation. "Marriage is a responsibility, sure, but you make it sound like I'm being crushed under the weight of it."

"That's not what I'm saying, sweetheart." Her tone was soothing but measured. "What I mean is, when a man you've never met is placed before you and you're told, 'Here's your husband, go love him,' it's understandable if your heart doesn't follow the command. It would make sense if you developed feelings for someone you had a less stressful, more natural rapport with instead."

They dodged two baby strollers approaching from opposite directions and took refuge beside the Brussels sprouts.

"It's not like I'm falling in love with another guy." Tears sprang to her eyes.

"Even if it's a crush, it's okay. Your father was sweet on one of the bank tellers who worked with him—I could tell by the way he talked about her—but it's not something he ever acted on. When you work with someone and see them all the time, these things happen. Like Stockholm syndrome, but less sinister."

Does Edward have a crush on Francesca? The possibility mollified her guilt over Peter, but only for a moment, because it raised a bigger question she couldn't bear to consider.

"Do you think Peter has feelings for you?" Madeleine asked.

"Doubtful. He's way younger than me. He'd never—and I'd never—it's naive to believe I have a special connection with him because of some easy banter. Maybe he's easier to talk to because he's closer to my real age. I *am* still twenty-one on the inside. But regardless, it's not like I'm gonna jeopardize my marriage over some silly crush." If it was even that. "Look at these, I've never seen Brussels sprouts this big." Oona scrutinized the baby cabbages.

"You hate Brussels sprouts." Madeleine waited until her daughter looked up at her. "Maybe your crush isn't so silly. What you need now may not be what 2003 Oona needed. You don't have to feel beholden to whatever arrangements last year's version of you made."

Before either of them could say more, a boy on a Razor scooter zipped by and came up short on the turn, knocking into the table beside them, which pitched forward. Brussels sprouts cascaded down like a mass of green golf balls. They rolled and scattered in all directions.

Oona was asleep when Edward came home that night, and he woke her by running kisses up her bare legs.

"Mm, that feels nice." Her murmur was tinged with slumber. She let him remove her nightshirt to give him access to more bare skin.

"I've been thinking of doing this all day."

As he touched her, without intending to, Oona stopped feeling her husband's hands—which were rough and patchworked with scars and burns resulting from years of food preparation. Instead, she imagined Peter's hands, warm and smooth, his long fingers gliding over her, inside her.

And that's when the bigger question loomed again, demanding to be considered.

Do I even want to be married?

17

Opening night at Clary's Pub was a relative success—not the star-studded affair Francesca had promised, but her networking did produce a number of journalists, local business owners, relevant industry taste-makers, and irrelevant celebutantes. Despite the promising start, business dwindled immediately thereafter. A lukewarm write-up in *New York* magazine two weeks later left her husband desolate. Oona was at the restaurant during a quiet lunch hour when Francesca brought in the review.

"'. . . not elevated enough to justify the prices for what is ultimately pub food dressed in frilly French garments. Chef and proprietor Edward Clary needs to lessen his reliance on truffle oil·and revisit the menu with a fresh and frugal eye. Small portions of stodgy food at exorbitant prices plus an out-of-the-way location puts Clary's Pub at risk . . .'" Edward stopped reading to take a long gulp of Guinness. "I knew we should've done a soft opening. It would've given us a chance to iron out problems before word spread. All this bloody hype for the grand opening when we should've come out of the gate quietly, not with our bollocks hanging out."

From the white-knuckled way he held his pint glass, Oona expected him to throw it across the room, but instead he hunched his shoulders, deflated, and set it down.

"It's one review. You've gotten some good write-ups, too," Francesca said.

"Yes, the *Brooklyn Paper* said my mash was the best in the borough. It's a shame nobody fucking reads the *Brooklyn Paper*."

He stomped upstairs to his office, taking the magazine with him. When Francesca went to follow, Oona blocked her path.

"I'll take this one," Oona said.

"Actually, I should go. He'll want to talk strategy, since business has been so slow." She stepped around a table to take an alternate route, but Oona was faster and blocked her again.

"You can do all that later. Right now, he needs his wife." Ignoring Francesca's dubious raised eyebrow, she pressed on and took brisk strides to Edward's office.

Barely across the threshold and—

"Not now, Oona." He was poring over the magazine again.

"It's only one review." She hated herself for echoing Francesca.

"It's a review that matters. I don't know why nobody else understands this. We've been open for three weeks and we're lucky if we clear ten covers at lunch. Luckier still if we do twenty at dinner. And this"—he clutched the magazine and shook its glossy pages—"isn't going to help. Why did I even make this place a pub? Nobody's going to be popping by for a pint and 'overpriced shepherd's pie.' We get zero foot traffic out here."

This wasn't the time for I-told-you-so's; instead, Oona played the supportive wife, going over to him and massaging his shoulders.

"I'm sure things will pick up. It's only a matter of time before this place is booked solid."

"We'll see." He bent his head and kissed her knuckles, then removed her hands from his shoulders. "Maybe doing a brunch menu will help. I'll run some ideas by Francesca. Could you send her up here? Thanks, love." Without waiting for a response, he returned to the magazine.

Oona stood with her hands suspended in midair like someone had paused the movie of her life. There was nothing else to say, so she did as she was told, focusing on Francesca's pointy red stilettos to avoid her inevitable smirk.

Weeks passed. The restaurant continued to lose money, Oona continued to play guitar and write checks, and Edward continued to come home late. So late, sometimes he never made it past the living room couch.

Clary's Pub was closed on Mondays, which was typically when Edward carved out time for Oona. One such Monday in late March, they went to a local Italian bistro for lunch.

Once they were seated and their server was out of earshot, Edward shook his head in disgust. "Is that hostess having a laugh? She barely looked up from her mobile when she greeted us. Like she was doing us a bloody favor calling over a waiter. And did you get a look at him? All rumpled like he just rolled out of bed, reeking of body odor. If he was my server, I'd send him home for a shower before letting him anywhere near my customers." Opening his menu with a grunt, he gave Oona an expectant look.

His vitriol left her too stunned to speak. Sure, he could be nitpicky about the eateries they patronized, but this level of hostility was new. "I guess the owner could learn a thing or two from you about managing staff," she mumbled, taking refuge in her own menu. "I did read a rave review of this place, so hopefully the food will make up for the service."

But the food didn't meet Edward's exacting standards, either. According to him, the pasta was overcooked, the broccoli rabe undercooked, and the sauce too salty. "Where did you read this so-called rave review, anyway?"

"Oh, um, some food blog." It had actually been *New York* magazine, but telling him the real source—or confessing her own dish was tasty— might've angered him further.

"Of course." His face soured. "Any pillock with a computer can be a food expert nowadays. Even if they can't tell their taste buds from their arseholes."

"Actually, I was thinking it might be worthwhile to host a dinner for bloggers to help with word of mouth. And I had a few other ideas on how we could drum up business." She took a bite of squid ink pasta, careful not to reveal her pleasure in the food. "I checked your marketing calendar, and it doesn't look like there's much planned besides some print ads and direct mailings. Why don't we splash out on bus ads or even some subway-entrance ads along the F line?" Unable to read his reaction, Oona kept going. "Clary's could also have a stronger online presence. The website could be better—that music *has* to go—and getting someone to help with search engine optimization—"

An outburst of laughter cut her off, though the way Edward bared his teeth was anything but jolly. "Jesus, Oona, when did you become a restaurant marketing guru?"

"I've just been doing some research—"

"And according to your research, it sounds like I've done fuck all to promote Clary's. What other insights can you share? Tell me what's wrong with the menu, the decor, the general operations." He propped his chin in his hand and stared in mock enthrallment.

Edward's sarcasm knocked the wind out of her. Was there any point in trying to reason with him? She was on the verge of backpedaling, but a queasy injustice made her bite back. "So it's okay for me to pay for *everything* as long as I shut the hell up? I'm giving you decent ideas here—and offering to fund them!—but you'd rather make me feel like a moron than consider what I have to say." Grabbing her purse, she fumbled around until she found her wallet. Oona stood, threw some twenties onto the table, and snatched up her jacket. "Here, let me cover lunch, too. Which, for the record, I thought was *delicious*."

Her mind was a nasty tangle of thoughts as she stormed out of the bistro. But before she could begin to unsnarl them, Edward appeared at her side.

"Oona, forgive me." Hands in pockets, he hung his head. "After everything you invested into it and working my bollocks off day and night—it's killing me that Clary's isn't doing better. I'm an embarrassment."

"You're not an embarrassment." She let out a slow sigh. "But you acted like a dick when I was trying to help you."

"An utter wanker. No disagreement there. And your suggestions were spot-on. But the thought of you sinking more money into this . . ."

"It's fine. The money doesn't matter."

After some further tussling with his pride, Edward relented and gratefully accepted the funding for Oona's ideas. Which brought in a few new customers. Too few. They hoped business would pick up in May when the weather warmed and Edward opened up the patio. It didn't. The stench off the Gowanus Canal kept the dwindling patrons indoors.

Meanwhile, Oona continued her lessons and her feelings for Peter only grew. She played regularly for her mother, who'd listen and nod with a knowing, thoughtful, oddly melancholy smile. Maybe she was still nursing a broken heart. They spoke little about Edward or Peter or the restaurant. They spoke little about much, so the music filled in their silence. It was a confusing time for Oona, and she found it easier to avoid parsing out her emotions and the mounting resentment in her marriage by pouring her energy into music.

By June, Oona and Edward's limited interactions had become more barbed.

"Oh, so it's fine to flake out on seeing *Avenue Q* with me last week, but *god forbid* you miss a single poker night with your buddies."

"I 'flaked out' because my line cook cut the top of his finger off and I worked a hundred hours last week. Forgive me for wanting a bit of leisure time that doesn't involve you."

By June, Peter was sharing more personal details of his life with Oona.

"Did I ever tell you I went to med school? I never made it past the first year."

"Did I ever tell you I almost studied at the London School of Economics? I never made it as far as Heathrow Airport. Good thing we both had music to fall back on."

By July, she and Edward barely had sex anymore.

"Mom's birthday is coming up. Should I even bother to make reservations for three?"

"Madeleine loathes me. Let's not pretend you won't have a better time if I'm not there."

By July, Oona had mastered barre chords.

"My brother ended up becoming a doctor, so at least my parents had one kid who lived up to their expectations. I tried, but I just couldn't do it."

"After my dad died, I always wondered what he would've expected from me. I think that's why I went to business school. Too bad I find actually running a business so dull. Maybe if I didn't, the restaurant wouldn't be failing."

By August, she and Edward were sleeping in separate rooms.

"I'm not saying your food isn't good, but it's too fussy and too expensive. Sorry if that hurts your precious ego, but how many bad reviews do you need to get before you change it up?"

"What *hurts my precious ego* is my bloody wife having no faith in me. No, don't touch me. I'm going out for a walk."

By August, she could play a flawless rendition of "Space Oddity."

"It's amazing how much you change over the course of each lesson. You usually come in looking upset or preoccupied, but by the end of the hour, you're a lot calmer, happier. Music is the best therapy."

"Definitely. Could we try 'Comfortably Numb' next? I think I'm ready to tackle those arpeggios now."

The restaurant continued to fail. Edward tried a variety of menus and price points, he hired different staff (though Francesca stayed on), but nothing worked. The food was good, but not good enough to attract customers in a culinary dead zone. Losing money didn't matter to Oona—the $100,000 she invested in Google's IPO would be worth $1.5 million in a little over a decade. This foresight didn't help their marriage in the short term, though; some problems couldn't be solved with money.

In early September, Peter invited Oona to play at a pediatric cancer benefit.

"I'm doing the music program," he said. "My friend's fourteen-year-old daughter was diagnosed with an inoperable brain tumor a couple of months ago. It's to raise money for her medical bills, with the rest going to medulloblastoma research. The music will be all Radiohead songs, her favorite band."

"I'm in."

A surprised smile at her swift acquiescence. "The strumming pattern for 'Fake Plastic Trees' is pretty easy. Would you be willing to take that one? We can get an accompanying singer—"

"I'll sing it, too. I love that song."

"Radiohead did an awesome version of it last year when they played BAM. Did you go to that show?"

Did she? Would she? "No. I don't think so." She coughed. "Hey, could we go over 'Sympathy for the Devil' again? I still don't feel like I've really nailed it."

When she got home that night, another postcard from Kenzie awaited her. This one was from Vietnam, the photo an emerald staircase of rice paddies. On the back:

It's hot and rainy here. Been walking around in the downpour like a big ol' drama queen. I'm less angry now. But I still need to stay out here.

—Kenzie

Did that mean she wouldn't see him at all this year? If so, why tease her with these postcards, give her hope for their reunion? How maddening for him to be out of reach like that. Had she done something to piss him off? Either way, she had no choice but to resign herself to the mystery of his absence.

Luckily, in the ensuing weeks, the upcoming benefit concert provided a more positive focus. The event would take place in the auditorium of a Jewish community center in Ditmas Park. After rehearsal one night, Peter offered Oona a ride home.

"I had no idea you could sing," he said as they drove down the expansive residential boulevard of Ocean Parkway. "How does it feel to play with a band again? Remind you of your Early Dawning days?"

"Yeah. It's a rush. When everyone plays in sync—there's something magical about it. It's a kind of high."

"I know what you mean. Music is the best drug." A swift glance at her. "Is your husband coming to the concert?"

Mentions of Edward in their conversations were rare. "Unfortunately, he can't make it. He's got some so-called important people coming for a business dinner that night."

"It's a shame he won't get to see you perform."

"It's okay." Her music was something she didn't like sharing with Edward, anyway. He asked her to play a song from time to time—when they weren't in the middle of a fight—but his interest was more perfunctory than passionate. If all she could elicit was politeness, she preferred not to play for him at all. "Marriage is complicated. You might find out for yourself one day."

"I've been married." His voice pitched high at the unexpected confession and he cleared his throat.

"You have? When, in college? Aren't you, like, twenty-five?"

"I'm thirty."

"Wait, what?" She scrutinized his profile.

"I've always had a baby face. Still get carded at bars."

"And you were married?"

"Right out of college. It only lasted a year."

"What happened?"

"Our families—both Korean—were friends, and we were set up. We liked each other well enough, but went into it with a sense of obligation." A sudden jolt as he slammed on the brakes to avoid a driver who cut him off, arm out to prevent Oona from hitting the dashboard. "You okay?"

"I'm fine." But her mind still reeled from these revelations. *Is ten years too big of an age difference?*

Peter showed no reaction to the rude driver. "Anyway, I started med school right after we got married. We barely saw each other because of my schedule, and I was always stressed out and miserable, which put a strain on things. I'm sure you can relate, with your husband and his restaurant."

"Definitely." But there was so much more she could add. How she felt like she had a roommate more than a husband. How she could relate to the rest of it, too, the assumption of intimacy you couldn't live up to yet couldn't escape because you didn't want to disappoint the other person. Or yourself. Even as you did both.

"I bet you felt trapped." Oona dug her nails into her palms, refusing to cry in front of Peter. She wanted to tell him about being tangled in thorns of obligation. About being robbed, yet again, of all the wonderful things that happen in the beginning of a relationship, the initial soaring feelings, the buoyancy that comes with falling in love.

"I did feel trapped," he said. "And depressed, and ashamed for feeling that way. I was raised not to express emotional problems. Do you know there isn't even a Korean word for *depression*? The closest thing is a phrase that translates as having a down heart."

"And did quitting med school help your down heart?"

"Yes. But it turns out my wife wanted to be married to a doctor, not a musician." He let out an ironic chuckle.

"So choosing to pursue music cost you your marriage . . . Was it worth it?"

They were at a stoplight. Peter turned to face her, chin out, pride glittering in his eyes. "Music is as essential to me as air. Do I miss my wife? I miss the companionship, but I don't miss the loneliness of being with someone who feels like a stranger."

The light turned green, and a car behind them honked. Peter kept his foot on the brake, kept his eyes on Oona. "Choosing music was choosing to breathe. It's not a question of being worth it as much as how long I would've survived living a life that wasn't my own."

Other cars joined in the honking and Peter resumed driving. Oona watched his profile. If only he'd say more, reveal a hint of his feelings. But he remained quiet the rest of the way.

The night of the benefit, Oona poured her heart into her performance. The melancholy strumming built into desperation as she sang of fake plastic love and other artificial things. She bled into the notes and soared over the audience. When the song ended, the roar of applause made her smile until her cheeks hurt, made her teeth feel like they were made of diamonds. The evening was an enormous success, raising over a million dollars, much of which was anonymously donated by Oona.

Backstage, Peter gave her a hug and murmured, "You were glorious," in her ear, which was nearly drowned out by the sound of blood whooshing through her body.

In the taxi home, she found he'd slipped something into her coat pocket: a key ring bearing a silver guitar pick. There was an engraving on one side: "Nice Dream," the name of the first Radiohead song he'd taught her to play.

That night, Oona waited up for her husband. When he finally walked in, just before three A.M., he gave a start when she accosted him in the foyer.

"You almost gave me a heart attack," he said. "How was the benefit?"

"I have a down heart," she said.

A baffled stare. "I don't know what that means."

"It means I want a divorce."

Edward followed her to the living room. "Hang on, love, please let's sit down. I have to tell you about my night. This could change everything."

As she took a seat on the couch, she noted his collarbone had become more prominent. *When did he get so skinny?* So much they had both failed to notice.

"Oona, I know the restaurant has been causing stress. I'm so sorry for that. I was sure I could turn it around, but I think the biggest reason Clary's hasn't worked out is the location. You were right to try to talk me out of it, and I wish I'd listened. But we can still save the situation. Tonight one of my mates introduced me to a condo developer who's interested in buying property in Gowanus. We stand to make a tidy profit off selling the building, and we could start over with a new restaurant somewhere else. Or even go modest with a food truck." He reached for her hand and clasped it between both of his.

"Exactly what situation will that save?" Her tone was leaden.

"We can recoup some of our losses, learn from our—*my*—mistakes. I'm utterly gutted at failing you." His voice cracked. "This time I'll do it right, hire more support staff so I don't have to spend so much time away from you. It's been a rough road, but please don't give up just yet."

Oona hadn't expected him to beg, to make it this much harder. With a gentle tug, she removed her hand from his grasp. "It *has* been a rough road. And I did what I could to keep us on that road, but at this point, we're driving toward each other, playing chicken. One of us needs to swerve."

"It doesn't have to—"

"It *does* have to. Our marriage doesn't live or die with your professional success. There are other reasons it's not working." Her voice wavered as an internal deluge of black, slippery feelings coated her insides. Shame. Guilt. "It's not fair to expect you to stay in love with me when I'm not the person you knew before." But it would be gutless to deflect the real reason, even if she couldn't tell him the full truth. "And it's not fair to expect this different me to pick up the thread of being your wife and fall in love with you all over again. I tried, but I couldn't do it."

A soft hiss escaped him as he sucked air through his teeth. "God, Oona, I'm so sorry for what I've put you through." His face flickered between dejection and desperation. He was the boxer taking punch after punch, refusing to stay down. "What if I walk away from Clary's and take a break from the food game entirely? We could take more time and really try—"

"There is no more time." She had to do it. She had to deliver the final blows. "I don't want to try anymore. I can't keep forcing it. I'm tired of the confusion and loneliness. I'm done."

That silenced him. What a pity the sheen of tears gave his eyes such vibrancy.

Edward moved out the following week.

Their parting was amicable, like two polite strangers who got into a car accident. Neither wanted to blame the other. They exchanged paperwork promptly, eager to repair the damage and move on. The Gowanus property was sold and they split the proceeds.

October was grim as autumn crispened the air and dried out the trees' leaves before denuding their branches. Where she should've felt relief at having the house to herself again, instead a fog of loneliness drifted in. Any kind of companionship offers a degree of reassurance, even the sporadic kind, even the wrong kind. Now that she'd been stripped of that companionship, stripped of her wedding band, a doomed mantra orbited her brain: *I'll always end up alone.*

How long was it supposed to take to recover from a divorce? She wasn't there for the elation at the beginning; couldn't she be spared the grieving at the end? Apparently not. Yes, being a restaurant widow was painful, but being a divorcée came with its own cocktail of remorse and failure. The self-blame pummeled her: she hadn't been patient enough, she could've tried harder to save the marriage—she could've fought her treacherous desire, found a new guitar teacher as soon as she began to fall for Peter. Maybe that's what 2003 Oona was trying to warn her about on the subway.

She continued the lessons with Peter, but dropped down to once a week. Sitting in his apartment across from that Velvet Underground poster, her confounded heart tugged in different directions, at once drawing her toward him and pulling her away.

Maybe things could be better.

Maybe your heart has been through enough for now.

Maybe . . .

By mid-November, Oona couldn't take any more uncertainty.

"I divorced Edward," she announced during one of their lesson breaks as Peter strummed his guitar.

The room went silent. "Oh." His hand hovered over the strings. "How are you doing?"

"It happened a couple of months ago. I'm okay. We weren't married all that long, and I knew we didn't have a future together. Actually . . ." She readied herself to ask him out, hesitated. How much of a future could she have with Peter, with her next leap six weeks away? *Those could be some special weeks, though. Unless this is all one-sided. I need to know for sure.* "I . . . Would you maybe want to get coffee sometime?" Such a hammering in her chest, would she even hear his reply?

"I would, but I recently started seeing someone. Unless you meant . . ." Tension between his eyebrows as if he wanted to say more.

"No, I didn't mean as friends. I was asking you out." If she was going to flame out, she'd own it. "I thought—you gave me that key chain—I must've misread things. And I'm sure the age difference doesn't help."

"Age difference? What are you, thirty-two, thirty-three?"

"Forty, but thank you."

"Oh. So ten years." He blinked away his confusion and shrugged. "That's not an issue for me. And you didn't misread things, it's just—

you caught me at a bad time." Loose hair fell into his eyes and he shook it off, distressed. "Otherwise . . ."

"Of course. Bad timing. Story of my life." *At least it wasn't all in my head.* She stood and packed her guitar in its case. "I hope you don't mind if we end a little early today." *It's the little things you end up missing. The way he shook his hair out of his eyes? She'd miss that.*

"No problem. I'll see you next week."

Though of course he didn't.

"Everything has its time," his tattoo proclaimed.

Not everything.

A week later, one last postcard arrived from Kenzie. Japanese cherry blossom trees on one side, and on the other:

I'm ready to come home. Next month. I'm sorry I won't get to see you this year. But look at it this way: 2005 Oona will have something to look forward to.   *—Kenzie*

A bitter laugh thundered through her. How perfect: a punishment for something Earlier Oona did. "Of course. Of course this is how my year is ending." But at least she'd have something positive to include in the letter she'd write to 2005 Oona.

On New Year's Eve, she invited her mother over. They cooked Edward's recipe for beef Wellington, which came out a little dry but the gravy salvaged it. Madeleine brought over several bottles of champagne and a birthday cake from an Italian bakery, for after midnight.

By the second bottle, they were laughing about Oona's childhood exploits and Madeleine's misadventures at Pan Am, when she paraded down plane aisles in a blue uniform and white gloves like she was working a catwalk. Oona was glad she'd begin her forty-first year with her mother, whenever she returned to it. At the same time, it was a relief to be leaving 2004.

Please let me be younger next year. Please *let the next leap send me into the past.*

Too bad she wasn't more specific.

PART V

Here Comes Your Man

2003: 39/22

18

A shiver on the precipice of sleep, a lurch to catch an invisible stumble, eyes open, and Oona was in her kitchen.

"Happy New Year, my darling." Madeleine leaned over and kissed her on the cheek. "Are you okay?"

Was she? Oona glanced around. There was an open bottle of champagne on the counter along with a birthday cake, yet to be cut.

"I was just here. Is it over? Am I done leaping?" A fifty-fifty cocktail of hope and dread. How thrillingly mundane it would be to live life sequentially. To be able to rely on where and when each year would begin. Though going consecutive now, in her forties, meant a sacrifice. Would it be worth it? She wasn't sure, but she leaned toward yes.

It was a needless internal debate. Oona shut down the mental pros and cons as she took in the slight differences in this birthday scene. The cake before her had blue icing, whereas moments ago it had been purple. The champagne glasses had beveled edges and gold rims instead of the plain crystal flutes they'd been drinking out of.

"It's not 2005, is it?" A smattering of wistfulness in the question.

"Close. It's 2003."

"Fuck."

It *had* to be 2003—the year she'd meet and marry Edward. The year she'd begin funding his restaurant, which would fail as spectacularly as their marriage.

At least I'm in my thirties now. Yay?

"I keep hoping it'll get easier for you."

Oona opened her eyes, her mother's concerned face inches away. She stepped back and lost her balance, grabbing the counter for support, which sent one champagne flute toppling into the other. Both crashed to the floor.

"Well, that explains why the glasses are different next year," Oona said.

"Are you all right?"

"I'm fine. I just need a minute to . . ."

". . . read this?" There it was, the now-familiar sealed white envelope.

"I guess." She took the letter.

"Why don't you read it in your study? I'll clean this up and bring you some cake and more champagne." Madeleine went in search of a broom and dustpan.

On the way upstairs, Oona glimpsed her reflection in a hall mirror. A little thinner and blonder but otherwise identical to next year's/last year's version.

At her desk, the letter untouched before her, a futile sigh. What was the point of reading it? She already knew what this year would bring.

Dear Oona,

Sometimes I wonder how much these letters help you. I write them to prepare you, reassure you. But what if my mistake is trying to prevent you from making your own? I haven't been able to protect you from the shitty things I know will happen, so maybe I shouldn't try to rewrite our future anymore. After all, you need to experience the lows along with the highs. Otherwise, you end up with a safe, sterile, painless life, and who wants that?

"*I* want that," Oona said aloud.

Don't waste your time wishing for it. No matter how much you try to protect yourself from misery and disappointment, it still waits around the corner.

As does Edward. You know you're going to meet him, marry him, and divorce him. So what?

Most people's lives are novels, but yours is a series of short stories. Enjoy the Edward story. After all, you experienced the ending. Why not indulge in the beginning?

All good things end, always. The trick is to enjoy them while they last.

Spoiler alert: your life will be bittersweet, no matter what. But every New Year's Eve, when that stupid clock strikes midnight, you have another chance at a clean slate and a remarkable year. I promise, some years will be glorious, and not just the younger ones. Youth and beauty aren't everything.

Stop micromanaging your life and just live it; joy and meaning will follow. Find the happy medium between being daring and responsible. Cultivate that balance. Do your best. Be good to yourself, even when—especially when—life isn't being good to you.

Love,
Me

P.S. Don't forget about that citywide blackout. Either stock up on candles or leave NYC in mid-August.

Great, more smug Earlier Oona. So enlightened, so damn patronizing. This Oona couldn't be as Zen. Pushing forty was frustrating when she should've been celebrating her twenty-second birthday instead of being cloistered in a house time travel built, with nothing but a doomed-to-fail marriage to look forward to.

What if I take a different path? What if I don't get married?

Question after question swam through Oona's mind. Time to put fate to the test.

I don't have to choose Edward. I can choose anybody. I could choose nobody.
Fuck enlightenment and fuck marriage. I'm getting out of here.

While Kenzie's postcards had stirred a curiosity for travel, this was the first real pull she had to leave the country. That was something she was supposed to do in her twenties. With Dale.

Maybe he and I will still see some of the places on our list, she thought as she browsed travel websites. *At least we'll have one more summer together, whenever that'll be.*

And in case she did get there with Dale, Europe was out. So where should she go instead? Should she follow Kenzie's footsteps and visit Asia? No, this choice needed to be singular, solely hers. This first trip abroad had to be extraordinary, filled with sights that would imbue her with awe and wonder.

As she paced her bedroom, the display case caught her eye. The crystal red Corvette was there, as was the Fabergé egg and the Venetian mask. But the glass igloo was missing.

Alaska?

No. Somewhere warmer.

Also missing was the pyramid snow globe.

Egypt.

She'd explore the Great Pyramids of Giza, the tombs in the Valley of the Kings, the temples of Luxor and Abu Simbel. Maybe she'd even try a Nile cruise to conquer her boat phobia. And while it would be too warm to bring the leather jacket Dale had given her, she'd wear the anniversary watch. In that small way, he could join her.

Flipping through the blank pages of her passport (did she get a new one periodically to avoid spoilers?), Oona promised herself to fill it with stamps, to unmoor the anchor that had kept her tethered to a fifteen-mile radius of her home.

"You sure you don't want to come?" she asked Madeleine.

"No thank you, my darling. This is an adventure you should have on your own."

So Oona bought a one-way ticket to Cairo. If that leg of the trip went well, perhaps she'd continue on to Jordan or Morocco. She could spend the entire year traveling and subvert her fate of meeting and marrying Edward.

Internally, she was wearier, more defeated than she expected to be at twenty-two, but externally, she was a youthful thirty-nine. At the airport, she caught an admiring glance here and there. The potential for a travel fling wasn't out of the question.

A new resolve and optimism suffused Oona as she boarded the Cairo-bound plane. There was no need to be trapped by her flawed chronology or supposed destiny. She wouldn't tiptoe around her life, suffer the frustration that resulted from chasing stability. She would not be defeated by her known future.

Clean slate, here we go.

She settled into her seat and peered through the thick glass of the window: planes taxiing, carts of baggage wheeled under a flat gray sky that threatened rain. Her destination was sunny and dry. Nothing to see here, so she put on an eye mask.

There was a rustling as somebody sat beside her.

What was that humming? A familiar tune, one that strummed the chords of Oona's heart.

"'Sunday Morning.' Velvet Underground," she murmured, settling into her seat.

"One of my favorites. Sorry if I'm bothering you, but I'm deathly afraid of flying, and the only thing that calms my nerves, short of being blotto or zonked out on drugs, is humming. Or talking to distract myself." A British accent. Less plummy upper crust, more working class; less royal family, more Michael Caine.

"I know the statistics," he continued. "How you're more likely to die in a car accident than a plane crash, but I can never get my head around being in a giant metal object that defies gravity. I reckon my fear of heights doesn't help. Well, not heights, really—falling from a great height. Is fear of plummeting a recognized phobia? Though I've heard it's not the fall that kills you, it's the heart attack you get from the terror of going down. Oh dear. Best not think of it. I've put off this trip for years, but I had to finally honor my mother's last wishes to scatter her ashes among the Giza pyramids. She had a lifelong fascination with Egyptology, should've been an archaeologist or history professor really, but became a hairdresser instead. God, I'm just prattling on. Feel free to tell me to shut my gob and I won't bother you the rest of the flight."

She didn't need to take off the eye mask to know who it was.

19

Oona lifted her eye mask and faced Edward. Blood coursed in her veins, colored her cheeks.

"Excuse me." She unbuckled her seat belt, stepped around him, and hurried up the aisle.

Nope. No way. Not gonna happen.

Before she could reach the bathroom, a flight attendant who looked like she'd been wearing the same beehive hairdo and blue eye shadow for the last thirty years stopped her.

"I'm sorry, miss, the captain has switched on the 'fasten seat belt' sign in preparation for takeoff. I'll need you to return to your seat."

"Actually, would it be possible to sit somewhere else?" Oona kept her voice low. "I'll take any available seat on the plane." *Preferably one in the back.*

The flight attendant mimicked her hushed tone. "Oh, I'm afraid we're fully booked. Now, if you could just—"

"Then I'll switch with someone. Anyone. I'm sure someone in coach would love a first-class seat."

"I'm sure they would." Her understanding tone hardened. "But you'll have to wait until we're in the air and it's safe to move around. I really do need you to return to your seat now."

Oona could've fought harder, even gotten herself kicked off the plane to avoid that flight with Edward. But she didn't. And once she was buckled in beside him, she could've put on headphones and pretended to sleep. But she didn't. Fate was an irresistible bastard.

Edward continued to hum "Sunday Morning."

"Sorry if I'm being a pain in the arse," he said. "It's just this song . . ."

"No, it's okay, it's a great tune. It's funny, the song is basically about paranoia, but it's strangely comforting."

His face took on a haunted look. "It's like you read my mind."

"Like magic. Which isn't to say I don't appreciate the Velvets' other music. There's something to be said for bands with some grit to their sound."

"I was about to say the same thing," he enthused.

Slyness played up the corners of her mouth. "I'm kind of intuitive about certain things. Like, I bet I could guess some of your favorite bands. You seem like a Sonic Youth guy, for sure. And Pixies. And . . ." She pretended to consider. "Nirvana?"

His mouth hung open. "Are you psychic? You just named my top three." Fascinated, Edward tilted his body toward her. "Where did you come from?"

While she initially tried to dodge his charms, he reeled her in with his open chatter, his curiosity, and that gap-toothed grin. He had her laughing as the plane took off and eased her into a conversation that lasted the duration of their eleven-hour flight, give or take a nap or two.

A few hours in, the flight encountered severe turbulence, which made Edward's lips go white. Seeing another opportunity to dazzle him with her "intuition," Oona stroked his arm and said, "Come on, Edward, we're gonna be like two little Fonzies here. I don't need to ask you what Fonzie's like, right?"

Picking up on the *Pulp Fiction* reference, he automatically replied, "He's cool." His fear softened into spooked amusement. "I can recite every line of that movie."

"Well, it happens to be one of my favorites, and I'd like you to prove it."

So he recited the rest of the movie scene until the plane found smoother air. He was so grateful, he took her face in his hands and gave her a big kiss on the mouth, which surprised them both. This was followed by a series of kisses that grew with intensity, culminating in a longer one that told Oona this was something she could not run away from.

We won't be divorced until next year, anyway. Why hide from guaranteed happiness?

The way she saw it, 2004 Oona already paid the credit card bill, so why shouldn't 2003 Oona enjoy the spending spree? True, she wasn't dealing with dollars but emotions, a more dangerous currency. But for once foresight was in her favor. She was sure her heart would be invincible this year, though no heart ever truly is.

So she explored Cairo with Edward. They rode camels and scattered his mother's ashes at sunset by the Giza pyramids. They went to hookah bars and smoked apricot-flavored tobacco, talking late into the night. They got lost in souks, where Oona searched for colorful souvenirs for Madeleine. They spent a day at the Egyptian Museum ogling the splendors of King Tut's tomb: stunningly crafted furniture, jewelry, chests, and urns; the ornate death mask. One night, craving stateside comforts, they went to the Hard Rock Cafe for burgers.

"I got this for you." Edward slid a small square box across the table.

"It's not the 'Walk Like an Egyptian' coffee mug, is it? I was kidding when I said my life wouldn't be complete without it." But when she opened the box, her breath caught in her throat. "Oh." She pulled out a snow globe containing a pyramid. "This is even better."

"I thought you would appreciate the snow-in-the-desert irony."

"You have no idea." A puzzled delight unfolded within her while gazing at him. She hadn't noticed the gold flecks in his sleepy blue eyes before, or the endearing way he giggled when something funny caught him by surprise. Who knew the withered could still blossom with new life? How unlikely.

Edward initially planned on a five-day trip, but he extended his stay to spend more time with Oona. While she offered to foot the bill, he insisted on paying his way, though he did agree to share her hotel room. The first week, even when sleeping in the same bed, she didn't let things go beyond kissing. The depth of their connection—the impossibility yet inevitability of it—overwhelmed her, and she needed to keep the physical at bay to process the rest of it.

But there was only so long she could resist their chemistry. Eight days into the trip, they had sex on a sleeper train to Aswan.

Those early days in Egypt were glorious—worth it. What was it about Edward that made him so damn alluring? There was the physical attraction, the things they had in common—beyond music and movies, a similar sarcastic sense of humor and a progressive political outlook. But it was more his effect on her: she felt drunk around him, out of her senses. She wanted to tell him every thought that came into her head, wanted to touch him all the time. He reciprocated her intensity. It was infatuation that could never be sated, two thirsty people drinking the ocean.

In Aswan, Oona ate some lamb kebabs that gave her a nasty bout of food poisoning. While she was bedridden for two days, Edward remained at her side and put a romantic spin even on her illness: he fed her soda and saltines; read her American newspapers and magazines; placed cool, damp towels over her forehead ("it's more for headaches and fevers, but my mum did this whenever I got ill, and I always found it comforting").

Once she recovered, the rest of the trip unfurled like an upbeat movie montage. Edward suppressed his plummeting phobia so they could take a hot-air balloon ride over the temples and farmlands of Luxor. In the Valley of the Kings, they climbed into tombs, humming the *Indiana Jones* theme song until the colorful, spectacularly preserved hieroglyphs within stunned them into silence. They traveled north to coastal Alexandria, strolling the Corniche waterfront promenade lined with palm trees, enjoying the city's refreshing salty breezes and relaxed Mediterranean vibe.

After a two-week loop around the country, they ended up back in Cairo, weary from sightseeing all day and having feverish sex throughout the night. Oona wanted to extend their trip, prolong this suspended state of bliss; she worried the magic might begin to dissipate the moment they returned to New York. But it was time to go home.

Their last night in Cairo, they dined in a restaurant with wooden lanterns hanging from the ceiling, votive candles in filigreed brass holders, and gauzy purple curtains woven with gold stars. Edward took Oona's hand in both of his and kissed her knuckles. "This may sound barmy, but I've never connected like this with anyone. I can't explain it. It's almost like we've met before."

"That's exactly what it is." It was hard not to cry, hard not to let knowledge of the future take away from the present.

"Mind you, I've never believed in past lives or destiny or any of that malarkey. But something about this—about *you*—feels . . ."

"Meant to be." Wax dripped down the sides of the candle holder between them, formed a small puddle on the wooden table. Oona poked at the wax, let it coat the tip of her finger and mask her fingerprint. "I wish it could be like this when we get back to New York."

"Real life will get in the way, to an extent, but whatever this is between us isn't going to go away, not any time soon. *I* won't go away. I'm mad about you."

They smiled until their faces hurt.

Back in New York, real life did get in the way, to an extent. Edward's hectic schedule at a Carroll Gardens bistro limited their time together, though not to the degree it would once he ran Clary's. Even so, Oona found herself with an abundance of free hours. To fill them, she volunteered at a food bank and the local library. She also resumed her guitar lessons, this time with an older, female instructor, and marveled at retaining a skill she hadn't yet picked up chronologically. As always, she studied the binder. (Boeing was a key position that year. After she bought the stock at $16 a share in 1982, it split four times, taking her from 600 to 4,050 shares; she'd sold off half in 1997 at $57 and would soon buy more shares at $26, letting the position grow to over $400 in years to come.) She also took regular walks in Prospect Park, a habit she'd maintained ever since Kenzie brought her there during her first leap, hoping she'd finally see him again that year.

All this waiting, filling the hours, treading water until the next time she saw Edward as she became more attached to him. Even her music room didn't provide its usual timeless solace, though it surprised her with two valuable guitars she didn't own in 2004, one originally belonging to founding Rolling Stones member Brian Jones, the other a 12-string Bowie had played on.

"Why would I get rid of these?" Oona mused to herself. "Charity donations, maybe?"

Each night she waited for a text message from Edward saying he was done with work and then rushed to his Kensington apartment. He smelled of smoke and fried potatoes and whiskey—which lingered even after he showered—but she didn't mind the pungent combination because it mingled with his own earthy scent, which made her heady. No matter how tired he was after a shift, he was always eager for her body. He might fall asleep right after, wet hair soaking his pillow, but would wake up hungry for her again.

This is what I would've missed out on if I tried to change my fate. A year where I finally get to be happy.

One night in early February, Oona got a one A.M. text from Edward saying he was finishing up a poker game with his friends and heading home. She waited at his place for an hour, growing increasingly panicked, until he finally turned up at two-thirty, drunker than usual, disheveled, wild-eyed.

"Edward, what the fuck?"

"Oh, bugger." He sniffed, wiped his nose with the back of his hand. "I thought I told you I was playing cards." More sniffing.

She followed him into his apartment. "It looks like you've been doing more than that. Why didn't you answer my texts? I was going nuts wondering what happened."

"Bloody hell, do you have to be so clingy?"

"Do you have to be such an insensitive prick?"

The argument escalated and their voices rose until the downstairs neighbors banged on the ceiling. This snapped them out of it.

"I'm sorry, love." Edward kissed her, sloppy and rough.

"I'm still mad at you." But she went in for another kiss. *Our first fight. How oddly romantic.*

"Show me how mad," he murmured.

Their makeup sex was insistent and explosive, tinged with remnants of anger.

Sex became a drug for Oona, a pheromone IV dripping a steady dose into her bloodstream. Her emotional fixation was obviously rooted in chemistry, but wasn't all love chemical? It was science. And while the inevitability of next year's divorce should've stirred caution in her, the expiration date made her want to experience all the love she could now, store it up for any lonely years that might follow.

There were two things she didn't tell Edward about: the time travel and her wealth. He must've known she had *some* money (she had no day job and had a penchant for exorbitant tipping), but he might not have realized the extent of her riches. She wore clothes that eschewed trends—well-made and expensive, but simple—and she didn't wear jewelry other than the watch from Dale or flaunt possessions that belied a grotesque or superficial relationship to money. There was only the house. He hadn't yet seen her mansion, and apprehension at being treated differently when he did made her put off inviting him over, using home renovations as an excuse (to avoid lying, she had the living room recarpeted).

In March, Edward complained of his apartment's lease expiring and a subsequent rent hike. With no sign of their passion lessening (that was a 2004 Oona problem), she suggested he move in with her.

"I haven't even seen your place. Is it big enough for the both of us?"

She laughed and laughed.

"What's so funny?" he asked.

"You'll see."

When he finally crossed the threshold into her foyer—which was the size of his living room—he laughed, too. And if the mansion impressed him, it didn't come close to his look of stunned adoration the following morning, when she served him kippers on toast for breakfast and fixed his tea just as he liked it.

"How could you possibly know? You really are a wonder, Oona."

The following month, Edward told her he had something special planned. Lou Reed was playing in concert that night, so it already promised to be a memorable evening.

I hope he doesn't propose. Not yet. Not tonight.

He took her to a narrow Indian restaurant on Curry Row, its low ceiling strung with lights shaped like chili peppers and tinsel stars. They ate vindaloo and discussed Edward's dreams of building a culinary empire. His enthusiasm was contagious, but she didn't offer to be an investor; maybe keeping business out of their relationship would salvage it the following year.

After dinner, they went to the Bowery Ballroom. Oona had gotten tickets to the show months ago, but Edward secured VIP spots for them in the balcony. That was his "something special." She was relieved and touched by the thoughtful gesture, though she would've preferred to arrive hours early and stand close to the stage.

Seeing Lou Reed was a religious experience for Oona. Though he performed only five Velvet Underground songs, she savored each one like a sermon. She pressed herself against the railing, wanting to sail over it and kneel beside the man on stage with the dark sunglasses strumming his guitar and speak-singing with a casual air of cool. Edward stood behind her, his arms wrapped around her waist. As much as she loved him, she wanted to shake herself free, to be alone in the crowd, to let the music engulf her. During "Candy Says" she wept, recalling how she and Dale listened to Velvets records in his basement, sometimes spread out like starfish on the rug with only their fingertips touching; other times on their sides, pressed together, legs entwined, kissing deeply. Kisses brimming with the blind optimism of first love.

After the concert, in the taxi home, Edward wanted to talk about the show, but Oona sat with her forehead pressed against the glass, eyes glossy with unshed tears, unable to say anything.

Though Madeleine was aware of Edward's existence, Oona put off

introducing the two. Even if her mother's unspoken but obvious dis-
approval came later, it was easier to postpone it. But once May rolled
around and they'd been living together for two months, there was only
so much grumbling Oona could stand from Madeleine about never being invited over.

"All right, all right! Come by for dinner next week. Edward will
make you shrimp fra diavolo." Maybe cooking Madeleine's favorite dish
would ingratiate him to her. In case it didn't, Oona also stocked up on
her favorite pinot grigio.

Good food and wine took them only so far.

When Madeleine walked through the front door, Oona held her
breath, waiting for something to go wrong.

"Mom, this is Edward."

He stepped forward, arms out because Oona had told him her mom
was a hugger.

But Madeleine held out a hand to shake instead, her smile lacking
its usual exuberance.

This set the tone for the rest of the evening. No matter how much
wine was poured, polite barriers stayed up and the conversation never
adopted a natural flow, despite Oona's frequent nudges to keep the chatter going.

When Edward left to use the bathroom, Oona turned to her mother
and hissed, "What is the matter with you? Why are you behaving like
a robot?"

Madeleine's eyes widened in mock innocence. "I'm being perfectly
nice."

"That's what's so strange. Nice has no personality. *You* have personality. You're nice, too, but why aren't you sharing any of your stories
or asking inappropriate questions or being too flirty or . . . being *you*?"

Madeleine put up her hands and pled ignorant. "I thought I *was*
being me."

"Why don't you . . ." *Like Edward?* But he returned to the dining room in the middle of her question, so she softened her tone and
course-corrected. ". . . let me get us another bottle of wine?"

"That would be lovely."

Oh, if she never saw another sickly fake smile from her mother.

After Madeleine went home, as they cleared the table, Edward asked, "Did I say something to upset her? Was there a problem with the food?"

"The food was fantastic. You were fantastic." She corked the last of the wine, resisting the temptation to guzzle it.

"Are you sure? Because I got the impression she didn't like me. Maybe she thinks I'm not good enough for you. I sometimes wonder the same thing."

His uneasy frown made her breath hitch. How dare Madeleine make him feel less than, unworthy. "Don't say that. You've made me happier than I've been in years. You're a great guy. And a phenomenal chef."

"One who can't even get his own restaurant off the ground. Who lets his girlfriend pay all the bills." He set a stack of dirty plates back on the table and bowed his head.

"Hey, you *will* have your own restaurant one day. I keep telling you to cut your hours at the bistro so you can focus on that, because I believe in you. And *I'm* the one who refuses to let you pay the bills, remember?"

"You must let me contribute in some way, Oona. My parents didn't raise me to take handouts, and I won't allow myself to be a kept man."

They settled on Edward's buying and preparing food as his household contribution. He also pared down his work schedule, which allowed him time to write up a business plan, scout locations for his future restaurant, and meet with potential investors. Would he ask Oona to fund the venture? She hoped he'd wait until she offered; otherwise, it could put an immediate tarnish on their relationship and make her question if money was the root of Edward's continued romantic interest.

In June, Madeleine got a boyfriend of her own: Nathan, a pharmacist at a small drugstore where she got her arthritis medication. Oona suggested a double date for them to get to know one another, but her mother said she preferred it be the three of them ("Nathan can be shy around new people"). Not the first time she'd excluded Edward, but Oona didn't press the issue. Instead, she made lunch reservations for

three at the River Café; with any luck, the stunning view of the Manhattan skyline across the Hudson would make up for any potential awkwardness.

It didn't.

Madeleine and Nathan were a half hour late, by which time Oona
had to bribe the hostess-slash-aspiring-model to keep their table, a mor-
tifying exchange for both women. When the tardy couple finally arrived, Oona was irate and immediately suspicious at the sight of Nathan.
Overgroomed was the first word that came to mind, from his slicked-back
silver hair to his fake tan. The teeth were a little too white, the eyebrows
too sculpted, the sides of his mustache and goatee too trimmed. *Loud* was
the second word, from his purple shirt and pink tie—both silk—to his
booming laugh to the cologne he'd doused himself with, which triggered
a sneezing fit from the hostess. Once that subsided, there was another
uncomfortable moment when she had to find him a suit jacket to wear
because of the restaurant's dress code. Madeleine was too captivated by
the bouquets of flowers filling the front entrance to notice Nathan ogling
the leggy hostess as she returned, but Oona noticed.

As he walked ahead of them, Oona turned to her mother. "I did tell
you jackets were required for men." A low singsong voice, teeth gritted.

"I'm sure you didn't," Madeleine replied.

"Pretty sure I did."

Things only got worse when they sat down.

After their orders were taken, a busboy filled their water glasses.
When he got to Nathan, he tipped the pitcher too far and an errant ice
cube landed beside his silverware.

"*Perdóneme, perdóneme.*" The busboy scooped the ice into his hand
and hurried away.

"You think he's running off in case I call immigration?" Nathan
tore off a hunk of bread and shoved it into his mouth.

Madeleine gave her daughter a preemptive kick under the table,
which did not deter Oona. "Did you really just say that?"

"This country is crowded enough with foreigners. There should be
some stricter rules about who gets to stay here, that's all I'm saying."

Snap went Oona's breadstick, which she kept breaking into smaller pieces. "And did your family come over on the *Mayflower*? Oh wait, those people were *also* foreigners."

"I was only joking." Nathan sat back and chuckled. "I like this one," he said to Madeleine. "She's a little spitfire, isn't she?"

Both women pasted brittle smiles onto their faces, which they wore for the rest of the meal.

"Did you tell her about our trip?" Nathan asked during dessert.

"I didn't." Shifting in her chair, Madeleine took a long sip of coffee before answering. "We're spending three weeks on the Amalfi Coast."

"How wonderful." Oona's tone was flinty. "Are you sure you'll be able to handle all the foreigners?"

Paired with the phony grin, Madeleine's glower gave her face a demonic look.

This time, Nathan's chuckle was forced. "Well, those are my people, so it's different."

"*Your* people, got it." Oona nodded. "Do pharmacists get that much vacation time? Or do you own the drugstore?"

"I don't. I had to pull some strings to get people to cover for me, but how could I say no to your mother's generosity, treating me to such a lavish trip?"

"You obviously couldn't. And yes, Mom is incredibly generous. Maybe too generous."

"I could say the same thing about you, Oona." Butter in her voice, venom in her glare.

Smiling through a mouthful of crème brûlée, Oona crunched down hard on the caramelized sugar.

The check came, and Nathan's lame reach for it was convincing to no one. There was a lot of halfhearted insisting until Oona waved everyone off and slid her credit card into the leather folio.

"Excuse me, ladies, I got an appointment with Doctor John." Nathan cocked finger guns at the bathroom and moseyed on over.

Eyebrows raised, Oona turned to her mother. "Doctor John?"

"He has his eccentricities." She waved her hand like dispersing smoke.

"Rich people get to be eccentric. *You* are eccentric. Is Nathan rich?"

"That's not your business."

"I bet he isn't, since you're paying for Italy. So he doesn't get to be eccentric. He's something else." She didn't complete her thought as Nathan headed back toward them.

Things were strained between mother and daughter after that lunch, but both were too romantically entrenched to acknowledge the distance building between them.

In July, Edward announced he'd found an investor for the restaurant and booked a long weekend in a private beachfront cottage on Cape Cod for the two of them to celebrate. By day, they kayaked, ate fresh clams and oysters, and lounged in the sand. At night, they went skinny-dipping and had sex on the beach.

The trip was idyllic, and this time Oona hoped Edward would propose. Despite her rising anticipation, he didn't.

One Thursday morning in early August, she woke up to Edward crouching by her bed.

"Let's go feed the ducks." He held up a paper bag full of rolls. "I thought we could enjoy a bit of the outdoors before the day gets too hot."

In the park, they followed the running path down to the lake and perched on a fallen log.

Come on, Kenzie, where are you? I better see you this year.

Oona forced herself back into the moment and joined Edward in tearing up bread and throwing it along the shore for the hungry birds.

When she reached into the bag for one of the last rolls, her fingers brushed against a velvet cube.

Oh!

Edward got on one knee and opened the box. "I've known since our flight to Egypt that you're the woman I want to spend my life with. You're smart, gorgeous, kind, and you have quality music taste. God knows what you see in a bloke like me." He offered a wink and self-deprecating chuckle. "But seriously, I just want to do whatever I can to make you happy. Before my mum died, she told me not to put off going after my dreams. 'We never have as much time as we think we do,' she said. I thought having a restaurant would be my biggest dream. Then I met you. I know it's fast," he concluded. "But life is bloody short and I know you're it for me. Will you marry me?"

The sky was piercing blue with perfect cotton clouds reflected in the water below, and the balmy air was punctuated with quacking ducks. Edward looked up at her with a tender, hopeful gaze.

Oona's heart softened and seized. She dropped to her knees across from him. "Of course I'll marry you. But there's something I need to tell you first."

20

A week after the proposal, Edward and Oona were married at City Hall.

A few days after that, Edward's investor pulled out.

"It's disappointing, but I'll move forward. Find another way." He offered Oona a tight, brave smile as desolation crept in behind his eyes.

I have so much. How could I not share it with him? After all, it's not like Clary's Pub will bankrupt me.

"I have another way," she said. "I'll be your investor."

"Absolutely not. I couldn't put such a burden on our marriage. Out of the question."

A vehement debate followed, and it took great effort for her to finally persuade him.

At least I know for sure he didn't marry me for my money.

"I have one condition, though," Oona said. "I'd like us to go on a honeymoon. Tomorrow. A week on a beach before things get insane with the restaurant." The timing would also put them out of town during the upcoming citywide blackout. There might've been a romantic element to experiencing twenty-nine hours of no electricity, but the prospect was less appealing in a sweltering metropolis. Besides, she and Edward were at their best when traveling.

He agreed to the trip, and she booked a last-minute flight to Barbados.

The following morning, in the kitchen, while waiting for their cab to the airport, Oona checked her watch. The clock hands stood at a right angle indicating three o'clock.

"Damn, I think my watch stopped," she said just as a car horn sounded.

"We can get it fixed when we get back. You're going to be on island time, anyway. Let's go, love, we don't want to miss our flight."

Oona unfastened the watch and left it on the counter.

Their honeymoon was blissfully uneventful, but when they returned, the overturned vase in the foyer signaled it was truly over.

"We've been robbed!" Oona scurried through the house, looking for anything missing or in disarray. Nothing until the music room: two of her guitars were gone, the Brian Jones and Bowie ones she hadn't owned during her previous leap.

The kitchen held worse news: her anniversary watch was no longer on the counter.

"Are you sure that's where you left it?" Edward helped her scour through the other rooms, in case she'd misplaced it, but the timepiece failed to turn up.

Back in the kitchen, Oona was queasy and weak-kneed. "Of all the things they could've taken. I'd trade this house for that watch." She burst into tears.

Edward wrapped his arms around her. "God, I'm so sorry."

"The blackout must've knocked out the alarm."

"Was anything taken besides the watch and guitars?"

Grabbing a paper towel, Oona blew her nose. "Not that I could tell. But the guitars are worth two hundred grand, so it was a good score for whatever scumbags did this. They didn't even need the watch."

One more tight squeeze and Edward stepped back. "I'll go call the police."

"I won't see those guitars again." She dabbed at her eyes. *But I will see the watch.* Because she'd begin 2004 with it in her coat pocket.

Or.

What if I don't have the watch next year, either?

Was it possible she'd done something to shift her fate? Maybe this new future included a lasting marriage to Edward. If losing a couple of guitars and the watch from Dale was the price she paid, she could do little but accept the obvious symbolism in the turn of events.

Within days, they put the burglary behind them, and within weeks, development plans for Edward's restaurant proceeded in earnest as they scouted potential properties around Brooklyn. Despite knowing how things would pan out, Oona tried to push for a promising site in East Williamsburg while Edward had his heart set on the space in Gowanus.

Save the restaurant, save the marriage? It was worth a shot.

"Clary's Pub is going to fail in Gowanus," she warned.

He recoiled as if slapped. "I thought you believed in me."

"I do." She touched his arm and he flinched away. "But I don't believe in this location."

"Does that mean you'll pull your backing unless we go with the East Williamsburg space?"

"No! God. Of course not. I just—"

"I'm sorry, love, but I have to be firm on this. Gowanus has to be the site of Clary's Pub."

But does it still have to fail?

He hired construction staff. And brought on Francesca as a consultant.

This time, Oona's dislike toward her was stronger and more immediate. Part of it was pure jealousy. Edward's fine cooking had caught up with Oona; she'd packed on fifteen pounds that wouldn't budge. And while she'd considered overcoming her fear of needles to get some Botox or Juvéderm, Edward had pleaded with her to age naturally. If only such a thing were possible, being twenty-two in a body seventeen years older. But she vowed to accept herself the way she looked, which was easier in Edward's presence than Francesca's, whose youth and smug confidence was tough to ignore. There was the way she'd explain things with a vague air of condescension, as if Oona didn't already know a deuce was a table for two and waxing it meant giving someone the VIP treatment. There was also the way she behaved around Edward, as if they had a secret shared history Oona wasn't privy to. It was more than their food industry expertise; it was the natural flow of their banter. They teased each other like old friends, though Edward swore she'd only ever been a professional acquaintance.

"Francesca is good at what she does, so I need to keep her around, but I don't let her forget I'm a happily married man," he reassured her.

So Oona quashed her jealousy and kept out of their way. While Francesca was busy creating operational systems and developing service protocols, Edward racked up invoices, which Oona paid. Every night he came home, weary but inspired, and drew her into deep embraces filled with gratitude. Even if the restaurant ultimately failed, it still felt good to fulfill his greatest ambition.

As summer transitioned into autumn, a new unease took root. The year 2004 would begin in the aftermath of a fight between Oona and her mother—it was only a matter of time before this blowout occurred. She tried to safeguard against it by minimizing contact with Madeleine after the wedding. Easy to do, since her mother was too caught up with Nathan to notice. The duo took up golf and spent long weekends up and down the East Coast at different courses. Once in a while, Madeleine returned with quaint gifts from their trips: glass jugs of maple syrup, mason jars filled with preserves, homemade candles.

One Sunday in November, Madeleine asked her daughter out to breakfast, just the two of them. "I have something I need to discuss, face-to-face."

They met up at Dizzy's, a colorful diner with terrible wall art and terrific eggs Benedict.

Madeleine drummed her nails against the table as she scrutinized the menu, glanced up when her daughter slid something across the table.

"Suzanne Vega's playing Joe's Pub next month." Oona nodded at the ticket. "I thought you'd like to go with me. It's been ages since we've seen a show together."

"Oh. Thank you." A startled look and she stashed the ticket into her purse before returning to the menu. "Have you had the French toast here?"

"I haven't. I always get eggs." Oona took a long sip of tepid water from a plastic tumbler.

"I think I'm in the mood for French toast."

"You always get eggs, too."

"French toast is made with eggs. Anyway, there's nothing wrong with trying something different."

It's just food, let it go.

Oona tore at the napkin on her lap with stiff fingers. "Funny, you always complain there are too many sweet morning foods and not enough savory ones besides eggs and breakfast meats—lox if you're lucky. Now all of a sudden you're switching over to the sweet side?"

"You make it sound like I've become a white supremacist or a Scientologist."

"Does Nathan like sweet breakfast foods?"

"He does."

"I knew it," Oona muttered.

"As does much of the human population."

"Including Nathan."

A waiter with muttonchop sideburns and a forearm tattoo of an abacus came over.

Oona ordered the eggs Benedict.

"I'll have the French toast," Madeleine said.

"Coffee?" he asked.

"Yes, please," they answered in unison.

When he left, Madeleine reached across the table and touched Oona's wrist. "I think Nathan is going to ask me to marry him." Her voice was gilded with giddiness.

Oona stared across the room at an awful painting of Jackie O done in neon colors. "I'm not surprised. You're quite a catch."

"So is he. Intelligent, charismatic, and you have to admit he's nice to look at." A dreamy smile as if he were standing before her. "Very well put-together."

"Oh, very. He puts the *me* in *metrosexual*."

"I know you don't like him."

"You don't like Edward—it baffles me why—but that didn't stop me from marrying him."

The waiter served their coffee. Madeleine poured sugar into her cup, the spoon a clanging soundtrack as she stirred and stirred. "I never said I didn't like Edward. I never said much about him at all."

"Which is how I knew you didn't like him."

"I just always wondered if he was right for you. Wondered what you have in common."

"Yeah, I know that feeling." *Keep it together. Keep it friendly.* "How do you know Nathan is gonna propose, anyway?"

"I saw him examining my rings when I took them off to do the dishes." A girlish excitement in her voice. "It looked like he was check-ing my ring size. We're going on a cruise next month, and I think he might pop the question then."

"Amalfi, long weekends playing golf, and now a cruise—does he even work anymore?"

Madeleine shifted in her seat. "If you must know, he's between jobs right now. What does it matter? We have such a good time together."

"Is he living off his savings? Or . . . living off you?" A crooked, bitter smile.

"I'm appalled you'd say something like that considering your situa-tion. How much money are you sinking into Clary's Pub? Do you know how many restaurants fail in their first year alone?"

"Edward is working his ass off to make Clary's a success." The nap-kin in her lap was in tatters.

"Oh sure, he works so hard, he's barely home. Meanwhile, you don't know what he's really doing when he says he's working. You just keep signing the checks, doing your good deeds, playing guitar, and pretending you have a healthy marriage."

"And you think you'll have a healthier one?" Oona balled up the napkin shreds and took in a long breath. As much as she wanted to avoid fighting with her mother, the presumptions about her marriage sparked an urge to retaliate. The words pushed against her closed lips the way floodwaters push against a cracked dam; containment was feeble and futile. "Have you *seen* the way Nathan checks out other women? There's being a flirt and there's being a skeeve. I could maybe forgive the heavy cologne and finger guns, but the not-so-veiled racism—I can't believe you'd dismiss it as joking around. It's like you purposefully picked the biggest creep you could find. Why? And don't even tell me about your bedroom activities, because I already feel sick. Come on, Mom, he's obviously using you. And you're completely blinded by his looks—unless it's those neon-white teeth. At least Edward is ambitious, hardworking, and has the decency not to ogle other women when we're out together. The nicest thing I can say about Nathan is that his hygiene is impeccable. I've tried to give him a fair chance, but the guy is a dud. Marrying him would be ridiculous."

A young couple in expensive workout clothes at a neighboring table pretended not to eavesdrop, but kept glancing over at Oona and Madeleine.

"As ridiculous as getting married when you hop around from year to year? How do you expect to maintain a marriage under such circumstances? At least I can have constancy with Nathan. You begin each year like an amnesiac. Yet Edward still readily accepted you. Don't you find that peculiar? Don't you think your money has something to do with that?"

"I promised myself I wasn't gonna do this—" Oona began. *Am I sure I want to— Fucking yes.* "But I have to, because you don't see what a mistake this is. Nathan is not a good guy. And your relationship with him is not going to last. Not even another year."

Madeleine's mouth opened ever so slightly and the electricity behind her eyes dimmed; the green and gold lost their luster, became flat and muddy.

The sight of her mother's crestfallen face made Oona's stomach knot up, but she plowed on. "That's right, Nathan is not part of your future. Edward's not part of mine, either, if it makes you feel any better. So you're right, I'm not able to maintain a marriage. But you won't even get that far with Nathan. You're better off cutting him loose now."

A downward gaze and Madeleine's body went still except for a small movement in her shoulders as she breathed in and out.

Oona pushed her chair back, dropped some cash on the table, and left before the food was served.

I did the right thing, she told herself as she walked home. *Didn't I?*

She made it three blocks before bursting into tears. But she didn't turn back.

21

Oona didn't call her mother in the following weeks. It was a cowardly way to leave things and she knew it, even if they'd make amends in January, less than two months away. Meanwhile, remorse trickled in and eroded Oona's justification for her outburst. In trying to protect her mother, how much had she hurt her? Maybe she hadn't given Nathan a fair shake and was too quick to sabotage their relationship.

It ate away at her, but Oona didn't mention the argument to Edward. Partly to cover up her bad behavior and partly to shield him from Madeleine's distasteful accusations, which Oona refused to believe. Despite his longer hours at the restaurant, their marriage remained solid. If anything, the fight with her mom made her more grateful for this blissful year with Edward, and more determined to subvert next year's divorce. She wrote her 2004 letter early and gave her husband the sealed envelope to return to her after the countdown.

But what about next month's Suzanne Vega concert? Would Madeleine go? If she did, was there hope for an early reconciliation or was Oona headed for an even bigger confrontation?

*   *   *

On a Monday night in early December, Oona took the N to Eighth Street and walked a few blocks to Joe's Pub. The doors hadn't opened, and a dozen people formed a line waiting to get in. Madeleine wasn't among them.

But standing off to the side, smoking a cigarette, was Kenzie.

Could it really—finally—be him?

He was in his late teens or early twenties, but it was definitely him. *Too thin. Is he sick?*

A black-and-gray leopard-spotted jacket hung off his gaunt frame, and his angular face was sharper than it had been when she'd last seen him—the cheeks hollow, purple half-moon shadows beneath his eyes. His hair, dyed blue-black and buzzed short on the sides, had also lost its luster; it fell like inky straw over one eye.

Oona had to talk to him, but was stuck on what to say. Should she pretend to be a smoker and try to bum a cigarette? Ask for directions?

"Excuse me." She approached him. "Have you seen a petite woman in her mid-fifties with curly black hair, probably wearing something inappropriate for her age?"

He gave Oona a weary look as he blew a stream of smoke out of the corner of his mouth. "Sounds like the lady who gave me her Suzanne Vega ticket."

It couldn't be. Her mother had claimed not to know Kenzie in 2004. Either she was hiding something or this was one hell of a coincidence.

"You never met this woman before?"

"Nope. I was just standing here, and she came up and asked if I wanted her ticket. I said I wasn't sure, but she handed it to me, anyway."

"Did she say anything else?"

The corner of his mouth twitched, impatient. "She said something about avoiding family drama and not wanting the ticket to go to waste."

A sting in the back of Oona's throat. While she'd expected her mother to stand her up, the confirmation of it was a blow. Yet in slighting her, Madeleine had also put Kenzie in her path.

"Life is too fucking weird sometimes," she muttered.

"A-fucking-men." Kenzie put out his cigarette and flicked the butt into the gutter.

They exchanged wry half-smiles.

"That was probably my mother you met. I'm the family drama. Hope you won't mind sitting with me."

"Yeah, the thing is . . ." He scratched the back of his head. "I'm not sure I'm up for this."

"Look, whatever she told you about me—"

"She didn't say anything. I'm just pretty beat. Not sure why I even came out tonight."

"Considering you did and ended up with a free concert ticket, maybe that's the universe telling you to see Suzanne Vega." *And me.* Desperation curled at the edges of her voice.

He raked the toe of his boot against the sidewalk. "I *have* always wanted to see her live."

"It'll be great, you won't regret it." Such a strain to keep her voice on the light side of cajoling, not to veer into pushy.

The line began to move as patrons were let into the club.

After tilting his head side to side, he landed on a decision. "Okay. I guess let's do this."

Yes!

"I'm Oona, by the way." *Your future employer and best friend.*

"Kenzie."

The venue accommodated less than two hundred, with a stage in the corner, tiny candle-lit tables, velvet banquettes, and ornate columns. Oona and Kenzie's table was two feet from the stage.

"Whoa, this is really close." Kenzie fidgeted in his seat, his face strained.

"I know, isn't it great?" She tried to evade his dismay. "So are you from New York?"

"No. I came here because . . ." His eyes swept the room and he chewed on a thumbnail.

"Because . . ."

"I, uh . . ." He stood. "I need to step out for a minute. One more cigarette before the show."

"Do you want me to order you a drink?"

"Gin and tonic, thanks."

Before she could say anything else, he wove around the tables in a swift path to the exit. It was hard not to follow him.

She'd prepared for a rough night when imagining Madeleine at the concert with her, but Kenzie? Though this was supposedly their first meeting, and Oona hadn't counted on instant rapport (well, maybe a little), she also hadn't expected him to be so nervous and haggard-looking. It was hard not to assume the worst. Was it drugs, illness, illegal activity? What else could explain it?

Oona ordered two gin and tonics from a passing cocktail waitress. They were brought over quickly, and as the minutes ticked by, Kenzie's drink sweated in a pool of its own condensation. Maybe she should try to find him, in case something happened. In case he was hurt.

The lights began to dim. If she was going to look for Kenzie, it was best to leave now. She slid her chair back and—

Someone headed her way, head down, in a gray-and-black jacket. Leopard spots?

They were. Kenzie slid into his seat. Everyone around them applauded as Suzanne Vega took the stage.

Oona leaned over the table. "I wasn't sure you'd come back."

"Me neither." He guzzled his cocktail as if it was a glass of water.

"Are you okay?"

The first song began before he could answer.

Oona shifted her attention from Kenzie to the performance. At least he'd returned.

Onstage, no frills: just a singer and her acoustic guitar. Her voice a buttery alto, her lyrics filled with shades of longing and loneliness, cautionary tales, and subdued desire. Between songs, her anecdotes were clever and self-deprecating, told by the shy girl you wish you'd befriended, grown up into the wise older sister you wish you had.

How sad, that this singer seemed more knowable to Oona than the young man next to her, who hugged his elbows like he was trying to fold in on himself. He applauded with the rest of the audience, but his face was inscrutable; his eyebrows pinched together like he was looking at something faraway and confounding. But he did remain seated, at least for the first dozen songs.

It wasn't until "In Liverpool" that he began to tremble, closing his eyes as Vega sang of missing something or someone impossible to have. Oona tilted her head back and breathed through her nose, a trick Cyn had taught her to impede threatening tears. Would he reveal the root of his suffering, allow her to try to ease it? Reaching a hand out felt too bold, so she kept her fingers entwined in her lap until the song ended.

At which point, Kenzie stood. "I gotta go," he said over the applause, and made a hunched-over retreat.

This time she followed him outside.

"Kenzie, what is it?" She walked double time to match his brisk strides. "Please, tell me what's wrong." A quick run and she blocked his path, forcing him to a halt. Never mind that she was acting too familiar for a supposed stranger. Ignoring his pain was not an option.

If Kenzie found her boldness off-putting, he didn't show it. Instead, he fumbled in his pockets for a cigarette, lit it with shaking hands. "I would've been fine if she didn't do that song. It always gets to me." A cloud of smoke gathered between them. "I'm sorry, I couldn't be there anymore. It was all too pretty and hushed and quaint."

He wasn't walking away, so that was progress. Surely there was a way to get him to open up. "Would you rather be somewhere loud and ugly?" No sarcasm in her question.

"Only if I can get blind drunk there."

"Then let's find you a dive bar."

A defeated shrug. "Why not."

Oona navigated them to St. Mark's Place, glancing at the Japanese restaurant that formerly housed Vamps (*Where's Crosby working these days?*) before stepping down into a dusty bar. Low ceilings; walls, floors, and furniture made of wood; a fat orange tabby curled up beside the jukebox. Being a Monday, the place was dead except for a couple of grizzled middle-aged men in flannel shirts watching a muted football game and a cluster of lanky NYU students playing darts. Kenzie selected a quiet corner table beneath a burned-out light.

"Beer okay?" Oona asked.

"If it also comes with a double shot of whiskey. But it's my round." He held out a twenty; the stern jut of his chin told her not to argue.

As she waited for the drinks, she kept glancing his way, as if he might take off again, but once he planted his elbows on the table and his head in his hands, he didn't move. The bartender filled the pitcher, and the sour whiff of beer reminded her of her father kissing her good night. A smell she associated with reassurance.

She returned with a pitcher of Bud, two mugs, and a double whiskey, which Kenzie knocked back right away. Something on his middle finger glinted.

"I like your ring." Oona motioned to the silver band made of two elongated wings.

"Yeah? Someone gave it to me when I was going through a shitty time. Though the last month has been even shittier." He poured the beer, handed her the first mug, and drained half of his before she even took a sip.

"Anything you want to talk about?"

"I don't know."

Sweat beaded on her upper lip. Choosing words was like choosing wires to dismantle a bomb—the right ones could tame the situation; the wrong ones could blow it up. "Sometimes it's easier to talk to a stranger."

"Sometimes it's easier not to talk at all." His response monotone and weary.

Don't push it. "Then we can just sit here and drink."

Kenzie leaned back and shrugged. "Fuck it." A gulp of beer and he began. "A few weeks ago, my moms died in a car accident."

"Oh my god, Kenzie." How badly she wanted to hug him, but the flinch in his body—the invisible barbed wire encircling him—said *keep away.* "I'm so sorry." Oona brought her beer to her face but didn't drink it. "I know how awful it is to lose a parent so young. My dad died when I was eleven. I was there when it happened. He fell off a boat and I *laughed* because he made such a silly face as he went over. I mean, he was a good swimmer, I didn't think for a second he might drown." She pushed the glass aside. "I still feel like an asshole for laughing."

For the first time that night, he didn't slide his gaze away when he looked at her. "I feel like an asshole every day. I was getting stoned and playing video games when my moms died."

"That doesn't make you an asshole."

"You don't know me."

But I do. I will. "I have a feeling you're a good kid."

His face crumpled, but he stopped short of tears, held on to the edge of the table as he composed himself. "I'm not a good kid, I'm a loser. I dropped out of school, put my mothers' house up for sale, and now I'm just wandering around."

"It's okay to be lost for a little while."

"I don't eat, I don't sleep. But I'm always hungry and always tired."

"Well, hey, I'm married to a chef who can feed you, I have a spare bedroom, and if you're looking for something to do, I'm in the market for a personal assistant." *Great, now you'll definitely scare him off.*

But his reaction wasn't fearful or discomfited. Instead, his eyebrows lifted and eyes grew shiny, like the offer both pained and pleased him. "I'm staying with a friend, but thanks." He got to his feet. "I need a smoke."

"Want me to get another round in the meantime?"

"Naw, I think I'm done."

Aching disappointment radiated within her. She gathered her coat and purse and followed him outside. "Are you getting a cab?"

"Subway."

They walked west toward Broadway, Kenzie setting a slow, deliberate pace.

"What gets me is how angry I am all the time. And not just about my moms' deaths, but stupid shit." He stopped in front of a Starbucks and pointed at it. "Like, why does Astor Place have two Starbucks across the fucking street from each other?"

"Not to piss you off further, but there's actually a third Starbucks in the Barnes & Noble across the street from that one." She tilted her head toward Lafayette. "It's one of those annoying New York things."

"It makes me want to punch a fire hydrant. Every day, it's something else. And . . ." His face twisted into a grimace. "A few years ago,

I had a bad falling-out with one of my moms. I never had a chance to tell her how much she hurt me, and I know it's time to forgive her and let it go, but I can't. I'm sad and I miss her, but I still need more time to be mad at her." A wrought-iron fence separated the tables outside the coffee shop from the sidewalk, and Kenzie gripped the railing like he wanted to tear it out of the ground.

"Then be mad at her." Was the same kind of rage gnawing at her mother? Perhaps Madeleine had come into the city intending to put the fight behind them, but found herself still angry. In which case, giving away her concert ticket wasn't meant to punish Oona as much as shield her. "Maybe you need to give it more time."

"Yeah. And distance. I thought New York would be a good place to shake it off. Get lost in the chaos. Or at least have company for my misery—all these people wearing black, looking like they'd rather be somewhere else."

"Maybe you haven't given New York enough of a chance." *Or me.* Such potential for perfect symmetry, for her to help him with his grief as he'd helped with hers.

"Or maybe I just need to be somewhere else. Get lost somewhere farther away." His grip on the fence loosened. "I've always wanted to visit Asia. Did you know Thailand is called the Land of Smiles?"

And there it was. "I didn't know that." Her windpipe narrowed and she blinked rapidly. "I've only seen pictures, but it looks like a beautiful country."

A thoughtful nod and Kenzie let go of the railing, resumed walking. "I've been reading up on it and it seems so damn cool. There are jungles and temples and all these different islands. On New Year's, they have a giant water fight, and every full moon, one island throws a big party . . ."

As he continued to speak of Thailand's wonders, his voice brightened, and Oona became more deflated. She couldn't keep him here; it would be selfish to even try.

When they reached the Eighth Street N/R station, Kenzie started down the steps, but Oona hung back. "I'm actually going to take a taxi." She didn't want to put a damper on his travel plans, and her supportive smile wouldn't hold much longer.

"Hang on." He bounded back up. "If you give me your address, I'll send you a postcard."

"Sure." She scrawled it on the back of a receipt; the paper quivered when she handed it to him. "Wait!" Even though he'd be out of harm's way when the tsunami hit Southeast Asia in 2004, she had to warn him, in case she was the reason *why* he ended up safe. "Get out of Asia in December. Something awful is going to happen. There's no rational way I can tell you how I know, I just need you to trust me on this."

Narrowing one eye, he said, "Um, okay, Nostradamus. Who knows, I might get bored after a couple of weeks and give New York another try."

But she knew it would be more than a couple of weeks. All this waiting, as if the scattered pieces of her life would ever fall into place.

As they regarded each other, Kenzie's smirk faded into a beseeching look.

Was he waiting for her to say more?

"I hope we'll meet again" was all she could think of.

"Me too." He gave a lingering nod and disappeared down into the station.

Oona took a cab home and found Edward hanging up his jacket in the foyer.

"Fancy meeting you here." A pleased smile and he took her in his arms. "How was the concert?"

"Strange" was all she could get out before a great weariness muted her.

"Hey, hey." He stroked her hair as she buried her head in his shoulder. "What is it, love?"

But she didn't have the words to articulate what "it" was, and she was too tired to cry, so she just stood there as her temporary husband held her.

22

The blowout with Madeleine and the heart-wrenching evening with Kenzie left Oona depressed, so she kept busy in the following weeks by converting her den into a home theater. She had a giant screen and surround-sound speakers installed, along with two rows of seating, microfiber love seats on the lower tier and reclining leather chairs on the upper. Red velvet drapes on either side of the screen and an antique popcorn machine completed the effect.

Every few days, she called her mother and got her voice mail. She never left a message.

The home theater was complete by Christmas, so they spent the holiday watching a marathon of Quentin Tarantino movies, enjoying other peoples' witty banter and cartoonish violence.

They hadn't discussed Oona's "memory condition" much since the engagement, but with her impending leap a week away and Edward's attention rooted in Clary's Pub, she had to remind him about it.

"It always happens at midnight, and it's going to be jarring, because I won't know who you are. That letter I gave you will help, though. Make sure I read it right away." Recalling her 2004 leap beginning on the subway, she added, "And let's not get separated around the count-down. Don't let me wander off."

Though the build-out was unfinished, Edward decided to throw a big New Year's Eve party at Clary's, and two days prior, he hosted a din-ner to thank key people involved in the restaurant. Oona and Francesca were there, as were the construction and kitchen staff. The furniture and light fixtures had yet to be delivered, so they set up planks of wood on sawhorses. Table linen and silverware that had arrived days before provided elegant touches, and nobody would've guessed the clusters of white candles in tall glass cylinders acting as minimalist centerpieces were purchased from a local bodega.

Everyone around Oona talked shop—the structural details of the restaurant, its menu and concept, the local food scene. She had little to contribute, so she ate slowly to have something to do, and drank too much wine. At one point, in the middle of a heated debate on the French school of cooking, Oona dropped her fork. When she bent under the table to retrieve it, she saw Francesca's yellow stiletto standing absent of its owner. She followed the line of her stockinged leg down to her foot, which was in Edward's lap. Revulsion flooded Oona as she scurried back up.

"French food is like the little black dress," Francesca said, eyes glinting. "It's timeless. But I think California cuisine is poised to have a moment."

"I think you're right." The corners of Edward's mouth twitched. "I'm going to take Alice Waters's lead and incorporate more local and organic fare into my menu."

The animated chatter around her grew louder as Oona stared at her plate. She'd left her fork on the ground. It didn't matter. She was no longer hungry.

All she could do was sit there, unable to move, unable to speak. When dessert was served, she excused herself, citing the onset of a mi-graine. Edward called her a taxi and promised he wouldn't be home too late. As soon as she got outside, she threw up in the gutter.

Oona didn't mention what she witnessed to Edward, not that

night. No doubt he would've found a way to brush it off or deny it. No, she needed more solid evidence to confirm whether what she saw indicated a larger betrayal. They'd still be married the following year, so how was it possible? Another part of her wondered how it could be anything else. Either way, she had to know for sure before she confronted Edward and warned 2004 Oona with a new letter. Rash judgment had already caused her to detonate her mother's love life; she'd learn from that and proceed with caution before taking a sledgehammer to her marriage. She wouldn't accept the bleak reality of Edward's cheating until she had proof.

So she did what many suspicious spouses have done before her: she went snooping. First stop: his dresser drawers and pockets, which yielded no evidence.

His electronic devices were next. The following night, she waited until he fell asleep, crept out of bed, and took his cell phone and Black-Berry into her study. The phone didn't take long to check. Edward wasn't one to save texts, so there weren't many to examine, and none were from Francesca.

The BlackBerry took hours to get through. As she skimmed hundreds of subject lines and emails, nausea churned through her. She focused on messages from Francesca, searched for any flirtatious traces or romantic subtext. Yet she found nothing incriminating.

Edward's laptop was trickier; it was at the restaurant's office, in a locked drawer. He kept a spare set of keys at home but would be waking shortly to spend the day at Clary's working and preparing for the New Year's party. Ah, but she'd be there that night. It was cutting it close, but she'd find a way to sneak off and search his computer.

That evening, after grabbing Edward's extra set of keys, Oona called for a car to take her to Clary's, aiming to get there around nine, but the holiday demand for cabs caused a delay and she didn't arrive until nine-thirty.

Still plenty of time. I just—what is this?

She stopped dead in the restaurant's entrance. Strung throughout the interior, a web of white Christmas lights.

"Do you like it?" Francesca greeted her, brimming with glee. "Ed-

ward was stuck on a last-minute way to jazz up this place for the festivities, and I suggested fairy lights. He'd mentioned some party you raved
about where the room was covered in them, so I thought it would be a
perfect solution here. In a way, I should be thanking you for the idea."
The spaghetti strap of her beige silk gown slid down her shoulder, but
she made no move to adjust it.

Resisting violent urges, Oona coerced her mouth into a grin.
"You're very welcome. Where should I put my coat?"

"The storage room down the hall."

How appropriate that Francesca played the party co-host and Oona
a mere guest.

Once in the back room, she was frozen in place. Wasn't anger a
fire? Her skin should've been glowing red and hot to the touch, yet she
stood in the dark, shivering.

An electronic jangle announced a text message from Edward asking where she was.

Please let me be wrong about this.

Time to join the party.

"There you are, love." Edward beckoned her over to a cluster of
guests. "Let me introduce you to the missus," he said to them.

A series of names and extended hands followed, which she shook.
But she made no effort to remember the names; she'd forget them all in
a matter of hours, anyway.

"How do you like them?" Edward motioned to the Christmas lights.

It was more theft than homage, but she lied and praised the decorations.

"Do try the Scotch eggs," Edward urged. "It's a new recipe, and if
they go over well tonight, I may add them to the menu."

As she stood around making polite chitchat, it was as if a fog rolled
in, surrounding her, dimming the voices around her, reducing her to
smiles and nods.

More guests arrived, and Edward went off to greet them. This was
her chance. She excused herself and checked her phone for the time:
10:05 P.M.

When she was sure nobody was looking, Oona stepped away.

Upstairs, she unlocked Edward's office and, with one final backward glance, slipped inside. She set her phone down and sat at his desk. Her hands hovered over it like a piano player poised to start a challenging piece. Why direct so much effort to discover her marriage was a lie? She *could* let it be and spare herself this pain. After all, once the clock struck midnight, this Oona would leap again, while 2004 Oona would remain clueless about the preceding months. What would the truth solve, anyway?

Nothing. The truth would be its own reward—or punishment. It was New Year's Eve, and if she didn't learn the truth about her marriage to Edward today, she'd never know if he'd deceived her. She *had* to know.

Oona unlocked the bottom desk drawer and took out the computer. Before she flipped it open, an idea tugged at the back of her mind like an impatient child.

What else is in here? What's important enough to be locked away?

The laptop had been on a stack of T-shirts bearing beverage logos, and the drawer also contained hanging file folders brimming with invoices and contracts. Except the last one, which held something different: a handful of Polaroid pictures. Francesca naked in each one. Except for the last one, which featured her with a shirtless Edward.

An oily disgust simmered inside Oona, but there was also a lightness, like her head might float away from the rest of her body. Relief. She hadn't been reading into things. She wasn't paranoid. A certain satisfaction comes with being right, even when it's something you'd rather be wrong about.

Is there more?

Sifting through the T-shirts, beneath them she found a rectangular jewelry box. Too short for a necklace, this one was sized for a bracelet. She opened the box. Inside was a silver watch, its face dotted with black stars, its hands stopped at three o'clock.

Oona gasped and held her breath.

It couldn't be. Her watch.

She clutched it in one hand, covered her mouth with the other, and ran into the adjoining bathroom. Nothing came out but heaving sobs as she bent over the sink, inhaling a sharp odor of pine-scented bleach. Any satisfaction at being vindicated was gone. Her legs began to give way, but she fought gravity and remained standing, even as the white tile floor beckoned. She wanted to sleep for days, sleep into the next year, sleep through several years.

If only she could curl up on the floor right now.

I'm sorry, Mom. I wish I'd listened. I wish you could help me now.

How badly Oona wanted to cry and cry and be wrapped in her mother's comforting arms. Madeleine would've surely set aside her own wounded feelings to soothe her daughter; she wouldn't be smug or petty or say she'd known Edward was rotten all along. Except Madeleine was off with her own rotten Romeo, on a cruise and unreachable. And Oona had less than two hours to confront her husband and write herself a new letter.

"Oona?"

Beside the desk was Edward. His eyes darted to the ransacked drawer, the scattered photos, and landed on her. "Look, whatever you think this—"

"Stop!" The word boomed out of her mouth, startling them both. "I *know* what this is. I saw Francesca playing footsie with you the other night. I just wanted proof before you found a way to make me think I was a paranoid, jealous wife. So I went through your things."

"Something a paranoid, jealous wife would never do, of course." His eyebrows knit together with amusement. "And you found 'proof' in some photos taken years ago?"

The blasé reaction made Oona stand up straighter, imagining her vertebrae were infused with steel. "Don't you fucking dare. I know you're a two-timing douchelord. But we'll get back to that. First, how the hell did you end up with my watch?" She held up the timepiece.

Rapid blinks, confusion flickering across his features. "I don't—I didn't—"

"I know it's the one Dale gave me, so spare me the bullshit."

Edward raked his fingers through his hair. "Let's sit down and talk this over rationally."

"You can sit, but I'm good standing."

Her sharp tone made him falter, but he also remained standing. They faced each other from across the desk.

"It *is* my watch, right?"

"Oona, I owe you an enormous apology. Yes, it's your watch."

"How did you get it?"

"You know how I play poker with the lads," he began. "One of my mates started inviting me to high-stakes poker games." Edward gnawed on his lower lip as he stared at his shoes. "I played well for a while. Then I cocked it up. Ended up owing scads of money."

"Why didn't you come to me?" Mouth pursed into a tight knot.

"And tell you the man you're about to marry is a loser who's two hundred grand in the hole?"

"Better than a loser who robs me of my prized possessions." There was a tickle in Oona's throat, a sourness in her mouth. "So you set up that burglary."

A sheepish grimace as he scratched the back of his neck. "It was a low thing to do. I'm so sorry. They weren't supposed to take the watch."

"But you got it back for me." Oona glanced down at its silver face. "How sweet." Spoken with venom.

"I just couldn't find the right moment—the right way to give it to you."

"And now I won't be able to wear it again, because it'll make me think of what you've done. You've ruined something so special to me. While we're returning things, you can have these." She pulled her engagement and wedding rings off and dropped them on the desk. "So how long have you been fucking Francesca?" The vile question caused a whiplash shiver to snake through her body.

Edward wore an expression ready for denial, but the hard look in her eyes made him change course. "Three years. On and off. But we stopped after I met you."

"Bullshit."

"All right, there was one slip after a late night working. One. But that was it. She keeps making advances toward me and I try to reject them. I've wanted to end things with her for a while now, but she's good at her job and she's my best chance for making Clary's a success."

"*She's* your best chance."

"Her expertise. And you—of course you," he sputtered.

"Well, thanks for using both of us to make your precious restaurant dream come true."

Her snide tone made him wince. "I'm not using you. You might not believe this, but I truly am in love with you."

Oona laughed even as hot tears flooded her eyes. "Don't insult me by lying more. On top of the cheating and the stealing, it's a bit much."

"I realize that. But Oona, look at it this way. You know the worst, so there's no reason for me to lie. What I did was unforgivable, but I *do* have feelings for you. I've been utterly smitten with you since Egypt. You can't deny our chemistry is real. You can't force that kind of connection."

She had to bite down on her tongue to keep from agreeing out loud. But there was no room in her rage for sentimentality. "That was just sex."

"It was never just sex. You know it was more than that." His eyes grew wistful. "I'd do anything to earn your trust back . . ."

It should've been the moment she boiled over with fury, roared at ear-piercing volumes. Yet she stood there, defeated, and managed only a whisper. "I thought this was something real."

"It is. And still can be. Won't your brain . . . reset or something at midnight?"

"In a way."

"Well . . . what if you let yourself forget this? Use that blank slate for us to start over."

"Are you out of your fucking mind? You want me to pretend you didn't betray me?" Oona snorted. "By the way, where's that 2004 letter I wrote to myself? I want it back."

"It's at the house. Listen, Oona, we could still have a great life together. I'll cut Francesca out of my life for good, I swear it. I *know* I can make you happy."

"Not gonna happen. For you to think I'd even consider it is crazy."

"Crazier than losing your memory at the stroke of midnight every year?"

She took in a long breath through her teeth.

"I didn't say that to hurt you." When Edward tried to come around to her side of the desk, she circled away from him. "I accept you for the way you are. I'm merely saying, there's a lot about our relationship that's crazy. I married you knowing you'd forget me in January. I can handle that, because I love you. And since we'd have this fresh start, you could—"

"I can't. I won't." It was like her head was being injected with helium while the rest of her body turned to stone. "What time is it?"

"A bit after eleven."

"Shit." She had to get home and tear up that letter. In case she didn't make it in time, she grabbed a blank server pad and pen off the desk to write a new one along the way. When Edward made to follow her, she gave him a deathly stare. "Don't come after me. If you do, I'll burn this place to the ground before it even opens for business."

How satisfying to see his face become a gruesome medley of fear, anguish, distress.

Oona ran downstairs. The party was in full tilt, OutKast's "Hey Ya!" blasting over the stereo, the lyrics about shaking it like a Polaroid picture mocking her. She got her coat and pushed past guests to get to the front door. Two steps shy of the exit:

"Have you seen Edward?"

"He's upstairs." A wicked leer as she turned to Francesca. "And you're a pretentious cunt."

Not waiting for a reaction, Oona bolted outside.

One happy, perfect year was all she wanted. What a price to pay.

I could've found Peter instead. I could've caught him at a better time.

It was windy, but Oona kept her coat open, let the bracing air wake her up, each gust whispering how gullible, how foolish. But she wouldn't be a victim. She'd eschew self-pity, harness responsibility, and take action.

Reaching into her pocket for her phone—"Fuck!" It was still on Edward's desk. She wouldn't be able to call a cab or check the time. And she wouldn't make it home on foot before midnight. At least she had her MetroCard.

So this is how I end up on the F train. Wait, let me guess: it gets delayed.

It did, arriving quickly but stalling short of the next stop due to a "sick passenger."

Near Oona's seat was a rowdy group of drunk twenty-something hipsters in skinny jeans and plaid scarves swaying, their complaints loud and slurred. The woman in the houndstooth coat was farther down the car reading a book.

Facing the blank paper, she got as far as "Dear Oona" and paused. How to begin this new letter?

Pent-up vitriol spilled onto the pages; she wrote with such vehemence, the words left grooves in the paper. Once finished, she read the new letter and her frenzy waned. It was too intimidating, too acrimonious. She needed to warn 2004 Oona, not scare the shit out of her.

Oona flipped to a blank page in the notepad and began again. Better to keep it to the headlines: *Local Time Traveler to Divorce Scoundrel Husband and Pursue Guitar Teacher.*

The revised note was more direct, less upsetting. A satisfied nod and she clipped the pen to the pad. Just then, the stalled train pitched into motion and one of the drunk hipsters lost his balance. He stumbled into Oona, knocking the pad and pen out of her hand.

Ignoring his indifferent apology, Oona jumped up to rescue the fallen notepad by the sliding doors, but his friends stood in her way.

"Excuse me, I need to get—"

A lurch as the train came to an abrupt stop. Before she could reach down, the doors opened and one of the hipsters shuffled forward, sweeping the notepad and pen into the gap between the train and platform.

"Shit!" she cried out.

"Next stop, Seventh Avenue. Stand clear of the closing doors."

The group gave her a confused look as they stepped off the train.

No air to breathe, like she'd been punched in the throat. A wheeze as she forced her lungs to obey.

The rumble of the subway and the bitterness of bad luck shook free her tears.

Oona rushed to the woman in the houndstooth coat.

"Please, I need a pen." Her voice was pitched high with hysteria. "I need to warn myself to divorce Edward and find Peter. I know you have a pen. Hurry, I don't have much time."

The woman looked up from her book. "I'm sorry, I only heard half of what you said. You wanna borrow a pen?"

"Yes, quickly. I—"

Another lurch and Oona was thrown off her feet.

She didn't get a chance to finish her sentence.

PART VI

On Some Faraway Beach

1995: 31/23

23

Time was a rubber band pulling her back, back, back, until—*snap*—and panic flung her forward, bolted her upright with a startled cry like she'd been pushed off a high ledge.

"Son of a bitch!" She burst into tears, covered her face.

Guttural, primal noises came out of her, a bitterness that choked her. Betrayal like razor wire coiled around her, cut into her.

Her sobs died down.

She was in bed, but not her bed. And this wasn't her room. Not her house. It wasn't even a house, more like a hut built by a castaway.

Clawing aside a veil of mosquito netting, she stood and did a slow spin of her surroundings: A-line thatched ceiling; bamboo blinds; minimalist geometric furniture, its wood stained the color of melted chocolate mixed with blood. At one end of the room was a set of double doors. Oona cracked them open and poked her head outside. There was a large patio, then a stretch of beach framed by palm tree silhouettes. The lapping tide a subdued roar, the balmy air threaded with a fermented, fishy odor. And at one end of the balcony, on a wooden recliner, a sleeping figure.

Oona shrieked, and the figure bolted upright, matching her scream.

"Mom?"

"Oona?" Madeleine rubbed her eyes, sat up straighter. "Darn it. Did I sleep past midnight? I can't shake this jet lag."

"Where the hell are we?"

"Come sit." She patted the space beside her, beckoning her reluctant daughter.

Residual anger pinballed within Oona, made her snippy. "Did we take a three-hour tour and get stranded here? That's the only thing missing from my stupid fucking life."

"We're in Phu Quoc. Vietnam. You said next year you'd be 'dealing with some shit' and would be better off getting lost somewhere far away."

Ah, so she'd followed Kenzie's anger-slash-grief-management strategy. "I'm surprised we're not in Thailand. Is Kenzie here?"

"Who?"

Then that would be a no. "What year is it?"

"It's 1995."

"Which puts Kenzie . . . probably in elementary school. Of course. Why would something ever work in my favor?" Oona slapped her knees, dug her nails into them as fresh tears threatened. It only took her mother's hand on her back to release them.

"I thought he was one of the good ones." Oona wept and wept, soaking Madeleine's silk blouse. "I knew it wouldn't last. But I hoped." The words were muffled against her mother's shoulder. "I thought I could change things. But it was all a lie."

"Oh, honey, I'm so sorry. What happened?"

"I . . ." But more sobs choked her, and her face twisted with anguish as she fought to catch her breath. All Madeleine could do was stroke small circles on her daughter's back and murmur shushing sounds the way she did when Oona had nightmares in the year following her father's death. After a minute, the cries ebbed into jerky breathing. "I—I need a tissue."

"Let's go inside."

They settled on the sofa, Madeleine armed with a glass of water and pack of tissues.

Oona blew her nose and wiped her damp cheeks. "I just don't get it. I couldn't prevent it when I leaped backward, but I *could* have the year before that. Yet there was no warning in the letter I read before I met him. Why wouldn't my earlier self try to stop me?" Why had 2002 Oona set her up like that?

"I'm sure she—*you* had your reasons. Maybe you believed the good parts of the year outweighed the bad."

"No. No." Fervent head-shaking.

"Look at it this way: whatever dreadful things happened, you won't have to live through them again."

"Or at all. Because it's 1995, so it hasn't happened yet." A thought like a firecracker set off in a dark room, bright and dangerous. "Maybe my earlier self wouldn't help me, but you could. If I tell you his name now, because I won't meet him until . . ." *2003*. The year dangled on her tongue, but she reeled it back in, uncertain. "You could warn me. Prevent the whole train wreck. If you knew his name, maybe . . ."

A grim heaviness weighed down Madeleine's features. "This is one of your early leaps, isn't it? How old are you on the inside?"

"I just turned twenty-three. If it's 1995 . . ." Oona flipped through a mental calendar. "I also just turned thirty-one. Ugh, this will never stop feeling fucked up." The end table beside her collected more balled-up tissues. "How'd you know this was one of my early leaps?"

"Because a more mature you would never ask me to help you change your future. Though I wish I could spare you this pain." Lips trembling, she pressed them into a line, blinked hard and asked, "Was he violent?"

A vehement no followed by a softer one. Fresh tears rolled down her face and she wiped them away. "He robbed me of . . . I just—want to undo the whole thing."

Madeleine put a hand on her daughter's arm in a gesture that said, *Slow down, think this through.* "You know I'm here to help you any way that I can, but even if you tell me his name, I won't sabotage your re-lationship."

That made one of them. Had Oona done the right thing sabotaging her mother's relationship? Even if Nathan was a certified creep and

Madeleine was funding his comfortable lifestyle, his presence bright-ened her life, brought a glimmer to her eyes that disappeared after being told it wouldn't last.

"Honey, please take some time with this."

Oona unclenched her fists, like she'd just put down a loaded gun. "You're right. I don't have to decide tonight." She launched into a stream of grievances. "God, I thought last year was gonna be awesome, but it ended up so shitty. Not only with—*him*. I thought I'd finally begin my friendship with Kenzie—you don't even know Kenzie yet—but we had one tense, weird night and then he took off. And you and me, we had the *worst* fight. It was awful. I never said sorry, because I wasn't ready and—god, I was a chickenshit. I should've stepped up." She clutched her chest; the pressure of thorny emotions festering within needed re-lease. "I'm *so* sorry. Even though you already forgave me. I didn't know what you were forgiving me for then, and now that I do, I can't tell you what I'm apologizing for. I'm just very sorry," Oona cried.

A flicker of fear swept away with a hurried smile. "My darling, if future me forgives you, so does present-day me." She squeezed her daughter's shoulder.

"I can't fight with you like that again. You're the only constant in my life." Oona grabbed a cushion and held it over her stomach. "And you were right about him, too. Don't you get tired being right about everything?" A single dejected chuckle.

"Of course I don't. And I've been wrong my fair share of times. I was wrong earlier tonight, thinking I could doze off and wake up be-fore midnight. It must've been frightening for you to come to like that, somewhere new, alone."

"It's always a little scary. And a little lonely."

"Well, I'll help make things less lonely." Madeleine stood and walked over to a mini-fridge. "How about some champagne? You can never feel truly sad if you're drinking champagne."

"I don't want any. I'm sorry." The promise of a buzz was tempting, but it would lead to the bad kind of drunk, the dark, self-pitying kind. Her eyes roved the hut, landed on a windowsill lined with potted or-chids. "So we're in Vietnam, huh?"

"We've only been here a few days, but my goodness, it's stunning."

Could it be stunning enough to cool her volcanic fury? To say nothing of the queasy shame that she'd allowed herself to be suckered, so eager to love and be loved. She'd gotten it so wrong. If she'd known the truth about Edward and warned herself in time, 2004 could've been a happier year. It could've been spent with Peter.

The lost opportunity burned in her throat and instigated fresh tears.

Madeleine brought over two cans of soda and more tissues.

"I feel like I'm never gonna get it right." The tinny pop of the soda can was a punctuation mark on Oona's self-pity. "As much as I've tried to shape my life to have some coherence, every time I try to bond with someone, either I fail or they don't stay—or I can't stay, because of leaping. I guess I should get used to the idea it'll usually be just me and you."

"Not every year." Madeleine bared her teeth, preparing to say something unpleasant but necessary. "Though some years, yes. It helps to look at it in the short term. Every year can be a tabula rasa, and once it's over, you can begin again."

"At square one."

"Not necessarily."

"That's how it feels." Oona put down her soda and twisted her hands in her lap. "Did I leave myself a letter?"

"No. This time it's a present." Madeleine handed her daughter a tiny crimson box.

Oona opened it and took out a platinum band made of two elongated wings. A small accompanying note in her handwriting read: *Anger can be an energy. Don't burn, soar.* Squinting, she checked the ring again. It had the same design as the one Kenzie wore in her last leap. "Is there anything else? Any letter?"

"That's it. Some years, you find letters unnecessary, especially as you get used to leaping."

Oona put the ring on her left middle finger. "There's no getting used to it. It's the worst. The *powerlessness* of it." She spat the words out, hot under her skin. How could she turn this anger into a fuel when all it wanted to do was incinerate her? "At least I'm far away. Maybe the distance will help." Her words held little conviction. "You sure you don't want to help change my future?"

"Ask me again at the end of the year."

The following morning brought a heat wave and unexpected optimism. Their hut was on a remote stretch of vanilla beach, the waters beyond an ombré of sapphire to blue topaz to palest jade. A rope swing hung from one leaning palm tree, a hammock strung between two others. It took effort to remain angry in such lovely surroundings. As the days passed and the temperature rose, the sun's fire served as a warped law of affinity; it quelled her internal inferno to a manageable flame. She still wanted to reveal Edward's name to Madeleine. But she kept her mouth shut.

They spent a week on the sleepy island, swimming, hiking the fringes of the dense jungle and virgin rain forests, eating fresh fruit and fish, singing along to songs Oona strummed on her guitar while swaying in a hammock.

Next they flew to Hanoi. The city was hectic but small, its commotion palatable and easy to navigate. Their hotel was on the Hoan Kiem Lake, a modest body of water that offered a modicum of tranquility amid the urban bustle. Roosters woke them at sunrise, and they began the day walking around the lake, sometimes joining the clusters of fellow early risers doing tai chi. They perused cramped shop stalls selling everything from fruit to flowers to party decorations. They visited the Presidential Palace and the monument containing Ho Chi Minh's preserved dead body. Every day they bought gooey pudding made of mung bean paste from a woman mixing it in a large silver pot in the middle of the sidewalk, sitting on low plastic stools as they ate the sugary spoonfuls. They visited the Hoa Lo Prison, better known as the "Hanoi Hilton," and balanced that somber outing by taking in a surprisingly elaborate puppet show. Distractions and delights abounded, but always Edward Clary's name was balanced on the edge of Oona's lips. She kept them sealed, but always her silence felt hard-won, a temporary thing.

The culture shock was a tonic for Oona. She found the machine-gun staccato of the Vietnamese language—and the surprising proliferation of Russian spoken—oddly soothing. She embraced the unknowable and indecipherable. While Madeleine grew nervous when they veered onto an unintended street, Oona was happy to get lost down twisty paths with faded, tattered awnings bearing signs she couldn't read, signs she mentally rewrote to bear the name of her former husband.

Sometimes Oona felt like she'd traveled back even further in time. There were weathered natives in conical hats carrying yokes across their shoulders balancing heavy straw baskets. There was a prevalence of bicycles and motorbikes over cars and buses, which they dodged daily at treacherous street crossings. There were the peeling facades of French Colonial buildings, crammed together like stale geometric pastries. Oona wanted to lean over their frilly balconies, smoke endless cigarettes, and pretend she was the sad heroine in an old movie, but instead she walked on and sought out more of the unfamiliar to distract herself. Besides, she didn't smoke.

When they had enough of the city, they took the train down to Ha Long Bay.

"I think I'm ready to get on a boat again," Oona said.

"Are you sure?" her mother asked.

"Not really. But I already missed the chance to cruise the Nile, and I don't want this stupid phobia to hold me back from seeing one of the coolest parts of this country. Those islands look hella gorgeous."

"Hella?"

"Very. Don't worry about it. Let's find us a boat."

So they rented a junk for three days. If it capsized, if she drowned, so be it. On their way to the dock, Oona thought of the incident in the Meatpacking District three leaps ago, mouthing off to a cinder block of a stranger before her neck ended up in the noose of his fist. Part of her then wanted him to crush her. Part of her now wanted the boat to do the job instead. But a bigger part of her wanted to endure and survive, and was certain she would. The knowable future was her safety net. It bolstered her courage.

This courage wavered on the dock. With great hesitation, she made it onto the boat. The first few hours aboard left her with aching fingers from gripping the railing so hard. But then she gave in to the soothing powers of the undulating horizon and the view, which was indeed "hella gor-geous." The boat took them around hundreds of limestone islands pok-ing out of the water like crooked mossy teeth. At night, when the waves lapped against the boat and rocked Oona to sleep, she whispered Ed-ward's name into her pillow and hoped the next day it would hurt a little less. And it did.

They took their time making their way through the rest of the country, down to sleepy Hue and picturesque Hoi An, where they rode motorcycles to the beach and had a new wardrobe of clothes made by expert tailors, which they shipped back to New York. They ate savory crepes with shrimp and pork, caramelized fish served in clay pots, sal-ads with sliced banana flowers and pickled carrots, and endless bowls of steaming pho.

After a month of travel, Oona's fury and resentment simmered down some; it only twinged now and again, like a healed broken bone does when it rains. Vietnam was equally enchanting and humbling. The impoverished conditions of many locals put her in her place. Here were people with real hardships, yet she continued to obsess over life's injustices against her. How ungrateful, to mope while staying in four- and five-star hotels, how tiresome this sullenness. As she traversed the country, she gave generously to hospitals, orphanages, schools. She prioritized seeing more, giving more, and her mental spotlight shifted away from Edward. She craved crossing more borders, experiencing more unfamiliar environments. And once she'd conquered her boat phobia, a new desire emerged: to escape landlocked areas and spend more time on the water.

While she wanted to provide support and companionship to her daughter, after two months, Madeleine missed the comforts of New York. The novelty of Vietnam had worn off for her, and she was desper-ate for some good bagels.

"Are you sure you want to continue on by yourself?" Madeleine asked. "It can be dangerous, a woman traveling alone, especially abroad."

"If it was so dangerous, I probably would've said so in a letter instead of leaving this for myself." She held up her hand with the carved plati-num band. "Or I would've written something different, like 'stay home.'"

Oona continued alone to Laos and Cambodia, then to Thailand, which she found most enchanting of all. As her wanderlust and appetite for novelty grew, she became less afraid of solitude. Of everything.

Even Bangkok—with its overwhelming swarm of concrete, color, chaos, its oscillation between holiness and depravity—didn't intimidate her. Granted, she began with the safer tourist attractions: the floating markets, the teak birdcage of the Jim Thompson House, the countless multi-spired majestic temples with Buddhas (this one made of jade, that one gold-seated, the other one reclining). She couldn't get enough of the smells: one street infused with jasmine, the next exhaust, the one after that fried pork. And there was the food: plentiful, inexpensive, and delectable. She ate and ate and ate street food—skewers of meat, bowls of noodles, crunchy papaya salad—her taste buds soaking in the key flavors of the native cuisine: sweet, salty, sour, and spicy.

After a couple of weeks in Bangkok, she went island-hopping, beginning in Phuket.

During the day, Oona baked in the sun until her limbs practically sizzled, then cooled off in the turquoise water. Sometimes she'd lie on the beach with her eyes closed and pretend Dale was beside her. Other times she'd join a group of backpackers for games of volleyball or evening gatherings around a bonfire, playing guitar as they sang off-key renditions of Nirvana, Pearl Jam, and Smashing Pumpkins songs (though when "Zero" got blank stares, she realized it hadn't been released yet, so she stuck to the band's earlier hits). The grunge movement was making its mark around the world, and its unkempt thrift-store aesthetic both suited and was popular with many young travelers. They favored torn jeans and baggy band T-shirts, layering on a flannel shirt when the evening temperatures dipped. They also stayed abreast of current events and had heated conversations about the O. J. Simpson trial, the bombing in Oklahoma City, the horrors in Rwanda, Bosnia, and Croatia. The talk of bloodshed was at odds with their paradisiacal environment, but Oona admired their commitment to stay informed when they could easily remain in a bubble of pretty beaches, as she was prone to do.

At the end of each day, Oona washed the sand and salt off her body and imagined shedding a layer of skin. The sun darkened her limbs and lightened her hair, which made her chameleon eyes glimmer like etched glass, her teeth pearly and blinding. Her face grew thinner, her chin and cheekbones sharper as the heat and tranquility of her surroundings absorbed her appetite. When she became restless on one island, she'd head to Ko Pha Ngan for a Full Moon Party, dance all night, and sleep on the beach. Or she'd move on to a different island, where she found new splendors even as the sand and surf provided a constant rhythm to her days. She'd felt like a castaway for so long, why not play at the real thing?

How foolish that she'd let her broken chronology confine her for so long. Even the trip to Egypt had been born of avoidance, running away from fate as she was catapulted toward it. But this year abroad wasn't about trying to hide or subvert, it was her rage giving her a choice, to fry or fly, say no or say yes. So she chose yes. She said yes at a snake farm, when offered a cobra's head to kiss for good luck. She said yes to playing guitar at a party of German divorcées at a beachfront café, and yes again all four times they asked her to play Sheryl Crow's "All I Wanna Do." She said yes at a shooting range, firing off rifle rounds at paper targets. She said yes to piercing her navel and yes again to removing the hoop a month later when the piercing became infected. If her future wasn't malleable, why put limits on the present? So she said yes, yes, yes, and sometimes she wished she hadn't, but mostly she was glad she did.

No wonder Kenzie had stayed away a full year. (Though how did he afford it? Working odd jobs? Family money?) It felt good to get lost and was tempting to stay lost. When December came, she thought, *Where to next?* India? China? If culture shock was now her favorite drug, either one should provide an ample fix.

But as she considered new destinations, the months apart from her mother became magnified. It was time to return to the familiar. It was time to go home.

Oona had called Madeleine regularly during the year, and though she hadn't felt homesick while exploring villages and jungles and cities and beaches, the moment she arrived at the airport for the journey back, she missed her mother with such ferocity, she could barely endure the day's worth of travel before reaching JFK.

Madeleine greeted her at the airport with a big bouquet of orchids, which was semi-crushed in their ensuing hug.

"How was it?" her mother asked.

"I didn't want it to end. But I'm also glad it did."

"Sounds like you had a lot of fun."

"Yeah, even though bad things also happened. I got pickpocketed and sunburned and my belly button turned into a horror show and I *never* wanna hear that Sheryl Crow song again. Still, it was one of the best years of my life."

"Pretty remarkable, considering how it started off."

Edward. A part of her still wanted to say his name aloud, the cinders within her still smoldering. But there was a freedom in making mistakes, feeling broken, falling into the void, and then climbing out. A freedom in letting go, setting aside, moving on.

She gave her mother a tired, exasperated smile. "Don't worry, I won't ask you to mess with my future again." *Doesn't seem like I can outrun it, anyway. And maybe that's okay.*

They ended the year drinking champagne in the Park Slope brownstone, Oona no longer feeling bereft or betrayed. She missed nobody and regretted nothing. If she could explore foreign countries with ease, she could handle yet another foreign timeline. She was ready for anything.

But there are some things *nobody* is ready for.

PART VII

More Than This

1999: 35/24

24

"Happy New Year! And Happy Birthday!"

Oona's eyes fluttered open as if from a refreshing nap. No shock, no queasiness, no physical jolt. She was getting used to leaping.

Normally, she'd be flooded with a yearning for a return to the sequential, for a remission from this time illness. But she didn't wish for any specific year.

Whatever comes next, I can handle it.

"Happy New Year, Mom." How steady her voice. How relaxed her shoulders, her hands folded in her lap. How wonderful to begin the year serenely instead of disoriented, to float instead of free fall.

"It's 1999 and you just turned thirty-five," said her mother from the other end of the couch.

"Great. I can't wait to see what the year brings."

Madeleine tilted her head, eyes bright with intrigue. "There's something different about you."

"There is." She offered a secret smile and glanced down. The light caught her platinum ring, the wings winking at her as she turned her hand. What was this? There was writing on her left palm.

"I never know what to expect when you leap . . ."

As her mother continued to speak, Oona surreptitiously read the note on her hand:

Ask Mom about tattoo/check her bag for answers.

". . . and even though it's still the same you each time, I swear, it's almost like your face changes somehow and—"

"Can you tell me about my tattoo? I think I'm ready for an explanation now." She tried to bury the note of strain in her tranquil tone.

Madeleine, reaching for her champagne glass on the coffee table, froze in the awkward position. Retracted her arm and sat back against the sofa. "Oh, sweetheart, you can't force these things. The right time will present itself and you'll know what you need to know when you need to know it." She stood and put her hands on her hips. "Shall we have some cake with this champagne?"

"Actually, I'd love some tea." Better to choose a beverage meant for warmth and comfort. Plus, it would keep her mom busy for a few extra minutes.

"Of course. I'll make you a cup." Madeleine pointed across the room. "In the meantime, your letter's on the mantel."

"Okay, thanks."

The letter could wait. Once Madeleine was out of the room, Oona went over to the armchair, to her mother's handbag.

She sifted through its contents: leather gloves, a day planner, a tube of hand lotion, receipts, two slim books (Saint-Exupéry's *The Little Prince* and Rilke's *Duino Elegies*), a key chain shaped like a miniature dream catcher, a pack of tissues. Would any of this help her figure out her tattoo? But then a flash of yellow in a side pocket caught her eye: a greeting card envelope. A birthday card? It couldn't be for Oona; she loathed yellow.

She slipped out the buttery envelope. Four capital letters were handwritten on it in black ink: *M.D.C.R.*

Her gaze ping-ponged from the envelope to her tattoo, from her mother's cursive to the permanent calligraphy on her wrist.

"I hope chamomile is okay." Madeleine came in with a steaming mug. "I put in extra—oh, shit." Hastily setting down the mug, she plucked the envelope out of Oona's fingers.

Her daughter stared at the space the yellow rectangle had occupied, hand still raised. "Sorry I went through your things, but . . . what's in the envelope?"

"I shouldn't have . . . I should've . . ."

"What's in the envelope, Mom?" In her head, a trickle of snowfall obscured logical thoughts, the cold white intensifying.

"A congratulations card." Madeleine slipped it back into her purse.

"For who? For what?"

"For Mackenzie. For winning an essay contest."

"Mackenzie who?"

Dread darkened her mother's eyes, and she spoke slowly, like she was inching along a narrow ledge. "Mackenzie Dale Charles Ray."

Her mental blizzard intensified, each gust of white blowing away half-formed questions.

"Let's sit." A guiding hand on Oona's arm, and she went from sitting to standing, from holding nothing to holding a mug of tea.

It was her only tattoo. She'd connected the hourglass and swirls of galaxies to Dale, but the initials had eluded her. Like an inept crossword solver, she'd always filled in the blanks incorrectly. Now Oona had the answer key. "Mackenzie. Dale. Charles. Ray."

"Yes." Beside her, Madeleine sat with her bag on her lap, tentative fingers hovering in the space between them.

"Mackenzie as in Kenzie?"

"Same person."

Perplexed, Oona asked, "Why would you not tell me he's my brother?"

"Because he's not your brother." There was a tremor in Madeleine's voice and a crease of dismay between her eyebrows.

"Then who is he?"

"Your son," said Madeleine.

Two syllables that spun the room sideways. If Oona's life had been a string of pearls, this would be when the thread snapped and they scattered. The mug in her hand shook. "There's no way I had a son. I've always been on birth control." The mug hit the coffee table with a clack as she set it down; tea sloshed over the sides. "I don't understand, how could—forget about the tea." She shooed away her mother's hand wiping at the spill.

"I just don't want it to stain the wood."

"You might want to reprioritize your list of things to worry about right about now." Oona massaged her jaw in a vain attempt to loosen it. Everything felt too tight: her clothes, her skin. Her skull a room with shrinking walls. "I . . . I don't even know where to start. I can't believe you've kept this from me. How could you betray me like that?"

"I never betrayed you, Oona. *You* were the one who decided to keep it a secret. Until he was older. Until you were ready. There was no way you could've raised a child with your—situation."

"I know!" Baffled anger clanged through Oona like a tower bell. "Hence the fucking birth control." The clanging quieted, replaced by a murmured mantra of four letters. *M.D.C.R.* The *D* stood for . . . "Dale. He was the father?"

Madeleine nodded like a bank teller in a holdup.

"Did I . . ." But there was no need to frame it as a question. "I got pregnant on purpose. Because I knew Dale would die. And since the band wouldn't be his legacy, this would be a way . . ."

"Part of him could live on." Madeleine's voice was full of tiptoes. "And once you knew your son as a grown man, it was inevitable you'd want to bring him into the world when you leaped back into your younger self."

I have a son. Dale's son.

"Kenzie was there in 2015 for my first leap."

A hint of relief, eyes brighter, Madeleine said, "He was? Oh, good. You intended for him to be part of your life after he was eighteen."

"No. You don't get to look happy about this." Her mother's face fell. "I thought he was my assistant! He never said anything about being my son—at most, a friend. Why didn't either of you tell me the truth?"

"I . . . I can't speak for something that hasn't happened yet."

"And what about when I met him in 2003? Why did he pretend not to know me? Was he even pretending?"

"Honey, none of this has happened yet, so I really don't know." She massaged her temples with her fingertips.

Unable to fully process the twisted timelines, she pressed on. "And where is he now?"

"A friend of mine adopted him. She even agreed to keep the name you gave him, provided he took her surname."

"How generous of her. What friend?"

"Nobody you'd remember. She moved out of New York when you were little."

"She's a lesbian, right?"

Madeleine dropped her hands. "That's right. How do you know that?"

"Kenzie told me he had two moms." Who'd both die in a few years. But Oona wouldn't make the same mistake again; she'd spare her mother this knowledge before it happened.

"They're taking great care of him."

"*Great care?*" Oona echoed with sarcasm. "Who are these women?" Dark clouds in her head. "Where do they live? Where is my son right now?"

"I can't tell you."

"Are you fucking serious?"

Madeleine recoiled and put a hand to her cheek. "We have an arrangement with them. I'm allowed to visit once a year under the guise of being a family friend, but he can't know about you until he's eighteen. I can assure you he's doing well. He's healthy. Happy. Thriving."

Thriving without me, his birth mother. Unaware his current mothers will be killed before he finishes college.

"He's . . . how old now?" Her head too muddled to line up the numbers.

"Fourteen. Fifteen in May. Born after Dale died." She gave her daughter a beseeching look. "You couldn't handle the leaping *and* being a mother. Plus, the grief over Dale—"

"What about the grief over intentionally having a kid only to give him away?"

"It wasn't easy. You learned one of the hardest lessons about being a mother early on: you have to put your child first. Your own happiness is less important."

It was a compliment like a piece of candy dusted with arsenic. Oona shook her head to refuse it. "Why couldn't *you* take him? Be more than a distant *family friend* to him."

"Oh, sweetie." A quiver in her voice. "It's not like I could've hidden him away from you. And there was no way of knowing what kind of impact your leaping would have on him. How could he grow up facing a different version of his mother every year? You wanted to protect him."

"And now I want to see him. Is he in New York?"

"No. I'm sorry, but you can't have any contact with him. The terms of the agreement—"

"You think I give a shit about any agreement right now? Show it to me, I'll tear it right up. I'll pay whatever fine—"

"It's more than a fine. You could go to jail. That wouldn't be good for you or your son."

"What would you know about it? You let me give away my own child and then lied about it for years. Stellar parenting there, Mom."

"Stop it," she snapped. "You *knew*. You knew Kenzie would grow up to be a fine man, because you'd seen the result. And when you gave birth however many leaps later, you knew he'd turn out well raised by others, hard as that was to accept."

Oona paused to consider the twisted logic of tangled timelines, her life like an M. C. Escher drawing, years like staircases turning in on themselves to form a tangible but implausible whole. She wanted to crumple that drawing and toss it aside. Get a blank sheet and create her own staircases instead of blindly ascending and descending steps already sketched out for her.

"You know what?" She held her mother's gaze, eyes and voice a flat sheet of ice. "I'm tired of accepting what Earlier Oona laid out for me. I've done it before and it fucking backfired. I'm sick of being treated like Present-Day Oona doesn't know what's best for her. And what's best for me right now is to see Kenzie. Now are you gonna tell me where he is?"

"I'm sorry, but I can't."

"Then *I'm* sorry, but you need to get out of my house."

Madeleine opened her mouth in slow motion but no words came. No sound at all as she stood, collected her things, and left.

The tea was tepid, but Oona gulped it anyway; it quelled the dryness in her throat, but not the ache. All this time spent missing Dale while part of him lived on, in secret. While her mother knew and said nothing. Yes, Madeleine was an easy target for her ire and betrayal—a betrayal that eclipsed Edward's, because this was a matter of blood—but she also had Earlier Oona to blame. How could she have abandoned Kenzie? It was confounding, this self-loathing for something she'd already done *and* had yet to do, like being a warped version of Schrödinger's cat.

Not warning herself of a doomed marriage was one thing, but hiding her own child from herself? Earlier Oona might've considered that to be sensible and wise, but this Oona wanted to tell her to fuck off, to beat the shit out of her, to punch and kick her to a bloody pulp.

Empty mug in hand, Oona reached back to throw it, aiming at the mantel. Except—there it was, the white envelope with her name on it. Her arm sagged.

"Fuck you . . . me . . ." she muttered.

Might as well see what her so-called sage self had to say.

Oona,

   Anger is a poison and forgiveness is the antidote.

"What kind of fortune-cookie bullshit is that?" she seethed.

   Of course, that's not going to help you right now. Your anger is totally justified. There's nothing I can tell you that'll make you understand certain choices I made. I keep thinking if I share some of the things I've learned, you won't have to learn them the hard way. Instead, trying to protect you often ends up making things more convoluted. So I'll keep it simple.

   In your top desk drawer is a plane ticket and a Post-it with an address.

   Kenzie is in Boston. More information awaits when you get there.

25

All Oona brought to Boston was a backpack, a small suitcase, and her guitar. The taxi dropped her off on a narrow cobblestone street in Beacon Hill lined with brick row homes. Snow dusted their black window shutters and old-fashioned gas lamps dotted the block. Picture-postcard perfect.

Is this where my son lives?

She matched the number on the door to the address on the Post-it. As she was about to ring the bell, she stopped, her finger an inch away from it.

What if Kenzie's life was as lovely and perfect as these homes? Could she really come stomping in amidst all this quiet charm? Could she cause such a disruption?

Then again, how could she *not* see her child? A child she had with her first—arguably *only*—love. However idyllic his home, however much he might be *thriving* under the upbringing of his adopted mothers, it was no substitute for his biological mom.

I'm doing a good thing here.

It shouldn't have required so much self-coaxing, but she rang the bell. Waited agonizing seconds before the door opened. A rotund rosy-

cheeked woman with wispy white hair and Ben Franklin–style eye-
glasses stood before her.

*Is this one of the women raising my son? She's old enough to be his grand-
mother. Older than his* actual *grandmother.*

Oona opened her mouth to deliver the impassioned speech she'd
silently practiced on the journey to Boston. All that came out was a
cloud of foggy breath.

"Oona, how lovely to see you. Happy New Year!" The woman drew
a shawl around herself against the cold, her face friendly, absent of
suspicion.

"Happy New Year," Oona echoed, though the phrase rang hollow.
Shocking New Year, more like. Bitter New Year.

"Come in, come in, it's nippy out there." She beckoned, opening the
door wider. "I've got your keys and paperwork close by."

Taking cautious steps, Oona set her bags and guitar case inside the
threshold.

Keys to what?

"How frightful, having your purse stolen. That's why I never ride
the subway when I visit New York. I'm glad you weren't hurt." She
sorted through a wicker basket on a side table in the foyer. "I changed
the locks as soon as I got your message. Now I know I put these keys in
here. Where are the darn things?" Jingling and rustling as she sifted
through odds and ends.

I have an apartment in Boston? Oona tried to remain quiet so she
could gradually piece together what was going on. But tempering her
impatience was tricky. "Do you . . ." Oona crafted the question as innoc-
uously as possible. "Do you know my mother, Madeleine Lockhart?" It
was unlikely, but she had to know if this woman was raising Kenzie.

"I'm afraid I don't." Her eyebrows scrunched together. "Do I look
like someone she knows? I get that a lot. I must have one of those faces."

"That must be it." Oona scraped her lower lip with her teeth.

"Ah, I remember what I did with them. I put them with the copy of
your lease in this drawer. Here we are." She held out a folded sheet of paper
and two shiny keys. "Now you *must* promise you'll be more careful."

"I will. Thank you. How much do I owe you for the locksmith?"

"You paid a year's rent up front, double what I would've charged for the place, so I won't accept an extra cent from you." A dismissive wave and firm shake of her head.

The address on the lease took Oona to a ground-floor apartment several doors down, a spacious one-bedroom decorated in black, white, and red—minimalist and modern. Many would've found the living space sterile, but Oona took comfort in its starkness.

Taped to the bathroom mirror was another letter.

Oona,

The situation with Kenzie is delicate. You must respect that he's being raised by caring, responsible women, Shivani and Faye, who are terrific parents. You must also be aware of a legal agreement in place with them. It includes terms akin to a restraining order. You're not allowed to contact Kenzie before he turns eighteen. But now that you know he's your son, I'm sure nothing will stop you from seeing him, so I've come up with a way for you to do so.

After school on Mondays, Wednesdays, and Fridays, Kenzie goes to High Strung, a coffee shop/record store, to do his homework.

At the end of 1998, I secured us this apartment so you could visit High Strung and see your son (he should be back from winter break in a few days). Three afternoons a week might not seem like a lot, but it was the best I could do.

Obviously, you can't tell him you're his birth mother. Maybe say you're a BU grad student. You may even want to use a different name and change up your look. If he or one of his adopted moms finds out who you are, the situation could blow up and hurt Kenzie. Before you consider telling him the truth or whisking him across state lines, remember the wonderful man he'll grow up to be, raised by Faye and Shivani. He has only a few years left with them—you'll be part of his life much longer than that. Plus, they have nearly fifteen years of experience parenting him—you have none (sorry if that's harsh). Just don't do anything extreme.

Even though I haven't been able to change my fate, I'll always wonder if it's possible. If I've already done it without seeing evidence of it yet. But playing fast and loose with my destiny is one thing. Now you need to take your son into consideration. His future is bound up with yours, so tread lightly for his sake.

Good luck,
Me

P.S. If you want to get on a fast track to bonding with Kenzie, remember Kate Bush.

Oona set aside the letter, her head pounding. She checked the medicine cabinet for aspirin. It was empty except for a box of black hair dye.

I have to pretend to be someone else to see my own son? What the fuck?

Grabbing the box of Clairol, she considered tossing it into the waste bin. Instead, she slumped down on the lip of the bathtub.

She twisted the ring on her middle finger, its message a liar. Anger did not equal energy. It was an anchor pulling her down. Oona was tired of being angry. So very tired.

It was too much, taking on these different roles, stepping into Earlier Oona's shoes. Girlfriend, Club Kid, investor, wife, world traveler . . . and now she was a mother. No role was more daunting than that. Even if she had to hide her true identity from Kenzie, she felt a massive responsibility to do right by him. But what was the right thing to do here?

It wasn't enough for Madeleine to say Kenzie was doing well; Oona had to see it for herself. To see what his life was like without her. To see if there was any way she could be part of his life now, lay a foundation for when he went from having three mothers to one. Developing a rapport would take time. Considering he was a teenage boy and she was a grown woman, her options were limited; she had to be careful, make sure her bonding efforts weren't perceived as creepy or weird. All things 1998 Oona had figured out and tried to safeguard against.

She held up the box of Clairol and sighed. *Okay, Earlier Oona. We'll try it your way.*

Monday afternoon, as Oona stepped through the entrance to High Strung, she felt she was entering a strange high-stakes costume party.

Between the black hair dye and closet full of black clothes left for her, she'd figured a goth ensemble was in order. The combat boots were already giving her blisters, but at least she had her trusty leather jacket to complete the look, providing some armor.

The smell of coffee greeted her, warm and invigorating.

High Strung was an open space with low ceilings papered in overlapping music posters. Along the right wall were racks of alphabetized used CDs, and the back wall held crates of used records, with higher-end collector's items displayed above them. A long low counter ran the length of the left side, the coffee machines in the front, register at the back. Mismatched chairs and wooden tables covered in graffiti and stickers dotted the space in between.

At the register, a greasy-haired college-age guy in a Marilyn Manson T-shirt argued with a twenty-something woman with black lipstick and cherry-red hair twisted into two buns.

"You wanna maybe stop shouting at me and help that customer?"

"You wanna maybe stop getting high on your lunch break?" The woman spotted Oona and hurried to the front counter. "Sorry about that. What can I get you?"

A stiff smile as Oona approached. "Large soy latte, please."

"Soy?"

"Sorry, that's not a thing yet. Large chai?"

"You got it."

After she paid for her drink, Oona chose a table facing the door and spread out her props—textbooks, highlighters, pens, and a spiral-bound notebook.

What am I doing? As she pretended to study, Oona tried to picture a teenage Kenzie doing homework at a neighboring table. As an adult, he hadn't told her much about his early life. Did he get good grades? Play any sports? Have lots of friends? Was he close with his adopted mothers? And what did he look like now? Would she recognize him? Would she love him?

An hour later, while Oona was at the counter ordering a second chai, the barista called out to someone behind her, "Look who's back!

If it isn't Mr. Mackenzie Ray. How's it going, Mack? You have a good winter break?"

Mack?

Oona turned and snuck a peek at her son. He held traces of the man he'd become, the young man she met years ago—in the eyes and mouth—but there was also a roundness to his features. A leftover layer of baby fat masked the cheekbones that would emerge as he grew taller and slimmer. The hair that he'd go on to experiment with was currently a brown wavy mop grazing his chin. If she looked closely, she could see a bit of Dale around the eyes and nose, but none of herself.

"Yeah, my moms took me on a surprise trip to London, which was awesome."

His voice, a few notes higher than its eventual timbre, was distinctly Kenzie, but the sight of him offered only vague hints of familiarity. If she saw this boy on the street, she might've walked right by, unaware she'd given birth to him. Oona felt a stab of dull pain at the thought.

"Ooh, London is wicked," the barista gushed. "When we visit my father's family in Manchester, we always try to squeeze in a few days there."

Eyes wide, he held up both hands and stepped back. "Whoa, Daphne. You're part British? I'm shocked 'cause it's not like you've mentioned it a hundred times before."

"Okay, okay, no need to be a smartass." A loud hiss as Daphne turned on the milk steamer. "So what was the best part of your trip?"

As if sleepwalking, Oona shuffled sideways to let Kenzie step forward, trying not to gawk at her son.

"Oh, the Tower of London, easy. The tour guide was in, like, Shakespearean costume, and he showed us where Anne Boleyn was *beheaded*. I thought the history stuff might be boring, but those Tudors . . . man, they were messed up."

Daphne chuckled. "Here's your chai." When Kenzie went to grab it, she swatted his hand out of the way. "That one's not for you." She slid the paper cup toward Oona with an apologetic smile. "Sorry, that's all he drinks."

"Yeah, sorry." Kenzie gave Oona a bashful half-smile.

Does he recognize me? Does he see a resemblance?

But there was nothing behind his eyes beyond blank politeness. Pointing to her hand, he said, "I like your ring."

Mouth dry, Oona was desperate to say something clever, but her tongue stuck to the roof of her mouth, her mind blanked, and she could do no more than mumble, "Thanks." As Daphne prepared Kenzie's chai, the two continued to banter, and Oona retreated to her table. She blinked away tears that threatened to ruin her thick mascara, catching a few salty stragglers with the knuckle of her forefinger.

It's just the initial shock of seeing him. I'm sure I'll find a way to talk to him later.

But her determination evaporated as the afternoon wore on. It took all her energy and focus just to pretend-study, hold back tears, and remember to breathe. Building a rapport with her son—even talking to him—was a mountain she was too winded to climb.

Meanwhile, when she wasn't bickering with the cashier, Daphne and Kenzie continued to lob quips, he from behind a nearby table strewn with books (just as Oona had pictured it), she from behind the counter. Their exchanges sounded progressively further away.

It wasn't until Kenzie packed up his things, put on his coat, waved to Daphne, and left, that it pierced into her, the truth an arrow and her heart the bull's-eye.

I'm a stranger to him.

26

Over the next week, Oona tried to settle into her new life in Boston. When not at High Strung, she took long walks around the city, read books, played her guitar, and had long imaginary conversations with her teenage son. She mentally tried out different parental versions: the cool mom, the strict mom, the doting mom. It made her wonder what kind of mother she would've been if she hadn't abandoned him; what kind of mother she could still be to him. These imaginary conversations always ended with Oona revealing who she was and Kenzie overcoming his shock to accept her into his life. They were far friendlier than the actual terse, brief conversations she had with her mother.

Oona phoned her using a calling card to ensure an untraceable number and named a different city each time Madeleine asked where she was. Neither one mentioned Kenzie. Did her mother know what Oona was really up to? Would she try to stop her? Had she warned Shivani? Hopefully Madeleine would stay out of it.

There were too many empty hours to fill in between visits to the coffee shop/record store, but that problem was solved one afternoon in mid-January.

As Oona entered High Strung, Daphne rushed by with a flyer in one hand and roll of Scotch tape in the other. She dropped the tape and both of them bent down to get it, banging heads together.

"Sorry," they said in unison.

"I'm having the day from hell," Daphne said. Her eyes grew wet and she fanned herself with the flyer—a help-wanted poster—to keep from crying. "Let me just put this in the window and I'll make your chai."

"What kind of help are you looking for?" Oona asked.

"A cashier. Preferably one who doesn't show up so stoned he can't work. Who doesn't quit and walk out on a day *nobody* can take an extra shift. At this point, I'd hire anyone familiar with a register."

"I know how to use a register. Maybe not this exact one, but I worked at a drugstore a while back." Not that she needed the money, but she needed more to do. "I love music, I don't smoke pot, and I could start right now."

Daphne looked her up and down with cautious curiosity. "What's your name?"

"Um . . . Nancy." A mental scramble to create a fake last name. "Nancy Jones."

"All right, Nancy." She gave a what-the-hell shrug. "Help me get through today without any major fuckups, and you're hired."

In between serving customers, Daphne gave Oona a quickie training session. When Kenzie came in later, Daphne was too busy to chat, but did introduce "Nancy" to him (*He still doesn't know my real name*). Work was a welcome distraction from thinking about her son nonstop. By the end of the day, Oona proved herself worthy, and Daphne offered her the cashier position.

In the weeks following, Oona was attentive to customers, kept the inventory organized, and perfectly balanced the cash drawer. She got used to being on her feet all day. She got used to being alone at night. She got used to her new name.

She did not get used to seeing Kenzie.

All the earnest and heartfelt internal monologues she composed, the cute or clever one-liners—every word vanished the moment her son came into High Strung. The confidence and cautious optimism she'd built up crumbled like a sandcastle beneath a tsunami. She could do little more than wave or say hello or offer tight little smiles.

What she learned about him came from observation and eavesdropping. He was a decent student (B+ average), wrote album reviews for the school paper, and was on the debate team. He sometimes brought friends to High Strung, classmates that ranged from quirky to nerdy to alternative. He spoke well about Shivani and Faye, though he grumbled about them bugging him to bring up his science grades and being overprotective.

There was no denying what Madeleine had reported. He was healthy. Happy. Thriving.

While she'd come to Boston believing her presence would improve Kenzie's life, the more she saw him, the more her self-doubt grew. How could she be sure her words or actions wouldn't do him harm? She was the butterfly flapping her wings with the best intentions, but what if she brought on hurricanes and tornadoes?

That's what kept her from speaking to him, following him, or asking Daphne about him.

As January neared to a close, Oona's uncertainty and paralysis around Kenzie had become routine—until one Wednesday afternoon.

She was going through a plastic bag full of used CDs someone had donated when the bag tore and a CD fell behind the counter before she could grab it. Oona bent to pick it up: on the cover, a brunette in blue jeans and red boots hugged a knee to her chest. Kate Bush. Of course.

Before any second thoughts could waylay her, Oona took the disc over to the stereo and replaced the Portishead album she'd been playing.

Silence followed by whale sounds replaced with a tinkling piano and high clear singing, an undulating melody like a flowing stream.

Kenzie put his pen down and lifted his head, squinting at Oona. "What's this music? Kinda sounds like a Tori Amos wannabe."

"Don't you dare," Oona hissed.

A flicker of surprise at her vehemence. "Hey, I like Tori. It's a compliment."

"Oh no, it's not. This"—she pointed to the ceiling—"is Kate Bush and she was *first*. *The Kick Inside* came out over a decade before *Little Earthquakes*." Oona pressed her palms on the counter like she might vault over it. "Kate Bush influenced and paved the way for singers like your precious Tori. Who's good, don't get me wrong. But Kate is *superb* and criminally underrated." Her skin tingled as heat spread through her chest, up her neck. "I'm surprised you don't already love her considering—" She stopped short of forecasting his music tastes. "Considering you spend so much time in a record store."

Maybe there is *something I can give him. Something nobody else can.*

Kenzie sat back, eyebrows as high as they could go, and shot Daphne a look. "How come *you* never played any Kate Bush?" he asked her.

"I like boy singers better than girl singers." Daphne offered a no-big-deal shrug. "Nick Cave, Tom Waits, that sort of thing."

"In other words, you like singers who sound like they're gonna kill you in your sleep if they don't drink themselves to death first," said Oona. She glanced at Kenzie, who was holding back a laugh.

Instead of getting defensive, Daphne raised her hands in an answered-prayer pose. "*Finally.*"

"What?" Oona asked.

"I was starting to think you'd never show any personality. Whew." An exaggerated swipe of her forehead with the back of her hand. "You want a chai?"

"I'd love one, actually." Shifting her weight to one foot, Oona put a hand on her hip. "If that drink has enough *personality* for you." Kenzie's low chuckle nearly made her lose her balance. There was an inherent satisfaction in making anyone laugh, but when it was your own kid? It felt like a superpower. "As for *you*, mister," she said to him, "for all your studying, you clearly need more of a music education. You think this album is good? Wait until you hear *Hounds of Love*. The second half of it—'The Ninth Wave'—is gonna blow your mind."

She shot him a wink and checked the floor. Nope, she wasn't levitating. But she still felt like she was defying gravity.

Sure, it was cheating, since Oona remembered a lot of Kenzie's future favorites (or was she shaping them?). But it was the bridge she needed.

The weeks that followed marked a series of "lessons." Kate Bush 101. Elements of Patti Smith. Introduction to Cocteau Twins. Fundamentals of PJ Harvey. She gradually wove in the handful of male-fronted bands she knew he enjoyed, including Pink Floyd and Roxy Music. He already had some foundational knowledge in Stevie Nicks and Suzanne Vega and, of course, Tori Amos, but there was much more she could teach him. At least when it came to music.

But would that be their only shared language? Their exchanges rarely meandered into the personal, what with his friends around some days and homework he semi-cared about vying for attention on others.

A few weeks later, it got more personal.

Kenzie came into High Strung alone on a Wednesday in February. At first he was bent over a textbook, but after an hour, he closed it, pushed his chair back, and glanced at Oona, who'd been watching but pretending not to watch.

"*The Wall*, right?" A finger pointed up to indicate the music.

"That's right."

"I like *Dark Side of the Moon* better." Before the conversation turned into a debate, Kenzie asked, "So did you get into music from working in record stores and stuff?"

"I, uh . . . Not really. I guess my mom got me into it. Pink Floyd and Velvet Underground, at least." She stopped short of telling him about the band she'd played in.

"I wish my moms were into cool bands like that."

"What do they listen to?"

"More mellow, folky stuff like Joni Mitchell—who's okay, I guess—and Neil Young." Kenzie made a gagging noise. "I don't know how I'm gonna convince them to let me see Garbage next week. Faye's working second shift and Shivani freaks out in big crowds. Like, Faye is a huge hockey fan, but I always have to go to Bruins games with her because the one time Shivani went to the Fleet Center, she had a panic attack in practically five minutes."

Oona's ears perked at his dilemma, but better not to pounce. "Is that where Garbage is playing? The Fleet Center?"

"Yeah." Eyes down, he doodled in a notebook and squirmed. "I got two tickets when they first went on sale before asking for permission. I figured I'd be able to talk Faye into taking me, but then her schedule changed, and I haven't come up with another plan." A heavy sigh and pout. "I can't wait until I'm old enough to do stuff whenever I want. Like, I wish I could be twenty-one *tomorrow*, so I could go to bars and concerts and clubs."

"You don't wish that. Trust me. But I understand wanting to be independent," Oona said. "You'll have lots of time to do those things. You'll also have a bunch of responsibilities you don't have to worry about right now. Plus, when you're older, you're only gonna wish you were younger."

Kenzie rolled his eyes. "I'm gonna wish I'm the only gay kid in my grade *and* the only kid I know with two lesbian moms? I'm gonna wish they nagged me about getting good grades and being true to myself, and telling them where I am every second of the day?"

"Well, maybe not that first part, but the rest of it? Believe it or not, yeah. When you're older, you'll look at it differently. Not as nagging as much as your mothers taking care of you. Being good moms." Her breath caught. "It's easy to take that for granted. You'll get more perspective when you're older."

"I have lots of perspective now. Being a teenager is a pain in the ass. Sometimes I feel like I'm already an old dude on the inside waiting for my outside to catch up."

She let out a startled laugh. "I'm the opposite. Every year, I feel too old on the outside. Then again, I don't know what a thirty-something person is supposed to feel like. All I can do is make the most of whatever age I am. It's not like you have a choice, right?"

Narrowing his eyes, he gave a reluctant nod. "I guess. That still doesn't solve what I'm gonna do about this Garbage show. I really wanna go."

"If only you could find a responsible grown-up with awesome music taste to take you . . ." A toe in the water to check his reaction.

He shot a sneaky (hopeful?) look her way. "If only."

"Someone who not only appreciates Garbage, but who'd also introduce you to Curve, a band that does the fierce female electronica thing even better—and who did it first."

A groan as he slid down in his seat. "Seriously? You're going to turn this into another lesson?"

"Do you want a chaperone for this show or not?" Mental note to pull back on the musicology so he didn't tire of it—or her.

"What I want is for my moms to stop treating me like I'm a little kid, but that'll probably never happen."

Since he'd gotten more personal, Oona braved asking, "Why do you call your mothers by their first names?"

"We tried doing Mama F and Mama S, but they sound too similar. I still call them my moms, though." He turned big hopeful eyes on her. "So about this concert . . ."

"I may have an idea . . ." *Why did I say that? I have no idea. But I don't want to let him down.*

"I hope it's a good one because I'll die if I can't go."

"Can't go where?" A long-limbed forty-something blonde strode up to Kenzie. Her short spiky hair and green coat gave her the air of an elegant cactus.

"Since when do you come get me?" Kenzie asked. "I'm usually waiting around the hospital for you to finish up."

"Scheduling mix-up had too many of us on first shift, so they sent me home early. Now why do you think you're going to die?"

"Garbage," he mumbled, stuffing his textbook into his book bag.

"What garbage? What's gotten into you, Mack? Did something happen at school?"

"He means the band Garbage," Oona said. She should've run into the stock room, hid until they both left, just in case. But she stood there, trancelike.

This woman has been raising my son. She knows him better than I do.

"Are you Nancy?" the woman asked.

"I am." After nearly two months, it was still odd responding to an alias.

"I'm Faye. Mack has been raving about all the great music you've turned him onto." Faye's arm stretched practically halfway across the room to shake hands. "I can't say it's my taste, but then what teenager likes the same music as his mother?"

I did. Kenzie does.

"He may not share your taste in music, but he's the only teenager I've come across who actually gets along with his parents and speaks highly of them." A lie to butter her up as a plan began to jell in her mind. "And I understand why you and Shivani would be so cautious—I should've consulted you both before I even offered the tickets." Two beats to let Faye's confusion build, then Oona continued. "I'm friends with some record promoters, and they give me concert tickets once in a while. Ken— Mack mentioned how much he loves Garbage, so I called in a favor and got him two tickets for their show at the Fleet Center next week."

A long breath drawn in, but Faye didn't shoot down the idea. "Is this on a school night?"

Kenzie saw the opening and raced to it. "It's on Monday, but I'd come here and do *all* my homework beforehand."

"But you know I—"

"I know you're working second shift, and I know Shivani can't do the Fleet. But Nancy could take me. And make sure I get home okay." Pleading eyes zigzagged between the two women.

"You can't inconvenience Nancy like that." Dismay in the corners of her mouth. "Dragging her to a concert in the North End and making her drop you off in the Back Bay after."

"He wouldn't be dragging me, not at all." She flashed her best you-can-trust-me smile. "I'm a fan of the band and was planning to go, anyway. And I live in Beacon Hill, so getting him home is no inconvenience, really."

Faye's apprehension receded, but only a few degrees. "It's very nice of you to offer. I know Mack adores you and would be thrilled to go, but . . . I just met you." She turned to Kenzie. "And you *know* Shivani would want to meet Nancy if she was going to let you go—big *if*." Back to Oona. "What if you came over for dinner so we could get to know you a little better? That would give me a better shot of talking Shivani into this scheme. We don't even have to bring up the concert. It could just be a dinner to thank you for letting Mack use your employee discount on all those CDs."

Oona hadn't wanted Kenzie to pay for them at all, but she'd fudged the numbers and paid the difference out of pocket.

"Are you free tomorrow night?" Faye's smile was expectant.

Meeting face-to-face with Shivani? Impossible. How could Oona be sure she wouldn't be recognized?

But what if this was her only chance to segue into a true friendship with Kenzie? Besides, that beseeching look in her son's eyes made it impossible to say no.

"Dinner tomorrow would be lovely."

What the hell am I doing?

27

Thursday night, Oona stood before a gray townhouse on Commonwealth Avenue.

No, really, what the hell am I doing?

She could forgo the dinner, skip the concert, remain acquaintances with her son for the rest of the year. It would be a sliver of the relationship she wanted, but better than nothing. Which is what she could end up with if her cover was blown tonight.

At least she'd see how he lived. And maybe the evening would go smoothly. Yet as she rang the doorbell, Oona couldn't escape the feeling she was in a car with no brakes, traveling full speed down an icy hill.

Kenzie opened the door. "What's up, Nance? You mind if I call you Nance?"

A fake name was bad, a fake nickname somehow worse. But she hid her cringe. "Of course not. I brought dessert. Éclairs." She held out a bakery box tied up with red string.

"Nice. Those are my favorite." He waved her inside.

I know.

"You can hang up your coat over— *Whoa*. You sure you're not gonna get arrested?" His eyes bulged out.

A sickened whoosh went through her. "What do you mean?"

"The pink." He pointed to her cardigan. "Aren't the goth police gonna, like, arrest you for wearing a color?"

"I just wanted to look nice for dinner." She glanced past him at a living room decorated in pastel tones with warm, homey touches: family photos, velvet throw pillows, potted plants. "Do you *not* want me to make a good impression with your mothers?"

"Yeah, okay." A sheepish nod and his face lit up. "Hey, did you hear Blondie is playing the Orpheum in May?"

"Funny, I was planning to play *Parallel Lines* for you tomorrow." On the one hand, this additional musical connection made her feel closer to him. On the other, now she had one less thing to teach him.

"Oh, I have all of Blondie's stuff. I kinda started listening because I read somewhere Deborah Harry is also adopted, but then I really got into the music, too. Anyway, if everything works out with the Garbage concert—"

"Was that the— Oh, hello." A petite Indian woman with a round face and a thick braid down to her waist came into the hallway. "Sorry, I had the blender going, so I wasn't sure if I heard the bell. You must be Nancy. I'm Shivani."

They shook hands, Oona hoping her smile read more affable, less terrified.

Shivani cocked her head. "Have we met before? There's something familiar about you . . ."

Well, shit. "Oh, um—I mean—" A bead of sweat ran down Oona's spine as she stumbled over her words. "You've probably seen me at High Strung."

"No, that is not it, Faye picks him up there because she works nearby. But I could swear . . ." Another searching look and Oona held her breath until Shivani shrugged. "I must be thinking of somebody else. Come on through." She led them down a hall with several closed doors, lined with more family photos.

He's smiling in all of these. He's been given a good life. I doubt I could've done better. Resisting the impulse to snatch the pictures off the walls and examine them more closely, Oona forced herself to keep walking. *I don't have a single picture of Kenzie.*

"I'm just putting the finishing touches on the soup," said Shivani. "I hope you like gazpacho."

"Who doesn't like cold soup when it's thirty degrees out?" Kenzie cracked.

A light swat on his shoulder and Shivani smirked. "Hey, mister, the last time I checked you loved my cold soup."

"Yeah, yeah." Kenzie turned to Oona. "She's right, I do."

"My mom also has a thing for cold soup in the winter." Oona's admission elicited another inquisitive look from Shivani as they reached the dining room. *Change the subject.* "Your home is so pretty."

Shivai offered a low chuckle. "That's Faye's doing. She has never met a knickknack or throw pillow she didn't like."

"Nancy, welcome." Faye set down a breadbasket and waved from the other side of a round oak table. "Please sit anywhere you like."

"Thanks for having me over."

"Nancy brought éclairs for dessert." Bragging as if Kenzie played a part in their appearance.

Shivani took the bakery box from him. "I guess I'll just have to take that carrot cake I made to work." Her eyes twinkled with mischief.

"Aw, come on, you know carrot cake is my *other* favorite dessert," he pleaded.

"I have an idea," Faye said. "Why don't we just skip the soup and roast chicken and go right to dessert?"

"As if you'd ever let me be so happy." Kenzie slumped into a chair beside Oona.

Taking the bakery box from Shivani, Faye said, "Hon, you've been going nonstop, have a seat."

"But I need to—"

"I'll get the gazpacho. Just sit and relax."

So much communicated in the smile they shared as Shivani sat on Oona's other side: teamwork underpinned by tenderness, understanding, love. And all of it would be gone too soon, wiped out in a tragic accident.

Once Faye left, Shivani turned to Oona. "Sorry if we seem a little frazzled. We're used to eating together most nights, and with Faye's schedule changing—"

"Mom! It's only for a week." An epic eye roll from Kenzie. "You're acting as if she's going to Antarctica for the next year."

"You know how families have their little routines." Shivani offered Oona an apologetic smile.

"I understand." *I wish.* "So Mack told me Faye's a hospital administrator, but he didn't mention what you do for a living."

"That's because my job involves feet, which my son thinks is 'the grossest thing ever.' I'm a podiatrist. I work in the Brookline Foot and Ankle Center."

My son. Oona's polite expression faltered.

Shivani's eyes sparked with a fresh idea. "Nancy, have you ever come in for treatment there? Perhaps that is where I have seen you?"

"Nope, I've never had any problems with my feet or ankles." *God, I hope this disguise holds up.*

"Ugh, we're about to eat here. Can we please not talk about feet?" Kenzie made retching sounds as he tore into a bread roll.

"See what I mean?" A weary chuckle. "So what about you, Nancy? How long have you been working at the record store?"

"Record-store-slash-coffee-shop." Half mumbled through a mouthful of bread.

Dale also talked with his mouth full. Is that sort of thing hereditary?

"Please finish chewing your food before speaking," Shivani admonished him.

Before Oona could reply, Faye returned carrying a porcelain soup tureen and announced, "Soup's on! Literally."

Kenzie and Shivani let out synchronized groans.

"Every time, Faye? Every time?" Mock exasperation from Shivani.

"Don't pretend you don't love it." Another secret smile and Faye came over to serve her gazpacho.

"Hey, Nancy, I forgot to tell you about this cool CD I found at Planet

Records." Kenzie waved his hands around animatedly, as if conducting an invisible orchestra comprised of his thoughts. *Something else Dale used to do.* "Sorry, I know they're the competition, but I thought the cover was cool and the guy at the store said it was rare. Candy Stranger. You ever hear of her?"

"I haven't," Oona said. "And it's okay, you're allowed to shop in other record stores."

"She was some kind of eighties one-hit wonder in Europe, but she sings in English. Always wore masks when she performed, so nobody knows what she looked like. Kind of a wacko, but the whole album is *really* good."

Faye came around to Oona with the tureen. "Here you go," she said, drawing up a brimming ladle.

As she navigated it over Oona's bowl, Kenzie knocked over his water glass.

Faye missed the bowl and poured soup down Oona's pink sweater.

"Oh crap, I'm so sorry."

"It's fine. It wasn't hot soup." Oona dabbed at the stains with a linen napkin.

Scrambling to her feet, Shivani said, "Here, why don't you take that off and I'll put it in the wash. It'll be dry by the time we're done with dessert."

Oona took off the sweater. The soup had seeped through to her black dress underneath, so she pulled up the sleeve to wipe off her clammy skin.

Kenzie spotted Oona's tattoo. "Cool ink! What does *M.D.C.R.* mean?"

There was a tap on Oona's shoulder. When she looked up, Shivani was staring at her, stone-faced. "I wonder if I could speak with you in the other room for a moment, *Nancy*."

Oh fuck.

"What's the problem?" Faye asked, still holding the gazpacho.

"God, Mom, it's just a tattoo. It's not like Nancy's in a biker gang." Exasperation tinged his voice as he took another peek at Oona's wrist. "*M.D.C.R.* . . . those are my initials."

The tureen slipped from Faye's hands, spilled red across the table. Kenzie knocked his chair over as he stood to avoid getting soup on him.

The ruined sweater shook in Shivani's hand as she held it back out to Oona. "I think you should leave."

"What's going on?" Kenzie asked.

"Mack, could you give us a minute? We need to have a word with your friend." Faye put her hands on his shoulders to steer him away, but he ducked out of her grasp.

If she left now, Oona could prevent further potential damage. But she stood rooted in place. "I'm sorry. I couldn't stay away once I found out."

Something hardened behind Shivani's eyes as her mouth became a flat line, but there was also a glint of fear, vulnerability. "What nerve you have to come here, trying to fool us."

Faye took a step toward Oona. "I'm sorry, but you need to go now. Madeleine should've told you—"

"What does Aunt Madeleine have to do with this?" Kenzie asked.

"You call her *Aunt Madeleine*?" Bitter injustice coursed through her.

"She's not really my aunt, she's—"

"Your *grandmother*." The words a runaway train barreling off their track. Oona turned to Kenzie. "Madeleine is your grandmother. Madeleine is also my mother. My name isn't Nancy Jones. It's Oona Lockhart. I'm your birth mother." Why wasn't it more of a relief to confess? Why did it hurt so much?

"I could have you arrested for this," Shivani said.

But Oona continued. "I named you Mackenzie. Except I think of you as Kenzie, not Mack. The *D* in your name is for Dale, your birth father. The *C* stands for Charles, my father."

Kenzie's gaze shifted between the three women, like watching a confusing, gory tennis match. "I don't understand. I thought nobody knew who my mother was. Some policeman found me in a diner bathroom."

"This is the garbage you've been telling him about me?"

"We needed to tell him something." Her voice cold and brittle, Shivani gave Kenzie a beseeching look. "We were going to tell you the truth when you turned eighteen."

He folded his arms across his chest. "How about you tell me the fucking truth now?"

"Language," Faye said.

"Are you serious?" A look of disgust as he shook his head first at Faye, then at Oona. "So you're not Nancy? Your name is Oona, and you're my mother?"

"Your biological mom, yeah. Your father died before I gave birth to you and I couldn't . . . I also have a condition . . . it affects my memory. I swear, I don't even remember putting you up for adoption. I wasn't able to raise you. And I wasn't supposed to find out about you so soon."

"Did Madeleine tell you?" Shivani gripped her braid with both hands, her knuckles white.

"No." Despite her earlier anger toward her mother, Oona felt an unexpected urge to protect her. "She had nothing to do with this."

Backing away until he was pressed against a china hutch, Kenzie's eyes grew round and his mouth trembled. "Do you even know how fucked up this is? What am I supposed to believe here? Everyone lied to me. *You*"—a hand waved between Faye and Shivani—"lied to me about my birth mother. You've known who she is all along but didn't tell me." An accusing finger at Oona. "And you made up a name and dressed all gothy, so—what?—you could spy on me? Teach me about music and become my friend? Were you even gonna take me to the Garbage concert or just try to kidnap me?"

"Of course I was going to take you to the concert."

"And then what? Lean over before the encore and go, 'Oh, by the way, I gave birth to you'?" Tears streaked his face.

Seeing Kenzie cry unmoored Oona's own tears. "I just wanted to know you. Be part of your life."

"You picked a creepy-ass way to do it. And this memory condition bullshit? I mean—you're nuts. You have to be nuts." A look to Shivani and Faye to back him up. "She's nuts, right? That's why she couldn't raise me. And the legal thing is some kind of restraining order? Shouldn't one of you be calling the cops right now?"

"As a matter of fact, we should," Faye said. "But we'll give Oona here a chance to leave on her own before we involve the authorities."

But the thought of leaving now was unbearable. "Please, you don't have to—"

"*Enough*." The word a shaky growl out of Shivani. "You must go now."

Shivani and Faye blocked her from Kenzie, the three of them gaping at her in unified horror, as if she were holding them hostage, wielding a deadly weapon. Anguish ripped through Oona as she pleaded, "If only we could all just sit down for a few minutes and—"

"Get the fuck out of here!" Kenzie's high-pitched holler caused Oona to stumble back. "And stay the hell away from me. I have two mothers. I don't need a third one. You're a stranger. You're nobody."

Another step back and another until she turned and fled the vitriol of his words, the loathing in his eyes.

Oona thought nothing could surpass the humiliation Edward had dealt her, but this indignity before her own son made her feel even smaller, plunged her to a new depth of shame and despair. Astonishing how, no matter how far you fall, there's always lower to go.

How many blocks did she walk before the streets became foreign to her? She'd left her stained sweater behind. Not that she'd go back to that house. Or High Strung. Or even her Beacon Hill apartment. This was over.

Oona flagged down a taxi. "Logan Airport, please."

Boston was over.

It was close to midnight when Oona returned to Brooklyn. Her mother was waiting on her front stoop.

"Can we do this tomorrow, please?" How could Oona have any tears left? So dry inside, so empty. Yet her eyes blurred and a fresh sob threatened at the back of her throat. "I can't do this right now."

"You don't have to do anything, my darling. Come here." Madeleine put her arms around her daughter. "Shh, shh." She tried to quiet Oona's low wailing. "Give me your keys, let's go inside."

Slow heavy footsteps to the kitchen. She slumped in a chair as Madeleine put the kettle on.

"I guess Shivani called you."

"She did. They won't press any charges but asked me to forgo my annual visit."

Eyes trained on the counter, Oona asked, "Is there any way for me to fix this?"

"Not until after they die."

An anguished jolt of her head. "You know about that?"

Madeleine stood with a spoon pointed at the ceiling, chewed on her lower lip. "You never told me how or exactly when, but you let it slip that they die when he's in college. Kenzie will come back to you then. He'll need you then."

"But he won't, not right away. And he doesn't need me now. Because he has two other mothers. Who know how to be good parents, which I clearly do not." The words wooden, trancelike.

"If it's any consolation, no parent really knows what they're doing. We're all faking it to some extent." A kind smile. "But, my dear, I have no doubt you'll be a wonderful mother to him when he's ready to have you in his life."

"When he's fully grown. And the years until then—"

"Until then, let him go. Let him be angry with you. Let him get over it. Give him these years with two women who love him like he's their own flesh and blood. It's what he needs most right now." The kettle whistled and Madeleine turned away to prepare the tea, a tremor in her shoulders.

Let him be angry with you.

That's why he was so tense when she met him in 2003. All that pent-up anger for his mother wasn't directed at Faye or Shivani. It was Oona. Years from now, after the women who raised him died, he wouldn't be able to spend more than a few uncomfortable hours with his birth mother before running away to Asia.

"Every time I try to change things for the better, I end up ruining them," Oona said in a low monotone. "No wonder I stopped warning myself. It's not like I ever pay attention. I end up doing what I want, anyway. But the way I hurt Kenzie tonight, I—I never want to hurt anyone like that again. Especially not my son." Bracing herself for another wave of pain, she let out a short breath when it didn't come. If only she could remain this numb indefinitely. "I never listen. But I'll listen to you, Mom. If this is what my son needs—if the only thing I can give him right now is . . . *my absence* . . . okay." A sensation like something precious was torn out of her and scattered to the wind. Like that night in 2003 infinitely magnified. "I'll stay away. I'll listen to you."

How many cups of tea had Madeleine served her, how many times had she consoled her? Whatever the year, whatever Oona's transgression, her mother was always there to forgive and soothe. The least Oona could do was heed her wisdom once in a while.

The rest of the year stretched out, unpromising, an uneventful blur. Time would be her penance and she'd serve it.

Oona kept her pact to have no contact with her son, with one exception. When his birthday approached that May, she mailed him her platinum ring with the elongated wings. The same one he'd wear in 2003. She included the same short note she'd left herself. Her anger had left her burnt, but his wouldn't; he would soar.

When New Year's Eve came, it would be the first time she'd actually wish to leap to a future year in her timeline, to be reunited with Kenzie. And she'd get exactly what she wanted.

Well, maybe not *exactly*.

PART VIII

Wish You Were Here

2017: 53/25

28

Quiet. Dim lighting. A tightness at her sides. Oona came to in a plush chair, elbows wedged between the armrests as if glued to them. She blinked to get her bearings. Was she home? Yes, in one of the guest rooms.

A thirty-something man leaned over her. He wore a furry green vest over a black turtleneck. Hair like a white bird's nest, big brown eyes filled with worry.

"Kenzie!" She wrapped her arms around him tightly.

Thank you.

"Whoa, easy, I think I heard a rib crack. Been a while, huh?"

"Yes and no." She loosened her hold to get a closer look at her son. Lean, but with healthy color in his cheeks, shoulders no longer hunched with adolescent uncertainty or anger, chin tipped up a few degrees, self-assured but not arrogant. "God, I missed you so damn much. I don't even care if I'm an old lady again, I'm just happy you're here." The best thing of all was how his eyes reflected warmth, love.

"Eh, you're only fifty-three. Happy Birthday, Mom."

A rush of awe and tenderness she'd never felt before. "Wow." The word came out in a dazzled whisper. "That's the first time I've heard you call me Mom."

"You'll hear it a lot now. You might even get sick of it."

Her laugh brimmed with delight. Before she could bring him in for another hug, his pained look stopped her. "I know. I owe you a million apologies. There's so much—"

"Oona." A voice from the other side of the room.

Her eyes shifted to the bed, where her mother lay nestled among a cocoon of pillows.

"Mom?"

Madeleine's head looked shrunken, her body dwarfed by the creamy peach comforter she was tucked into, like a fragile figurine encased in bubble wrap. Her curly hair still thick and dark but with an artificial sheen. Apart from two pink circles colored onto her cheeks and matching lip gloss on her inflated mouth, her face was the color of ashes. Eyeliner and fake lashes didn't do much to mask her lusterless bloodshot eyes. An attempt had been made to cover the bruises beneath them with concealer, but the shadows came through.

Oona rushed over to the bed and sat down, causing her mother to wince as she disturbed the mattress.

"Happy New Year, my sweet girl. And Happy Birthday." Her voice, too, was sapped of its vitality; the words took extraordinary effort to articulate, like she'd just run a great distance. "How old are you on the inside?"

"Twenty-five." How light her mother's bony hand was as she took it, how prominent the veins, how little flesh beneath the skin. "Mom, what happened to you?" There was no mistaking the gauntness of Madeleine's features. No amount of makeup could mask a weight loss this drastic.

Oona touched her mother's hair. "Why are you wearing a wig?" But she didn't need to be told, nor did she need an explanation for Madeleine's diminutive appearance or her inability to hold a smile. Learning the name of the illness was secondary when a more terrifying question loomed. How much time did her mother have left?

"I'll explain everything later," Kenzie said, his hand on Oona's shoulder a necessary anchor as she drifted away from the moment. "She insisted on champagne, but neither of us could bring ourselves to open it." A nod to the silver bucket beside the bed.

"Yes, please, let's have a toast." Madeleine's eyes grew heavy, her nod more like her neck was protesting her head's weight.

How can you ignore a dying woman's wish? Oona reached for the sweaty bottle and removed it from its icy bath. Her fingers fumbled with the foil and metal fastener, and she imagined herself as a glass bottle, a cork holding in frothy tears. She poured two full glasses of champagne and went to pour the third.

"Only a sip for me," said Madeleine. "It's the good stuff, no point in wasting it."

The three held their glasses aloft. Only Kenzie's hand remained steady.

"I'm sorry if it's upsetting for you to see me like this, my darling," Madeleine began. "Kenzie helped me get dolled up, but I know I look ghastly. Not that you'll give me any bull about looking pretty when I don't. That's something I love about you." She paused to take a few breaths. "I'd like to make a toast to the wonderful times we've had together, and the time we have left. When I first got pregnant and had to leave Pan Am, I saw motherhood as something that might hamper my life. Instead, motherhood completed it." She aimed a dazzling smile at Oona, all traces of fatigue momentarily vanished. "You were a fascinating child and grew up to be an even more fascinating woman. You've given me . . . a marvelous life. Because of you, I got to see the world, something I deeply missed when I first became a mother."

The hand holding the champagne glass faltered, but she tightened her grip on it. "As you got older, you developed your independence, but I never felt like you stopped needing me. I'm so grateful for that. It's a bittersweet thing to see your child become self-sufficient, and it's easy to slip into irrelevance. But that never happened with us. Even when you were technically older than me and arguably wiser, I never stopped feeling important to you. And you never stopped being important to me. I've gotten nearly everything I've wanted in this life, much of it thanks to you. My extraordinary girl. My best friend."

"To Oona," Kenzie said, his jaw trembling.

They brought in and clinked their glasses.

"And to Kenzie," Madeleine continued. "My incredible grandson. You were handed a complicated family situation, and you adapted, time and time again. I'm so proud of the fine man you are today. I see the best of all of us—Oona, Shivani, Faye, even me—in you. But you've also become your own person. With so much compassion and strength and kindness." Another pause to take a few breaths. "Thank you for coming back to us, believing our crazy stories, and forgiving us. Thank you for completing our family and sharing your beautiful self with us. I only wish . . ." But whether she lacked the will or the energy, she stopped there.

"To Kenzie," Oona's voice wobbled.

Another gentle clink of glasses.

"Oona, I have to apologize to you." Her voice smaller and weaker now. "I did my best for you . . . but I couldn't always shield you from so much pain."

"Of course. None of that matters now." And it didn't. What mattered now was making sure Madeleine knew how loved she was.

"And, Kenzie, I owe you an apology, too." Madeleine was down to a whisper. "For lying about who I was when you were growing up, and for not being able to save Faye and Shivani. Oona knew when—and I tried so hard, but—"

"No, Mom, I shouldn't have put that on you. I—"

"Both of you, stop it, please." Kenzie stepped between them. "Madeleine, you have nothing to be sorry for. You can't hold yourself responsible for something like that. I've made peace with what happened—with all of it." A look back at Oona, his eyes pleading for her to jump in.

But what could she say? Not many could claim such an exceptional mother. Words were flimsy, ephemeral, incapable of conveying how much Madeleine meant to her. Oona waited for the lump to form in her throat or the prick of tears, neither of which materialized. Instead her body felt hollow, as if her internal organs had been scooped out and replaced with dry ice.

A whispered "Mom" was all she could manage. Her mother's gaze, ardent and steadfast, told her nothing more needed to be said.

"I hate to break up the party, but I need some rest." Madeleine set her glass on the bedside table. "Please, take the rest of the champagne and celebrate without me. Yes, celebrate. I'm still breathing, so don't you dare mourn me yet. Try to have a little fun tonight."

"*Have a little fun tonight?* Really?" The air pulling out of her throat like a long silk scarf.

"I'll clean this up and meet you in your study," Kenzie said to Oona.

In the hallway, she leaned against the wall, braced for impact. But still no tears. Over the years, she'd wept at countless things less significant. How dare she remain dry-eyed now? She should be doubled over, blind and racked with sobs. She should be an open wound, an endless wretched wail. Because she got more than she gave, because she could never be the mother Madeleine was. Oona needed tears to drown out this self-loathing; otherwise, what would?

Down the hall, to her study, she went over to the drinks cart and poured a glass of scotch. Downed it and shuddered at the searing path it traced down her throat.

Kenzie poked his head in the doorway. "How are you holding up?"

"It's . . . always a surprise."

"Yeah . . ." A conflicted smile. He stepped into the room and closed the door.

"What? Why are you looking at me like that?" If only she could return to the earlier elation of seeing her son. Instead, all she could think of was her mother, painted to hide her frailty and eminent demise.

"I never know what to expect on January first."

"You and me both, kiddo." Her nod was sluggish, unsure. "It's surreal to see you all grown up again. The last time we met was . . . complicated."

"Complicated. I swear, sometimes I think that's *really* what the C in my initials stands for."

A shared tired smile.

"I like the new hair." She pointed to the bleached tangles. "What about the music blogs? You still freelancing?"

"A little. I've cut down on assignments since Madeleine got sick."

"Right." She uncapped the decanter, refilled her glass. "Want some scotch? Doesn't feel right to drink champagne tonight."

"It doesn't, but I'll pass on both. I'm too sad to get shitfaced. You might want to take it easy, too. I know it's tempting to drink until you get numb—"

"Oh, but that's the thing. I'm numb now. I'm drinking to feel *something*. I should be bawling my eyes out, hysterical. But . . ." She waved a hand across her face and blinked rapidly. "Nothing. I'll cry over a paper cut, but not my dying mother. What kind of an asshole am I?"

"Come here." Kenzie took the glass out of her hand and hugged her. She buried her face in his furry vest, wanting the soft fabric to smother her. "There's no right or wrong way to react to something like this," he said. "Not crying doesn't make you an asshole. You're just in shock. The tears will come later. Knowing you, maybe sooner than later." He gave her a playful nudge.

Bobbing her head, eyes vacant, Oona stepped back from the hug and took a deep breath.

I don't want to know.

But she needed to know. "Cancer?"

Kenzie nodded. "Lymphoma."

"How much time does she have left? Months? Weeks?"

"Weeks, hopefully."

The two words together were jarring, like a fist slammed against a piano. What was hopeful about living mere weeks?

"The best we can do now is help her manage the pain," he said.

"Is she in a lot of pain?" *I should be in pain, too.* Oona wanted to slap, scratch, pinch herself—anything to feel less disconnected.

"Madeleine is a strong woman, but this disease is a motherfucker. It's wearing her down. We'll want to keep her suffering to a minimum."

"What does that mean? We'll feed her a morphine milkshake if the pain becomes too much?"

Kenzie stared her down, his eyes dark and unflinching. "If we have to, yes. We considered sending her to this resort off the coast of Peru where some people spend their last days, but Madeleine decided she preferred to be close to home. A hospice nurse comes in every day, but it might get to a point where her palliative care falls on us."

"Oh . . ." The alcohol had begun its blurring trick, but also made her limbs feel heavy. "Well . . . I'm glad you're still around."

"Good, because I'm living here now. Don't worry, I know you like your privacy, and I'll stay out of your way when you want to be alone."

"I don't want to be alone." Her mother would be gone so soon. The thought left her on the precipice of a dark chasm. "Did I leave myself a letter?"

Kenzie looked down. "No. You tried writing one a bunch of times, but could never find the right words. So you decided it was better to say nothing and make the most of the time left."

"I guess that makes sense." She reached for the bottle of scotch, but set it back down. "What can I do?"

"There's stuff I've been trying to take care of on my own, because it was hard for you. But . . . it's getting hard for me, too. I'll need your help with certain things."

"Of course." A dark wave engulfed her. *Am I ever a good mother to my son?* "Is her will up-to-date?"

"That's one of the things."

"And . . . funeral arrangements."

"Yes. But we don't have to get into any of that tonight."

"Okay." Tamping down the quiver in her voice, she spoke with calm determination. "I'll help you with anything you need." How much had she burdened Kenzie with last year? To say nothing of other years. "Last year must've been horrendous."

He tipped his head side to side, considering. "The last couple of months weren't so hot. Seeing Madeleine get sicker was awful. Then there was the presidential election—wait until I fill you in on *that* shitshow—and 2016 had some other low points. Losing Bowie, Prince, and Leonard Cohen sucked—"

"Wait, they're all dead?" Her eyebrows shot up.

"Yeah, that was a brutal 'Rule of Three.' But on a personal level, overall, last year was pretty epic. You made sure of that." He gave her a nod of approval, a flicker of light and warmth that she clung to in the dank darkness.

"What did I do?"

"As if I'm gonna tell you. But you did good, Mom. Real good. Now come on, let's go downstairs for some cake and éclairs." He tugged on her arm, but she remained immobile, staring at the empty fireplace.

"I wish this could be a happier reunion." If only there was an actual fire sizzling and crackling, even though it wouldn't warm the cold in her bones. "I wish this wasn't going to be a terrible year."

29

It *was* a terrible year.

And then it wasn't.

The weeks leading up to Madeleine's death were dull, oppressive, and downhearted. Every day there was a little less of her as the illness tightened its grip, her abdomen swollen and skin yellow, liver failure making her unable to eat. Unable to sleep without heavy sedatives, waking up disoriented in a pool of her own sweat. Oona was desperate for her mother to live, but this wasn't living. It was a multipronged horror in which she was waiting out the clock on Madeleine's suffering, while dreading each minute in case it was the last.

"Look at it this way, my dear girl," Madeleine said one evening, through parched lips. "You're going to see me again, maybe even on your next leap. We'll have many more years together, and you won't have to live through my death again. Think of it as getting the worst out of the way."

"And what about the years I have left without you?" Her voice a raspy whisper.

"They'll be peppered in with the years you do have me. It'll be easier in some ways. If you were living a normal person's chronology, I'd be out of your life forever. At least you'll be able to look forward to seeing me again. And when I'm not here, you'll have Kenzie."

But rarely both together. How bitterly unfair. Oona jerked her head side to side, tried to shake out some tears, but her eyes remained dry.

As if sensing her troubling thoughts, Madeleine added, "All three of us have had some marvelous years together, too. Last year in particular—" Her racking cough provided the perfect dramatic pause. Taking a hasty drink of water, she continued. "Why, it was nothing short of glorious. We saw and experienced more in a matter of months than many do in a lifetime." She held up a finger as a spasm of pain coursed through her.

"Do you need more morphine?" Oona's face echoed a different pain.

"Not right now." After a moment, her body relaxed. "Last year, you must've known about my impending diagnosis, because you insisted we not waste a single moment. And we didn't. No spoilers, but . . ." A mischievous gleam still shone through her fading eyes. "Let's just say, the only thing left on my bucket list is the figurative bucket." Her wink made Oona want to fall to her knees.

"Please don't go crossing that off yet, Mom. There are some things I still need to say." She'd had days to string together a tribute, and though it would never do her mother justice, there wasn't much time left to vocalize it. Imperfect was better than unspoken.

"You know how Dad always called you a force of nature? Well, I saw you more as a force of chaos. Growing up, you did these little disruptive things that drove me crazy—like how I'd comb my hair until it was perfect, and you'd come and tousle it. Or how you bought me orange tennis shoes after I asked for plain white ones. And after Dad died, when the last thing I needed was more chaos, you still brought it. Making me cut class, ride roller coasters, go to concerts . . . But I get it now. You weren't adding chaos to my life. You were adding color." What would a world without Madeleine possibly look like? Oona could conjure only a gray canvas. A wave of cold exhaustion swept over her, but she continued.

"That's the amazing thing about you, how sneaky your wisdom is.

And how quiet your sacrifices. You've done so much to put me first. I'm sorry I took that for granted. And I'm sorry for the times I pushed you away or acted like there was nothing I could learn from you. I actually learned a lot. You taught me to be brave and curious, to make mistakes, to be my boldest and truest self, to find a path through this tangled-up life of mine and . . . Thank you. For everything." Oona had to stop. Her words, though heartfelt, were beginning to resemble a eulogy, which she'd have to write soon enough—such grim, unavoidable homework awaiting her.

When Madeleine fell asleep, Oona checked to make sure she was still breathing (faintly, but she was), then asked Kenzie to join her in the study.

"Could we sit?" She motioned to the plum-colored armchairs across from the fireplace. "I swear, every year, the chairs in here are different."

"Yeah, you do swap them out a lot. You say you can't seem to get them right."

"If only it was just the chairs." A dark chuckle. "But I do like these." She settled into the plush cushioning. "So listen . . ."

"Uh-oh. You have your 'we need to talk about Kenzie' face." Elbows on knees, he leaned forward.

"More like, we need to talk about my shitty mom skills. My last leap was 1999."

"Did you party like Prince told you to? Laugh at all the Y2K— Oh, 1999." His smirk evaporated. "Yeah, that was rough."

"I didn't know I had a kid before that leap." She clasped her hands as if in prayer. "What happened in Boston . . . it was such a crazy thing to do, but I wanted to see you so badly. I couldn't think of a better way to do it without causing more disruption."

"And you would've gotten away with it, too, if it wasn't for that pesky gazpacho," he said in a cartoony old man voice.

Her earnestness interrupted, she sat back. "You've heard all this from me before."

"Yeah, and we're cool." A breezy wave of his hand.

"*I'm* not cool. I'm so sorry for lying to you, for damaging your relationship with Shivani and Faye."

"It took a hit, but we moved past it. You and I did, too, eventually. Though, you have to admit, what you did—that *Undercover Boss* bullshit—was pretty messed up. But we've reached a point where we can even laugh about it now."

Oona couldn't imagine laughing about that (or much of anything) right then.

"You're not a shitty mom," he said. "When that whole showdown happened . . . it took a while for it to sink in. I thought there was no way this goth chick with the cool music taste actually gave birth to me."

"And yet . . ."

"And yet."

How peculiar, to see her smirk reflected in a young man she hadn't even become pregnant with in her timeline. A man older than her externally than she was internally. "You must've thought I was a deadbeat or mentally ill."

"Kinda, and that's before I found out about the time travel. Which—spoiler alert—Madeleine filled me in on."

Her brow puckered, then smoothed out. "Was that in 2003?"

"Yeah." Kenzie's face grew somber.

"I've always wondered about the night of that Suzanne Vega show. Chronologically, I thought you were meeting me for the first time, so that's why I pretended not to know you. But if you already knew who I was, why go along with my act?" Her hands orbited each other, urging him to fill in the blanks.

A hissing sigh preceded his response. "I was out of my head when my mo— when Faye and Shivani died. Madeleine stayed with me for a while, helped me get their affairs in order, then convinced me to return to Brooklyn with her." Silence as he shifted in his seat, crossed one leg over a knee, then the other. "She tried to get me to see you, tried to explain your leaps, but I wasn't ready to deal with that, not on top of everything else. So she tried a different tactic, suggested I take her concert ticket, pretend I didn't know you. Said I could feel out the situation and leave if I wasn't comfortable."

"Wow." The fog thinned and another obscured corner of her life became visible. "So that was the first time you'd seen me since the Boston incident. No wonder you could barely look at me." Shock flashed across her face. "I just realized something."

"Uh-oh?"

"The first time I met you"—she counted off on her fingers—"in 2015, you pretended you weren't my son. The second time, in 2003, we both pretended not to know each other. The third time, I pretended I wasn't your mother. This is the first leap where neither of us are pretending."

They shook their heads in sync, a web of perplexity and tenderness strung between them.

The following morning, Madeleine passed away. Kenzie found her in bed. He didn't want Oona to see the body, but she insisted. "Mom made me look at Dad's body again before he was buried. She said I needed to do it for closure, so my brain truly registered that he was gone. In a weird way, it helped."

When she saw her mother, Oona didn't outwardly react. Madeleine was gaunt and waxy, but her closed eyes looked as if they could still open and glint with traces of life. Seeing her this way resolved nothing, helped nothing. Oona remained in a catatonic state of agony, like a surgery patient whose anesthesia had worn off mid-operation, paralyzed, cut open.

They made funeral arrangements.

Madeleine Lockhart was scheduled for burial in a Queens cemetery on a Thursday, though the services would be held in Coney Island. That morning, the funeral home called. When Oona picked up the phone, her heart jackhammered, believing for a second it was because there'd been a mistake, that Madeleine was still alive. But they called only because Oona had forgotten to provide them with a pair of her mother's shoes for the burial, which had to be messengered over.

"Are you ready?"

In the mirror her eyes were glossed over, somewhere else: Dale's basement, that fateful New Year's Eve. An indulgent dose of nostalgia, but a necessary reminder (*Look at how much joy you are capable of*). Any respite was allowable today, any barricade against the encroaching gloom.

"The Uber's gonna be here in ten minutes . . . Mom?" Kenzie asked from her bedroom doorway.

Her gaze shifted over to her son standing in the threshold. "Come in, I'm almost ready."

"That's a great color on you."

"Thanks." One of Madeleine's final requests was that nobody wear black to her funeral. White was fine, but brighter pigments were encouraged, so Oona had gone out and purchased a purple wool dress. Probably not as vibrant as her mother would've liked (Kenzie's fuchsia suit would've garnered higher approval), but it was the best she could do. "Could you help me with this?" She held out the gold necklace made from clockwork parts Madeleine had given her.

After he helped her fasten it, Oona screwed her eyes shut and took a deep breath. "I can't do it."

"It's the worst, but you can't miss your mother's funeral."

"Not the funeral. The eulogy." She went to her purse and took out a folded-up piece of paper. "I've written and rewritten the thing a dozen times, but when I think about standing up there and reading it out loud . . ." Though still dry-eyed, her breathing quickened, became jagged.

"Shh, it's okay. Calm down." He put a hand on her back. "I'll give the eulogy for you."

"It's too much to ask." But her eyes begged for a contradiction.

"It's not too much. I got this." He pocketed the paper.

His mercy made it easier for her to breathe, even as guilt crept in. "You're an amazing kid. Stronger than me."

"Naw, I'm just more mature than you this year. You have no idea how much you'll kick ass in later leaps. Now, come on, Mom. We need to go."

Before she died, Madeleine had given Oona a cheat sheet of extended family and friends they'd spent time with in recent years, but when the strangers began their parade before her in the funeral home that smelled of musty lavender, Oona failed to recall a single name. The mourners took her blank silence for grief and offered tentative hugs, pats on the shoulder, and versions of the same scripted condolences. So many iterations of *I'm sorry* and *My deepest sympathies* and *If there's anything I can do.* She gritted her teeth and waited out the generic kindness.

Though she wouldn't have to deliver the eulogy herself, Oona still worried that seeing Kenzie at the podium would end her drought of tears and bring about a messy emotional display. But her written words didn't make her cry, nor did seeing other mourners weep, not even her son. She didn't cry at all that day. Why wouldn't the sadness overcome her? Sad would've been familiar, sad would've been easier. This was more like being mummified in an arid, airless room. All she heard was a faint ringing in her ears, and all she felt was a tingle in the tips of her fingers.

Days later, Oona was heating up Chinese leftovers on a glass plate in the microwave. When she took the plate out, it slipped from her fingers and crashed to the floor. The glass shattered, lo mein noodles and sesame chicken scattering. She dropped to her knees and bawled.

Skinny arms around her. Kenzie shushing her as she rocked back and forth. "No use crying over spilled lo mein."

She paused her wailing. "Terrible joke."

"Yeah, it is. We used to call that 'Faye funny.'"

"We? Oh." She frowned. "You mean you and Shivani . . ." A quieter, thoughtful grief came over her.

"I'm sorry, last year you were fine with me talking about—"

"No, it *is* fine for you to talk about them." She wiped her nose with the back of her hand. "I was just thinking . . . I lost my dad, but I still had my mom right there. I can't imagine what it would've been like losing both of them at once."

"It sucked a hell of a lot." A grim nod. "But I had Madeleine. And you, even if I did take some time to come around. You both helped me through it. And I'll help you through this."

"But what about you? You lost your grandmother. I'm crying into Chinese food wondering how many leaps it'll be before I get to see her again, but you . . ."

He looked away and cleared his throat. "I'll be fine. I've still got you, right?"

"Goddamn right you do." They got to their feet. "Now let's clean up this mess. You grab the paper towels, and I'll get a sponge."

As they tidied the floor, Kenzie said, "Can I tell you something weird?"

"Always."

"I know your whole time travel condition has fucked up your life, but sometimes I'm jealous of it. Sometimes I wish I inherited it from you, even a little bit."

Oona paused, wet sponge in midair. "Really? Is it so you could . . . see them again? Shivani and Faye?"

"That's part of it, sure. And also . . . I don't know, when you're experiencing time in order, there's probably so much you take for granted. But when you go from year to year randomly, I bet you see things differently. Notice more. Appreciate more."

"Yeah, you'd think so, but sometimes you're too busy dealing with what a pain in the ass it is." *Notice more. Appreciate more. Damn, how did I end up with such a wise kid?* Not that she could take too much credit—if anything, it was another reminder of the excruciating decision she'd have to make after he was born.

"No doubt it's a pain. But you also get to look forward—or is it backward?—to these other moments in your life that are gone for the rest of us." A wistful smile. "And once in a while you get to be young again. Youth isn't wasted on you."

"Oh, I've had my share of wasted youth. And come on, you're only in your thirties. You're too young to be sounding like such an old man. Though I'm still in my twenties, so technically you're older than me. Wow, Mom was right, this does get confusing." She switched on the faucet to rinse out the sponge. "Trust me, you have nothing to be jealous about."

"You obviously haven't lived through your European eighties adventure then."

"I haven't lived through most of the eighties yet. Wait." Off the water went as she abruptly turned around. "What kind of European eighties adventure? Is it with Dale?"

"Shit." Gnawing his lower lip, he shook his head. "I'm not supposed to tell you. Please don't make me say anything else."

"It's okay, I won't." Because he'd already said enough. And she no longer wanted to shield herself from tragedy. Which meant—yes, a flood of horrendous feelings awaited her: sorrow, guilt, regret. But it also meant letting her love for Kenzie buoy her. It meant being present for him this year. It meant being hopeful about the years to come.

As the months went by, Oona and Kenzie muddled through; their grief was ever-present, but lessened by degrees.

Despite routines and distractions, Oona and her son often felt Madeleine's absence, as if the color and volume on the world had been turned down a notch. They mourned her in the moments when they turned to each other with heavyhearted smiles that said, *Madeleine would've loved this.* Like when they came across a tiny East Village shop selling Indian and Tibetan textiles and trinkets. Or when they caught a TV documentary about the history of flight attendants. Or when they saw a six-foot inflatable bottle of champagne while passing by the grand opening of a liquor store. So many things Madeleine would've loved.

The loss of her mother made for a bittersweet reunion with Kenzie—a balancing act of enjoying his company while accepting his inevitable absence from her life, depending on what year awaited her next leap.

One morning in late October, while they sat on a log in the park, feeding the ducks and geese, Oona turned to Kenzie and said, "I haven't lived through being pregnant and giving birth to you yet, but . . . do you ever wish I hadn't given you up for adoption?"

"That's not a fair question." He plucked bits off a loaf of bread and let them fall at his feet. "It's not fair to you or to Faye and Shivani. Because I love having you in my life, but I also loved having them in my life."

"But losing them so young . . . what if I could spare you that pain?" Noting his suspicious scowl, she hurried to add, "Not by keeping you from them. I saw what a happy family the three of you were. I'm talking about the accident. I've tried to change certain parts of the future, but I've never been able to. Maybe I didn't try hard enough. Mom couldn't prevent the accident, but there has to be another way—"

"No."

"But what if it would give you more time with Faye and Shivani?" *Even if that means less time with me.* "What if it could mean a better life for you?"

"Mom, you need to stop." He faced her with a stubborn jut to his chin. "Of *course* I wish the accident never happened. After they died, there were times I would've *killed* for just one more day with them." Oona opened her mouth to retort. "Hang on, you need to let me finish. Every time we have this conversation, you try to talk over me." Chastened, she chewed her lip and nodded an apology. "You have no idea how tempting it is when you start talking about this, how my brain goes crazy wondering if maybe this time you *would* be able to change the future or send me off into a happier parallel timeline or whatever." He pointed his palms to the sky. "But there's no way to know what the cost would be—would other people die in their place?—or if it would guarantee a happier life. Maybe I've seen too many movies where that kind of thing goes horribly wrong or maybe I've just accepted things as they are. I just wish you would, too. Mom, you have to stop trying to mess with your fate. Or at least mine. You need to let the bad shit happen and stop trying to undo it. What went down with you and me in Boston, Faye and Shivani's accident, let it all be."

"Are you sure?" Always this nagging remorse that she'd made the wrong choices, took the wrong turns in the maze of her life.

"I'm sure." He put a hand on her arm and softened his voice. "I have an awesome life. Yes, I've lost some good people and I'm a little aimless. I'm thirty-three, single, still figuring out what I want to be when I grow up, still living with my mother. But I'm okay with that. And it's up to me to change anything I'm not okay with."

"Fair enough." A slow nod. "I hope your aimlessness isn't my fault. When I was with Dale, he had such a clear vision for our lives, which I admired, because I never had a path like that mapped out for myself. But then I was selected for that year abroad and suddenly had two paths to choose from, and then—just as suddenly—none . . ." She watched two ducks fighting over a crust in the shallow end of the water. "I'm sorry you didn't get to know your father."

"Not something you had any control over." A heavy shrug. "Hey, do you think he would've had a problem with me being gay?"

"God no. But he *definitely* would've had a problem with you being a Pink Floyd fan."

Kenzie laughed and Oona joined in.

"So . . . um . . . are you doing okay these days?" he asked.

"Fine, I guess. Why, what's up?"

"I was . . . I was thinking of taking a trip."

"Ooh, where to?"

"New Zealand."

"What's in New Zealand?" Reading the glimmer in his eyes, she amended the question. "Who's in New Zealand?"

"I've been chatting with this guy online the last few months."

"A sheep farmer? Lord of the Rings tour guide?"

"Mom!" But he held back another laugh even as he admonished her. "He's a tech guy. Web analytics."

"Tell me all about him."

"His name is David . . ."

As Kenzie recounted their digital courtship, Oona's heart gave a little squeeze at the joy splashed across his face. Was this how she looked in the early days when she told Madeleine about Dale or Crosby or Edward? Had her mother experienced the same surge of elation mixed with trepidation? Elation because how beautiful to see your child's heart soar. Trepidation because how delicate the flight, how easy to crash.

"I think he's a good guy, Mom. And I've always wanted to visit New Zealand."

"Well, don't let me stop you." When his smile faltered, she said, "No, really. You should go. I'll be fine here." Oona forced a breezy tone. "I was actually thinking of going on my own trip." She wasn't. "Maybe I'll take a cruise around the Greek islands." She wouldn't.

"You sure you don't want to do New Zealand with me?" But it was a hollow invitation.

"Maybe some other time."

"It'll only be for a few weeks."

"Get a one-way ticket just in case. Maybe things will go well with David and you'll want to stay longer." She thought of exploring Egyptian tombs and markets with Edward, the added enchantment of falling in love in a foreign country. Hopefully, Kenzie's romantic luck would exceed hers. But better not to think of sour endings or her impending loneliness.

Kenzie did end up staying longer in New Zealand, two months during which Oona continued her routines, feeling both suspended in and fleeting through time. Sleep often eluded her, as did hunger. She'd begun the year thinner than she was in her first leap and continued to lose weight, but it was born out of grief, not health consciousness. No Madeleine plus no Kenzie equaled no appetite.

To distract herself from all the absence, she studied her financial binder, memorizing every page (pragmatic but wishful thinking that the next leap would take her to an earlier year). She also found volunteer work, at an animal shelter and a library. Dogs and books, two excellent defenses against solitude and despair.

In early December, she received a package from New Zealand: a small blue ceramic bird with a red beak. The attached note read:

> This is a pukeko, one of NZ's native birds. It's reluctant to fly and tends to run and hide when it's disturbed. But when it does fly, it can cover great distances. Sound familiar? I thought it would make a good addition to your tchotchke menagerie.
>
> XO Kenzie

She added the ceramic bird to the display case in her bedroom. It held numerous knickknacks still missing their origin stories—the Fabergé egg, the Venetian mask, the glass igloo, many others. There was no telling when her collection would be fully known to her, or when it would be complete, but each year was another blank page filled.

Finally, her son sent word he was coming back to New York for Christmas. His flight would get in Saturday afternoon, and that morning, she worked her final volunteer shift at the library. On her way out, in the hallway, she heard guitar strumming and followed it to a room with its door ajar—open far enough to reveal a circle of kids sitting around a middle-aged Asian man playing the opening bars of Pink Floyd's "Wish You Were Here." Gray at the temples, wearier behind the eyes, but his face filled with warm recognition when he saw Oona in the doorway.

Peter Han. They hadn't crossed paths since that last guitar lesson. *You caught me at a bad time,* he'd said. And now?

He sang the entire song over the heads of the children straight at her. And when he got to the line about lost souls swimming in a fishbowl, she grinned even as a few sneaky tears slid down her face. Because it was nice to feel less lost and alone, even for a moment. Because *of course* this would happen right at the end of the year.

After the song, he excused himself and went over to Oona.

"What, no Radiohead?" she asked.

"Oh, you got here late and missed 'No Surprises.'" Hair a little thinner, but it still fell into his eyes the same way, and he still flicked it aside the same way.

"You sing about suicide to little kids?"

"Eh, they focus more on the lyrics about pretty houses and gardens than carbon monoxide."

"And I see you've gotten over your stage fright," she said.

"Playing for eight-year-olds is different." A quirk of his mouth. "It's good to see you, Oona. Really good. It's been, what—"

"It doesn't matter how long it's been. It's just stupid time."

"Stupid time," he said as if casting an insult, then snickered.

Was she smiling too much? If she was, then so was he.

"Can I take you to lunch?" A sweet bashfulness in his question.

"Yes." The word out of her mouth before she glanced at the wall clock behind him. "Wait, no. I can't. I have to leave for the airport in a half hour. I could do a quick coffee?"

"Let me just grab my guitar."

They went to a café around the corner with exposed brick and a chalkboard proclaiming all tips were donated to a women's shelter. Peter paid for their coffee, but when he wasn't looking, Oona slipped a hundred-dollar bill into the tip jar.

Once they were settled at a corner table, hot beverages untouched before them, at first all they could do was stare at each other, tentative, a gossamer anticipation strung between them like fairy lights. The noise of customers and jangly Christmas music receded into the background, like the hush in a dark theater before the show begins. They tilted their heads. Hesitated. Then both spoke at once.

"So how long have you been playing for kids?"

"So what time is your flight?"

They laughed. Paused. And when neither moved to answer, they both did, at the same time.

"I was just filling in for a friend."

"I'm just picking someone up."

More laughter. It was okay. They'd have time to get their rhythm right.

"I thought maybe you were also a volunteer," Oona said. "Because it would make perfect sense for us to spend all this time in the same building but never run into each other until my last day there."

"Come on, don't have such a low opinion of fate. That was actually the first time I'd even set foot in that library. But you know, I *did* see you a couple of years ago, in Prospect Park." Peter took a long sip of coffee, eyebrows raised as if reliving the surprising moment. "I would've said hello, but you were having this intense conversation with someone—a guy."

"Did he happen to be young and handsome, with cool Tilda Swinton hair?" Her smile mysterious, dreamy.

"I think so."

"Yeah, that was Kenzie, my kid. That's who I'm picking up at the airport." Had Peter seen her during her very first leap? How awkward it would've been if he'd approached them, only for her to have no idea who he was.

"I didn't know you had a child."

Neither did I. "It's a long, complicated story."

"Is it now." His eyes flashed, playful, ready to accept a challenge. His fingers made a slow path along the table, stopped in the center. "Funny, because you never struck me as the least bit complicated."

"Yeah, neither did you. Not even a little." She slid her hand forward until it was just shy of his. There had always been an invisible wall between them, but now he flipped his palm up, and the wall became an open door. The only thing left to do was walk through it, so Oona crossed the threshold and slid her hand into his. He gave one soft squeeze, a greeting: *Welcome home.*

"I gotta admit, it killed me a little when you stopped your lessons—don't get me wrong, I understand why."

"Can you even imagine how awkward it would've been if I kept coming? It makes me cringe just thinking about it."

"I would've endured that awkwardness if it meant seeing you. Any day."

"Even if it made things with your girlfriend weird?"

"Oh, you mean the woman I ended up marrying and having three kids with?" Before Oona could pull her hand away, he grinned. "Kidding. We broke up after a couple of months. I . . . I wanted to call you. But I didn't want to be that guy. I also had this sense—I don't know, like I needed to wait. Like things had to play out a certain way."

"'Everything has its time,'" she quoted his tattoo.

"Exactly. I'm just glad we're sitting here right now."

"Me too." She kept her eyes fixed on their clasped hands. So rarely does a fulfilled wish live up to the anticipation of it and even exceed it. "It's too bad I need to leave so soon."

"Maybe we could get dinner sometime?"

"I'd love to." She looked up at him. "But it can't be until after the new year."

Any disappointment smoothed over with an understanding nod. "Of course. I'm sure you have a lot going on for the holidays. With your son."

"That's part of it. But also . . . I want to give 2018 Oona something to look forward to."

He tapped a finger to his chin, weighed the statement. "Then I guess 2018 Peter will also have something to look forward to."

When the year ended, she wouldn't be ready to go, but the clock would have no sympathy. Her next leap would always hover on the horizon, unavoidable, waiting to whisk her away.

In some cases, waiting to grant a wish from years ago.

PART IX

All Tomorrow's Parties

1983: 19/26

30

"Happy New Year!"

Warm lips pressed against Oona's and firm arms wrapped around her as the room erupted in celebratory shrieks. Eyes closed, she returned the kiss and tightened her arms around a man who'd always felt like home. Eyes closed, in case it wasn't really true, in case it was a figment.

I need to be sure.

Oona opened her eyes.

She was back in Dale's basement, back in the mirrored room, surrounded by her motley group of friends. A small television across the way showed Times Square ushering in 1983 while all around her, people popped streamers and created a cacophony with noisemakers and their own hooting.

This better not be a dream.

It wasn't.

Seven years of disorientation and strange navigation. Seven years of wandering and wondering. Seven long years until she returned.

Oona stepped back and there he was. Dale. His smile lopsided, his big brown eyes full of all the love in the world. She glanced down at her sequined dress and leather jacket, then back up at him.

"It really happened." A flood of joy, so acute it hurt. "I'm really back. *You're* back." She held a hand an inch away from his face, scared to touch him in case he dissipated before her.

"What's the matter with you?" Dale cocked his head.

But it wasn't a mirage. His hand against her cheek said he wasn't going to disappear, at least not tonight. Barely able to keep her head above water as vacillating emotions threatened to drown her, she threw her arms around him and buried her face in his neck. "It's you. It's finally you."

He pulled back and squinted at her. "Are you okay? Did you have too much champagne?"

A wild laugh. "No, I'm fine. I'm great. So thrilled to see you, you have no idea."

"I've been here all night. You make it sound like it's been years or something."

Seven. Seven years.

"Sorry to interrupt your sickening lovey-dovey moment, but I need to borrow this man for a minute." Wayne tugged on Dale's sleeve and jerked his head upstairs. Oona took in her friend's Jheri-curled hair, red leather getup, and fingerless gloves, and she laughed again.

"What are you grinning at, missy?"

"Just . . . eighties fashion is the best."

"Any idea what's gotten into this one?" Wayne asked Dale.

"I'm trying to figure that out myself."

"Clearly, the girl isn't drinking enough." A soft elbow to her side and a wink. "Why don't you have another while we take care of something upstairs."

Oona nodded, too choked up to speak. But she wouldn't take his advice, because she wanted to remember the rest of this night relatively sober.

The partygoers swayed to the mid-tempo synths of a Yaz song and even Pam did a cautious two-step to the music. As if sensing she was being watched, she looked over at Oona, who gave her a sad smile. *I promise I'll visit you in London.*

A moment later, the music was cut off, the basement lights dimmed, and Dale and Wayne came downstairs with an ice-cream cake lit up with twenty candles, nineteen plus one to grow on.

The room burst into a rendition of "Happy Birthday." The cake was decorated with music notes, her name spelled out beneath it in blue icing. Oona couldn't hold back any longer. The tears came so thick and fast, they extinguished two of the candles before she blew the rest out. Everyone around her cheered and the lights came back on.

"Did you make a wish?" Dale put an arm around her waist.

"Yes." *Though it'll never come true.*

Wayne whisked away the cake to cut pieces for everyone.

"I've got one more surprise for you." Wiggling his eyebrows, Dale held out a tiny box wrapped in silver paper.

Inside was a gold chain holding a miniature hourglass pendant.

"That's real sand in there, too," he said.

"Several galaxies' worth, I bet. It's lovely," breathed Oona.

"We had the best summer," he whispered as he helped her fasten the clasp.

"This summer will be even better." She sneaked a peek at the inside of her wrist, but of course: no tattoo.

What would happen to the necklace in the coming years? Why didn't she have it later in life?

Later could wait.

"Come here." She pulled him close, inhaled his cologne and hair gel, mixed with the smell of her new leather jacket.

What'll happen to Dale's jacket after he dies? Will he be buried in it? Another lump formed in her throat, but she swallowed it down. This line of thinking was no good. She had to cast aside the future's certainties—getting pregnant in the late summer, giving birth to a son Dale wouldn't live to see the following spring. She had to pretend she didn't know what would happen next year. It was the only way she'd enjoy this one.

Suppressing tears and sighs and future wisdom, Oona wrapped her arms around Dale's neck and kissed him hard on the mouth, oblivious to the whistles and hollers around her. The kiss opened a gulf of bright light inside her. She'd lost count of all the men she'd kissed in the last seven years, but none came close to Dale D'Amico. None kissed her back with such transcendent passion. (Maybe Peter Han would, but that was for Future Oona to determine.)

And still the sorrow threatened at the edges like a tidal wave on the horizon. How could she keep it from engulfing her?

Corey came over. "Hey, so should we go ahead and tune up?"

In the corner of the room, a wooden platform had been erected as a makeshift stage. On it were Corey's drums, Oona's Yamaha keyboard, and a couple of amps, which propped up Dale's guitar and Wayne's bass.

"Shit," she said under her breath. There was no way she could play. It had been years since she touched a keyboard. Oona's mouth went dry. "I need to call a band meeting. Could we go outside for a minute?"

Corey, Wayne, and Dale exchanged curious looks but followed her to the backyard.

The air was so cold it singed the inside of her nostrils. "I have a couple of announcements to make. First of all, I'm going to drop out of school, to spend as much time with the band as possible. And you." She pointed to Dale but held him back when he moved toward her. "Hold on, you might not like this second part as much." Big breath in. Out. "I hate playing the keyboard. I've been taking guitar lessons and I've gotten good. I'm going to keep playing the guitar no matter what, and I'd like to stay in the band, but I never want to touch that Yamaha again."

Corey and Wayne exchanged a wide-eyed look; each took a step back.

"You've been secretly taking guitar lessons?" Dale stood with his arms folded, eyebrows up, mouth turned down.

"I couldn't tell you right away. I didn't even know if I'd be any good. You've always been so adamant about me playing keys and . . ."

"I was adamant because the band needed a keyboardist. Not a second guitarist." The confusion in Dale's eyes turned to pleading, for the woman before him to transform back into the one he'd known mere moments ago.

"Lots of great bands have two guitarists. Talking Heads. The Rolling Stones. Velvet Underground. Radiohead has *three* guitarists."

"Who the hell is *Radiohead*?" Dale glanced at the other two guys, who shrugged and stepped farther away.

"Just some . . . you wouldn't . . . It doesn't matter," Oona stammered. "The point is, we can make two guitars work. And if we need to, we can find a new keyboardist."

"None of this makes any sense." He walked in tight circles around the yard. "You say you're quitting school to be with me, be with the band, but you learned a new instrument behind my back . . . What else are you hiding from me?"

Plenty, she wanted to say, but she merely shrugged. "I still want to be in the band. Maybe you should ask the other guys what they think. At the very least, you should hear me play. I'm a good guitarist." *Better than you, but I've had years more practice.*

"Factory Twelve asked us to tour with them based on our sound, which has keys. I don't know if they'll want us without them. I don't know what our sound will be like now." Dale stopped pacing and examined her face closely. "I can't put my finger on it, but you're different."

"Early adulthood is a formative period in a person's life."

"See? Even the way you're talking right now—it's not like you."

"It *is* me. The real me."

Corey stepped back into the circle. "Hey, since we're changing things up, can we also change our name?"

"What's wrong with Early Dawning?" Dale asked, hands up in exasperation.

A reluctant forward shuffle from Wayne. "I hate to say it, but . . . everything."

Brow furrowed and jaw set, Dale braced for an argument. But when he caught Oona's eye, his face softened.

"As much as I love the Velvet Underground reference, I'm not crazy about Early Dawning as a band name, either," she said. "But we could still find something with a nod to the Velvets. How about . . . Candy Says?"

"I don't know, do we have to be so obvious about our influences?" Wayne lit a cigarette and blew smoke above their heads. "What if we mix it up a little more? How about . . . Strangers with Candy? Or just Stranger Candy."

The four of them stood a little straighter, a new hum of energy running through them.

Oona's ears buzzed with the echo of something Kenzie had mentioned in 1999, about a European eighties one-hit wonder. Wasn't her name Candy Stranger?

"Stranger Candy," murmured Dale, his face full of fire and mischief.

"You're already picturing the marquee, aren't you?" Oona knocked her shoulder against him.

"I think we all are." Corey chewed his thumbnail, nodded. "So you think Madeleine is gonna mind you dropping out of school?"

Mom. Mom is alive.

Another hard swallow and, "I think she'll be fine with it. Hell, she'll probably ask to be our tour manager."

Wayne stubbed his cigarette out on the heel of his boot. "Can we go back inside now? It's freezing out here."

Lagging behind, Oona grabbed Dale's sleeve to hold him back. "We'll follow you guys in a minute."

When they were alone in the yard, he gave her a nervous look. "Any more bombshells?"

"Nothing bad. You know how we planned to go to Europe this summer, after the tour?"

"Don't tell me you changed your mind about that, too."

"No way, I still want to go. But I want to stay longer. I think we should stay the rest of the year. Work odd jobs along the way if we need to . . ." *But we won't need to, because in March, Croeso will win the Florida Derby, paying out 85–1 odds.*

"And what about the band? If the Factory Twelve tour goes well, we should use the money to cut a better demo, follow up with our own tour."

"The band will still be there."

"Europe will still be there," Dale said, following her logic.

You won't be here. She wished she could tell him enough to convince him: that nothing would ever come of the band regardless of their name, that he should enjoy his last days because he had only fourteen months' worth of them left.

"We won't get another shot at Europe," Oona insisted. "It may sound morbid, but . . . this is our one chance to go." Taking both of his hands in hers, she begged him with her eyes, with her skin, with her mouth against his. Dale's side of the kiss asked many questions, but hers offered no answers—only that he had to trust her.

When they broke apart, he half smiled and let out a long decisive sigh. "We'll find a way to get to Europe." Oona moved in for another kiss, but he put out an arm. "I'm still figuring out how this band is going to sound with no keys and two guitarists. If it doesn't work, we'll need to find a new keyboardist. So there'll be five of us. And I can't make any promises about Europe beyond the summer. Let's see how the tour goes."

"Let's see how the tour goes," she agreed.

Even though the band wouldn't make any significant mark on the world of music, she'd have the year to experience the high that comes from creating and playing songs. And even though Dale would die young, it wouldn't be this year, and she'd cherish every moment with him, cultivate memories she'd savor during any lonely days to come.

Beyond that, she couldn't know what the rest of the year had in store, to say nothing of subsequent ones. The future had shown her previews of what lay ahead, but there were always surprises mixed in with the spoilers. Glimpses, but not the full picture. And whether she went by her internal age of twenty-six or her external age of nineteen, she was still young, and she had decades of living to do, even if it was out of order.

Oona would always try to create continuity and meaning in her life—she couldn't help it—but she'd also seize these moments of happiness and relish them. Whichever way the years flowed, it was impossible to outmaneuver their passage. Even chronology doesn't guarantee security. All good things ended, always. The trick was to enjoy them while they lasted. Oona was still learning.

Every time she leaped, no matter the year, someone important would be absent from her life: Dale or Madeleine or Kenzie. Every year, bittersweet. But that was okay.

There would be bad days, there always would. But she'd collect these good days, each one illuminated, and string them together until they glowed brightly in her memory like Christmas lights in a mirrored room.

"How about we go back inside and you show off your guitar skills for us? I bet you're impressive." Dale winked as he held the door open for her.

And maybe youth isn't wasted on the young; maybe the young know how to spend their youth just right.

It was going to be a glorious year.

Acknowledgments

Philippa Sitters: thank you for fishing me out of your slush pile and setting us on this incredible journey. You, Lisette Verhagen, and Kirsty McLachlan have been instrumental in making some of my biggest writer dreams come true. I'm deeply grateful to have you three working on my behalf at DGA.

James Melia: you read my story with a big heart and a keen editorial eye, and you challenged me as a writer in the best possible way. Thank you for your wisdom and compassion, and for helping me make the unbelievable more believable. I'm also grateful to everyone at Flatiron and Macmillan involved in bringing the book to readers, especially Megan Lynch, Bob Miller, Cristina Gilbert, Nancy Trypuc, Marlena Bittner, Tricia Cave, Caroline Bleeke, Keith Hayes, Jaya Miceli, Katherine Turro, Erin Gordon, Samantha Zukergood, Jordan Forney, Emily Walters, Lena Shekhter, Meg Drislane, Omar Chapa, Nancy Inglis, Christina MacDonald, Ryan Jenkins, and everyone in the sales, audio, contracts, finance, and operations departments.

Rachel Winterbottom: your editorial insights made me dig deeper and take a closer look at character nuances and relationships. I'm thankful to you, Brendan Durkin, Katie Moss, and Anna Morrison and everyone at Gollancz and Orion for embracing Oona so warmly and giving her a home across the pond.

Erin Foster Hartley: you're always there to read a draft, help with brainstorming, give me a pep talk, or recommend a good show or podcast. I'm grateful to have you as a friend and CP. Please don't ever sashay away.

Kelli Newby: you offer constructive criticism with so much warmth and encouragement. Thank you for that, and for never letting me fall off the radar for too long. You're awesome.

Lauren Scovel: you gave me some tough editorial notes, and I'm glad I eventually had the good sense to follow them. I'll always be grateful for your critiques; this book wouldn't be what it is today without your input.

Many thanks to others who took time to read early versions of all or part of this book:

Emily Colin, Bridget McGraw, Jennifer Hawkins, Rachel Lynn Solomon, Shannon Monahan, Sarah Bruck, Nina Laurin, Amy Carothers, Mary Ann Marlowe, Tracie Martin, Kelly Calabrese.

Traci Cappiello: your support and hospitality meant so much to me when I was tackling revisions. There aren't enough pineapples in the world to convey my gratitude.

Michelle Hazen and Zoje Stage: thank you for your openness, insights, and candor in helping me navigate the publishing industry.

Speaking of the publishing industry... I got a *lot* (hundreds!) of rejections in the years I've been trying to make it as a writer. Sometimes they buoyed me because of a bit of nice feedback, sometimes they left me indifferent, and more than once, they plummeted me into deep despair. But the rejection gave me grit and tested how much I wanted this dream. And it made this moment so much sweeter because it didn't come quickly or easily. So to every agent and editor who said no, thank you. And to writers still trying to get their stories out there, keep fighting the good fight.

Mom: Thank you for surviving, believing, and loving unconditionally.

And finally, Terry Montimore: You deserve another shout-out. Nobody would even be reading this right now if it wasn't for your ongoing faith and support. You made this all possible. Thank you for giving my heart and the rest of me a home ("thank god I don't live there!"). P.S. The jerk store called—they've never heard of you.

Credits

We would like to thank everyone at Orion who worked on the publication of The Rearranged Life of Oona Lockhart in the UK.

Editorial
Rachel Winterbottom
Brendan Durkin

Editorial Management
Charlie Panayiotou
Jane Hughes
Alice Davis

Audio
Paul Stark
Amber Bates

Contracts
Anne Goddard
Paul Bulos

Jake Alderson

Design
Lucie Stericker
Joanna Ridley
Nick May
Helen Ewing
Clare Sivell

Finance
Jennifer Muchan
Jasdip Nandra
Afeera Ahmed
Elizabeth Beaumont
Sue Baker

Marketing
Katie Moss

Production
Paul Hussey
Fiona McIntosh

Publicity
Stevie Finegan

Sales
Jen Wilson
Victoria Laws
Esther Waters
Rachael Hum
Ellie Kyrke-Smith
Frances Doyle
Ben Goddard
Georgina Cutler

Barbara Ronan
Andrew Hally
Dominic Smith
Maggy Park
Linda McGregor
Sinead White
Jemimah James
Rachel Jones
Jack Dennison
Nigel Andrews
Ian Williamson
Julia Benson
Declan Kyle
Robert Mackenzie

Operations
Jo Jacobs
Sharon Willis
Lisa Pryde

About the Author

After receiving a BFA in creative writing from Emerson College, **Margarita Montimore** worked for over a decade in publishing and social media before deciding to focus on the writing dream full-time. She lives in New Jersey with her husband and dog.